Prais
Eden's

"Hagberg may have out Clancied Clancy. . . . Better strap in for this ride." —Stephen Coonts on *High Flight*

"Not only do Hagberg's novels have a ring of truth; sometimes they become the truth." —Dean Ing

"David Hagberg runs in the same fast, high-tech track as Clancy and his gung-ho colleagues, with lots of war games, fancy weapons, and much male bonding."

—*New York Daily News*

"I've been a Hagberg fan for years and he's certainly come a long and enviable way . . . he now takes his place alongside such masters as Tom Clancy and Clive Cussler."

—Ed Gorman

"David Hagberg is one of the more interesting writers of thrillers in the new millennium . . . his work rivals that of Clancy, Koontz and Cornwell."

—*The Midwest Book Review*

"Hagberg is one of the finest, if not the finest thriller writer today." —*Rave Reviews*

"Hagberg delivers a payload of action, suspense and political intrigue." —*Publishers Weekly*

Novels by David Hagberg

Twister
The Capsule
Last Come the Children
Heartland
*Without Honor**
*Countdown**
*Crossfire**
*Critical Mass**
Desert Fire
*High Flight**
*Assassin**
*White House**
*Joshua's Hammer**
Eden's Gate†

Writing as Sean Flannery

The Kremlin Conspiracy
Eagles Fly
The Trinity Factor
The Hollow Men
Broken Idols
False Prophets
Gulag
Moscow Crossing
The Zebra Network
Crossed Swords
Counterstrike
Moving Targets
Winner Take All†
Kilo Option†
Achilles' Heel†

(*Kirk McGarvey adventures)
(†Bill Lane adventures)

EDEN'S GATE

David Hagberg

A TOM DOHERTY ASSOCIATES BOOK
NEW YORK

EDEN'S GATE

A Forge Book
Published by Tom Doherty Associates, LLC
175 Fifth Avenue
New York, NY 10010

www.tor.com

ISBN: 0-812-54440-4
Library of Congress Catalog Card Number: 2001023177

First edition: June 2001
First mass market edition: July 2002

Printed in the United States of America

0 9 8 7 6 5 4 3 2 1

Although it's true that there are nefarious characters living in Montana, that is also true of every other state. My apologies to the good people of Montana, and especially to Kalispell. I've not only set bad deeds afoot there, I even changed places to suit the needs of the story. Nothing I have written in any way should be taken as the truth, or as a representation of real people. It's just fiction.

For Laurie,
as always

Special thanks to my son Kevin Hagberg
for the nifty idea, his support, and
his constant love

PROLOGUE

REICHSAMT 17
JUNE 1, 1945

Water was rushing somewhere, the sound hollow and frightening in the confines of research Chamber Gamma. A very slightly built man dressed in striped pajamas, the Star of David patch sewn on his left breast, stopped to cock an ear. Rows of beakers, chemicals, bunsen burners, two gas chromatographs, and six powerful microscopes were arranged as final, silent, terrible witnesses to the horrors that had gone on down here since 1943.

The other sound he'd been hearing since early this morning came again; deep throated, almost below the level of hearing, in that place where you can only feel it. A thudding, like a pile driver. Distant. Somewhere above.

Manny Goldfine went back into the connecting tunnel between labs and shined the weak beam of his dying flashlight on the rough concrete ceiling. The thump came again, and dust filtered down. Explosions? He'd been trying to locate the exact source for three hours, and the sounds were bringing him, as he feared they would, toward the main elevator shaft. They were trying to get in. But that way was blocked for now. He and Sharon had seen to that last night. Then, around two in the morning, he wasn't exactly sure of the time, he'd held her frail body in his arms and watched her die like the others, with long, wheezy gasps as she fought to bring air into her blood-filled lungs. In the end she'd looked up at him with love, and somehow managed to reach up with clawlike fingers to brush at the fleck of blood she'd coughed up on his shirt. She'd been fastidious all her life.

"I'm sorry, my darling," she had whispered, and then she'd died.

For a long time Manny sobbed because of the life he and his wife had never had; for the children they'd not been allowed to conceive and raise; for the picnics, and plays, and concerts they'd not seen; for the trip to Paris she'd talked about since they were kids together in Berlin.

Then he had gone on a berserk rampage against the bastard Nazis who had done this horrible thing, not only to them, but to all their friends and relatives, and to their beautiful country. He'd raged against the bodies of the German scientists and SS guards, especially *Leutnant* Grueber, whose body lay in corridor B. He'd kicked the heartless bastard until his skull was crushed.

Afterward he'd lain in a heap in the corridor near his wife's body, and waited for his own merciful death to come. The Germans would never again reach this place. He and the others had sealed off all the passages leading to the surface one hundred meters above. They were on the shores of Lake Tollense, so water had always been a problem; now it would be their salvation. They'd sabotaged the pumps and placed explosives against the west wall, on the other side of which was the bottom of the lake. When the wall went, this place would flood instantly with no way of pumping it out short of draining the lake.

For some reason he had lasted longer than the others. He'd been alone with the bodies of five hundred Jews, some of them test subjects, some of them scientists like him, and one hundred Nazis plus the SS guards. During the night he was sure that he could hear them crying out in anguish; crawling toward him, seeking help, or revenge. Do research or die, they had told him. Do it *well* or your wife will die in front of your eyes. And their souls were coming for him now; for the terrible things he and the others had discovered and perfected.

Something in his heritage, he supposed, made him survive while others died. *Grossvater* Goldfine had lived to his hundredth birthday, and uncles Benjamin and David were both in their nineties when the Nazis came for them. They'd probably still be alive if they had not been murdered. Gassed, cremated. They'd all heard the stories, even down here. He was weak from hunger and overwork, but he was not sick. No heaviness in his chest. No blood in his stools, in his nostrils, none on his handkerchief.

Another much heavier thump came, and this time small pieces of the ceiling rained down on his head, the dust so bad now that it made him cough. He hurried to the end of the corridor and opened the heavy steel door. It was the last one in the complex. All the others, down every interconnecting tunnel, all the way back to the dormitories that butted against the west wall, were in the locked open position. When the waters came the bunker would flood in seconds. Nothing would live down here. Nothing would *ever* live down here; the horrible secrets would be buried forever.

Looking back the way he had come, he could just make out the detonator switch lying on the floor next to Sharon's body where he'd spent the night. Wires led all the way back to the explosives on the west wall. He could have turned the switch last night. He should have done it. He certainly wanted the peace; to be with his wife; no pain, no suffering, and especially no sorrows or loneliness. But something inside of him, some curiosity about how the end would play out had gotten the better of him. And then the explosions had begun. The SS was trying to get back in to save its own, or to reclaim the weapon hiding down here. Use it against innocent women and children. The indiscriminate killer. He had to see, to make sure.

He stepped through the doorway into the arrivals and security hall as an even larger explosion came from directly overhead. He was shoved back by the concussion as a big section of concrete ceiling caved in; tons of rubble, dirt, stone, concrete, reinforcing bars half buried the room and knocked him off his feet.

"It's our responsibility to ourselves to live, Manny," Sharon had told him. But she was wrong, God bless her. They had a greater responsibility to the human race. But she didn't understand, and she was frightened, so he had comforted her at that moment.

Goldfine picked himself up and staggered back to the half-buried doorway. He'd lost his flashlight, but the tunnel was no longer in darkness. For a second or two he thought that he was hallucinating, but then he realized that he was seeing daylight for the first time in more than two years.

Mindless of the sharp rocks and jagged steel that tore at his hands and knees, he crawled up the pile of rubble so that he could look outside. There was light streaming down through the thick dust.

Something moved above. Figures. He could suddenly feel a cool breeze, and then he saw them. Soldiers. Two of them; no, three or four. Peering down from twenty or thirty meters up the jagged shaft the explosions had opened.

Soldiers, the thought solidified in his mind. They were SS. He was sure of it.

Scrambling backward, he hit the rubble-strewn floor of the tunnel running. They were coming. He was already too late. God in heaven, forgive him.

Someone was shouting at him from above. His ears were still ringing from the last explosion but he didn't think they were speaking German. It was another language. Polish, maybe. He couldn't be sure. Possibly it was a trick. The bastards did that sometimes.

He stumbled and fell, smashing his face on the floor so hard that he blacked out for a moment. When the fuzz cleared he was lying next to Sharon's body. Her mouth and chin were bloody, the front of her striped pajamas black with crusted blood. Her eyes were half open, and milky; her hair was matted, and her skin was deathly white. But he loved her. She was the most beautiful creature that God had ever put on earth. Kind, gentle, understanding.

The shouting was much louder now, and there was more light. Goldfine tenderly kissed his wife on the lips, then without further hesitation picked up the detonator, raised the handle, and twisted it sharply to the right.

A huge explosion rocked the foundations of the bunker. Goldfine looked up as a solid wall of water raced down the tunnel directly toward him at the speed of a freight train.

"God have mercy—," he said, and he joined his wife.

Captain Second Rank Aleksei Konalev, standing in the turret of his tank twenty meters from where the Special Bunker Demolitions Squad had been working all morning, felt, rather than heard, the deep underground explosion. His first instinct was to duck; he'd been fighting without leave for nearly three years. But then he thought that something terrible had gone wrong, and the team had either had an accident with their explosives, or they had run into another booby trap.

"*Yeb vas*," he swore. It was the goddamn Nazis. The war had been over for more than a month, and yet they were still finding their deadly little surprises lying around.

They were just above the lake here; the windows in the church steeple in the town of Neubrandenburg a few klicks to the north twinkled in the bright sun. A second after the explosion a huge depression appeared on the surface of the lake a couple of hundred meters off shore.

Konalev reached for his binoculars at the same moment a tremendous geyser of water shot out of the shaft the squad had excavated into the bunker. Mud, concrete, rocks, steel, and bodies were blasted one hundred meters into the pale blue sky. In three years of war, Konalev had never seen such a fantastic sight, and his mouth dropped open. The sound was like a thousand tanks bearing down on him, and he looked up in time to see something very large and black falling out of the sky directly toward him.

"Move, move, move!" he screamed at his driver. He ducked down into the turret and slammed the hatch shut an instant before his tank was hit with a solid, metallic bang so hard that the turret jammed on its track, and the entire tank was shoved backward at least ten meters.

But his crew had been under fire before. The driver had the engine in reverse and was racing backward, as more debris rained down on them, hitting them like heavy caliber machine gun bullets being fired from above.

The gunner, blood streaming down from a gash where he'd hit his forehead, was peering through the periscope. "I don't see any enemy fire!" he shouted. "Where are they, sir? I can't see them!"

"Easy, Yuri." Konalev shouted him down. "We're not under fire. It was an explosion." Konalev keyed his radio, but all he was getting was static. The antenna had probably been knocked out by whatever had hit them.

The driver, looking through his periscope, backed off the accelerator, and the tank ground to a halt. He looked up, a confused expression on his battle-hardened features. "Fish," he said.

"What is it?" Konalev demanded.

"It's raining fish, sir," the driver said in wonder. "Out of the sky, fish were falling."

"Still?"

The driver turned back to the periscope. "No, sir. They're all over the ground, but they've stopped falling."

Konalev climbed back up into the turret, and he had trouble opening the hatch, but it finally gave with a squeal of metal on metal.

The scene was like something his old grandmother used to read to him out of the Bible. Water swirled around a large depression where the bunker entrance had been. Fish lay everywhere. Huge waves raced across the lake, and debris of all kinds littered an area at least two hundred meters in diameter.

But Konalev's eyes were drawn to a steel door lying on the front deck of his tank. It was the object that had been blasted out of the bunker and had fallen on them. A large skull and crossbones was painted on the door, beneath which was the legend: VORSICHT. Danger.

PART ONE

Present Day

1

KALISPELL, MONTANA

The Grand Hotel was old but elegant, and as Bill Lane looked down on Main Street from his third floor front window the police were setting up traffic barricades for the Fourth of July parade due to start in a couple of hours. The morning was cool, in the high fifties, and the sky was perfectly clear, the Flathead mountain range to the east like a Chamber of Commerce poster.

Someone knocked at the door and he went to answer it. He was a husky, thick-shouldered man in his mid-forties with blue, observant eyes. He still had the graceful movements of an athlete and this morning he was dressed in a light cashmere sweater, Pierre Cardin jeans, and hand-sewn soft leather boots. A small pixie of a girl smiled sweetly up at him when he opened the door, a serving cart in front of her.

A fire engine gave a single blast on its siren, and she giggled. "I've brought your breakfast, Mr. Clark," she said. "But you're going to want to get downstairs pretty soon if you want to get a good spot."

"I thought I might watch the parade from up here," Lane said, smiling. The girl couldn't have been more than seventeen or eighteen, with the all-American fresh-scrubbed look of small town. She had freckles and a complexion that was otherwise flawless with no makeup. Frannie would be a little jealous, though not much.

"No, sir, it wouldn't be the same."

"You don't say."

"Yes, sir. And after the parade there'll be the festival in the park. It's worth going to see. Lieutenant Governor Branson is coming in, and there'll be speeches and all that stuff. But it'll be cool."

The fire engine gave another test blast on its siren, answered by a couple of police cars. Lane had to laugh. Kalispell was like something out of his midwestern childhood, and he'd forgotten how sweet and uncomplicated places like this could be. Or at least appear to be on the surface.

"Let me set this up for you before it gets cold, sir," the girl said, and Lane stepped aside so that she could push the serving cart to the table by the windows.

With a population of just over twelve thousand, the town was Montana's seventh largest. The surrounding mountains, lakes, and forests were achingly gorgeous. But coming in early last night by air he'd been able to pick out only a few lights here and there outside of town. Most of the state was scarcely populated. And the people liked it that way for one reason or another.

The girl opened the serving cart's leaf and handed Lane the bill and a pen to sign it with. "You don't have to add anything extra. There's already a service charge. They do it at all the hotels around here now."

Lane signed it, added a good tip anyway, and handed it back to her. "It sounds as if the natives are getting restless out there already."

"Oh, no, sir. The Flatheads won't be coming in for the parade, mostly. They usually don't. But they don't ever cause any trouble."

"Do you mean Indians?"

The girl put the pen and bill in her apron pocket. "Yes, sir. But the reservation is south of the lake, down around Polson. They don't come up here much. But it used to be different. My dad told me about it."

"Maybe they want to be left alone," Lane said. "I think that a lot of people come out here for the same reason. Nobody bothers them. Just like they want it."

"Where did you hear something like that?"

"I don't know. Read it somewhere, I guess."

A flinty, suspicious look came into the girl's eyes, and she didn't look so young or innocent as before. But it only lasted a moment, and then she was smiling sweetly again. "I'll be going. Enjoy your breakfast."

"I don't suppose the real estate offices would be open today, would they?"

"Not until tomorrow. Are you thinking about buying something? My aunt May has her own agency. Kalispell Realty. Over in the mall."

"I'll look her up," Lane said, and he saw the girl to the door, locked it when she was gone, and secured the safety chain.

He checked the window again; already people had begun to gather for the parade, bringing their lawn chairs and picnic coolers with them. The town was all decked out in red, white, and blue bunting swinging from streetlamps. A squad of men who looked to be in their fifties, wearing bits and pieces of military uniforms, marched by. A blue and white police car was parked on the corner, but the cop was nowhere in sight. Nor were the people he'd come here to make contact with. But that would change soon.

He stepped away from the window and took his 9mm Beretta from the waistband beneath his sweater at the small of his back. He cycled all nine rounds out of the breach to check the action, then removed the magazine, reloaded the rounds in the same order they had come out, and stuffed the gun back in his waistband.

Breakfast was softly scrambled eggs, a rasher of medium-done bacon, hash browns, tomato juice with a slice of lemon, and unsweetened hot tea, also with a slice of lemon. He sat down to it, one eye toward the goings-on down on the street, and the other on the door. He was a man who did not like surprises not of his own making, and he had a feeling that this town, or at least the surrounding countryside, had plenty of them.

After breakfast he had a smoke by the open window. The street was filling up with people now, many of whom had already set up along the curbs. There were kids and dogs everywhere. In the distance to the northwest he could hear several different marching bands warming up, and every few minutes the fire engine would give a blast on its siren.

Lane used his cell phone to make a local call. Everything would depend on timing, he thought as he waited for it to go through.

Frances Shipley answered it on the first ring, her husky British accent mellifluous and out of place almost anywhere except in London or on stage. He and Frannie, who was a lieutenant commander in Her Majesty's Secret Intelligence Service, had been married for one year. Lane could not imagine a life without her. Together they headed a super secret and very tiny organization of troubleshooters for the White House and number 10 Downing Street called simply "The Room."

"Yes," she said.

"I'm getting set to head downstairs. Is everything ready on your end? Tommy's in place?"

"He's about a half-block out. Looks like he's eating an ice cream cone. Cheeky bugger."

"Ah, some people have all the luck."

"Yes, don't we, darling?" Frannie said sweetly.

"Any sign of our people? I haven't seen anything from here yet."

"They're in town."

"Okay, don't call me, I'll call you." Lane said, and he was about to switch off.

"Watch yourself, William," Frannie cautioned.

"You, too. Ta-ta." Lane broke the connection, pocketed the phone, and pulling on a light Gucci leather jacket, left his room and headed downstairs.

The parade was a half hour from starting and downtown was full. Shops such as clothing stores and hardware stores, and banks, post offices, city hall, and libraries were closed for the holiday. But places like restaurants, gift shops, bakeries, and ice cream shops were open and doing a land office business. There was probably no one left in town who wasn't here, and the tourists were easy to spot because their boots and jeans were too new, and they stood around self-consciously.

Lane spotted the woman across the street coming out of an art gallery specializing in Indian and cowboy artifacts. She was very tall and slender, wearing a light yellow dress with large blue polka dots, and a very large, gay nineties sort of summer hat that on her looked fantastic. Her maiden name was Gloria Swanson, and like her namesake she had wanted to become a serious actor. But because of a lack of talent she'd never made it. In her late forties, however, she still turned heads.

Lane waited in the crowd as she made her way across the street and went inside the Grand Hotel. He followed her inside in time to see her enter the lounge and take a seat at the empty bar. She took a cigarette out of her handbag, but before she could get out her lighter he was there with a match.

"Just like in the movies," he said.

She turned to look at him, her eyes soft, almost unfocused, her expression supremely indifferent. Close up he could see the lines under her makeup. "Thank you," she said, taking the light.

"Mind if I join you?"

"Yes," she said. "I do mind." She turned as the bartender, a young man with a large mustache and thick arms, came over, and she ordered a Sapphire martini; up, very dry, very cold. "Two olives, darlin'," she reminded him.

"Yes, Mrs. Sloan."

If her husband had used his real name hers would have been Mrs. Helmut Speyer, wife of a former East German Stasi intelligence officer and hit man. The West German BND had lost track of him after the Wall came down, and it wasn't until a few weeks ago that he was positively identified masquerading as Herbert Sloan here in Montana.

The bartender took his time making her drink, and when he was finished he came to the end of the bar where Lane had seated himself.

"What'll it be, sir?" he asked. His smile was fake.

"I'll have the same as hers, but if it's not as cold as outer Siberia you'll have to do it again."

The bartender leaned a little closer. "Whatever your game is, pal, it's not going to work. Just a word of advice? She's a married lady, and her husband and his pals don't take kindly to assholes."

"Nice speech." Lane grinned at him. "But I don't think the management would take *kindly* to its guests being treated like this."

"Let's see your room key."

Lane laid it on the bar. "Make that a Gibson, would you? Olives give me gas."

The bartender's brows knitted for a second, but then he nodded stiffly. "Sorry for the misunderstanding, sir. But this time of year we get all kinds in here." He glanced down the bar at the woman. "We tend to take care of our own."

"An admirable sentiment."

The bartender went to fix the drink and a moment later two men walked in. One of them was tall and very husky, his light brown hair cut very short in the military style. He wore khakis and a bush jacket, and he remained standing by the door to the lobby. If he was carrying a gun, Lane decided, it wasn't in a shoulder holster. He wore an earpiece.

The other man, much shorter, more compactly built, with short steel gray hair, a thin mustache, dressed in gray slacks and a blue blazer over an open collar white shirt, came directly across to the woman, who turned to him and offered her cheek.

"I thought I'd find you here," the man said with a hint of irritation. He was Helmut Speyer, aka Herbert Sloan.

"I was tired of waiting," his wife said languidly.

The bartender broke off from making Lane's drink. "Good morning, Mr. Sloan. Care for something?"

"A glass of beer."

"Yes, sir."

Speyer glanced briefly at Lane, and then turned back to his wife and said something too low to be heard. Lane looked over at the man standing by the door. He was Ernst Baumann, aka Ernest Burkhart, Speyer's chief of staff and bodyguard. He was staring at Lane. The German Federal Police also had warrants for his arrest on several charges of murder, arson and kidnapping, including three car bombings.

Lane nodded pleasantly and smiled at the man, then turned around as his drink finally came.

"No trouble, sir," the bartender warned softly. "Please."

"There'll be no trouble from me as long as my Gibson is cold," Lane said loudly enough for the others to hear.

"Finish up now," Speyer told his wife. "The parade is just about to start."

Lane sipped his drink, and he had to admit that it was a lot better than he expected it would be. "This is just fine," he said. "Tell the lady for me that she has good taste."

An old man, wearing a tired sport coat at least two sizes too large, his right hand in a pocket, came shuffling up Main Street. He was obviously in a lot of pain. A few people in the crowd gave him sympathetic looks, but most ignored him. He looked like a bum. He stopped in front of the Grand Hotel, hesitated for a few moments as if he was trying to make up his mind about something, then threw the last of his ice cream cone in a trash barrel and went inside.

The front desk clerk spotted him, but before he could decide what to do, an attractive woman dressed in a short cotton skirt, a brightly colored blouse, and sandals entered from the street. She took off her large sunglasses and came over.

"Good morning, madam," the clerk said.

"Ms.," Frannie corrected him, smiling sweetly. "I was rather wondering if you have a king size nonsmoking for the next five days. Everyone else in town seems to be booked."

"I'm sorry, no," the clerk said. He was a married man with three children, but he was so captivated by her looks and by her English accent that he didn't see the old man enter the lounge.

"Could you just check to make absolutely certain, ducky?"

"Certainly."

The old man walked into the barroom. He looked so harmless that Sergeant Baumann took a moment to react. Jew, he thought, but it was already too late because the old man had pulled a gun out of his pocket and pointed it directly at Speyer's head from a distance of only a few inches.

Speyer turned around and grinned, a hard, flat, expressionless look in his dead gray eyes. "Well, it's the Fourth of July and a patriot is here to celebrate. Care for a drink, old-timer?"

The old man cocked the hammer on the military Colt .45 which had to be as old as he was, and Baumann, who had started forward, stopped short. "I know who you are, *Schweinhund*."

"Then you have me at the disadvantage," Speyer replied calmly. "I don't think I've ever seen you before, but I've met so many people." He turned to his wife, who sat with her mouth half-open in a smile. "Do you recall this gentleman from your Hollywood days, my dear?"

"He looks like a Jew," she said, and she turned back to reach for her drink, slopping a little of it on the bar.

"There you are," Speyer said. "But you must forgive my wife's rudeness. Do you have a name?"

Baumann edged closer, and the old man caught sight of him in the mirror behind the bar. All of a sudden he thrust the muzzle of the .45 forward so that it touched Speyer's left cheek just below the eye. His hand began to shake. "You son of a bitch, before I kill you, you're going to remember." He raised the gun barrel and slashed it across Speyer's face, opening a small gash which instantly started to bleed.

The bartender had eased to the end of the bar where he picked up a phone.

"Put the telephone down, young man, or I'll shoot this man first, and then you," the old man called out. His accent was German. The bartender did as he was told and spread his hands out.

"Whatever the problem is, mister, we can work it out," he said.

"Two or three hundred grams of pressure on this trigger should do the trick nicely, I think," the old man said. "One month before the Wall came down. Me, my wife, my son, and my daughter could wait no longer, so we decided to escape. With all that was happening, Hoennecker on the way out, Gorbachev turning his back on us, I thought it was time. The guards were lax. So many were going over to the west. Nobody cared any longer, but nobody knew when another crackdown would come."

"Is that what this is, a case of mistaken identity?" Speyer asked. Blood ran down his cheek but he made no move to try to stanch the flow. "You think that I was a German border guard?"

"I never said that," the old man said calmly.

Speyer pursed his lips, realizing his stupid mistake. "I thought I heard—"

"*Kapitän* Helmut Speyer. The East German Secret Police, Stasi. Just happening by that night." The old man shook his head, the memory obviously painful. "You shot and killed my son and wife while I was atop the wall trying to help them over. Then you took my fourteen-year-old Lisa and offered to trade her life for mine."

"You took yours, obviously, though I don't know what you're talking about."

"I took mine because the West German police were right there and pulled me the rest of the way over. I had no choice. And by the time I could get to a place where I could see, you and she were gone."

Speyer shook his head. "I was never there—"

"I saw the records," the old man shouted. "You raped her first, and then you gave her to the guards who raped her until she was dead."

"No," Speyer said.

"Oh, yes," the old man said. His finger tightened on the trigger.

Bill Lane fired two shots, the first catching the old man in the left armpit, spinning him around, and the second catching him in the heart. His hand went to the fatal wound which erupted in a spray of blood as he fell to the floor, dead.

The sudden silence in the barroom was deafening. The bartender's mouth dropped open. "Holy shit, man, you shot him."

"I didn't like the odds," Lane said. "Besides, I know the crazy old bastard. He tried to come after me in Washington a couple of months ago." He slipped off the bar stool, and cocked an ear to listen. So far there were no sirens. "So what's the story, folks? Self-defense?"

"Who are you?" Speyer demanded.

"Let's just say that I'm a friend," Lane said. "And as of this moment I'm a murderer, unless you can help."

Speyer helped his wife down. "Get the car and bring it around back, *Liebchen.* And hurry, would you please?"

Gloria gave Lane a worried look, then gathered her purse and left.

"What happened here, Willy?" Speyer asked the bartender, but keeping an eye on Lane. "Was it an accident?"

"Whatever you say, Mr. Sloan."

"Okay, we have about two minutes, maybe less," Speyer said. "Who the hell are you and what are you doing here?"

"Like I said—" Lane had begun when the muzzle of Sergeant Baumann's pistol touched his temple.

"Mr. Sloan asked you a question."

"Do you trust the bartender?" Lane asked casually.

"That doesn't matter. You just have to trust that I'm not going to pull the trigger if you piss me off," Baumann said.

"John Clark. Until a few years ago I worked for South African Intelligence. I'm a freelance now."

"What are you doing here?" Baumann asked.

"Looking for a job."

"Working for me?" Speyer said, surprised.

"I'm good at what I do."

"Killing old men?" Speyer asked.

"Shit," Lane said, flinching. It was enough to throw Baumann's concentration off. Lane grabbed the sergeant's pistol, twisted it out of his hand, and stepped aside as he brought his own gun to the man's face. "Actually I do pretty good disarming stupid people, too."

"Son of a bitch," Baumann swore.

"Actually my mother was a saint, and I'll thank you to remember that in the future, or I'll take you apart bit by bit, *verstehen*?" Lane said. He handed Baumann back his gun. "Are you going to help me?" he asked Speyer.

"Are you wanted by the police?"

Lane hesitated. "Not in the United States."

A siren sounded outside. This time it was continuous and headed their way, not a test blast for the parade like earlier.

"The old man came in with a gun, and this gentleman shot him in self-defense. Have you got that, Willy?"

"Yes, sir," the bartender stammered.

"We were never here."

"No, sir."

"There'll be a coroner's hearing. When you're released, come look me up and we'll talk," Speyer told Lane.

He turned, stepped over the old man's body, and headed to the back door. Baumann followed him, and at the end of the bar he turned and gave Lane a look that was anything but friendly.

"Don't try to follow me, or I'll kill you," Lane told the bartender when Speyer and Baumann were gone. "I'm not going to be arrested here."

"No, sir."

Lane safetied his gun, stuffed it back in his waistband, and walked out into the lobby. The clerk was gone, and Frannie was crouched down in front of the front desk. She blew him a kiss. Lane reached the front door, but the cop car was stuck in the crowd a half block up Main Street. No one outside had heard the gunshots, which meant that the call to the police had probably come from the desk clerk. And there had already been so many sirens this morning that this one was being mostly ignored. It was better this way, he thought. Less chance of an innocent bystander getting in the middle of things, something they had worried about. Or some trigger-happy cowboy jumping up and taking potshots. That would have been great.

He worked his way through the crowd in the opposite direction from the cop car and turned right on First Street. The primary scenario was for him to show up at Speyer's ranch outside of Crazy Horse on the Flathead River northeast of town sometime tonight. The local police would have issued an all-points bulletin for his arrest by then; armed and dangerous. And they would have called the state police for help. The manhunt would hit all the radio stations and television feeds, and it would be on all the police frequencies, something they were pretty sure Speyer's people regularly monitored. John Clark would be legitimized.

When he reached the dark blue Range Rover that had been left for him this morning three blocks from the hotel, there were more sirens behind him converging on the murder scene. A big Lincoln Navigator SUV with dark tinted windows came around the corner. Lane unlocked his car and opened the door as the Lincoln pulled up. The back door opened and Speyer beckoned to him. "Come with us."

Gloria was in the backseat with him. Baumann was driving. "I'm not going to leave my stuff behind," Lane said.

"Don't be a fool," Speyer said. "The police know your name, and they'll be looking for this car."

"It can't be connected to me."

"Where the hell do you think you're going?"

"I was going to find out where you live and come out to see you tonight."

"You'd be dead before you got within a mile of me," Speyer said with mounting frustration. He said something to Baumann who was watching the rearview mirror. His bodyguard nodded. "I'm sending Ernst with you."

"Whatever you say." Lane got behind the wheel and closed the door. He took out his phone and, keeping it below the level of the windows, hit the speed dial button. Baumann and Speyer got out of the Lincoln and said something else to each other.

"Yes?" Frannie asked, breathless. She wasn't expecting his call so soon.

"Change of plans. Baumann is coming with me."

Speyer climbed into the Lincoln's driver's seat and Baumann shut the door.

"Are you in the Rover?" Frannie asked.

"Right," Lane said. He broke the connection and slipped the phone in his jacket pocket. Baumann came over and got in the passenger seat as Speyer took off.

"What do we do now?"

"We're going back up to Center Street where we can pick up Highway Two. That'll take us out of town, and give us some time to figure out what you're up to."

"What about the cops?"

Baumann pressed his earpiece a little closer. "They're still busy at the hotel." He was receiving police frequencies in the earpiece.

Lane started the car and pulled out. By the time they reached the highway a half-dozen blocks west of town the Lincoln was nowhere to be seen. Traffic was very light. The sirens behind them had finally stopped.

"You were told to stay at the hotel. Why didn't you?"

"I didn't want to get arrested."

"Why not? You said you didn't have a record, and Willy would have backed up your self-defense story. In a few days you'd have been in the clear."

"The gun I'm carrying isn't registered, and it doesn't have a serial number, for starts."

"Let's see it," Baumann demanded.

"Not a chance in hell," Lane told him. "At least not until I'm someplace that I consider safe."

The highway went east past the fairgrounds back into town, crossing Main Street a few blocks noth of the hotel. The crowds were thick downtown, but there were no signs of the police.

"You said that you worked for South African Intelligence?"

"That's right, until about five years ago."

"Who was your boss?"

"Roger deKlerk, and he was a dumb son of a bitch."

Baumann's lips pursed. "What brought you to the States?"

"I had a job in Vienna, and when it was over I had a choice of going to South America or coming here. I chose here."

"Why?"

"Seemed like the right thing to do at the time." He took out a cigarette and lit it without offering one to Baumann. "I don't like being crowded." He laughed. "And this is virgin territory, isn't it? Ripe with opportunities and all that?"

"Who was the old man?" Baumann asked.

"That one will wait until I can talk to your boss. I think he'll be interested in making a deal."

"Why did you come to Kalispell?"

"I was following . . . the old man."

"What was he doing here?"

"What, are you dense or something? He came here to find Speyer and kill him. And he damn near succeeded."

They crossed the Stillwater River, a couple of fishermen on its banks, as they headed toward the airport. A Delta jetliner was just coming in for a landing.

"And you just happened to be there in the bar, hustling the captain's wife, when all this happens," Baumann said. "What the hell are you trying to pull?"

"For Christ's sake, you dumb kraut, the old man was Meyer Goldstein. He used to work for the Wiesenthal Center in Vienna as a special investigator."

"So that story about his wife and children at the Wall was a lie?"

"I don't know. But Speyer was high on Goldstein's list because your boss helped hide some old SS officers with ties to the KGB in trade for Nazi gold left over from the war. It's what financed your move here, I expect. The Wiesenthal Center wanted to get its hands not only on those guys, but on what they figured was a major stash that Speyer might know something about. But Goldstein got unhinged and he wanted the past buried. Most of his family was gassed in the Holocaust, and he wanted to put an end to it."

"You said he tried to kill you."

Lane shrugged. "I lied. I followed Goldstein who I knew would lead me to your boss sooner or later. And I figured that one favor might deserve another."

"You want a part of the gold?"

"Very astute," Lane said disparagingly. "Next question: How did I know about Goldstein in the first place?"

Baumann's jaw tightened. "I was getting to it."

"My job in Vienna was for a client in Buenos Aires who wanted some records destroyed. Easy enough, but one thing led to another and I stumbled on Goldstein."

Baumann gave him a very hard look. "You expect me to believe such a story?"

"I don't care whether you do or not," Lane said

cheerfully. "I didn't come all this way to hold your hand. I came to save your boss's life—something you should have been able to do yourself—and ask for a job. One down, one to go."

State Highway 2 merged with State Highway 40, and a sign said HUNGRY HORSE, 10 MILES. Baumann told him to turn right, and they headed east toward the mountains, Glacier National Park, and the Continental Divide, one of the very few wilderness areas left in the entire United States.

Except for its large size, Speyer's mountain enclave would have looked at home in the Swiss Alps. A split-rail fence followed a crushed gravel driveway to a sprawling chalet. A sweeping veranda faced a broad, meandering stream and natural trout pools that reflected the not so distant snow-capped mountains. Several outbuildings, at least two of which looked like barracks, were across a field. A Bell Ranger helicopter sat on a pad beside a grass runway. A Gulfstream bizjet was parked in a hangar whose door was open. The entire compound was in a large clearing surrounded by dense forests.

There were at least a half-dozen men dressed in plain BDUs (Battle Dress Uniforms) doing work around the place. They looked up as the Range Rover came up from the highway and pulled up in front of the chalet.

"I didn't spot any surveillance on the way in," Lane said conversationally. They were five miles off the highway here.

"That's the whole idea," Baumann replied.

"Then my hat's off to you. I should have seen them."

One of the workmen in BDUs came over as Baumann and Lane got out of the car. He was a large, hard-looking man. He carried a Glock 17 in a shoulder holster, and he wore a flesh-toned earpiece.

"The captain is expecting you, sir," he told Baumann. "He'll meet you at the pool."

"Get this under cover, Carl, and take it apart. I want to see an inventory as soon as possible."

"Yes, sir."

"I wouldn't do that, if I were you," Lane warned him.

"I think we can handle it, sir," the guard said with a smirk. He made to get in the driver's seat.

Lane shrugged. "Just take it back in the woods, or somewhere else, if you would. It'll minimize your casualties."

A glass door in the veranda opened and Speyer came out of the house. He beckoned to them.

"Just a minute, sir, we have to take care of something first," Baumann called up to him. A couple of the other guards, sensing that something was going on, stopped what they were doing and looked up.

"Like I said, Ernst, I think we can handle this," Carl said politely. He was clearly not liking the situation he was in.

"What did you bring with you?" Baumann asked.

"A few weapons, some fragmentation grenades, a couple of LAWs rockets, a few RPGs, and fifty kilos of Semtex," Lane said. "Wasn't time to pick up the rest. I was traveling light."

Carl reached inside for the car keys, but Baumann stopped him. "Are they wired?"

"Of course. I don't want just anybody pawing through my stuff. That's one of the reasons I thought it wasn't wise to leave the car parked in town. Killing a Jew is one thing, but blowing up half of Kalispell would be another."

Carl strode around to the back of the Rover, and

inspected the door lock, hinges, and the window glass and frame. The back of the car was packed with what appeared to be ordinary luggage. He looked up. "I don't see any leads."

"Inside the door," Lane told him. "The mains are fiber-optics, embedded in the glass. You can't see them."

"Can we take it from the inside?"

Lane shook his head. "Pressure switches behind the backseat."

"We could put it up on a hoist and take the floor out."

Lane had to laugh. "Crude. But it'd be a neat trick if I was in a hurry and had to get my shit out of there."

"All right, smart-ass, we'll trace the circuitry—"

Lane wagged a finger at him. "Take the fuse cover off and it blows. Put a multimeter in the cigarette lighter and it blows. Disconnect the battery and it blows. Break the back window and . . ." He grinned. "Boom."

Even Baumann had to smile. "Are you going to tell us, or do we have to lose a few men to find out on our own?"

"Pop the gas filler door," Lane said. "The button is on the floor left of the driver's seat."

"Thank you," Baumann said. "As you suggested, we would like to minimize our casualties." He nodded for Carl to get to it, and he motioned for Lane to precede him up to the house.

They started away from the Rover, but Lane snapped his fingers and turned back. "By the way, Carl, tell your demolitions man to take it slow."

"What the hell are you talking about now?"

"Oh, if he's any good he'll figure it out," Lane said pleasantly. "But you might just mention to him that I had a Swiss connection in my wild youth."

* * *

A large indoor pool with a curved, tinted glass ceiling and walls looked down on a long valley rimmed by the mountains. A large section of the wall had been slid back, and four ceiling fans made it pleasant. Speyer, a bandage on his cheek, was seated at a patio table, sipping a glass of wine. Baumann led Lane over to him and they sat down.

"Mr. Clark, finally. I wanted to thank you for saving my life back there, although your timing was a little close."

"I had the advantage, I knew it was coming," Lane said.

"Let me have your gun, please."

Lane took out his pistol and started to eject the magazine, but Speyer held him off.

"No, don't unload it. Give it to me as it is." He held out his hand and Lane gave him the gun.

There was another patio table on the deck outside the pool enclosure. A brown pottery hurricane lamp sat on the table. Speyer fired one shot, and the lamp disintegrated.

"A nine-millimeter bullet carries a terrific impact, but have you thought about using a higher velocity weapon? Perhaps one whose magazine holds more rounds?"

"This gun's an old friend. We've been through a lot together, and it's never let me down."

Speyer carefully lowered the hammer and switched the safety lever. He put the gun on the table. "The name you used to register at the hotel is a fake, although interestingly enough the credit card is valid. What does that mean?"

"John Clark was a real person who died eight years ago in Arlington, Virginia. Car accident. It's one of the American passports I use."

"What's your real name?"

"John Browne, with an e."

"Social security number?"

"I'm not an American, so I don't have a social security number. But I have a South African national identity code." Lane gave him the number.

Baumann picked up a phone and repeated the information.

"Don't you want to take my fingerprints?" Lane asked.

"We already have them," Baumann said.

Speyer was watching him closely. "So, Mr. Browne with an e, late of South African Intelligence, what do we make of you?"

"I came here looking for a job."

"You took a big chance, didn't you? Shooting a man in the heart in cold blood and in front of witnesses is extreme in the least." Speyer poured another glass of wine. "Carrying an unregistered weapon, driving around in a car not licensed to you, and loaded with illegal weapons and explosives. Weren't you concerned about getting stopped?"

"No," Lane said unconcernedly. "I knew that you would hire me. You'd be a fool not to. I have the skills that your organization needs."

Speyer considered that for a moment. "We could kill you, I suppose. Dispose of your body and that would be the end of it. Nobody would come here looking for you. Willy is trustworthy. The local police are thinking about turning over the investigation to the state police who will in time turn it over to the FBI. But that might take weeks because so far there's no identification on the man you killed."

"Interpol will have his prints."

"This is Montana. The investigation might not go that far."

"Then you have nothing to worry about."

"I never did. It's you who has everything to worry about."

Baumann tensed a little. Lane knew that this could go either way. Speyer was in the middle of something big. They knew that much from the German Federal Police, who had asked for help, but they did not know what it was. Speyer would have to be very sensitive right now, alert for anything that smacked of a coincidence.

"I don't think that you're a man who throws away valuable assets, Herr *Kapitän*. And that's exactly what I could be to you. In part because I am expendable."

"That's a good point," Speyer said. "You're handy with a gun, and from what I'm told you know something about demolitions. What else can you do that would make you a valuable asset?"

"I can fly the jet and the Bell Ranger I saw coming in. My French and German are pretty good, and I can get by in Spanish in a pinch." Lane grinned. "I'd like to say that I carry a five handicap in golf, but I never did like the game so I couldn't beat a nine. Do I have a job?"

"What else?" Speyer asked.

"The usual. Hand-to-hand combat, survival training, codes and code breaking, surveillance and tailing, wiretapping, sport diving, and I'm a C-rated fencer in foil and épée."

Speyer and Buamann exchanged a look. "What if I say no? What then?" Speyer asked.

"I would think that you were damned ungrateful," Lane said. He shrugged. "I would hope that there'd be no trouble here. I mean you'd let me go and all that. I suppose I'd go down to Buenos Aires. I can get another job there. But I was looking for a change of scenery. Something different."

"Gold?" Baumann asked.

"I wouldn't turn down some serious money if it came my way," he said. "But I'm willing to earn it, if you know what I mean."

Speyer took a drink. "Did you leave anything of interest in your hotel room?"

"Toiletries kit, a few items of clothing, an overnight bag. All bought here in the States, and all untraceable."

"You mentioned that the car is untraceable, too."

"I bought it from a chop shop in Miami two weeks ago. It's registered to Paul Asimov in Detroit. I have a valid driver's license in that name, too."

Speyer sat back. "I'll give you marks for inventiveness and balls."

"Thanks. What about the job?"

"We'll see," Speyer said. "You'll stay with us until we can do a background check. If everything looks good we'll talk some more. I may have a use for you after all."

Baumann rose and motioned for Lane to do the same.

"Ernst will show you to your room," Speyer said. "One thing, though, don't try to leave the property just yet. I'd hate to see something happen to you out there in the valley. There are wolves and bears around here. We don't mess with them and they don't mess with us unless someone wanders around where they shouldn't be. We've placed bait stations around the perimeter."

"I catch your meaning."

"Good," Speyer said.

The chalet's great room soared three stories to the sloped ceiling. A spiral staircase led to a broad balcony off which the bedrooms were located. A massive stone fireplace dominated the center of the room, while the main wall was glass, the view nothing less than spectacular.

"No one bothers you up here?" Lane asked.

"The captain has a number of investments in the area, and his privacy is respected," Baumann said.

They crossed the great room and went upstairs to a large, very well-appointed bedroom at the end of the hall, with a view only slightly less spectacular than from downstairs. A big bathroom included double sinks, a mirrored wall, walk-in shower, hot tub, and a toilet and bidet. A television was set in a large armoire just like in a hotel. But unlike the hotels Lane had stayed in, this room was equipped with a closed-circuit television camera mounted in the ceiling.

"Am I going to be locked in here until mealtimes?" Lane asked, looking around the room, opening drawers, trying the lights.

"On the contrary, you have free run of the compound. But don't wander off, as the captain suggested; it could be dangerous to your health in more than one way. The helicopter and hangar are off limits for the time being of course, and if you happen upon a locked door—don't try your luck."

"I have a couple of suitcases with my clothes and other things in the car that I'd like to have."

"When they're cleared they'll be brought to you," Baumann said at the door. "A word of advice, Mr. Browne, don't fuck with us, you'll lose."

Lane spread his hands and smiled. "I don't want to give anyone a bad impression. I'm here for a job. And if I get it, you and I will be working together, so I want us to be friends, or at least be able to tolerate each other. Deal?"

"Dinner is at eight. Stay out of trouble in the meantime," Baumann said. He left.

Lane took off his jacket, tossed it over a chair and went into the bathroom where he splashed some cold water on his face. The door was not locked, nor were the windows secured. The telephone had a dial tone, but the red light on the closed-circuit television camera was glowing, indicating that he was being watched. He turned on the television and switched to a local channel in time to catch a news bulletin about the fatal shooting of a so far unidentified old bum in the Grand Hotel by John Clark, a hotel guest, who had disappeared after the shooting. The only witness was William Hardt, the bartender, who told police that Clark had been seated at the bar. When the old man came in, Clark jumped up, shot him in the heart as cool as could be, and walked out.

No one had ever seen the old man before, and a manhunt was currently under way for Clark.

Speyer was leaning against a fence in the horse paddock thinking that he was going to miss all of this. Baumann came over from the house with a file folder, and said, "He checks out, but I don't trust him."

"Do you trust anybody, Ernst? Even me?" Speyer looked at his sergeant.

"Only you, sir. But the bastard showing up here was too coincidental for me. Are you going to hire him?"

"If he's who he says he is, he'll be useful."

"Apparently he is."

"The dive is going to be very dangerous, no telling what we're going to run into down there even with the engineering diagrams to guide us. It's been almost sixty years. If he can find the package, attach a line to it and guide it to the main entrance, it wouldn't matter what happens afterwards."

Baumann looked out across the paddock to the

river valley and the mountains beyond. "I hate it here."

"This was never more than a temporary safe haven, Ernst. We discussed that in the beginning. And it has served our purposes admirably."

Baumann laughed. "He was screwing deKlerk's wife, and got out of Cape Town about two steps ahead of a firing squad. Afterwards they decided to keep quiet about it, didn't want the embarrassment, I suppose."

"Then perhaps my wife will be useful after all," Speyer said.

"Sir?"

"He dresses well, and he's obviously a ladies' man. Perhaps Gloria can keep an eye on him."

Baumann didn't know what to say. He was obviously uncomfortable.

Speyer clapped him on the arm. "Take it easy, Ernst. We have a lot of difficult, dangerous work ahead of us, but afterwards it'll be Eden." A snatch of some Americanism came to him, and it was annoying. *Be careful what you wish for, you might get it.* He shook himself out of what he knew could become a bad mood if he allowed himself the luxury. "What about the Swiss connection he mentioned?"

"The Rover's wiring was very sophisticated. Hans had a hell of a time with it. He told me that without Browne's clue he might have screwed up. The son of a bitch used Swiss-made superfast electrical switches that are used on American nuclear weapons. You have to wonder how the hell he got them."

"Interesting," Speyer said. "What else?"

"He has money, or at least he did have. His suitcases—all of them matched Louis Vuitton—are filled with Armani suits, Gucci and Bruno Magli shoes and boots, silk ties, handmade shirts; everything first-class. And damned expensive."

"He came here looking for gold," Speyer said, suppressing a smile. "He's a man of expensive tastes who is probably broke, or else he wouldn't have taken such a chance. Sounds good to me, Ernst. Just the man we're looking for, and at just the right time we need him."

"That's what I mean by coincidence," Baumann said glumly.

Speyer laughed, the sound harsh, and he gave his sergeant a hard look. "Thank God for some coincidences. What would you have done if the old man had actually shot me?"

"I would have killed him."

"A little late for me," Speyer said. He took the file folder from Baumann. "Ask our guest to join us for dinner, please. Cocktails at seven-thirty, I should think."

The dining room was across the back of the house, and floor-to-ceiling windows afforded them a magnificent view of the mountains. The long table was set for four. Speyer was dressed in a smoking jacket with a bright red ascot, while his wife wore an extremely tight black cocktail dress with almost no back and a deeply plunging neckline. At her age she nearly looked ludicrous, but not quite.

"It seems as if you are who you say you are," Speyer told Lane.

"I'm glad to hear it. I was starting to get a little paranoid," Lane said. He was dressed in an Armani linen suit, Gucci loafers without socks, and a collarless white silk shirt buttoned at the neck.

A white-coated waiter came up. "Would you care for a drink, captain?" he asked. He was one of the men from outside whom Lane had seen in plain fatigues earlier in the day.

"Whatever Mr. Browne is having," Speyer said graciously.

"Dom Perignon vintage. Let's say ninety-three. But I want it very cold."

"Yes, sir," the waiter said and he left.

"Not Cristal?" Gloria asked.

Lane shrugged. "But then this is Montana, madame, not Los Angeles."

She smiled vacantly.

"Do you have any family back in Cape Town?" Speyer asked. "Wife and kiddies, mother and father?"

"My mother's in a nursing home in Willowmore, my father, who was an only child, died ten years ago, and my wife and son died in a car accident five years ago."

"How did it happen?"

Lane's eyes narrowed, and his lips compressed. "Some bloody bastards were chasing us. There was an accident and they were both killed instantly."

"Who was chasing you?"

"A couple of Russian intelligence officers."

"What happened to them?"

Lane looked up. "I killed them. Why did you want to know?"

Speyer shrugged. "Something more to check. You mentioned that you were a sport diver."

"Actually a bit more than that. I was a Special Guards UDT officer before I transferred to the Secret Service."

"Mixed gasses?" Baumann asked, curiously.

"Some, but not under combat conditions. I was trained to two hundred meters."

"Did you like that job?" Baumann persisted.

"I don't know, it was okay, I guess. Where are you taking this?"

"How hot are you in Germany?" Speyer asked.

"There's a warrant for my arrest in Austria and one in Switzerland for currency violations. They're at least three years old, and since I broke only a couple of banking laws, and nobody, especially not the Swiss, were screwed out of anything, I don't think they're looking very hard for me."

"Tell us, are you broke, Mr. Browne?" Gloria asked with some amusement.

Lane chuckled. "I'm not impecunious, if that's what you mean. But I'm not rolling in it either. I wouldn't have come here looking for a job otherwise."

The champagne came. After it was poured, Speyer proposed a toast. "To our new associate, Mr. Browne with an 'e.' That is, if he wants the job after I tell him about it."

Lane raised his glass and took a drink. The wine was very cold and quite good. "What are we after, gold in some old Nazi bunker in Germany?"

"A Nazi bunker is close, but it's not gold we'll be seeking," Speyer said. "But all that will be made clear to you as and when you need the information. The problem is water, and a lot of it. What we want is at least a hundred meters deep. The dive would be very dangerous."

"I've done worst things, I suppose."

"The rewards would be very handsome," Speyer said.

"Don't you have any competent divers on your staff?" Lane asked.

"Frankly, no. It was an issue that we were just starting to come to grips with. Will you take the job?"

"What if I say no?"

Speyer just laughed.

Lane grinned. "Well, I did come all this way looking for employment, and I have put my arse on the line." He turned to Gloria. "Pardon the expression, madame." He raised his glass. "I'm yours, Herr *Kapitän*. Let's drink to, if not a long association, at least a profitable one."

"*Prost*," Speyer said, and they all drank.

After dinner Lane went outside on the porch to get some fresh air and have a smoke. Gloria joined him, and took a cigarette.

"It gets cold here," she said. "I'm glad we're finally leaving."

"Where are we going—that is, if I'm included in the move?" Lane asked. It was dark, and there were a billion stars in the moonless sky. The temperature had already dropped to the low fifties.

"Helmut will tell you when the time comes," she said. She wasn't wearing a wrap, and she shivered. "It's too cold out here for me. I'm going in."

"I'll stay awhile," Lane said.

At the patio door she gave him an oddly appraising look. "What does impecunious mean?"

"Flat broke."

"I see," she said, and she went inside.

Lane walked down from the house toward the river. A hundred yards to the west was a small orchard of apple trees. He angled over to them, and when he was certain that no one was following him, pulled out his phone and hit the speed dial for the Kalispell number. Frannie answered on the first ring.

"Shipley and Hughes Accounting. Our office hours are from ten A.M. to six P.M. Eastern. At the tone please leave your message."

"What if this were an emergency, and I had to wait for all of that?" Lane asked.

"Don't get testy on me, love. Are you all right?"

"So far so good. They've offered me a job, diving, but according to Speyer it's not gold they're after."

"What then?"

"I don't know, but apparently we're going to Germany, to a Nazi bunker, so our BKA friends in Berlin got at least that right."

"I'll pass it back to them, and see if they've come up with anything new."

"Baumann is suspicious of me, so I don't know how long it'll be before they discover this phone and take it from me. It looks like we'll be leaving here soon, so keep on your toes, but don't crowd us."

"Don't take any unnecessary chances, William. This isn't rocket science, after all."

"We're in the wrong business for not taking chances," Lane said. Someone had come out of the house and was smoking a cigarette on the porch. Lane could make out the figure, but not who it was. "How is everything at your end? Is Tommy okay?"

"The dear old man is about to have a heart attack laughing at me," Frances said seriously.

"Let me guess, it was because you called the hotel clerk ducky."

"I am a Brit."

"But ducky?" Lane demanded. The figure moved off the porch and headed down the hill. "Got to go, love. I'm about to have some company."

"Take care, William."

"You too."

Lane got halfway up the hill before he could see that the figure was Baumann. He waved and Bumann stopped and waited for him to come the rest of the way.

"What were you doing down there?"

"I was trying to spot one of your bears," Lane said. He grinned. "But they mustn't be out and about yet."

"You were told not to wander around."

"I didn't know that accepting a job offer meant that I'd be restricted to quarters."

"It meant that you follow orders."

Lane shrugged. "Whatever." He glanced back toward the river. "How about tomorrow? Is there any trout in that stream? I'd like to try my luck."

"There won't be any time. We're leaving first thing in the morning."

"To where?"

"You'll find out when we get there."

"What about my car?"

"It stays here," Baumann said. "And that'll be all the questions. You'll be told what you need to know when you need it."

In the distance to the southwest a Fourth of July rocket burst very low on the horizon. "Too bad we couldn't be in town tonight to catch the celebration. I'm in a mood to party."

"I wasn't aware that South Africans were so interested in American holidays."

Lane laughed. "Lighten up, Ernst. A party's a party. It's got to get pretty boring up here after places like Berlin. Not much to do, unless you like trout fishing or dodging bears."

Baumann's eyes narrowed. "Don't fuck with me, Browne. If you so much as fart at the wrong time I'm going to jam my hand down your throat and rip your heart out."

"Right," Lane said. He stepped around Baumann and headed back up to the house. He got two steps and he turned around. "Don't bother coming up to tuck me in, Ernst, I think I can manage on my own."

Speyer was on the veranda, drinking a beer and watching the distant fireworks. Baumann went up to him. "I don't trust the bastard."

"Don't be tedious, Ernst. We've already had this discussion, unless you've learned something new."

"He could be a plant."

"What, a BND agent all the way here from Munich? You said he checked out."

"Creating a background isn't all that difficult," Baumann said.

Speyer considered it for a moment but shook his head. "If German intelligence suspected that we were up to something, let alone where we had gotten ourselves to, they would have sent more than one man to check us out. And I don't think they would have gone so far as to kill a man just to get in my good graces."

"Maybe they faked the shooting."

"I saw the blood with my own eyes. And Browne's gun checked out. The APB is on all the wires. If the BND wanted us, they would have asked the CIA for help, and with that bureaucracy they would have raised a dust cloud all the way from Washington that we couldn't have missed."

"I hope you're right," Baumann said.

"I know I'm right, Ernst. I did some checking of my own. There is no CIA operation against us in the works. Guaranteed."

"What about the FBI?"

"My Washington contact would have heard if anything was in the wind. And there's nothing. Browne is a smart-talking bastard, but he's the right man for us at the right time and place. The moment he retrieves the package, he's yours. Until then he's mine. Do you understand?"

Baumann nodded. "Yes, sir."

"Fine," Speyer said after a beat. "Now be a good sergeant and fetch me another beer, would you?"

Speyer retired to his quarters around midnight after making sure that the night shift was on duty and nothing was going to blindside them. Gloria was lying back on the couch in the sitting room, the lights low, watching the closed-circuit television monitoring Lane's room. He was in bed and apparently asleep.

"How long have you been watching?" Speyer asked, more amused than annoyed.

She was half-drunk on champagne. She looked up and grinned. "For a couple of hours. Since he came back."

"Did he leave the bathroom door open for you, my dear?"

"Yes," she said. "He doesn't have as much hair as you, Helmut, but he has more muscles. Does that make you sore?"

"Not at all," Speyer said. "As a matter of fact I want you to keep an eye on him for me."

"He's got a big prick, too," Gloria said. She was baiting him, but it wasn't working tonight. He no longer gave a damn.

Speyer laughed. "I hope you find him amusing."

"Oh, anything but that."

"Well, we're getting an early start in the morning, so if I were you, I'd come to bed soon." Speyer kissed his wife on the cheek, then headed for the bathroom.

"Helmut, do you know what impecunious means?" she called to him.

"Of course. It means he's dead broke. Didn't you know the word?"

She turned back to the television without answering him, the vacant look back in her eyes as she poured another glass of wine.

2

WASHINGTON, D.C.

Everything Speyer did seemed to be first-class, down to the plush carpeting and leather upholstery in the Gulfstream jet. But reading between the lines Lane got the impression that all of this—the plane, the cars, the lavish spread in Montana—was straining him to the limit, and he'd been forced into working on something very dangerous that would somehow fill the coffers once and for all. The big score.

Like a lot of ex-Stasi officers, Speyer was nothing but a two-bit thug, albeit a well-to-do two-bit thug.

They landed at Washington's Reagan Airport a few minutes before 5:00 P.M. local, where a Lincoln Town Car limousine driven by a uniformed chauffeur was waiting for them. Speyer dismissed the captain, copilot and steward for the night, but cautioned them to remain on call and sober. They would be staying at the Holiday Inn Downtown on Thomas Circle, and Speyer did not want to chase around town trying to find them if he needed to take off in a hurry.

With the last of the rush hour traffic it was after six by the time Speyer, Gloria, Baumann, and Lane crossed the Key Bridge into Georgetown, and another fifteen minutes before they pulled into the circular driveway of a lovely old three-story Georgian mansion just off R Street across from Montrose Park. The house was owned by Thomas Mann, a distant cousin of the famous writer.

It felt odd to Lane to be back like this, because he

and Frannie maintained a house a half-dozen blocks away in a back alley called Rock Court. But he didn't think there was much risk of being recognized here, not unless they went out to dinner someplace public tonight.

A slight man with thinning white hair, who walked with a stoop and was impeccably dressed in a three-piece London-tailored suit, waited for them in the flower-filled conservatory at the back. When the doorman left, the man gave Gloria a warm hug, and then shook hands with Speyer.

"It's good to be back in Washington, Herr General," Speyer said.

I'm glad that you're here, and of course you can count on me to help," Mann said in a comradely tone.

"You remember Sergeant Baumann," Speyer said.

"Of course. You're looking fit, Sergeant."

"Thank you, sir."

"And this is a new associate of ours, John Browne, until lately with South African Intelligence. I've hired him because of his . . . unique talents."

Mann sized him up coolly, and then shook hands. "How is it that you met Helmut?"

"Let's just say that I was in the right place at the right time," Lane replied.

"He saved my life," Speyer explained.

Mann smiled thinly. "A valuable talent to have around."

"Not only that, but he's a diver. South African UDT. Two hundred meters."

"So you're going after it finally," Mann said with some interest. "You must have found the key."

"Only the means to the key," Speyer said. "Which is why I'm here in Washington, and which is why I'm going to need your help, Herr General. But with your connections in Washington I don't think it should present a problem."

Mann poured them each a glass of sherry. "All right, what can I do for you?"

"I need to know the chief of Russian intelligence here in Washington, and I need to know how closely he's being watched by the FBI."

"Ivan Lukashin. Has a nice house over in Arlington. Three car garage, pool. A couple of golf and tennis memberships. He's better connected here in Washington than your congressmen from Montana. The FBI was watching him because there was a rumor that he was somehow involved with a drug smuggling ring. Russian mafia. But they couldn't come up with any hard evidence, so they backed off a couple of months ago."

"Is he connected?"

"If you mean in the Mafia, I frankly don't know, but I wouldn't be surprised. He can't afford that lifestyle on his *rezident*'s pay, so he's getting help from somewhere."

"How about in the Kremlin?"

"His father was a missile service general, and his wife's father was just appointed to Putin's special advisory staff," Mann told him. "What are you getting at?"

"I need his help, and I'm looking for a weakness that I can exploit," Speyer replied easily. He'd seemed tense before, but now he seemed relaxed.

"Obviously it will be money. I can set up a meeting and secure the introductions. But what do you need him for?"

Speyer took a leather-clad notebook and Mont Blanc pen from his vest pocket, jotted down the names of four men, tore out the paper and passed it to Mann. "I need to hire these four men, and I must be assured of their loyalty to me, and their complete discretion."

Mann read the names and looked up. "Russians still in Germany?"

Speyer nodded. "They are deep cover, and so far as I know they want to keep it that way. But they have some information and the connections with German Television One that I need."

"The fewer the people involved, the better off you'll be," Mann warned.

"I know. But if the information I have is accurate, and if it fits with what these four can tell me and do for me—providing they'll cooperate—then we'll be home free."

Mann sat back, sipped his sherry, and gave Speyer a long, appraising look. "You have been after this holy grail—whatever it really is—for a long time, Helmut. I'll help even though I don't know what it is. I owe at least that much to you."

"Thank you, Herr General," Speyer said. "And believe me that you don't want to know the details. How soon can you arrange the meeting?"

"Later tonight, I should think. If that's not too soon for you."

"Just perfect," Speyer said.

"You must understand that you are playing at a dangerous game. The Russians no longer want to be connected with us; they have their own problems. The old ideologies are gone. It's purely a matter of money now, and personal gain. Lukashin is a master at it."

"I'll keep that in mind, my old friend," Speyer said. "Thank you."

Sitting alone in his second floor study, Thomas Mann had another thought. The arrangements for the meeting tonight were set, but something didn't seem right with the new man. He phoned an associate in Helena, Montana. "I have a mutual friend with me here in Washington," he said.

"I shouldn't be surprised, with the trouble in Kalispell," said Konrad Aden. Like Mann, he was a prominent attorney and businessman, but he was also the western chief of staff for the Friends, a loose worldwide organization of former Stasi officers in hiding around the world. He dealt with only the most prominent of men in the U.S. west of the Mississippi.

"Is he in any immediate trouble?"

"No, nothing like that. He has friends out here. But he was seen coming out of the Grand Hotel after the shooting. I have some reliable people on their way down to cover his tracks. He may have missed something."

"I've heard nothing about a shooting."

"It won't hit the national news," Aden said. He told Mann everything that had happened, including the current lack of progress in the police investigation.

"It sounds like a set-up to me. I suspect he's actually brought the shooter here with him. Tall, well dressed, says he's John Browne, former South African Intelligence."

"He could be the same man," Aden said. "What are they up to?"

"I don't know yet. But clean up the mess out there, and if you find out anything new let me know."

"Is Browne legitimate?"

"Helmut seems to think he is, but I'll do my own checking. The problem is one of coincidence, I should think."

"I agree." Aden chuckled. "Helmut was always the brash one. Our risk taker."

"Age has not changed him," Mann said, and he rang off.

* * *

They had their own beautifully appointed, spacious rooms, each with a bathroom. Speyer came down to Lane's sitting room, and tossed him the Beretta. "You might have use for this."

"Thanks. I was wondering when I'd get it back." Lane said. He checked the action and then the load, before stuffing it in his belt at the small of his back.

"Have you ever heard of this Russian?" Speyer asked. "Lukashin?"

"It's a new name to me."

"He's supposed to be one tough son of a bitch, and he'll almost certainly not come to the meeting alone."

"Is that where I come in?" Lane asked.

Speyer nodded. "Just keep in the background, and keep your mouth shut. But if the need should arise, kill him."

"I had a silencer in my luggage."

Speyer took it out of his pocket and handed it to him. "We're meeting with them at the Lincoln Memorial at ten o'clock, and it could go either way."

"I'll be ready," Lane said. "But it would be helpful if I knew what the hell I'm putting my life on the line for."

"Money," Speyer replied coolly.

"There's money, and then there's money, if you catch my meaning."

"You're right," Speyer said after a slight hesitation. "You're either going to walk away from this operation a rich man, or you're going to end up dead. So you might as well know what you're in for."

"That's fair enough," Lane said. "What's at the bottom of a flooded Nazi bunker that has you interested enough to hire me and to talk to the Russians? Gold?"

"The bunker was one of Hitler's research centers for *Wunderwaffen*."

"Rockets?"

"Something better than that."

"Nukes?"

Speyer shook his head. "That part's not important. They were using a special catalyst for their experiments, and they drained nearly all the Third Reich's entire supply—most of which came from Jews gassed in the concentration camps."

"If it's not gold, what then? What's worth all this effort? Platinum? But that would be too heavy."

"Diamonds," Speyer said. "From engagement rings, heirloom jewelry, that sort of thing. A lot of those Jews were rich. There's maybe three hundred million dollars' worth down there stored in a safe in the main research laboratory."

"Why hasn't anyone gone after them before now?"

"In the first place, those records came into our hands in East Germany, and were buried until I came across them. And secondly, it would be impossible to get down there unless you had the engineering diagrams of the bunker system. There was an explosion right after the war, probably a booby trap, and the entire place is filled with water, and no way to drain it or pump it out. The Russians capped the entrances with a few hundred tons of concrete and marked it as a mass grave."

"But they really didn't cap it."

"Not that one, nor did they completely seal a dozen others. It's those records I want, and I know the four men who have access to them. Lukashin's the key."

"What's the connection to German television all about?"

"We're going to do a documentary. That's how we're going to get inside without attracting any government attention."

"Okay, I'm with you so far. But what about the Russians, do they know what's there?"

"I destroyed that part of the record."

Something wasn't adding up for Lane. The German Federal Police were interested in what Speyer was going after, and the Russians knew the layout of the bunker and how to get into it. Why hadn't something been done by now? "What do the Russians think is there?"

"A bunch of dead Jews."

"Besides that," Lane insisted. "They'll want to know why you want to get down there. What are you going to tell them?"

Speyer gave him a calculating look. "You don't miss much, do you?"

"Diving into a flooded bunker to retrieve something is only part of it. I want to know who'll be coming after me when it's over, and why. It has to be more than diamonds."

Speyer was silent for a long time. But then he nodded. "The Nazis were doing human research, genetics. They supposedly created some monsters."

Lane gave him a skeptical look.

"I don't mean bogey men. I mean *monstrousities*. And the present German government, as well as everyone else who knows anything about the program, called Reichsamt Seventeen, doesn't want to dredge it up again. The program was ten times worse than the gas chambers, and a thousand times worse than even Josef Mengele. Inhuman beyond belief."

Even for you, Lane wanted to say. "And they used diamonds as a catalyst."

"A lot of diamonds."

"What happens afterwards?"

"To you?" Speyer asked.

"That's a start."

"You'll get paid off, and then you'll have to make a decision. Either go off on your own or come with us."

"Where might that be?"

"Eden," Speyer said.

Lane laughed. "Okay, assuming I buy into your Eden, wherever it might be, what about the Russians? Once they figure out what we've brought up they'll want a share."

"We're going to kill them."

"They still have a long reach."

"It won't matter. We'll be beyond it," Speyer said with supreme confidence.

"Why not kill me, too?"

Again Speyer hesitated for a long time. "Because Eden won't be the end of it. There'll be other projects. If you prove out on this one, I'll have further use for you. As you so astutely pointed out at the ranch, I'm not a man who throws away valuable assets."

"No, I don't expect you are. But I think your friend General Mann is right. You *are* playing a dangerous game. The Russians are not nice people, and they have very long memories."

Speyer threw back his head and laughed. "That's rich," he said. "That's very rich."

The evening was lovely. Lights from the Lincoln Memorial sparkled in the reflecting pool. Straight up the Mall the Washington Monument rose into the night sky, and beyond it the mass of the U.S. Capitol building was like something out of Gibbon's *Decline and Fall of the Roman Empire*. There was still plenty of traffic on Constitution Avenue and Alternate 50. Some pleasure boats were on the river. Lane drove a Lincoln Town Car, Baumann and Speyer in the backseat. He came down Bacon Drive as far as traffic was permitted, and parked.

There were a few other cars parked here and there, and a Capital City Tours bus had pulled up to the west of the entry. The passengers were getting off while the driver walked away and lit a cigarette. The imposing statue of Lincoln sat serenely behind the thirty-six columns.

"Keep your eyes and ears open, and your mouth shut," Speyer said.

"They'd be fools to start anything here," Lane replied. "Too public."

"Don't count on it. They have diplomatic immunity, a privilege we do not enjoy."

Lane opened the car door for them. Speyer got out and Baumann slid across right behind him.

"Watch your sight lines," Baumann warned.

They started up the stairs, Speyer in the lead, when three men came from inside. They wore suits and ties, but the one in the center was much better dressed. He obviously had a sense of fashion unusual for a Russian. The other two looked like typical Russian muscle.

Speyer picked up on it immediately. "Mr. Lukashin," he said.

"Yes, and you're Helmut Speyer," the Russian said, his English barely accented. They shook hands.

"Thank you for agreeing to meet on such a short notice—"

"Let's take a walk," Lukashin said. "This way, if you don't mind."

They went across the circular drive and took the stairs down to the reflecting pool where there were only a handful of people out and about, most of them heading to the Vietnam War Memorial. Lukashin's two bodyguards kept close to their boss, and Lane and Baumann flanked them.

The Russian Washington *rezident* had come to his post in the past six months, and Lane had the troubling thought seeing him now in person that he'd met the man somewhere. He was tall, but slender like a soccer player, and his eyes were blue, his hair blond. Very unusual for a Russian man. Lane tried to think where he might have met him. It was worrisome because he thought he'd seen the spark of recognition in Lukashin's eyes.

"Thomas was somewhat mysterious," Lukashin said. "But we've always had good dealings in the past. And you come highly recommended by him."

"This isn't a social call," Speyer said unnecessarily.

"No, I didn't expect it was." Lukashin glanced at Lane and Baumann, but didn't bother asking for introductions.

"I need some help from you, and I'm willing to pay handsomely, but only on one condition," Speyer said.

"I'm listening."

"Once we conclude our business you will make no attempt to find my whereabouts, or in any way contact me, or even mention my name to anyone. When this operation has been completed I'll need to make myself very scarce. Perhaps for a very long time."

"I can live with that. What do you want from me?"

Speyer took an envelope from his pocket and handed it to Lukashin. "These are the names and brief dossiers of four former KGB officers who worked with Stasi in East Germany. They're still there, under deep cover working for the SVR. I want to hire them, but they will have to be discreet, and they'll have to understand that once this project has been completed, their covers will be blown and they will have to leave

Germany forever. Where they go after that makes no difference to me."

Lukashin held the pages up to the light from a lamppost and briefly glanced at the information. "You want these men because of certain knowledge they have?"

"That, and their contacts in Germany."

Lukashin thought about it for a moment. "I don't think that they would be welcome at home afterward," he said. "In any case the cost of their repatriation would be very steep. I'll leave that part of the deal to your discretion. What will you have them do?"

"We're going to film a documentary."

Lukashin glanced at the four brief dossiers again. "Under the noses of the BKA, without anyone being the wiser." The BKA was the German Federal Police Bureau.

"That's exactly it."

"Afterwards everyone disappears, and in time even the documentary will be forgotten. I, on the other hand, have a very good memory."

Speyer handed him another envelope. "You might find this interesting."

Lukashin opened it and examined the documents that Mann had supplied Speyer. When he was finished reading he looked up, a very interested expression on his face now. "Very generous," he said.

"I take care of my friends."

"What if I were to hand these back to you and demand ten percent of whatever it is you hope to recover?"

"It's a risk that you could take, I suppose," Speyer said. He held out his hand for the envelopes.

After a moment, however, the Russian put them in his breast pocket. "What if I don't go through with my part of the bargain?"

"The checks will bounce, and word will get back to Moscow."

"How soon will you be ready to move?"

"The entire project should be finished within a couple of weeks from the time you supply me with the four men."

Lukashin nodded. "I see no problem with this," he said. "I'll get back to you soon. Where can I reach you?"

"Through Thomas Mann."

"Good enough."

Speyer, Baumann, and Lane walked back to the car while the Russians stayed behind at the reflecting pool. "Have you ever met Lukashin before?" Speyer asked Lane.

"I don't think so. But his face sure looked familiar. Maybe I saw a photograph."

"Well, he gave you a double take when he first saw you." Speyer turned to Baumann. "What do you think, Ernst?"

"I didn't notice anything. But if he knows Browne from somewhere, wouldn't he have said something?"

"Maybe," Speyer said. "When we get back I want you to do some checking. Perhaps Lukashin was stationed in South Africa."

Lane let a look of surprise cross his face. "Do you think the bastard was involved with the accident that killed my wife?"

"I don't know. But I'm going to find out."

When Lukashin got back to the Russian embassy on Wisconsin Avenue in Glover Park, he went with his number two, Nikolai Mironov, directly into the *referentura*—the secured room. When the door to the suite was shut and the electronic countermeasures activated, eavesdropping by any means was utterly impossible.

"I know one of Speyer's bodyguards, and it wasn't from Germany," Lukashin said.

"You should have demanded his name."

"Doesn't matter the name he would have given me, Nikki, what matters is who he really is."

"What are you thinking?"

"It might give us a clue to what Speyer is really after. Whatever it is, it has to be big because he's willing to pay plenty for it."

"What did he offer you?"

Lukashin had to smile. "He's going to pay off my house mortgage—that's about seven hundred thousand—and all my credit cards—that's another couple of hundred thousand. And you'll get some."

"He's serious."

"That he is," Lukashin said. "I'll pull up a recognition program from the mainframe, but in the meantime I want you to get his fingerprints."

"How?"

"I got the license tag number when they drove up. Run it through Metro DMV. I suspect it's one of Thomas Mann's cars, which means they're staying over there with him in Georgetown. That guy was driving and he wasn't wearing gloves, so I expect his prints will be all over the driver's side."

Mironov nodded. "I'll take care of it myself once they get bedded down over there. Do you know anything about their security?"

"No, but you should be able to find out which agency they use and pull something up from their website," Lukashin said. "Before I start cashing in favors I want to know exactly who I'm dealing with."

* * *

Lane parked the Town Car in the back and he, Speyer, and Baumann went into the house. Thomas Mann was still at a formal dinner at the British embassy. It was only a few minutes before eleven and Speyer was keyed up.

"Anyone care for a nightcap?" he asked.

"I'm going to get on the computer and check out Lukashin," Baumann said.

"I'll have a drink with you," Lane said. He and Speyer went back to the library where Speyer poured them brandies. They raised snifters. "Success."

"Yes, success," Lane said, and they drank. "I was wondering. What if Lukashin knows me from somewhere? Will that create a problem?"

"We'll have to see. But that might depend on you."

"In what way?"

"Let's say that he was involved in the deaths of your wife and child."

"I see what you mean," Lane said slowly.

"Revenge would interfere with my plans. I need Lukashin for the moment."

Lane looked up, a wicked smile curling his lips. "For the moment," he said.

"Afterwards what transpires between you and Comrade Lukashin is strictly your own business." Speyer finished his drink. "Are we in accord?"

"What if I were to need some help?"

Speyer considered it for a moment. "You would get it, within reason, of course."

"Of course," Lane said. He reached for the bottle of brandy and poured them each another drink. He raised his glass. "Success."

At two in the morning Thomas Mann's house was dark for the evening. Only dim hall lights showed from within and security lights shone in the driveway and parking area. There were no night watchmen, Mironov decided, as he waited across the street.

After fifteen minutes he crossed the street and slipped into the driveway, keeping to the deeper shadows as much as possible. There was a three car garage in back, but as luck would have it the Lincoln Town car that Speyer and his two bodyguards had used earlier in the evening was parked outside.

He inserted an electronic key in the trunk lid lock, attached the leads to an encoding device the size of a small electronic calculator, and attached its magnetic backing to the trunk lid. A few seconds later the lights turned green and the Lincoln's entire electronic system went dead. The door locks popped open.

He crab-walked to the driver's door and opened it. The interior lights, also defeated by the encoder, did not come on. Keeping low, he spread his fingerprint kit on the floor, and quickly dusted the steering wheel, gear shift lever, and interior door handle. Several clear prints showed up under a UV penlight. Holding the light in his teeth, he used tape to lift three separate prints, bagged them, then wiped off the powder residue.

Checking to make certain that he'd left nothing behind, no traces that anyone had been here or what they had done, Mironov closed the car door with a soft click. At the back of the car he reset the encoder, waited until the row of lights shifted back to red, then lifted the device off the trunk lid and removed the key.

When Lane first spotted the figure waiting in the shadows across the street, he had a fair idea who it might be, though at first he couldn't figure out why Lukashin had sent someone to spy on the house. When the man crossed the street, Lane went downstairs to the conservatory where he watched from the darkness.

Baumann came up behind him. "What are you doing down here?"

"Watching him," Lane said.

Baumann came up beside Lane and looked out the window. Mironov pocketed the device and key from the Lincoln's trunk lid. "Who the hell is he?"

"A Russian, I think. Looked like he lifted a couple of fingerprints from the driver's side."

"Yours?"

Lane grinned in the darkness. "I don't think anybody trusts me."

"If you have something to hide, they're going to find out," Baumann said. "If it's something that will interfere with our business, Helmut will kill you. What do you want to do?"

"I think we ought to help the poor man out."

"What do you mean?" Baumann demanded.

"Come on, Ernst, and I'll show you what I think of people who sneak behind my back looking for answers instead of asking me what they want to know face to face."

Mironov was heading up the driveway as Lane and Baumann slipped out the front door and intercepted him. He reared back and reached inside his jacket.

Lane was on him before he could pull out his gun. He grabbed the man's wrist with one hand and shoved his bent elbow up over his head, practically dislocating his shoulder.

Mironov stepped back and grunted in pain.

"One more step and I'll tear your arm out by the root, comrade," Lane said agreeably.

Mironov stood stock still, although he was obviously in a great deal of pain. "What do you want?"

"The question is, what are you doing here in the middle of the night?"

"Watching you."

"Wrong answer. You were lifting my fingerprints out of the car I drove tonight," Lane said. He shoved Mironov's elbow a little higher. "Why?"

"Fuck you—"

Lane squeezed the nerve bundle just above the man's elbow, and Mironov's complexion instantly went ashen; his knees started to buckle, but Lane backed off the pressure.

"I asked you a question."

"Ivan knows you from someplace," Mironov grunted. "He wanted to check it out."

"Fair enough," Lane said. "He looked familiar to me, too." He let go of Mironov's arm, and took the Russian's Makarov automatic out of his jacket. He ejected the magazine from the pistol, grabbed it firmly with his thumb and four fingers. Then, careful not to smudge the prints he had left, replaced the magazine in the gun and replaced the gun in Mironov's holster.

"Now what?" Mironov asked, holding his arm as if it were broken.

"Now you get out of here and let us good people get some sleep," Lane said.

"I'll be back—"

Before he could get the whole sentence out, Lane grabbed him by the throat and shoved him backward, almost off his feet. "If I ever lay eyes on you again, Russian, I'll kill you," he said, his voice guttural. "Think about it. Think real hard about it."

Lane let him go, then disdainfully turned his back on the man and headed back into the house, Baumann right behind him.

* * *

Speyer came down to the kitchen and Baumann made them some coffee. Gloria got up to see what was going on, but Speyer sent his wife back upstairs. Lane poured a little brandy into his coffee.

"What are they going to find out?" Speyer asked.

"Nothing more than I've already told you," Lane said. "But I don't like people sneaking around behind my back. And I especially don't like Russians."

Baumann had a new respect for Lane. "I don't think that *Schweinhund* will forget what happened tonight." He told Speyer everything.

"What'd you find out about him on the computer?"

"Well, he was never in South Africa," Baumann said. "Germany four years ago, France, Iran, Libya, Mexico City, and a few years back he was on some sort of a special assignment in Brazil. Rio."

"That's where I saw him," Lane said. "There was a joint Russian-U.S. war game down there. Every arms dealer in the world showed up, including some from Cape Town. Which was where I came in."

"Will that queer the deal?" Speyer asked.

"I don't think so," Baumann said. "Lukashin wants the money you've offered him. And he wanted Browne's fingerprints, which he now has. So he's got everything he wants."

"But if you missed something on the computer, and he was somehow involved in South Africa he might suspect that Browne is out for revenge."

"Even if that was the case, I don't think it'd stop a man like Lukashin," Lane said with a smirk. "Even if he screwed me over once, he wouldn't see any reason why he couldn't do it again." Lane shook his head. "He'll cooperate. He needs the money."

"That's assuming there was a South African connection after all," Speyer said, thinking out loud. "It's probably the thing in Rio. A coincidence." He focused on Lane and nodded his approval. "You did a good job tonight. I had my doubts, but I think you did okay. We're not going to kiss anyone's ass for this deal. Lukashin either does what I've asked him to do, or he can go fuck himself, and we'll get somebody else."

"That won't be necessary," Lane said. "He'll come along."

"We'll see," Speyer said. "As soon as this is settled we're heading up to New York."

"I thought we were going to Germany," Lane said.

"Not so fast. We have a few things to take care of first." Speyer smiled a knowing smile. "There are some other considerations as well. You'll be told when the time comes. In the meantime we need to take your picture so that we can get you a new passport. Wouldn't do for John Browne with an 'e' to be traveling on anything but bulletproof papers, now would it?"

Lane sat by an open window in his bedroom looking down on Avon Place while he smoked a cigarette. His door was locked and the bedside radio was playing just loudly enough to interfere with someone who might be listening in the hall when he used his phone.

Frances answered on the first ring. "Shipley and Hughes Accounting."

"I miss you," Lane said.

"That's nice to know. Are you safe?"

"Reasonably. Anything new from the Germans?"

"Nothing yet. Where are you?"

"About six blocks from home. On Avon Place, a house owned by Thomas Mann."

"We'll check it out. We lost you after the airport, but Tommy didn't want to get too close."

"We're heading to New York soon, maybe tomorrow. Looks like we're going after diamonds at a place called Reichsamt Seventeen, some kind of a Nazi genetic research lab where they supposedly used diamonds as a catalyst in their experiments."

"That doesn't make any sense," Frances said.

"It didn't to me either," Lane said. "But a problem has come up that you and Tommy are going to have to help me with. Ivan Lukashin, the SVR Washington *rezident*, thinks he knows me and the feeling is mutual. Maybe the Rio war games, but I'm not sure." Lane told her everything that had happened starting with the meeting at the Lincoln Memorial.

"I'll check on him."

"They have my fingerprints, so Tommy will have to plug the leaks," Lane said.

"Okay. As I've already pointed out, darling, this is not rocket science. So if it looks like Lukashin is on to you, I'm ordering out the marines for a rescue mission with or without your cooperation. *Capice?*"

Lane chuckled. "I love it when you talk dirty."

Frances got up and walked across the hall into Tom Hughes's office on the third floor of what supposedly was a U.S. Navy think tank, Omnibus Projects. Most of the rest of their very small staff had long since left for the evening, though because Lane was in the field they were all on call.

"He sounded in good spirits," Hughes said.

"The cheek. You eavesdropped. Is nothing sacred?"

"Not in this place." Hughes chuckled. He was a very large man, pushing three hundred pounds on a bad day, and he was not handsome: His face looked like an alcoholic's with broken red and blue veins, puffy, red-rimmed eyes, and a round, pockmarked nose. But he was brilliant and he was kind. He had a Ph.D. in foreign studies from Georgetown University; he read, wrote and spoke eleven languages fluently;

and his wife of twenty years, their six girls, two cats, one dog, and an assorted menagerie adored him. In his home he was benevolent king; and if the girls could eat, drink, or sleep for their father to save him the trouble they would fight amongst themselves for the honor. Uncle Bill and Aunt Frannie were family, and nothing they could ever do or say would change that. They had been adopted.

He had brought up Lukashin's SVR file on his computer. "He was down in Rio at the same time William was there, which is actually a break for our side. Dear William was masquerading as a South African intelligence officer that time, too."

"What about his fingerprints?"

"Already done, Frances. Whatever databases the Russians turn to, including their own in Moscow, they'll either come up with nothing, or they'll run into a blank wall in Johannesburg."

"Which is all they would find if he had really worked for South African Intelligence."

Hughes smiled, his eyes twinkling. "They do tend to protect their own."

"What about the business with the diamonds?" Frances asked.

"I'll make a couple of telephone calls in the morning, but I know just enough about genetics to know that I don't know. In the meantime you can get started on Reichsamt Seventeen. There should be some sort of a record somewhere, one would think."

"I'll check with the BKA in Berlin."

Hughes looked up at her. "Actually why don't you go home and get a few hours' sleep, my dear? We can call the Germans later this morning."

"What, and leave you here all alone?" Frances said. She shook her head. "Not a chance, you nasty man. Moira asked me to keep an eye on you at all times."

"Why might that be?" he asked in mock indignation.

"Because she knows that if you're left to your own devices for too long, you'll start smoking again."

"Gads!"

Gloria Speyer lay in bed staring up at the ceiling as her husband paced back and forth. She'd never seen him this agitated.

"The Russians have taken the hook," he said.

"How did Browne do tonight?" Gloria asked.

"He did all right," Speyer said.

Gloria looked at her husband; he was staring at her. "You still don't trust him, do you," she said.

"I don't trust anybody."

"Am I included?"

"You especially."

She laughed, and she could feel a warm glow in her belly. "Then you most definitely have a problem, my darling. You want him to work for you, and you want me to watch him." She laughed again. "Maybe I'll fuck him. Is that too high a price for you to pay?"

"On the contrary, sweetheart, that's exactly the price I want to pay, because it'll give me something to use against both of you. It's all about control, you know."

She plucked the ashtray off the nightstand and threw it at him. But he just stepped aside and laughed at her.

As the sun came up, Lukashin stood at the window of his office looking out toward the wooded grounds of the U.S. Naval Observatory, his thoughts lost in the new start the German had offered him on a sliver platter. He was drinking a cup of coffee, another habit besides going deeply in debt that he had picked up in the States. For the first time in as long as he could remember he could see the light at the end of the tunnel.

Mironov knocked once and came in. "He's South African. Name of John Browne."

Lukashin turned away from the window. "I was never in South Africa. How could we have met?"

"You were both in Rio de Janeiro for the war games four years ago," Mironov said. He laid the thin file folder on Lukashin's desk. "He worked for South African Intelligence until two years ago when they fired him. He was down there working with some arms dealers, but now they have a warrant for his arrest, though they're not pushing it with much vigor."

"What'd he do?"

"I couldn't find out," Mironov said. "Leastways not about that. But he has no love for us." Mironov explained what he'd come up with from Browne's record. "I checked with Moscow but there was no record of any such operation against him or his family."

"Things like that tend to get lost," Lukashin said. "Is he a threat?"

Mironov thought about the question for a moment. "Not to this operation, as long as we keep him at arm's length."

"Then I'll give Speyer what he wants."

"What about me, Ivan?"

"What do you want? Money?"

"Browne."

Lukashin grinned evilly. "When our business is concluded, you may have him. You've earned it."

"Yes I have," Mironov said with some relish. "Oh, yes I have."

3

NEW YORK CITY

The Gulfstream took off from Washington a few minutes after ten that morning. Lane and Gloria were the only passengers aboard. Speyer and Baumann were staying behind to wait for word from the Russians.

"Change of plans," Speyer had told him this morning. "I want you and Gloria to take the jet up to New York. Check into the Grand Hyatt and wait for us."

"Wouldn't it be easier if we all went together?" Lane asked. He had an idea what they were up to. They didn't trust him, even yet, and he couldn't blame them. But siccing Gloria on him was an exercise in futility, really sophomoric, and there was no way he wanted to get in the middle of some sort of a domestic dispute, whatever the reasons.

"You've already caused enough of a stir, and I want you out of here." He laughed tightly, his expansive, friendly mood of last night gone. "And there are times, frankly, when my wife gets on my nerves, if you know what I mean."

"Right," Lane said. "But I didn't sign on to be a baby-sitter."

"If you work for me, you'll do as you're told," Speyer said. "When you get to New York send the jet back for us; we should be ready by then."

Gloria sat across from Lane. She kept crossing and uncrossing her legs, giving him a good look at her thighs. She was dressed in a transluscent silk blouse, a lightweight cream-colored skirt and no nylons. She had probably been a beautiful young woman, Lane thought, but now she bordered on the edge of garish, though she still held her figure. He had to smile to himself. Under any other circumstances it would be amusing to see just how far she would go.

"It's nice to be with a man who is in a good mood all the time," she said.

"I can't see any reason not to be. I'm going to make a lot of money."

"Is that terribly important to you?"

Lane shrugged. "Not really," he said. "Having it is okay, but being without can be a drag."

"I've been there," she said with a little bitterness.

He supposed she had, and there wasn't much he could say. "Helmut seems to do okay for himself. Did you know him in Germany?"

"No, we met in LA about five years ago. He bankrolled a movie I was in and it just went from there. He was the life of the party." She focused on Lane. "But he can be a royal pain in the ass sometimes."

"We all can."

"I mean a real fucking Hitler. It's not *all* about money and power."

"That's too bad," Lane said.

"Yeah, I get tired of it sometimes."

"No, I mean that he has to take this kind of a chance to make some money. But Kalispell has to be expensive, and Eden won't come cheap."

"What are you talking about?"

"The mission. Germany. The diamonds. That's what this is all about, isn't it?"

Gloria shook her head. "I don't know what you're talking about, I really don't. Do you want to start making some sense?"

"Look, I took a chance coming out to see him because he's supposed to be connected. So I get out there, save his life and what happens?"

She shook her head, confused.

"You, Mrs. Sloan. He's sent you and me to New York together so that you can seduce me." Lane lit a cigarette with his Vacheron et Constantin gold lighter, handed it to her, and lit another for himself. "I'm flattered and all that, naturally, you're a beautiful woman, but what's the point? What does he want?"

He was in her territory now and she gave him a shrewd, appraising look. "Everybody has their own idea of Eden."

"If I take you to bed I'm being disloyal, is that what he wants to know?"

"I didn't discuss it with him," she said with amusement. "But if you would like to ask him, there is a phone beside you."

"Maybe I should. I wonder what he'd do?"

"He might kill you."

"He might try."

Gloria laughed, the sound deep in her throat, and she wet her lips. "Actually he didn't suggest that I sleep with you. That was my own idea. What do you think about that?"

"I think that when we get to the hotel I'm going to lock my door and make sure it stays that way," Lane said. He put out his cigarette, got up and went forward to the drink cabinet. It was well stocked. "How about a Bloody Mary?" he asked her.

"That would be nice," she said, still laughing. "Do you know what, John?"

"No, what?"

"I think that this is going to be more fun than I thought it would be. Infinitely more fun."

* * *

They took a limo to midtown Manhattan. The day was warm and hazy, the traffic light.

"We could be here alone in New York for days," Gloria said.

The UN was a block down the street. Despite his upbringing and his job with the National Security Agency and now working directly for the president, Lane had always been naïve. He'd always thought that ideas like the United Nations were a good thing. He called it his Superman complex. Truth, justice, and the American way. He firmly believed it. Frannie and Tom laughed at him, but with affection and not derision, when he argued for a world peace with the U.S. as the benevolent policeman. Of course what they were doing amounted to just about the same thing.

He focused on Gloria. "Why did you quit the movies? Didn't you ever get your big break?"

"You'd be better off asking why I started in the movies in the first place. Well, the answer is simple. I was looking for a husband and I found one."

"Nothing wrong with that. But Helmut might not have been your best choice."

She had brought a glass of champagne from the airplane and she drank it, looking at him over the rim of the glass. "Now you really are being disloyal. I don't care what business a man is in, as long as he treats me right. And Helmut did okay. He'll do okay again as soon as whatever's biting his ass goes away. But in the meantime I'm his wife, not a piece of property." Her thick, sensuous lips curled into a smirk. "And if that doesn't sink into his thick skull maybe it'll be me who kicks *him* out."

"Then what?"

"Whatever I want to do. I still have plenty of options, and Helmut is not in any position to try to stop me."

"He might kill you."

Gloria laughed. "That's rich," she said. "The son of a bitch wouldn't dare."

They checked into the Grand Hyatt a few minutes before one. The hotel, with its soaring atrium lobby, was a half-block from Grand Central Station, and comfortable if not elegant. Speyer had booked them adjoining suites that looked down on 42nd Street. Champagne and flowers were waiting in Gloria's.

She knocked on the connecting door after the bellmen were gone, and Lane let her in. She was a weak link in Speyer's defenses, and even though he disliked using her like that, he couldn't afford to pass up the opportunity.

"I'm not going to play games with you," he said, as he opened one of his bags on the luggage stand by the closet. "If you have a problem with your husband, work it out, but if you want my advice, just get the hell out."

"Are you trying to justify taking me to bed, John?" she asked. She walked into the bedroom, flopped down on the bed, and kicked off her shoes. She'd brought the bottle of champagne and a glass from her room. With the drinks she'd had on the way up from Washington she was beginning to get drunk. "I wonder what hubby dear would say if he were to walk in on us right this moment?"

Lane stepped around the corner. "If you want to fool around, okay, I'm game. But how about let's wait until the mission is done. I need the money and I don't want to screw up here."

"But I don't want to wait." The telephone rang. She

reached over and switched it to speakerphone. "Hello."

"Sweetheart, I thought the switchboard was connecting me with John's room," Speyer said tightly.

"They did," Gloria replied lightly. "Did you want to talk to him?"

"Yes, please."

Lane shook his head. "I'm right here, Mr. Sloan."

"Did you send the jet back for us?"

"Yes. We just got here ourselves, but it should be on its way back by now. Is there any problem in Washington?"

"None whatsoever. But there's been another change of plans."

"I'm listening."

"We're flying to Frankfurt tonight. The information we wanted has arrived safe and sound."

"I'm very glad to hear that."

"I want you two to check out of there this afternoon and get over to JFK no later than six-thirty."

"I'm not going anywhere without a passport."

"I have it. We're booked on Lufthansa zero-zero-nine, which leaves at seven-thirty. Meet us in the first-class lounge."

"What if there's a delay?"

"There won't be. Now listen. I want you to do exactly as you're told. Your special equipment that won't fly well, you need to get rid of it."

He meant Lane's pistol. "I understand, but what about when we get to Frankfurt?"

"You'll have your choice of the best available."

"Sounds good."

"Very well, we'll see you at six-thirty."

"Right," Lane said.

Gloria reached over and broke the connection, purposely hiking up her skirt to give him a long look.

She was wearing no panties, and Lane almost had to feel sorry for her. She was crude. She flashed him a big smile. "At least we have the rest of the afternoon."

"Not a chance," Lane said. "I have to get rid of my gun, and then I need to catch a couple hours of sleep. I was up most of last night."

"I have just the cure—"

"Out," Lane said. "Now."

She shook her head. "You don't know what you're missing." She got languidly off the bed and, carrying her champagne with her, brushed past him, gave him a wet kiss on the cheek, and left the room.

He locked the connecting door then went back to the bedside phone and called the hotel operator. There'd been something in Speyer's phone call that should not have been there, and he wanted to make sure he'd not been hearing things.

"Operator, how may I direct your call, Mr. Browne?"

"I just received a long distance call. I think it was from Washington. Could you find out that number for me?"

"One moment, sir." The operator was back a half-minute later. "Sir, there was only one telephone call to your room, and it was local. Would you like the number?"

"Yes, please."

The operator gave it to him, and he hung up. During Speyer's call he had heard the distinctive note of a ship's whistle. An ocean liner's whistle.

Using his cell phone he called Frannie in Washington, and gave her the New York number that Speyer had called from.

"Hold on a sec, love," she said. She was back in just a few seconds. "It's a pay phone."

"Somewhere near the docks."

Frannie was silent for a long moment. "How did you know that, William?"

"I heard a ship's whistle when he was talking to me. You have to wonder why he didn't come up on the jet with his wife and me."

"Maybe he wanted to meet someone without you knowing about it," Frances suggested.

"I think you're right. But who, and why?"

"Okay, love. What next?" she asked.

"We're off to Frankfurt tonight. Lufthansa zero-zero-nine from JFK. Call the Germans and make sure they give us plenty of room. In the meantime, have you come up with anything about the Nazi research bunker, and the business about the diamonds?"

"Nothing yet, but Tommy's working on it."

"Okay, tell the old scoundrel to step on it. I have a feeling that I'm going to be needing all the hard information I can get, and soon."

"Oh, you were right about Lukashin, too. He was in Rio during the war games, so he must have seen you there."

"Okay, that's not going to create a problem. The only other loose end is my gun. I'm going to check it here at the hotel. Have someone pick it up for me."

"Will do, luv."

"Tell Tommy to do whatever it takes to find out about Reichsamt Seventeen."

"William, listen to me, don't take any unnecessary chances. I'm worried about these people. We have enough right now to turn this over to the German federal police."

"Not yet," Lane said. "This isn't just about money, or at least not the diamonds. It's something bigger than that. I've got a feeling."

"Well, be careful," Frances said. "I want you back in one piece. In the meantime you're calling from a suite in the Grand Hyatt. What *are* you and the man's wife doing alone in a hotel?"

"Bridge," Lane said. "She's a marvelous bridge player. Honestly, darling."

"Peachy. We'll have to have the dear over one evening when this business is finished," Frances said sarcastically.

"Sounds good. Ta-ta," Lane replied and he broke the connection.

The first-class lounge was three-quarters full when Lane and Gloria showed up after picking up their tickets and checking their luggage. They got some champagne and walked over to where Speyer and Baumann were waiting at a window seat.

"Ah, I was wondering if you two were going to make it," Speyer said.

Their 747 was pulled up to the jetway, surrounded by service trucks and luggage handlers. The pilot and first officer were doing a walk-around. All routine. All normal. Yet Lane was beginning to wonder just what it was that Speyer was getting himself into. There was something sinister to the business; something much more than a mere snatch of a cache of diamonds hidden in a Nazi bunker for more than a half-century.

"Did you just get to New York yourself?" Lane asked, sitting down.

Gloria gave her husband a peck on the cheek and sat next to him, an amused expression on her face.

"About an hour ago."

"How about the Gulfstream?"

"We won't be needing it for now, so I sent it back to Kalispell," Speyer said. "Is there anything else you'd like to know?" he asked with a raised eyebrow.

"Sorry. But I tend to get a bit hyper in the middle of an operation. I want to know what's going on around me, and I want all my ducks in a row. Especially when it's my life on the line."

"Perfectly reasonable," Speyer told him.

"Is the bunker very far from Frankfurt?"

"It's in what used to be East Germany, of course," Speyer said. "But first we're going to Hamburg to meet with someone. Then we'll continue on to Neubrandenburg, on the Tollense See. It's just a couple of hundred klicks, not far."

"Then what?"

"Then we'll meet another old friend who'll put us up, and after that it's up to the Russians and to your diving skills." Speyer held up a hand before Lane could ask another question. "That'll be all for now. You'll be told the rest as and when you need to know."

"That's fine by me," Lane said. "But I'll want to know what's coming my way in plenty of time to get ready for it. I don't jump into dark closets unless I have a flashlight."

"We're in this together," Speyer said. "I'm depending on you just as much as you're depending on me and Ernst."

Gloria laughed softly, but then turned away as Speyer glared at her. The animosity between them was palpable, and Lane had a feeling that there would be trouble because of their problems.

OVER THE ATLANTIC

The overnight flight was smooth and the first-class accommodations comfortable. "I suppose that you're used to traveling like this all the time," Baumann said to Lane.

They were seated together, Speyer and Gloria, who was already sleeping, across the aisle. Dinner was a very good Wiener schnitzel with a passable Piesporter Michelsberg, then coffee and Asbach-Urhalt cognac afterward. The movie had started but most of the first- and business-class passengers were either asleep or working on their laptops.

"I've always figured that if you can't travel first-class, why bother? Why not just stay at home?"

"You have expensive tastes," Baumann said. "You must have to stay busy to keep up with them. And it has to be hell when you don't have the money to live that way. I know that it would bother me."

"I suppose it would," Lane said. "But personally I've never been in that position." He glanced over at Speyer, who had also reclined his seat and looked as if he was asleep. "What about your boss?"

"What about him?" Baumann asked, his voice low.

"He must be getting short of funds, otherwise he wouldn't be taking such a chance."

"What the hell are you talking about?"

Lane turned back to him. "Going back to Germany. I'm sure that a man of his background has to be wanted by the BKA. I'm sure that the German Federal Police would love to get their hands on him."

"He's done nothing wrong in Germany to warrant his arrest."

Lane laughed. "You have to be kidding. Ex-Stasi? They're still after all those guys with even more enthusiasm than they went after the old Nazis. You guys were in bed with the Russians."

"New papers, you should know about things like that."

"Now you're working with the Russians again. Must be like old times."

"You're working for us," Baumann observed. "It

means that you too are working with the Russians. And that after they killed your wife and child."

"Don't go any further, Ernst," Lane warned easily.

Baumann shrugged. "Necessity makes strange bed fellows, that's all I'm saying. We were good and loyal Germans working for our government. We followed orders."

It was the same stupid argument Nazi sympathizers had used after the war, and nobody bought it then. Didn't these guys read history? Maybe it was something in the German spirit, Lane thought.

"All I'm saying is don't look back. Just do your job and get on with it," Baumann said earnestly. "Life is too short otherwise."

"You're right," Lane said, working hard to keep a straight face. But it took nearly everything in his power not to reach over and break the bastard's neck.

FRANKFURT AM MAIN, GERMANY

It was eight-thirty in the morning, local, when they touched down at Frankfurt's Rhein Main Airport in a light rain from a solidly overcast sky. They went through passport control without a hitch, and in customs their bags were X-rayed but not opened.

If Speyer was suspicious because of their ease of entry into a country where he was wanted by the police, he didn't say anything. They took a cab over to the Hauptbanhof and forty-five minutes later boarded an InterCity Express train to Hamburg.

The first-class car was only half-full. They got facing seats, a low cocktail table between them, at the back of the car away from most of the other passengers. Ten minutes after they started out of the city the conductor came by to check their tickets, and then an attendant came with a drink cart. Gloria, who was hung over, ordered a glass of champagne, while the rest of them got coffee.

"It's good to be back like this," Speyer said heartily. "If those fools in Berlin can keep their heads above water while they pay the bills for rebuilding the east zone, it'll end up like the old days."

"Don't forget about the skinheads," Lane said.

Speyer chuckled. "They're just kids having some fun, you know. Blowing off steam."

"Killing people."

Speyer shrugged. "Yes, but they're mostly Turks, and some Greeks."

"It won't be like the old days, though," Baumann said with genuine nostalgia.

"Nothing ever is, actually," Speyer admitted. "But once you get used to the good life, Ernst, you won't miss the old very much."

"Even three hundred million doesn't go all that far," Lane said. "That's providing you can get the full dollar amount. In all likelihood you'll only get ten percent of that."

Speyer and Baumann exchanged a knowing look. "I think we'll manage to get by," Speyer assured him.

"What?" Lane asked.

Speyer put his coffee down and glanced out the window at the passing countryside. They were out of the city now and traveling at least two hundred kilometers per hour. Everything was precise and neat; the Germans were almost as bad as the Swiss on that score. *Alles in ordnung.* Everything in order.

"You might as well know the next part now that we've come this far. After all, it's going to be your life on the line down there."

"If you're going to talk business all the way up to

Hamburg, I'm going to find the bar car," Gloria said. She got up and made her way unsteadily forward.

"Please forgive my wife, she's been under a lot of strain lately," Speyer said, with a smirk. "I don't think that she ever completely adjusted to Montana."

"I understand."

"Well on with it, then," Speyer said. "Ernst and I didn't stay in Washington as I told you. In fact we got up to New York just an hour after you did."

"You met someone and you didn't want me to know about it. Is that it?" Lane said.

"That's right. And to be honest I won't trust you completely until this entire mission has developed."

"If I were in your shoes I wouldn't either. Who did you meet?"

"A representative of the Cuban government. When we're finished here, we're going to Havana."

"Eden?" Lane asked.

"That's been the code name."

"The Cuban government is guaranteeing you a safe haven for a specific sum of money. Is that it?"

"A very specific sum of money," Speyer said. "But they're going to earn it, because they're going to guarantee that I get the entire three hundred million, or maybe even a little more, for the diamonds, no questions asked."

"I'm listening."

"The Nazis were doing human research in that bunker, as I told you they were. And it was so horrible that no one, especially not the present German government, wants anything about the place to see the light of day. The Germans, like the Swiss, are having enough trouble as it is giving back the gold that they took from the Jews. Nobody wants to open *this* can of worms."

Lane had to admire the plan, and he grinned.

"That's really very clever," he said. "You're going to sell the diamonds back to the German government in exchange for your silence."

Speyer nodded with a smug smile.

"But you need the Cuban government to broker the deal for you, otherwise the Germans would just make their own deal with Washington and have you arrested, maybe even shot and killed on the way to jail."

"Cuba is our insurance policy, it's our safe haven, and with the casinos and hotels I plan on building, it'll be a cash cow that will last us for the rest of our lives." He nodded in satisfaction. "In short, it's Eden."

HAMBURG

It was raining in Hamburg, too. A stiff, cold breeze came off the Elbe River; there weren't many tourists visiting the harbor. Dozens of ships were tied up, busy loading or unloading cargo from around the world in Germany's busiest port. They'd rented a Mercedes at the train station, and Baumann parked it at the east end of the container terminal just across the quay from the 17,500-ton motor vessel *Maria*, registered in Athens, Greece. He stayed in the car with Gloria. Speyer and Lane got out.

"Is this how we're getting to Havana?" Lane asked.

"This is it. They'll hide us until we clear customs. It'll take almost two weeks to cross the Atlantic, but if there's any dust to be settled from the operation it'll be over by the time we arrive. No surprises. That's how I like things, and that's how this operation will proceed."

"We'll also be sitting ducks if the crew decide they

don't like our looks." Lane glanced back at Gloria seated in the back of the Mercedes. "Or like the looks of some of us just a little too much."

Speyer seemed unconcerned. "Anything's possible. But since they won't get the second half of their money until we dock in Havana it's not too likely."

They went up the boarding ladder, entered the superstructure, and took the stairs up five decks to the captain's quarters—just aft of the bridge. The ship was reasonably clean, though the interior spaces smelled like a faint combination of diesel oil and disinfectant. She was about six hundred feet long with a beam at the center of eighty-two feet.

"How many crew are there?" Lane asked.

"Seventeen including the officers, but she can accommodate twenty-two, so there's plenty of room for us."

Captain Horst Zimmer turned out to be a ruggedly handsome man with a short gray beard and well-trimmed hair. He wore a thick fisherman's sweater which made him look like a German version of Ernest Hemingway.

"Helmut, you old bastard. I wondered when you were going to show up," he shouted. He and Speyer shook hands and clapped each other on the shoulders like old friends.

Speyer handed him a thick manila envelope. "These are your bills of lading and clearances for us once we reach Havana." He stepped aside. "This is my new colleague, John Browne from South Africa."

Captain Zimmer sized up Lane and they shook hands. "Any friend of Helmut's is a friend of mine," he said with gusto. Lane thought that he was caught up in the middle of a B movie, but the captain was dead serious. He wasn't playing a role.

"Good to meet you, Captain," Lane said.

"John will be doing the diving for us," Speyer said.

Zimmer looked at Lane with new respect. "You've got balls, I'll say that much for you, my man." He shook his head in puzzlement. "I wouldn't go down there under a hundred meters of black water for *all* the gold in Fort Knox. If there was any gold still stored there." He laughed at his own joke.

"We're going up to Neubrandenburg this morning. What's your schedule?"

"It's getting tight," Zimmer said. "I can give you seventy-two hours, no more. By then the gear box will be back together and I'll have no further excuses to stay in this berth. We'll have to sail."

"That gives us plenty of time. I wouldn't want to stay here much longer than that in any event."

"It's settled then," Zimmer said. He looked past Speyer to the corridor. "Where's that beautiful wife of yours?"

"Waiting in the car."

"You brought her after all?"

Speyer nodded. "She insisted," he said, and Zimmer's expression darkened.

"Well, it can't be helped, I suppose."

"No," Speyer agreed. "We'll be back within three days."

"I can't wait any longer than that."

"I understand," Speyer said.

"Good luck, then, Helmut."

NEUBRANDENBURG

They were on the German plain east of Hamburg and well north of Berlin in the state of West Pomerania. Farmland, broken with stands of trees, stretched in every direction for as far as the eye could see, some of it at or actually below sea level.

They passed through the tiny village of Neustrelitz then turned north on the secondary road around Lake Tolense. A ski chalet, the smaller version of Speyer's house outside of Kalispell, was perched on a slight rise above the lake. The town of Neubrandenburg was ten kilometers to the north. The water of the lake looked steel gray except for the whitecaps. There were no fishermen or recreational boaters out today.

"It's usually very nice up here at this time of the year," Speyer apologized.

"A regular hotbed of tourism now that the Wall is down, I suppose," Lane quipped.

"Actually I was born here, and until I went away to Gymnasium in Rostock I practically lived on this lake in the summers," Speyer said.

"It must have been pleasant."

"But there's nothing here, Helmut, except farmland and the water," Gloria complained. "What in God's name did you do with yourself for entire summers?"

"About the same things you did in South Dakota when you were a child," Speyer replied with a vicious little note in his voice.

Gloria sat back and glowered at her husband, as Baumann drove up to the chalet and parked in the back by a large, weatherworn garage. An older man, perhaps in his mid-sixties, wearing a yellow foul-weather jacket, blue jeans, and boat shoes emerged from the house and came over to the car as they were all getting out and stretching.

"Welcome home, Captain, it's been too long since you were here," he boomed. Everybody in Germany shouted.

"It's good to be back, Otto, even if for only a couple of days," Speyer said warmly. "*Alles ist in ordnung?*"

"*Ja, natürlich, Herr Kapitän.*"

Everything was the same in this chalet as in the Kalispell house except that it was smaller and older. It smelled a little musty, too, as if it had not been occupied for a long time. The old man brought them beer and Gloria some wine.

"When the captain said that he was a married man and would be bringing his wife with him, he neglected to say how beautiful you are, Frau Speyer," he said.

"Thanks," she slurred insincerely. She glanced over at Lane and rolled her eyes.

"Sergeant Schaub was my top sergeant in East Berlin before our unit was dissolved," Speyer explained. He introduced Lane.

"The captain told me yesterday that you were handy with a gun," Sergeant Schaub said.

"I was at the right place at the right time." Lane took a deep draught of his beer. It was very good. "I didn't think you could get beer like this up here."

"It's not from here. That comes from Munich."

"Otto never drank a bad beer in his life," Baumann said, chuckling.

Schaub reached over and gave Baumann's belly a playful pat. "It looks as if that cheap American beer has done you no harm."

"Pisswater," Baumann pronounced. He raised his glass. "Now this, on the other hand, is beer that you can sink your teeth into, roll your tongue around, enjoy."

"Please," Gloria begged sarcastically.

Baumann was about to say something to her, but Speyer shot him a dirty look, which shut him up.

Eden, Lane decided, if they ever got there, was going to be lively and interesting.

Schaub offered them another drink and Lane held out his glass. "So what's the situation? How far are we from the bunker?"

Schaub poured more beer, then glanced at Speyer, who nodded. "The bunker entry is just a couple of kilometers from here, but we might have a problem. There've been some men here over the past few days, and some questions. We may have to delay the mission."

"What kind of men, Otto?" Speyer asked. "*Bundes*?"

Schaub nodded. "Yes, probably federal police. They asked in town if there'd been an increase in visitors over the past few weeks."

"To the lake, the town, the bunker? An increase in visitors exactly where?"

"They didn't specify."

Speyer thought about it for a moment, but then shrugged. "Maybe it was a government survey."

"That is possible under the new order," Schaub conceded. He brought out a bottle of good cognac. "Perhaps Frau Speyer would like something a little stronger?"

A back room of the chalet was devoted to hunting and fishing trophies which were mounted on the walls along with the weapons used to bag them. Schaub pushed a large wool rug aside, and lifted several boards of well-worn wood flooring up, revealing a storage area five feet long, half that wide, and eighteen inches deep. From this he withdrew several bundles and aluminum cases which he laid out and opened on a long, deeply scarred table.

In addition to a variety of pistols including Sig-

Sauers, Glock 17s, Walthers, and Berettas, along with the appropriate magazines and silencers, were a number of sniper rifles, automatic weapons, including the M-17 and AK-47, as well as a half-dozen LAWs rockets and two RPGs.

"The demolitions and other equipment are out in the garage," Sergeant Schaub explained. "I thought it was safer out there, away from the house."

Lane picked out a Beretta 9mm, the same as the gun he'd left in checked luggage at the Grand Hyatt, a Polish-made silencer, and two magazines of ammunition. "That's quite an arsenal. Have you been expecting trouble for a very long time?"

"It's better to be prepared than wanting," Schaub said.

Baumann picked out a seventeen-shot Glock, and Speyer one of the Walther PPKs, which was a very compact, flat weapon that was easy to conceal, though it didn't have much stopping power.

"If we have to use all of this we might just as well kiss off the project," Lane prompted, looking for a response.

"If you mean shooting German authorities, I don't think it'll come to that," Speyer replied. "But we'll almost certainly have a problem at some point with the Russians."

The map was very large scale, the type used by surveyors. A legend in German at the bottom advised that the starred benchmarks had been verified by satellite measurement. "It was designated Reichsamt Seventeen," Speyer explained.

"Reichs department seventeen," Lane translated. "Anonymous."

"That's how they wanted it in those days. And it

was smart, considering what was going on down there."

On the map the place was marked as the Neubrandenburg War Memorial, and a small black square at the spot along the lakeshore indicated that it was a point of special interest.

"What's on the site?"

"A small parking lot, an open pavilion with an eternal flame, and a small concrete structure with a steel door made to look like a maintenance shed of some sort," Schaub reported.

"The shed covers the actual entrance," Speyer said.

"Guards, caretakers?"

"One—" Speyer began, but Schaub interrupted.

"Sorry, *Herr Kapitän*, but in addition to the one guard, there have been two maintenance men doing repairs and painting the pavilion over the past few days."

"In the rain?" Speyer asked.

Schaub nodded solemnly.

"Well, we'll just have to see about that, won't we. And right now might be the best time of all."

The memorial was much larger than Lane thought it would be. The pavilion with its eternal flame was large enough to hold a hundred visitors easily, and the concrete shed was about the size of a small garage. Baumann was driving the Mercedes. He pulled into the parking lot. The wind off the lake was raw.

"You said that the bunker is flooded. Is it open to the lake?" Lane asked.

"There was an explosion, probably sabotage, and it opened a passage directly to the lake bottom," Speyer replied.

"Why hasn't anyone gone in that way?"

"The walls are far too unstable, and by now they're probably collapsed."

The grass and hedges were well maintained. There were several picnic benches above a small beach. They could see the town farther up the lake, but only woods and farmland on the opposite side two kilometers away. There was no sign of the two extra caretakers.

The guard, in a green wool uniform, came out of the small office at the rear of the pavilion and looked up at them. Speyer waved and the guard waved back.

"Even if the other two don't come back, he'll want to know what the hell we're up to when we start breaking into the place," Lane said.

"No he won't," Speyer assured him. "He'll be too busy to even notice."

They drove back to the chalet. Inside the shed Sergeant Schaub showed them the rest of the equipment.

"Everything that you asked for is here," he said. "Two mixed-gas diving outfits, including closed circuit masks, dry suits, lights, gauges, underwater navigational equipment, and buoyancy vests."

"You didn't purchase all of this from the same place, I presume," Speyer demanded.

"I used different suppliers in Hamburg, Berlin, Frankfurt, and Rostock, under four different names and on four different days."

"Who else is going down with me?" Lane asked, checking the equipment. It was all German made and first-class.

"Just you, I'm afraid," Speyer said. "I was unable to find anyone else."

"If something goes wrong I'm dead."

Speyer smiled. "But this way you'll get the pay of two divers. That should help alleviate your concerns."

* * *

"We're going to meet with the Russians tonight, and unless a problem comes up, we make the dive tomorrow," Speyer told them.

They were in the chalet's great room, a fire burning on the grate in the big stone fireplace. Sergeant Schaub had put on a wild boar stew, and the entire house smelled like baking bread. Even Gloria roused herself enough to go into the kitchen and help with the hot cabbage salad and other side dishes. It reminded her, she said, of when she was a little girl.

"And it wasn't so long ago at that," Sergeant Schaub offered gallantly.

"It bothers me that the two maintenance men were missing this afternoon," Baumann said,

"Don't worry about it. They probably finished their job and went to another," Speyer reassured them. He turned back to Lane. "The Russians will be bringing a German Television One panel truck with them which they'll park directly in front of the entrance shed. The three of us will be inside watching everything on the television monitors."

"What if the guard gets suspicious and wants to check on them?" Lane asked.

"It'll be okay, because these guys really are filmmakers. They're working on a number of freelance projects."

Lane nodded. "I assume that they'll keep the guard and any visitors who might show up busy while we peel the steel door and get inside. What then? I've never even heard of the place, let alone seen it."

"The Russians are bringing the engineering diagrams of the entire bunker system. They'll leave them with us tonight, which will give us time to study them and figure out your route."

Lane glanced over at Baumann, who was chewing his lip. "Of course that's providing that the explosion sixty years ago did nothing more than merely flood the bunker. There could be blown-out walls, collapsed ceilings, God only knows what other hazards."

"It's a risk that I'm willing to take," Speyer told him with a straight face.

"Oh, are you diving with me?"

"No. And if you want to back out now, go ahead. Ernst will drive you back to Hamburg in the morning. Of course I would have to have your word that you wouldn't say anything to anyone about the project. I could give you five thousand dollars for your efforts to this point. I think that it would not be impossible to find another diver willing to take the risk."

Lane looked away for a long moment. "Okay, so I locate the diamonds, then what?"

Speyer smiled. "Good man. The diamonds will be sealed in a black metal box about half a meter on a side. There'll just be the one."

"Weight?"

Speyer shrugged. "I don't know, but not so heavy, I think, that it would be impossible for one man to handle it underwater. In any event you'll be wearing a buoyancy control vest. A little extra gas in the vest should give you the needed lift."

"Wouldn't it be easier to open the box, and empty the diamonds into a dive bag?"

"No," Speyer said a little too quickly. "Without bringing them back in the original sealed case we have no way of proving that these are the actual diamonds from the bunker. They could be any diamonds. This could be a confidence game."

Lane couldn't help himself from laughing. "That's a good one," he said.

KALISPELL, MONTANA

Kalispell Chief of Police Carl Mattoon was just coming out of the Justice Building when a plain gray Chevy Caprice with federal plates pulled up. A tall, solidly built woman got out and came over, pulling an ID wallet from her purse. She flashed her badge.

"Chief Mattoon, my name is Linda Boulton. I'm the new SAC in the Helena FBI office. Could I have a couple minutes of your time, sir?"

"It's late and I haven't had my lunch yet. Why don't you come back tomorrow?"

"I understand, sir. This won't take but a minute."

Mattoon did not trust women. He'd been married twice, and divorced twice, both times to women cops. There was something not quite right about a woman carrying a badge, in his estimation. He gave her a long, hard stare, but she did not back down.

"Sir?"

"Oh hell and damnation, if you insist."

They walked back inside and Mattoon took her to his office. His deputies and clerks were surprised, but they said nothing, because he had the "look."

The FBI agent waited until the door was closed, but she didn't give Mattoon a chance to sit down before she unloaded on him. "Would you like to tell me what the fuck you people are doing down here? Because from where we sit it looks like you're all a bunch of incompetent bastards and screw-ups."

That was another thing Chief Mattoon didn't like: women who used foul language. "Now if you want to sit down and clean up your act, sweetheart, I'll let you explain what you mean."

"It's you who have the explaining to do."

"What the hell are you talking about?" Mattoon demanded.

"Murder."

Mattoon took off his cap, tossed it on top of the file cabinet, and sat down behind his desk. He'd been warned that the FBI might come snooping around, and to hold them off for as long as possible without doing anything illegal. Until this moment, however, he wasn't sure that he wanted a confrontation with the Bureau.

"That's a local matter, we're working on it."

"Well, that's real interesting, chief. But is it possible that I could interview your suspect, Mr. John Clark? The credit card that he used at the hotel comes up with a Washington, D.C., address. Makes it federal."

"We haven't made an arrest yet, but as soon as we do I'll give you a call and you can come on down here to talk to him."

"I'm not holding my breath. Mr. Clark has probably already left the state. Fleeing to avoid prosecution, now that's another federal offense." Her face was a mask of indifference, and Mattoon couldn't read her. That made him uncomfortable.

"That it is," he said.

"How about the victim then, Mr. Meyer Goldstein."

"What about him?"

"I'd like to see the results of the autopsy, and then have a look at the body." She rocked forward a little and gave him a smile.

"I'll surely see what I can do for you."

"Funny thing about that, too, you know. There is no body at the hospital, and no one over there can explain what happened to it, or if an autopsy was ever performed. Don't you find that odd?"

"What the hell are you doing here, Agent Boulton? What do you want?"

"Mr. Goldstein was a foreign national, he worked for the Simon Wiesenthal Center in Vienna, Austria." She snapped her fingers. "Actually I should have said *is* a foreign national. I talked to him by telephone this morning. He's never been to Montana in his life, and he's never even heard of Kalispell."

"Well, then, it's just a case of mistaken identity."

"I've had about enough of your shit—" Agent Boulton said, but Mattoon interrupted her.

"No, it's me who's had enough of your shit, Special Agent Boulton. Until I formally ask for your help, this is my jurisdiction and my investigation. So why don't you just skedaddle on out of here like a good little lady, and drive the fuck back up to Helena and lay siege to some Posse Comitatus or something."

She took an eight-by-ten photograph from a file folder and handed it to Mattoon. "Do you recognize this man?"

Mattoon looked at it and handed it back. "Herbert Sloan. He's a businessman, an investor of some kind. Owns a few hundred acres north of town."

"The German government thinks that his real name is Helmut Speyer, a former officer in the East German secret police."

"I wouldn't know about that. Why don't you go out there and talk to him?"

"That's the problem, you see. He's not out there. In fact he left two days ago, the morning after the murder." She put the photograph back in the file folder. "It's even possible that Mr. Sloan, or Herr Speyer, whoever he really is, along with his wife and another man, were in the bar at the time of the shooting."

"I don't know anything about that."

"Oh, but I think that you do, chief. And that's why I came down here to talk to you. A murderer missing. A victim's body missing. Witnesses missing." She smiled harshly. "I don't think that you're going to get lunch today. In fact I even wonder if you're going to get supper, considering all that we have to talk about."

Konrad Aden got back to his room in the Grand Hotel in time to order a drink from room service and take a shower before dinner. Sitting at the open window, sipping his martini, and looking down at Main Street, he used his cell phone to call Thomas Mann in Georgetown.

"Good afternoon, Konrad. Are you making progress?"

"I'm afraid that there may be some complications of a somewhat disturbing and puzzling nature. The FBI is here looking into the shooting."

"Will there be trouble for us?"

"That's the hell of it, General, I don't know. But my gut reaction is telling me to tread very carefully. There's something going on out here that just doesn't add up."

"Can you be more specific?"

"For starts, the body of the old Jew that Browne shot to death is missing. No one knows where it is, nor does anyone know anything about an autopsy. It's almost as if there never was a shooting in the first place."

"Helmut and Ernst were there and saw it."

"Well, the body is gone now. And it looks as if Helmut and his wife and Sergeant Baumann may have been placed at the scene. The FBI has been out to the ranch asking questions."

"Were they satisfied with the answers?"

"The FBI agent in charge of the Helena office is here talking to the chief of police."

"Who you have assured me knows nothing about Helmut's actual identity."

"That's not the problem yet," Aden said. "But we do have one loose end that I believe must be taken care of immediately."

"Go on."

"The only other witness is the bartender, William Hardt. Do I have authorization?"

"Do you feel that it is necessary?"

"Jawohl, Herr General."

"Then you have the authorization. I assume that you will use your usual discretion."

"Of course."

The Grand Hotel bar closed at ten this evening, but Willy wasn't finished shutting down and ready to go home until after 10:30. It had been a bitch of a week, and he didn't think that he was out of the woods yet. Someone was going to be coming around to ask more questions that he wasn't going to be able to answer. He just knew it. And no matter what he said or didn't say, he was going to be in some deep shit.

He flipped off the last of the lights behind the bar, and walked back through the kitchen where the only light was over the back door.

"Hello, Willy," Aden said from the shadows near the old walk-in freezer.

Willy stopped short, his heart in his throat, as a man with a very large pistol stepped into view. "What the hell do you want?"

"Nothing terrible. You just need to be put out of circulation for the rest of tonight. By morning everything will be settled. It's for Mr. Sloan. Do you understand?"

"Okay, that's cool," Willy said, relieved it wasn't a robbery or something. "But you don't have to point a gun at me. I'll do whatever you guys want me to do."

Aden opened the freezer door. "The compressor is turned off, so you can stay in here. By the time the morning kitchen crew comes in and finds out that something's wrong with the freezer, they'll let you out. You can tell them that you got locked in by mistake."

Willy was about to tell the man that the freezer could be opened from the inside with the safety latch, but he shrugged instead. "Fine by me. But you know that I wasn't going to open my mouth to the FBI."

"We understand."

Willy shuffled across the kitchen and into the freezer. Even as the heavy, soundproof door was closing, he realized that the compressor had not been turned off, and in fact it had probably been turned down to maximum cool, and the push rod for the safety latch was missing. When the light went out he understood that he was in some very big trouble.

4

NEUBRANDENBURG

Daylight lingered at this time of the year, although a low overcast hung over the lake and a chill wind blew from the north. Lane, dressed in a soft leather Gucci jacket, cashmere turtleneck, tan slacks, and half boots, went outside after dinner to have a smoke and take another look at the equipment in the garage. He had done some thinking about the dive that he was supposed to make tomorrow. He didn't have the experience that he said Browne had. But he did have some mixed gas training with the U.S. Navy about eight years ago during a project in the Azores. He'd actually made one dive to four hundred eighty feet, but it had been in the open sea, not into a dangerous bunker, and his total bottom time had only been about three minutes.

Inspecting the heavy closed-circuit diving mask and regulator, he decided that a lot of knowledge could be forgotten in eight years, and if he was going to survive the dive he had to first make sure that he completely understood his equipment.

He heard someone at the door, put down the mask, and turned around. Baumann came in.

"What are you doing out here?"

"Checking out the equipment before I put my life on the line tomorrow," Lane said. "Is that okay with you?"

"I don't care. If it was up to me I wouldn't go down

there for all the money in the world. It wouldn't do me any good if I was dead."

"What are *you* doing out here?"

"Helmut asked me to check on you. See if you needed any help. He figured that you were out here looking over things. This close to a mission he gets a little nervous, that's all."

"From where I stand I'm the only one who has anything serious to be worried about."

Baumann picked up the bulky mask and inspected it. He looked up at Lane. "Do you really know how to use this shit?"

"I've never used this specific equipment before, but it's all about the same. Same principles and all that."

Baumann put the mask down. "The Russians won't be here until midnight, so you have all the time you want. I'm going back inside."

"Tell Helmut that I might want to take another look at the memorial."

"Tonight?"

"Probably. I'll let you know."

Baumann nodded. "Whatever you want," he said, and he left the garage, walked across to the chalet and went inside.

Lane, watching from the deeper shadows just inside the doorway, saw a movement in the woods fifty yards behind the house. He stepped back a little farther into the garage, then went to a window. Five minutes later he saw a movement again, and this time he picked out a figure holding up what might have been a pair of binoculars. Someone was watching the house, and he had a pretty good idea who it was.

He went back to the doorway where he could watch the back of the chalet and the woods at the same time, but not be seen himself. He didn't want anyone sneaking up on him. He took out his cell phone and hit the speed dial number for the service provider here in Germany that would automatically transfer his call to his office in Washington. It took less than ten seconds for the connection to be made. Frances answered immediately.

"Yes."

"It's me, and I'm all right. I'm near a town called Neubrandenburg in what used to be East Germany."

Tom Hughes came on the line. "Are you in a secure location, William?"

"For the moment."

"There's nothing in the records about a Reichsamt Seventeen, and nothing on a need for diamonds for any sort of human guinea pig research. Speyer is either lying through his pearly whites, or he knows something that we don't. And the way the BKA is carrying on, I'd say that the latter is the most likely."

"What about the Russian Washington *rezident*?"

"Lukashin? He's in a fair amount of financial trouble even for a modern Russian. From what I can gather he's in to the Russian Mafia for something approaching a half-million dollars. And those folks don't accept excuses. So the man is well-motivated. But Mironov, his number two, is a rather nasty character with Russian Mafia ties up in Brighton Beach. He's got a vendetta for some reason against a South African by the name of John Browne."

"Don't worry about it—" Lane said, but Hughes cut him off.

"He's on his way to Germany, William, even as we speak. He flew over this noon. Should be arriving in Frankfurt am Main around midnight your time."

"Okay, I'll watch for him. But we have another problem. I spotted what looks like a surveillance operation behind the house that we're staying at. It's on the Tollense See. My guess would be BKA."

"They probably followed you from Frankfurt. Maybe it's for the best." Hughes, who was sometimes a Dutch uncle to Lane, was concerned.

"Tell them to back off. I still don't know what the hell Speyer is up to, and I don't think the Germans do either. But they're worried."

"So am I," Hughes said.

"That makes three of us," Frances broke in. "What now, love?"

"I'm going to take another look at the bunker entrance; a little later tonight we're meeting with the Russians, and in the morning I'm going for a swim."

"Dammit, William—" Frances protested.

"Take it easy, kiddo, I'll be okay," Lane said, and he rang off before they could give him more of an argument. He stood in the relative darkness for a long time staring at the woods, wondering just what the hell was down in the bunker that had Speyer so willing to face the risk of returning to Germany, and for the German Federal Police to take such an interest that they asked for American help. He also wondered why he was pushing this operation so far, but he wasn't quite willing yet to examine his motivations too deeply. It was Satchel Paige who once said don't look over your shoulder, something might be gaining on you. Lane figured that he knew exactly what the man had been talking about.

WASHINGTON, D.C.

Hughes hadn't been home in the week since Lane had gone off on assignment. His wife Moira and the girls understood perfectly. Lane was Uncle Bill to them, a part of the family. If Lane was in any danger it was only natural that Tom remain at his post to do whatever was necessary. What surprised him, however, was how badly Frances was taking this.

Their offices were near the vice president's residence in what had once been the chief astronomer's quarters on the grounds of the U.S. Naval Observatory. Normally there were a half-dozen staffers on duty, mostly communications specialists and analysts, but this afternoon it was just him and Frances.

He went down the hall to her office, and found her standing by the window, looking toward the observatory. There were a lot of tourists today, but she didn't seem to be watching them. He walked over and took her into his arms. He was a very large man, and she was slight of figure, almost boyish. She looked up and gave him a smile.

"If you've come to cheer me up, I can use it," she said brightly, though he could see that her eyes were troubled.

"On the contrary, we're finally alone and I'm a lecher."

"Good, I need that, too." Her lower lip quivered.

"He's a rather remarkable man, you know. He'll be okay."

She thought about that for a moment, then shook her head. Her face was round and pretty. Her eyes were wide and startlingly green; clear, honest, warm. "I didn't think it would be this way when I agreed to sign on."

"Fiddle faddle. You're a full commander in Her Majesty's Secret Intelligence Service, you knew exactly what this was all about." Hughes gave her a large smile, one that couldn't be resisted. "The fact of the matter is you're jealous. He's out having all the fun, while you're sitting home knitting booties."

Something flashed in her eyes, but then was gone.

She grinned. "You *are* a masher, and at the first opportunity I plan on telling Moira."

"She already knows," Hughes said. "But you're safe for the moment because I have to make a call to the Germans."

BERLIN

It was beyond his dinnertime and Chief Inspector Dieter Schey was about to leave for home when he took the call from Tom Hughes in Washington. When they had asked for help from the Americans he hadn't counted on this, and the dark brows on his narrow, pinched face knitted in anger.

"Of course it is your jurisdiction, but William has simply asked for a little elbow room," Hughes said.

"We've given your man enough latitude as it is," Schey replied tightly. He considered himself to be a reasonable man, but there was an unusual amount of pressure from above to get this case settled quickly and as quietly as possible.

"In for a penny, in for a pound. But I suppose I can understand your position, Chief Inspector. I'll get word to him to break off."

"*Verdammt*," Schey swore softly. "We came to you for help, so if it's room he wants, it's room we'll give him. But I'll have to clear it with my superior. We had hoped to keep a reasonably tight rein on what's happening up there."

"And I don't blame you," Hughes commiserated. "Of course it would be a great help if you could tell us exactly what he's going to run into down in that bunker—if it gets to that point."

"I sincerely hope it doesn't. All we want is Speyer

and Baumann behind bars, and their organization, the Friends, closed down permanently. They're all a bunch of murderers and thieves, just like the old Odessa. And they have an agenda."

"Which includes Reichsamt Seventeen, on which I can find no information whatsoever."

"The bunker is of secondary importance. They're probably after gold. What we're interested in is what he's going to do with his money."

"That's what we mean to help you discover if you'll give William the room."

"I'll see what I can do."

"*Grüss Gött*," Hughes said, and rang off.

Schey sat back for a moment, not at all happy that he had been maneuvered so easily, but then got up and went down the hall to the office of the director of BKA Special Operations, General Bruno Schaeffer. The general's secretary passed him straight in.

Schaeffer was a bull of a man, with a one meter, sixty centimeter chest, a farmer's square face and broad eyes. But he was smart, and it was said that most of the time he knew what you were thinking even before you knew it yourself.

Schey came to attention. "I've just spoken with the Americans. They want us to discontinue our surveillance operation at Tollense See."

"As a condition for their continued assistance?" the general asked mildly.

"Yes, sir."

"Then give them what they want," General Schaeffer said. Four lines on the telephone console were blinking. He ignored them, giving Schey his undivided attention. "Or at least make it appear as if you have given them what they want. Evidently your men up there got careless. Tell them to withdraw, and then return without being so obvious."

Schey allowed a smile. "I understand, Herr General. But it would be helpful if I had more information. For instance—"

The general picked up his phone and answered one of his calls as if Schey wasn't in the room. After a brief moment Schey turned on his heel and left. Supper would be late tonight. Very late.

NEUBRANDENBURG

Lane got a glass of beer from Schaub in the kitchen then went into the great room to sit by the fire. The evening was raw and he'd gotten chilled in the garage, made all the more worse by thinking about tomorrow's dive. Gloria, a crocheted afghan over her shoulders, sat with her feet tucked up under her at the end of the long couch. She was drinking champagne. The bottle was on the floor at her hand.

"Maybe you should think about laying off the booze for a while," he said. "Give your liver a rest."

"Screw yourself," she said mildly. She took a drink, looking at him over the rim of the glass. "I haven't noticed that men much give a damn whether a woman is drunk or not. In fact most of you bastards would prefer it that way."

"That depends on the class of men you're trying to seduce," Lane said. He went over and took the bottle from her. "You've had enough."

There wasn't much left in the bottle. What there was he poured into the edge of the fire, a champagne steam rising up into the chimney with a hiss. Standing by the massive hearth, with the tall windows at the end of the room looking out across the lake, boars' heads and deer racks hanging on the log walls, they could have been in another time, the thirties in Nazi Germany, for all the rustic malevolence here.

"What do you give a damn for?" Gloria asked.

"I don't like to see people destroying themselves," Lane told her. "Or being destroyed. It's a stupid waste of time."

"Like your wife and child?"

Lane drank his beer. Someone had put some new logs on the fire and they were going good, the changing pattern of flames mesmerizing.

"I'm a movie buff, and I saw the one picture that you were in," he said.

"I didn't think anyone had seen it, but I'd hoped that those who did would have had the decency never to say so."

It was a practiced line, dripping with contempt, and yet there was a sad expression on her face, as if she was grateful that at least one person had seen her film and wasn't laughing at her.

"You weren't God's gift to acting, but you photographed well. I think you could have probably made a decent career for yourself. What happened?"

She waved a hand dismissively. "That," she said.

"That what?"

She knocked back the rest of her champagne, and casually threw the glass into the fireplace. She hunched deeper into the couch. "That's a very long story."

"I wouldn't think that it would be a short one," Lane said. "What happened?"

"I was a woman of principles, if you can believe that." She laughed bleakly. "When sleeping around could have done me some good. I behaved myself. But by the time it was too late and no one gave a damn, I said the hell with it and let myself go." She appealed to Lane. "Kinda dumb, don't you think?"

"Kinda dumb," Lane agreed. "But drinking yourself to death won't solve anything."

She laughed again. "Did I mention that I was offered a role in a porn film last year?" She shook her head. "I turned them down, of course. But a couple of months ago I said what the hell. But when I called the producer, he turned me down. I've got a bad sense of timing."

Speyer came from upstairs. "Regaling John with your Hollywood exploits?" he asked.

Lane looked up. "Actually we were talking about the weather. Doesn't it ever get to be summer here?"

"The Baltic is only sixty kilometers north of here," Speyer said. He took a cigarette and a light from Lane. "Seems as if the FBI is interested in your handiwork in Kalispell."

"Did they find out anything?"

Speyer shook his head.

Gloria threw off the afghan, got up and stepped into her shoes. She was wearing tight jeans and a thick turtleneck. "I'm going upstairs to take a bath."

"You might want to hear the rest, my dear," Speyer told her, and she gave him a worried look. "The FBI came poking around at the ranch, but of course there was nothing for them to find."

"What about my car and the ordnance I brought with me?" Lane asked.

"It's well hidden, trust me," Speyer assured him. "They were asking questions around town, too, but they didn't find out anything there either. Nor will they."

Gloria stood quietly, as if she knew that she was going to hear some bad news.

Speyer glanced at her, but then turned back to Lane. "You see, the only weak link was Willy Hardt, the bartender. Besides the three of us and Ernst, Willy was the only other witness to the shooting. And he's been taken out of the picture. Permanently."

"You bastard," Gloria said softly. She brushed past him and went upstairs.

"That was a little extreme," Lane suggested. He should have thought of that. They could have arranged to take Hardt into custody on something unrelated.

"On the contrary, as I said, he was a weak link," Speyer replied. Gloria had stopped at the head of the stairs and was listening. Speyer ignored her. "Besides, I tend to take exception to men sleeping with my wife."

"I see."

"Ernst tells me that you'd like to take another look at the memorial tonight," Speyer said. "It's a good idea. I was going to suggest it myself. Why not right now?"

Schaub took them to the memorial in his old Mercedes 300TD station wagon, figuring that the familiar car on these roads at night would attract less attention than a fancy new car from out of the area. There was a padlocked chain across the driveway to the parking lot.

"Don't stop. Just drive by," Lane told him from the back seat.

Schaub did as he was told, and as they passed they saw a momentary flash of light as if someone had opened a door or a window curtain and then immediately closed it.

"There's a caretaker on duty overnight," Schaub explained.

"Is that something new?" Speyer asked.

"No, it's always been this way."

"What about at other war memorials?" Lane asked.

"Are they guarded around the clock, too?"

"Some are and some aren't. It depends."

"On what?"

Schaub glanced at Lane's reflection in the rearview mirror. "It depends on how important the memorial is. The Tomb of the Unknown Soldier in Berlin, places like that. And it also depends on whether there's been any vandalism. There's been a lot of that over the past few years because of the skinheads."

"Boys having fun," Speyer said dismissively.

"Which is it here?" Lane asked. "The importance or the vandalism?"

"Well, there's been no vandalism, I can tell you that much."

A Mercedes panel truck turned off the lake road and bumped up the gravel roadway to the rear of the chalet a few minutes after midnight. The legend DF 1, GERMAN TELEVISION ONE, was painted on the side. Two men got out.

"I thought there were supposed to be four of them," Lane said softly in the darkness of the back entry.

"There were," Speyer replied. "Maybe the others are still in the truck, or maybe they felt that there was no need for all of them to meet with us tonight."

"Or maybe something has gone wrong." Lane signaled to Baumann, who was waiting across the driveway in the garage.

Baumann moved forward slightly just out of the darkness so that Lane could see him. Like Lane, he was armed. There was no telling how the Russians were going to act tonight. They were in Germany under deep cover that was now possibly blown, and they did not want to go back to Russia. Life was a lot better here than it was in Moscow. They might simply shoot and run once they received the first half of their payment. It was a possibility that Lane had suggested, and Speyer had reluctantly agreed. Thus the precaution.

"Let me handle this," Speyer said. "I want you and Ernst to remain in the background unless something goes wrong."

"If I'm going to do the dive, I'm going to have to ask some questions."

"Only when the time is right. Until then let me do all the talking." Speyer was grim-faced. "These guys aren't going to screw around. Their lives are on the line."

Lane nodded. "And they know it." His Beretta was holstered under his sweater at the small of his back, the silencer already screwed on the end of the barrel. He had a spare magazine of ammunition in his pocket.

Schaub was waiting with a silenced Heckler & Koch 9mm pistol in the shadows at the head of the stairs overlooking the great room. He would act as their final backup should things go really wrong. Gloria had agreed to remain in the master suite at the rear of the house until the meeting was over. In fact, she was no problem because she had gone to bed around ten and had passed out shortly thereafter.

All their ducks were in a row, and yet Lane still felt a deep sense of uneasiness. There was something else going on that was just beyond his ken. He couldn't shake the sensation of foreboding.

Speyer stepped outside to the veranda as the two Russians walked over from their truck. They stopped in mid-stride when they saw him.

"Where are the other two men who were supposed to come with you?" Speyer demanded.

"Your information is old," the taller, huskier of the two said. They both wore dark trousers and matching jackets, of the kind worn by workmen and truck drivers. "Doronkin and Ranow are no longer in Germany."

"Where are they?"

"Dead."

"Do you have the equipment and the documents?" Speyer asked. "Did you bring them with you?"

The taller one nodded toward the other man, who held up a battered leather briefcase. "May we come in and get started?"

The Mercedes panel truck was okay where it was for now. Speyer stepped aside and motioned them forward.

Lane took up a position beside the fireplace where he could keep an eye on the two Russians. They introduced themselves as Vladimir Golanov and Danil Cherny, formerly KGB field officers. They were a scruffy-looking pair, and could have been gangsters out of a thirties American movie with slicked back hair. They sat on the couch. Cherny started to open the briefcase, but Golanov held him off.

"We have the film equipment in the truck, and the engineering diagrams here," he told Speyer. He glanced at Lane, but he didn't appear to be nervous, just cautious. "First I would like to see the money."

"Half tonight, the remainder tomorrow after we recover what we've come for," Speyer said.

"That's acceptable."

Speyer picked up a nylon gym bag sitting on the floor beside the chair, and tossed it to Golanov. The Russian opened it.

"Two hundred thousand marks," Speyer said. "Count it if you want. You'll get the rest when we're done."

Golanov and Cherny exchanged a look of relief,

but they were hiding something. "Okay, we have a deal. So let's get down to business."

Cherny opened the briefcase and spread out two dozen faded and crumbling engineering diagrams, along with eight twenty-by-twenty-five centimeter grainy black-and-white photographs that looked equally old. While their attention was diverted Lane happened to look up and spotted Baumann in the doorway from the kitchen.

"I'm the one who'll be doing the dive in the morning," Lane said, turning back.

"In that case you'd better pay attention, because there's going to be a lot of shit down there that's not on these drawings," Cherny said. He talked and acted like an engineer.

"There was an explosion which probably collapsed a lot of the ceilings and walls, right?"

Cherny nodded. "They set their charges against a granite wall separating the bunker from the lake. When the wall went, the water came rushing through the hole and vented up the elevator shaft with a considerable amount of hydrostatic force." Cherny wore glasses. He pushed them back up on the bridge of his nose. "I've read the report of a tank commander who happened to be there when it happened. He said that fish rained out of the sky."

"It probably scoured out the inside of the entire complex."

"Well, it certainly rearranged the furniture," Cherny agreed. "But not everything came out of the hole. A lot of what was down there either got jammed up in the rooms and the labs, or was so firmly attached to the floor or walls that it survived. The point is there's no telling what you'll find down there now—there's been sixty years of rot, too—so you damned well better memorize the layout according to the plans. It's the only way that you'll have any chance of finding what you're looking for." Cherny looked up from the drawings. "And getting back out of there alive."

"That's the object of this exercise," Lane replied dryly. Speyer had a strange, petulant look on his face, but Lane ignored him. "We're looking for the primary laboratory."

"That's here," Cherny said, stabbing a blunt finger on a spot down a broad corridor from the elevator shaft. "It's marked 'Laboritorium A.' The present day shaft is in the same location as the old elevator shaft, so you'll bottom out on the correct level and less than twenty meters from the lab."

"Providing the shaft hasn't collapsed, and there's nothing blocking the corridor."

Cherny shrugged. "You couldn't fill this house with enough money to tempt me to dive down there." He pursed his thin lips. "I think the chances of finding what you want in all that confusion and wreckage, in absolute darkness, and in water that's just a half a degree above freezing is almost zero, and your chances of getting back out alive are even less."

Golanov laughed nervously. "Don't exaggerate, Danil. The gentlemen are willing to pay us money for our information. Let's not talk them out of the project."

"No chance of that," Speyer said. "Leave the drawings and photographs with us tonight. Pick us up at 0800."

"Sounds good," Golanov said. He zippered the gym bag and he and Cherny left. When they were gone, Baumann came in from the kitchen, and Schaub came down from the balcony.

"It sounds very dangerous," Schaub said.

"Tomorrow will certainly be interesting," Lane replied. He looked up in time to see Gloria standing at the head of the stairs, a frightened expression on her face, before she turned and left.

Baumann and Schaub went to bed and Lane went out to the garage to make a final check on his dive equipment. The plan was to load everything into the back of the DF 1 truck and ride out of sight to the memorial. While the caretaker was being distracted by the Russians they would break into the maintenance shed and Lane would make the dive.

Any of a hundred things could go wrong. Equipment failure, hypothermia, hypoxemia, even nitrogen narcosis—the bends—if the oxygen-helium mixture wasn't just right. He could run into blocked passageways, unexploded ordnance, jagged pieces of metal or concrete that could rip his suit apart or shatter his mask. He could get disoriented; or simply moving through the tunnels he could cause the entire complex to collapse around his ears.

He had enough on all of them now to call in the BKA and have them arrested. But he couldn't do that. Not yet. Not until he found out what he was diving for. Certainly not diamonds. Speyer's story was ingenious, but Lane thought it was *too* ingenious to be true.

Back in the house Speyer was still up, studying the engineering diagrams. Lane poured a cognac against the chill and joined him.

"Is everything okay with the equipment?" Speyer asked.

"As far as I can tell," Lane said. "It's state of the art gear. Whoever picked it out knew what he was doing."

"It was Sergeant Schaub. He's a good man. I offered to take him to Cuba with us, but he turned me down. He wants to stay here. It's home."

"We're not going to kill the memorial caretaker tomorrow," Lane said.

Speyer shook his head. "There should be no reason for it, if everything goes well. But I can almost guarantee that we'll have trouble with the Russians. They're going to want whatever we bring out of the bunker, or they're going to want more money."

"What do you want to do?"

"If it comes to that we'll kill them."

"What about the bodies?"

"Sergeant Schaub will take care of that end of it for us," Speyer said. "He's very good at cleanup work."

It was the old German practicality. Everything in its place; everything neat and tidy; *alles in ordnung*. But it was cold and emotionless. Lane hated it.

Speyer turned back to the engineering diagram. "The diamonds will be locked in a large safe in the main laboratory. It should be just inside the door, a few meters to your left."

"Drilling out the lock is going to take too long, and blowing the hinges could be risky."

"You won't have to do either," Speyer said. He wrote a series of four two-digit numbers, each below sixty, on a slip of paper and handed it to Lane. "This is the combination to the safe."

"That'll come in helpful," Lane said. He glanced at the numbers, then handed the slip back.

A flash of irritation crossed Speyer's face. "I suggest that you keep it so that you can write it down on your plastic dive card."

"Fifty-eight, seventeen, forty-one, twenty-three," Lane said. "Now it's time for me to get some sleep." He started toward the stairs, but then thought of something and turned back. "Leave a note for Sergeant Schaub, would you? Since I'm diving I'm going to need a big breakfast. Steak, eggs, potatoes, toast, and a lot of black coffee."

Speyer just stared at him, and Lane grinned, a single word coming immediately to mind: *Prick.*

The DF 1 truck pulled in and parked behind the country house of Adolph Lauerbach a few kilometers northeast of Neubrandenburg. The family was not in residence, but then it very often was not because in reality this was one of the old KGB safehouses that had fallen through the cracks when the Wall came down. And if the local residents had learned nothing else over the last sixty years, it was to ask no questions.

Golanov shut off the headlights, then the engine, and turned around to face the rear. "I think that the South African suspected something."

"It doesn't matter, because the advantage will be ours," Nikolai Mironov said.

"If he's as handy as you say he is, once he gets out of the water he'll become a problem again."

Mironov nodded. "You're right. That's why we're going to kill him and the others as soon as he surfaces."

"If he suspects something, he might expect that we'll try to do just that," Cherny, the engineer, said.

"Look, both of you are expendable. Once they've got what they came for you'll be killed. That was the deal Speyer made with Lukashin. Nobody wants you back home, and you're costing too much money to keep here."

Cherny looked uncomfortable, but he didn't say anything.

"Do you understand what I'm telling you?" Mironov demanded. "Nobody gives a shit about you or any of the other KGB bastards here. Not Berlin and definitely not Moscow. If someone could push a button to get rid of you there'd be a line around the block waiting to do it. So if you want a chance to save your lives and get the hell out of here, you'll do what I tell you to do. Clear?"

Cherny and Golanov exchanged doleful glances, but they nodded.

"We don't have much of a choice," Golanov said.

"No, you don't. It's either them or you."

"Then we'll do whatever we have to do," Cherny said. "I for one don't feel very expendable."

5

NEUBRANDENBURG

Lane awoke at 3:00 A.M., got up and went to the window that looked out toward the lake. It was still blustery and it looked cold outside, whitecaps on the lake and no stars in the still overcast sky. But there was no one down there lurking about that he could see.

He used the bathroom and then went back to bed. He lay in the darkness thinking. The Russians were not going to try anything until he surfaced with the diamonds. They would not take the risk of coming that far and then losing the ultimate prize. The only wild card was Mironov, who was here in Germany by now, and probably with the two ex-KGB men.

He might be wanting revenge for the roughing up Lane had given him, and because he'd had to return to his boss with his tail between his legs. Russians were long on vengeance and very short on forgiveness these days. Especially when it involved money. The problem was that Lane had no way of telling what the man was going to do in the morning.

He had willed his mind to go blank so that he could get a couple more hours of sleep when he heard someone at his door. He silently snatched his pistol from the nightstand, slipped out of bed, and went to the even deeper darkness in the corner beyond the window. The door opened and he saw Gloria silhouetted; the light from the fire on the grate downstairs made her thin nightgown transparent.

Lane put the gun down on the chair beside him. "Go back to your husband," he said softly.

Startled, she turned toward his voice, but it was apparent that she could not see him. "I couldn't sleep," she said in a small voice. "I've been thinking about you all night."

"I'm sorry, but get out of here." He listened for someone else awake and up. But the house was silent except for the crackle of the fire.

"Your wife is dead, John."

"Not to me."

She came the rest of the way into the room and closed the door. Now Lane couldn't see her, but he heard her come across to him, and then she was naked and in his arms. She was shivering.

"You can't know how long it's been," she said, theatrically, her body tight against his. He was dressed only in his shorts, and she felt soft, almost slack, not in the least appealing.

He turned on the floor lamp. She reared back in the sudden glare, her hand going to her eyes. He gently pushed her back, picked up her nightgown from the floor and handed it to her.

"Go back to your own room before we both get into trouble," he told her. "I'm going to have a busy day of it starting in a damned few hours, and I'd like to get some sleep."

She didn't bother trying to cover herself, and an ugly look came into her face. "Fuck you," she said harshly, her lip curling into a sneer. "All the money in the world couldn't buy what I was offering you for nothing." She brushed past him and left his room.

"Well, that was nicely done," Lane muttered.

Mironov couldn't sleep either. He got up, put on a pair of slacks and a light jacket, and went out to the back porch, out of the wind, to smoke a cigarette. When he was finished he called Lukashin on his cell phone.

"Don't tell me that you're already finished with your little project," Lukashin said. It was about ten in the evening in Washington. There was music in the background.

"No, we're going first thing in the morning," Mironov said. "The good part is that I don't think he suspects anything. From what I could hear on Golanov's wire, the dive will be straightforward."

"A hundred meters down in total darkness into a destroyed bunker?" Lukashin asked. "I'd say that will be anything *but* straightforward." He laughed. "Whatever you do, don't show your hand until after whatever he's bringing up with him is safely out of the water. Unless you want to jump in after it."

Lane got up again a little before six, took a long, hot shower, got dressed in Pierre Cardin jeans and his favorite cashmere sweater, soft half boots on his feet, and went down to the kitchen. Sergeant Schaub was already up and had breakfast started. He handed Lane a steaming mug of coffee and poured a healthy measure of Asbach-Urhalt cognac into it.

"Something to brace you up, *Junge*. It's going to be damned cold down there even in a dry suit."

"I don't plan on staying long."

"See that you don't. With that helium-oxygen mixture the cold is going to hit you harder than normal. Is the equipment what you need?"

"It'll do fine," Lane said. He took a sip of the coffee. "Just what the doctor ordered."

Schaub went back to the stove where he was cooking fat sausages in a large skillet. There were fried potatoes, chopped spinach, cheese, and *Brötchen*, the small, hard German bread rolls. "How many eggs?"

"Three," Lane said.

"What about a weapon?" Schaub asked, attending to the cooking.

"I don't think there'll be any ghosts down there."

Schaub turned back, an impatient scowl on his square face. "I never trusted the bastard Russians, and I don't trust them now. I suggest that you carry a gun with you in case something goes wrong on top."

"I see what you mean," Lane said. "I can strap a pistol to my chest under my dry suit."

"Good idea," Schaub said, satisfied. "Now sit down and I'll fix your eggs."

Speyer was in the bathroom shaving. Gloria got out of bed and went to the door. She could smell breakfast from the kitchen downstairs, and her stomach turned over. She'd had too much to drink last night, as usual, and she felt like hell.

"Well, it worked," she said. "The bastard took the bait."

Speyer looked at her in the mirror. "What are you talking about?"

"Your pal, John Browne." She came into the bathroom, raised her nightgown, and sat on the toilet. He hated it when she relieved herself in his presence.

He waited until she was done. "What about him? Did you find out anything?"

"Nothing much, except that he's no different from any other man." She took off her nightgown, made sure that he got a good look at the self-inflicted bruises on her breasts and flanks, then stepped into the shower, closed the curtain and turned on the water.

Speyer pulled the curtain back. "Stop playing games, *Liebchen*, and tell me what happened."

Her eyes went wide and suddenly she began to cry. "You wanted me to tease him. Try to get him to tell me things. I tried last night, and he raped me."

"Why didn't you cry out?"

"I couldn't. He said that he would kill me. He's crazy."

Speyer turned away, angry, and Gloria closed the curtain again. She turned the water warmer and smiled. All men were easy.

Lane finished his breakfast and took his coffee outside to the front veranda where he could see the lake and have a smoke. It was still very cold and blustery with no signs that the weather would break soon. He was going to be very vulnerable while he was in the bunker. It was possible that because of the windy weather, which roiled up the surface of the lake, currents could be running through the bunker. There was no telling what he was going to run into when he got down there.

He tossed the cigarette aside and went across to the garage. In the back, behind a stack of cardboard boxes and some folded burlap bags, he found an opening in the wall boards. He wrapped his cell phone in a burlap sack and stuffed the bundle as far down inside the wall as he could reach. He didn't want someone finding it when he was inside the bunker.

"Browne," Speyer called from outside.

Lane shoved the rest of the burlap bags in front of the opening, and went back outside just as Speyer came across from the house.

"I was just making a last-minute check on the equipment."

"It's off, you son of a bitch," Speyer shouted. He sprinted for Lane, who stepped aside at the last possible moment and stuck out his foot, sending Speyer sprawling on his face.

Baumann and Schaub came out of the house. "What's happening?" Baumann demanded.

"I don't know."

Speyer got up and Lane tried to give him a helping hand but he batted it away. "You're fired. I want you to get the fuck out of here right now before I kill you."

"*Was ist, Herr Kapitän?*" Schaub asked as he and Baumann hurried across the driveway.

"The bastard wanted everything for himself," Speyer shouted.

"I don't know what you're talking about," Lane said, keeping his tone of voice casual, though he had a pretty good idea that it had something to do with Gloria.

"My wife came to talk to you last night." Speyer turned to Baumann and Schaub. "I wanted Gloria to find out as much as she could about him. I didn't trust him and I was right. He raped her."

"That's not true," Lane said. He held himself loose. He had the pistol in his belt at the small of his back but he didn't want to have to use it. He wanted to bring up the diamonds, or whatever it was, from the bunker and then find out what Speyer's ultimate plan was. Killing him now, or calling in the German Federal Police and arresting him, wouldn't provide the answers.

Schaub shot Lane a look. "What time was that, Herr *Kapitän*?"

"Three o'clock," Gloria said from the doorway. She was dressed in jeans and a sweater, but she hadn't fixed her hair and she wore no makeup.

"I'm sorry, Herr *Kapitän*, but Mr. Browne was with me in the kitchen," Sergeant Schaub said. "We couldn't sleep so we were having a smoke and some schnapps. Talking about the mission."

"He's a fucking liar," Gloria shrieked.

The animation suddenly drained from Speyer's face. For a moment he looked like a kid caught with his hand in the cookie jar. But a kid capable of killing anyone who got in his way or challenged him. When he raised his head he was smiling with embarrassment. "Sorry about that."

"You bastards," Gloria screamed, but then she realized that no one believed her, and she went back inside.

"Your wife did come to my room last night to try to seduce me, but I sent her away," Lane admitted. "That's the second time she's tried since Kalispell. Either keep her on a shorter leash, or the next time you send her to me I might not send her back."

"She said you hit her."

"I don't hit women or children. Only men who deserve to be hit."

Speyer stared at Lane with hatred. "I don't trust you."

"Well, I don't trust you either," Lane replied. "Nor do I particularly care for your brand of leadership. So if you want me to get out, I'll go. But first I'll take the five thousand you offered me. I didn't come all this way for nothing. Besides, I figure that saving your life is worth at least that much."

Speyer looked at Schaub and Baumann and then stared at the whitecaps marching across the lake for a few seconds before turning back. "I'd rather you didn't leave just yet," he said. "As a matter of fact without you we'd have to abort this mission until I could find someone to take your place. In the meantime keeping the Russians in place would be difficult if not impossible."

"Ten percent," Lane said.

Baumann started to object, but Speyer held him off. "That could be as much as thirty million dollars."

Lane shrugged. "I figure that it's worth it, don't you? Ninety percent of something is better than one hundred percent of nothing."

Speyer nodded, a wry smile on his lips. "It's a deal, Mr. Browne with an 'e.' Under the circumstances I don't have much of a choice."

"No, you don't," Lane said.

"What I want to know is what the hell is down there that's so important," Golanov asked.

"I don't know myself, but whatever it is, they want it badly enough to risk coming back to Germany and spending a lot of money," Mironov replied.

They were outside at the DF 1 truck, ready to head out. Golanov was driving and Cherny rode shotgun. Mironov would drive over to the chalet as soon as the filming began and the diver was down in the bunker. Speyer's wife didn't know what he looked like. To her he would be nothing other than one of the Russian team.

"Just remember nobody makes a move until Browne is out of the bunker and has the package," Mironov cautioned them. "I'll be waiting at the chalet, but if you see an opportunity, take it. Save us all some trouble. But I want Browne for myself if at all possible."

"What if the caretaker gets suspicious, or if a tourist should wander by?"

"Kill them," Mironov said. "Dump their bodies in the bunker, and seal it up."

Lane had the equipment he needed piled just inside the garage door. He'd taped his Beretta to his chest, and then donned the dry suit. He thought about carrying another pistol in his equipment bag or somewhere else under his suit, but he decided against it. If he couldn't defend himself with nine shots then he would be in enough trouble that reaching for another gun might well be impossible.

Schaub came out to the garage with another cup of brandy-laced coffee. Lane took it and warmed his bare hands. It was colder here this morning than Washington, D.C., usually got in the winter.

"They'll be here in a minute or two, are you ready?" Schaub asked.

"As ready as I'll ever be," Lane replied. "Why did you lie for me about Gloria?"

"Did you touch her?"

Lane shook his head.

"I didn't think so," Schaub said thoughtfully. He glanced back toward the house. "Helmut has told me about her. She's bad news all the way. He should never have married her in the first place, let alone bring her here." He shrugged. "But he is a jealous man, so he couldn't leave her behind."

"What about you, Otto? Are you coming with us after we're finished this morning?"

"This is my home, so I'll remain unless it becomes impossible for me."

"Why get involved in the first place? Just stay here this morning."

"I wish it were possible, *Junge*. But Helmut and I go back a long way together. I owe him."

"I see," Lane said. "Stay out of sight, then. Maybe we can pull this off without killing anyone."

They loaded the dive equipment in the back of the truck, and Lane crawled inside with Speyer, Baumann, and Schaub. It was a big truck, but with all the equipment they were cramped for space. The Russians were in front. Golanov, who would play the role of narrator, wore a sport coat and a white turtleneck. Cherny would be the cameraman. He wore white coveralls with "DF 1" stenciled on the back.

"Are we all set back there?" Golanov asked.

"Let's get it over with," Speyer ordered.

The drive down to the memorial took only a few minutes. When they turned onto the entry road Golanov headed directly over to the maintenance building, where he pulled up and parked.

"The parking lot is empty," he told them. "But keep your heads down until we can get the caretaker to the other side of the pavilion."

"Here he comes," Cherny said.

"Okay, you'll be able to hear everything over the headset. When we tell him that it'll only take an hour, that's your signal to start. And that's how long you'll have to make the dive and get out."

As soon as Golanov and Cherny were out of the truck with their camera equipment, Lane assembled his diving gear and put it on. Schaub helped him, while Speyer listened on the headset and Baumann kept lookout.

"They're showing him the authorization for filming from the Federal Parks Bureau," Speyer said. "Can you see them, Ernst?"

Baumann rose up so that he could look over the back of the driver's seat. "They're inside the pavilion, looking toward the lake."

"He's not sure what he's supposed to do." Speyer pressed the headset closer. "Stupid bastard." He looked up. "Has anyone else shown up?"

"*Nein.*"

Speyer listened a little longer. "Is there any sign of the two maintenance men?"

"Nothing."

"You may have to go out and kill the caretaker—" Speyer held up a hand. "Wait."

Lane lowered the chest zipper on his dry suit so that he could reach his pistol. He wasn't going to allow them to kill the caretaker. He met Schaub's eyes, but the sergeant said nothing, though it was obvious he knew what Lane meant to do.

"Okay, that's the signal," Speyer said, grinning like a death's head. "One hour. Do the lock, Ernst."

Baumann slid open the truck's side door, which was only a couple of feet from the steel door into the maintenance shed. Using a pair of hydraulic shears, he cut the shackle, removed the lock and opened the door. There was just enough clearance for Lane to slip inside.

It took a couple of moments for his eyes to adjust to the darkness, but then Baumann and Schaub squeezed their way inside and switched on flashlights.

A double-wide steel trapdoor was set into the concrete floor about twenty feet below the gallery they stood on. Metal stairs led to the lower level. There was nothing inside the shed; no equipment, no tools, no lights.

They went down to the base level. The trapdoor was secured by a padlock. While Schaub held a flashlight, Baumann cut and removed the padlock and swung the doors open to reveal the shaft into the bunker. The opening was ten feet on a side, water coming to within six inches of the top. There were no handholds, no ladders, nothing except the square of ominously black water.

"It's time, *Junge*, if you've got the stomach for it," Schaub said.

Lane had marked the locations of the bunker's main intersections and primary lab on a plastic marker board. He made sure it was secure in a leg pocket, then held up a thumb. "In for a penny, in for a pound."

"Try not to touch anything you don't have to touch, and don't brush up against the ceilings or walls," Schaub cautioned.

Lane nodded. Holding his mask in place with one hand, he switched on his dive light with the other and stepped off the concrete floor into the water. It immediately closed over his head like a coffin lid, and he began his long, slow fall to the bottom, three hundred feet down.

It was working exactly as they had planned it, Mironov thought as he came around the bend in the road. The memorial was up ahead, and although he couldn't see Golanov and Cherny with the caretaker, he could hear them talking over his headset as if they were actually making the stupid documentary.

He carried an Austrian-made 9mm Glock 17 self-loading pistol with a nineteen-round box magazine in a shoulder holster. He felt in his jacket pocket for the extra magazine of ammunition, and inside his belt on his right side for his second gun, a small, reliable, 5.45mm Russian-made PSM.

"How deep is the lake at this point?" Golanov's voice came over Mironov's headset.

He slowed as he passed the driveway down to the memorial. He saw the DF 1 truck in front of the maintenance shed but there was no sign of Golanov, Cherny, and the caretaker, though he could hear them. They were allowing one hour for the dive, but they would not be expecting the reception they were going to get.

* * *

After the first fifty feet Lane let a little gas into his buoyancy control vest to slow his rate of descent. As he dropped he spread his legs and looked down, shining the powerful beam of his halogen helmet light between his flippers. Shadows and dark, twisted shapes loomed all around him. Cables emerged from the side of the shaft at one point, dropped thirty or forty feet and then disappeared back into the shaft wall. A swastika was painted on the wall about halfway to the bottom, and directly beneath it was a skull and crossbones with the single word: VORSICHT! Danger! At another point his light flashed on the remains of a stairway, only four concrete steps remaining after nearly sixty years.

For the most part the shaft had been scoured clean by the blast, and by the sudden uprush of water which carried every loose object before it: cables, elevator cars, stairs, equipment, rubble, bodies. Silt had settled on every surface so that his movement made the water above him opaque. Below him, however, the water was pitch-black everywhere except in the beam of his light, where it was crystal clear.

His electronic depth gauge began beeping at 85 meters, which was about 280 feet. He let more air into his BC, and his rate of descent slowed to almost zero.

Below him the floor of the shaft was twisted upward at a steep angle, as if the concrete slab the bunker was constructed on had been tilted. But as he slowly worked his way down, he began to realize that the side of the shaft itself had been undercut and had collapsed into the main tunnel, half burying an opening to the left.

He jackknifed and followed the beam of his light to the base of the shaft where he directed it through the opening. This apparently was the main corridor that ran roughly east to west. He could make out a doorway and what appeared to be blown-out windows.

There was some debris, but mostly the tunnel was clear. Nor was there any appreciable current.

Lane backed up and took out the plastic card with his notes and sketches. The cold had already begun to seep into his bones, and he felt his strength being drawn off. But it was deceptively slow. Almost comforting.

The rubble he hovered above covered what had been the final security checkpoint at the bottom of the elevator shaft and stairwell. The opening into the bunker had been secured by a steel door, much like those aboard a submarine. But that was gone now.

He swam closer and once again shined his light into the main corridor, checking what he was seeing against his plastic dive card. His light wouldn't penetrate twenty meters; more like three or four. But the corridor seemed to be unblocked and stable. The ceilings and walls were not bulging, and so far as he could see there were no other collapsed sections ahead.

Replacing the dive card in his leg pocket, he eased his way through the opening and down into the corridor, a cloud of silt rising behind him, completely obliterating the opening.

He hovered again for several seconds to make sure that the ceiling wasn't going to fall in on him, and then swam to the first doorway. He shined his light inside what could have been a laboratory. All that was left now were several heavy workbenches bolted to the floor, some shelving along a wall, and a twisted pile of what might have been desks, file cabinets, and other things jammed into a corner.

Back in the main corridor he almost lost his bearings because rising silt was so thick he could not see his hand in front of his face mask, nor would the beam of his flashlight penetrate more than an arm's length.

With his hand trailing along the wall he swam forward, coming out of the silted water all of a sudden as if a thick gauze curtain had been pulled away from his eyes.

He passed two other doors, one of which opened into another scoured-out laboratory, and the other of which was closed. He didn't bother trying to open it. Instead he continued to another open door which he figured was the right distance, about twenty meters from the shaft, to be Laboratory A.

The steel door to this laboratory had been held in the open position by an iron bar jammed into the hinges from inside. Like the other labs, this one had been all but scoured clean of whatever equipment it had once held, except for several heavy workbenches and a very large two-door floor safe jammed into a corner.

There were two chairs and a tangle of wire, wood, pieces of concrete, a big microscope, and some other piece of laboratory equipment in front of the safe. Lane carefully removed these things, setting them aside in a dense cloud of silt.

He was so cold now that his joints were beginning to hurt, and he was getting sleepy. He raised his wrist to look at his dive watch. At first he couldn't make sense of what he was seeing. According to the watch forty-eight minutes had already elapsed. Was that possible, he asked himself. He pulled his dive computer and gauges over and studied them for several long seconds. His oxy-helium mixture was more than half gone, confirming his watch. But it seemed as if he had been gone for only a few minutes.

He shook his head to clear it, then waved the silt from the big combination lock, and cleared the mechanism by turning the knob three full turns to the right.

He hovered for several seconds, his mind drawing a blank, until the first number popped into his head. He turned the dial to 58. The mechanism, apparently sealed from the water, still worked smoothly. He turned to 17, right back to 41, and finally left to 23, but when he tried the latch handles they wouldn't budge.

Lane hovered motionless again, staring drunkenly at the dial. After all these years they couldn't expect the mechanism to still be in working order. Yet the dial was free and smooth.

He reached to turn it back to zero to start over, but first he tried the latches again. This time they opened smoothly.

A big bubble of air escaped from the safe, rising to the ceiling where it spread like quicksilver, brightly reflecting his light. A pair of inner doors, secured with a recessed latch, opened easily to his touch, and as he drew them open an even larger bubble of air escaped.

The safe was empty except for a single black metal box, a nearly perfect cube about twenty inches on a side. There were handles left and right. A bead of metal, what might have been lead, ran completely around the seam, sealing the container's lid. Skull and crossbones decals were painted on each side of the box with the single German world for danger in bold red print: VORSICHT!

In Lane's befuddled state he stared at the box for perhaps as long as a minute. It rested in a compartment in the exact middle of the safe. The compartment was held in place by a series of springs, like shock absorbers. Whatever was sealed in the box had to be sensitive to vibration or else the Germans would not have gone to such lengths to protect it.

If they were diamonds, Lane thought, they were unusually delicate stones.

He slid the box out of its compartment and was immediately weighed down to his knees, the box sinking at once to the concrete floor, silt rising in thick clouds. The damned thing had to weigh at least one hundred pounds.

Working almost completely by feel, Lane wrestled the box up to his chest where he braced it against the edge of the safe as he pushed the pressure button on his chest, dumping gas into his BC. He rose off his knees. The box was still as heavy as before, but he wasn't being weighed down by it.

He dumped a little more gas into his BC, turned and slowly made his way through the almost completely opaque water to where he thought the door was. He bumped into the wall, and he remained motionless for a second or two, until he gathered his wits enough to follow the wall to the left.

Five feet later he came to the opening and swam out into the corridor where he stopped again. He had come down the shaft and through the opening. But which way had he turned after that? There were other laboratories, and he vaguely remembered that one of them had been sealed.

He swiveled to the left and tried to peer through the silted water. He was very cold; his throat was dry and raw. Think. He swiveled to the right. He'd come stright down the main corridor and then turned . . . left into the laboratory. It meant that to get out he had to turn in the opposite direction. Right. But he was already facing right.

With agonizing slowness Lane swam to the end of the tunnel and half-swam, half-crawled up the pile of rubble, through the opening, and into the shaft. Home free now, except that he could no longer hold the box in his arms. He eased it down on top of the rubble, let go, and shot upward immediately.

A huge pressure stabbed his eardrums as if someone had driven hot pokers into his skull, and his lungs felt as if they were being ripped out. He was rising too fast.

He fumbled in the darkness with the pressure valve on his BC, finally making his fingers work to release some of the gas. His rise slowed immediately. He released more gas until he was ascending at a slow, even rate and the pressure in his head and lungs cleared as did the cobwebs in his brain.

He passed the stairs and the skull and crossbones and the cable, finally breaking the surface, the beam of a flashlight directly in his face.

"Did you get it?" Baumann demanded. His voice was hollow in the chamber. Lane pushed his face mask back. "I need the rope. It's too heavy to bring up by hand."

"Where is it?"

"At the bottom of the shaft. I managed to get it that far."

"Wait," Baumann ordered. He raced back up the stairs and slipped through the door.

"We were ready to give up on you," Schaub said. "It's been over an hour. The filming is done and the Russians are on their way back to the truck."

"Tell Helmut to stall them if he wants his diamonds," Lane said. "But I don't want anything to happen to the caretaker. Do you understand?"

Schaub nodded, his face ghostly in the reflected light from his flashlight beam. "He's my cousin. Nothing will happen to him."

"Does Helmut know that?"

Schaub shook his head as Baumann returned from the truck and rushed down the stairs. He carried the big coil of nylon rope, which he undid and handed an end to Lane.

"I'll secure it up here," he said urgently. "When you're ready, give me a couple of pulls. But for Christ's sake hurry, they're on the way back."

"It's heavy, so be careful," Lane warned. "I don't want it coming back down on top of me." He secured his mask, released some pressure from his BC, and started back down into the shaft.

Golanov led the way back up the hill from the pavilion. Cherny, carrying the camera and bulky battery pack, was right behind him. Hans Mueller, the caretaker, was heading back to his office for his midmorning tea and schnapps break. With the bad weather he wasn't expecting any tourists this morning.

"Do you think that he suspected anything?" Cherny asked.

"No, he's got an authorization document to file."

"What if he calls somebody?"

"He won't call anybody, Danil," Golanov shot back impatiently. They were no longer filming so the sound equipment was off and there was no chance that anyone in the truck could overhear them. "I want you to get into the truck through the driver's side door. Keep whoever's in there busy. I'm coming in the back way, and with any luck we'll end it right here."

"Only if you have a clear shot," Cherny said. "I don't want to end up at the bottom of the bunker."

"Just do your part and I'll do mine."

Cherny went to the front of the truck, and Golanov went around back. The side door was ajar as was the steel door into the maintenance shed, but there was nobody about.

He took out his Glock 17 and silently made his way along the side of the truck to the open door. He overheard Cherny say something, though he couldn't make out the words. Then Speyer replied, "No delays."

Golanov swung around the corner and into the truck. Speyer reared back in surprise and grabbed for his gun from the top of the radio.

"The instant you touch it you're dead," Golanov said.

Speyer's hand stopped. "I don't know what the fuck you think you're doing, but you're throwing away a lot of money."

Golanov laughed. "From where I'm standing I'd say that you're in no position to be giving orders now." He turned his head slightly. "Keep a sharp watch for the caretaker, Danil," he said. He backed up and motioned with his pistol for Speyer to come along. "You first, Herr *Kapitän*."

Speyer did as he was told, but very slowly, obviously looking for an opening. Golanov backed up, keeping a respectful distance, and waved Speyer inside the maintenance building.

Inside, they started down the stairs, Speyer in the lead. Below, at the open shaft, Baumann and Schaub looked up in surprise.

"Gentlemen, I want you to raise your hands right now," Golanov said. "If you try anything your captain will take the first bullet."

For a long second neither of them moved.

"Do as he says," Speyer told them.

Schaub tossed something into the water with a soft splash and he raised his hands.

"Where's Browne?"

"Still in the bunker," Schaub replied. "And it looks as if your timing is perfect. For a fucking Russian, that is."

At the bottom of the shaft Lane tied the rope to the container's handles. It was all by feel because of the silted water. He turned and gave a couple of sharp tugs on the line, but it was slack. Baumann had paid it out meter by meter as Lane descended so that he could feel when the two pulls came, but Lane continued to bring the line down, hand over hand, until he had ten or fifteen meters of it. Something had gone wrong.

Looping the rope through his weightbelt, Lane started to the top, conserving his energy, letting the BC do most of the work.

There was no telling exactly what he was going to find, but he suspected that the Russians had gotten the drop on Speyer and the others and were waiting for him to surface with the diamonds. If it was Mironov, he wouldn't hesitate to shoot first and ask questions later.

Lane stopped his ascent a few meters from the surface. He could see the beams of two flashlights shining down into the water. He swam to the forward wall of the shaft directly beneath their feet. Hopefully they were watching for him to come up in the center and might not spot him until it was too late.

Very slowly and precisely, so as to make absolutely no noise, Lane's head broke the surface. He pulled his mask off. Baumann and Schaub, their hands up, were directly above him. To the left he could make out Speyer's figure in the light reflecting crazily off the water. Behind him there was someone else. One of the Russians.

Pumping more gas into his BC, Lane rose even

farther out of the water. He unzippered his dry suit, took the Beretta out of his holster and switched the safety off. There was no one else down here with them, and he didn't know what that meant. But the present situation would not last much longer. If he was going to do something it had to be now.

"Help," he shouted, his voice echoing throughout the chamber.

Schaub pushed Baumann aside, and swung his flashlight around so that the beam caught the Russian in the face. At that moment Speyer stepped to the right, giving Lane a clear shot.

"Put it down," Lane shouted.

Golanov fired into the water, forcing Lane to fire back, hitting the Russian in the middle of the chest, and driving him back off his feet.

"Where's the other one?" Lane demanded.

"In the truck," Speyer said. He grabbed Baumann's gun just as Cherny appeared in the doorway above. Schaub shined his flashlight on the Russian, who dove to the right. Speyer fired two shots, both of them ricocheting dangerously off the concrete walls.

Cherny rose up from the shadows, a pistol in his hand, but Lane fired twice, at least one of them hitting the man, sending him tumbling down the stairs and half into the water, dead.

"I'll check the caretaker," Schaub shouted, and he raced up the stairs.

Lane untied the rope from his waist and handed it up to Baumann. "Careful with it, the damned thing is heavy."

He levered himself out of the water, and as Baumann started hauling the container up from the bottom of the shaft, Speyer came over and helped Lane out of his diving equipment. He was very excited.

"You actually found it? You got it?"

"Yeah. So let's clean up this mess and get the hell out of here now. I don't want the German police barging in here, guns blazing."

"You're right," Speyer agreed. He helped Baumann pull the container the rest of the way out of the shaft, and they manhandled it up onto the concrete floor. They all stared at it for a long moment, but then Lane finished pulling off his equipment. He bundled it in his dry suit, wrapped his weightbelt around it all, and dumped the lot into the bunker shaft. Speyer and Baumann rolled the two bodies into the water.

They lowered the double doors. Baumann took a new padlock out of his pocket and secured the latch. "It's not an exact match," he said. "But it'll pass unless they try to open it."

Schaub appeared at the doorway, out of breath. "It's all right," he called down. "He didn't hear a thing."

"How do you know?" Speyer demanded.

"I went down to the pavilion and looked in the window. He's having his tea, and you can hear the television all the way up the hill."

"No tourists?"

"Nobody else."

Baumann carried the heavy container up to the DF 1 truck. When it was loaded aboard, he replaced the lock on the maintenance door. Speyer got behind the wheel, and as they headed out of the memorial parking lot he thumped his fist on the steering wheel. "We did it. Son of a bitch, we did it."

Mironov, his pistol to Gloria's head, watched from the front entry hall as the DF 1 truck came up the driveway. The big grin on his face died as he saw who was driving. He pulled Gloria back into the living room. "Say one word and I'll blow your goddamned brains out." He was glad now that something had prompted him to park his car out of sight behind the garage. Something had gone wrong, and now it was just him.

Gloria said nothing, her eyes flicking back and forth between her captor and the kitchen.

He could hear them outside, laughing, as they got out of the truck. They came onto the back porch to the kitchen. Mironov hauled Gloria around and, using her as a shield, covered the door.

Speyer was first into the house, but he didn't spot Mironov and Gloria in the living room until he was halfway across the kitchen, and Schaub and Baumann were inside. He pulled up short, a look of surprise and consternation on his face, and he started for his gun.

"I'll kill her," Mironov warned.

Speyer stopped. "What the hell are you doing here? What do you want?"

"My car is parked in back of the garage. I want whatever you pulled up from the bunker put in the trunk." Mironov knew that he was in trouble. Without Golanov and Cherny it was just him against the four of them. "And where's Browne? I want him."

"Here I am," Lane said from the front entry hall.

Mironov twisted around, but before he could bring his gun to bear, Lane fired one shot, hitting him in the temple just above and forward of his right ear. The Russian slumped like a felled ox, dead before he hit the floor.

Gloria jumped back, Mironov falling at her feet, but she didn't utter a sound.

"How did you know he was going to be here?" Speyer demanded.

"Just a hunch," Lane said, putting away his gun. "I didn't think that Lukashin could keep his nose out of it. And this one certainly had a grudge."

"I like your hunches," Speyer said. "But now we have to get to the ship. Are you coming with us, Otto? This'll be your last chance."

"I'm staying," Schaub said. "I'll take care of everything here so you don't have anything to worry about."

"Once we're gone we'll be well out of it. They won't make the connection no matter what they find. At least not until it's too late."

"I'll get rid of the body just the same, along with the truck and his car by the time you sail tonight."

"I left some gear in the garage—" Lane said, but Schaub waved him off.

"Just get out of here, all of you. Leave this part to me."

There was an awkward moment, but then Baumann shook hands with him, and went out to put the container in the Mercedes' trunk.

"If you need anything let me know through the usual channels," Speyer said.

"Take care of yourself, Herr *Kapitän*," Schaub said. They shook hands, and Speyer went to the door.

"Thanks for your help," Lane said, shaking his hand.

"I saw what you were willing to do for my cousin," Schaub said, half under his breath. "I am a good judge of men after all."

"I'll bet you are at that."

Speyer came back. "Take my wife to the car," he told Lane. "I want a last word with Otto."

"Okay," Lane said. He took Gloria by the arm, gave Schaub a final nod, and went out.

BKA Special Agent *Leutnant* Alois Hegel had set up his operational base post in the Neubrandenburg Protestant Church steeple looking down the hill at the lake. From his vantage point he had a direct line of sight not only to the war memorial, but to Otto Schaub's chalet. Using state of the art Krupp Atlas charge-coupled image devices and sound intensifiers they had been able to all but look over the shoulders of Helmut Speyer and his henchmen.

They were connected via a real-time data link with BKA Special Operations in Berlin, and Hegel was waiting for the green light to make his arrests. He was young and this was his first taste of the real action he had been trained for.

His people were in place on every highway and dirt track within five kilometers of the chalet, and the perps were simply not going to get more than one kilometer away before they were taken down.

The phone chirped. "Alpha one, base."

Hegel answered it. "Alpha one."

"Well done, *Leutnant*," Chief Inspector Schey said. "Your unit may stand down now until Black Bishop has cleared the area."

Hegel couldn't believe it. "Sir, they're on the road now. I was going to order Red Range One."

"*Nein*. We know where they are going, and we'll take it from here. As soon as they're gone I want the crime scenes secured. Am I clear, *Leutnant*?"

"Yes, sir," Hegel said. He was seething inside. But he was a German and he knew how to obey orders.

Lieutenant Hegel stood just inside the chalet's kitchen. It was a few minutes before noon, and Speyer and the others would be up in Hamburg by now, leaving this one last surprise behind. The special BKA evidence team that had been standing by from the start of the operation had divided into two sections;

one for here and the other for the memorial. Both teams had their hands full.

"Alpha one, this is Alpha two." The comms unit in his left ear came to life.

"Go ahead, two."

"We have two bodies in the shaft. Golanov and Cherny. Do you have Schaub in custody?"

"*Nein*," Hegel replied. One body lay in a pool of blood on the kitchen floor, the other in the chalet's great room. "He and the Russian are dead. Both of them shot in the head."

"Doesn't pay to be friends with that bastard, does it. What the hell are they playing at?"

"I don't know," Hegel said. "But I sure as hell would like to find out."

HAMBURG

From the loading dock the M/V *Maria* looked deserted. There was no movement on her decks, and all of her hatches were closed. But when Lane and the others reached the top of the gangway, Captain Zimmer appeared from a doorway.

"You got it then?" he asked.

Lane stepped aside for Baumann, who was straining to carry the container. "Someplace secure, I should think, before poor Sergeant Baumann gets a hernia."

"Right, come with me." Captain Zimmer went back into the passageway and took a stairway down ten decks to what Lane figured had to be the bottom of the ship, or very close to it.

Baumann propped the box against a bulkhead as Zimmer undogged a waterproof door. "It'll be safe in here," he said. He reached inside and switched on a light.

The *Maria* was double-hulled, and this was the space between the outer hull and that of the aft cargo hold. A catwalk curved back to the stern of the ship. It smelled very badly of diesel oil, garbage, and perhaps rotting sewage.

"No one lingers very long back here," Zimmer said.

Gloria waited at the foot of the stairs while Zimmer led them the rest of the way aft to a special compartment he had built beneath the catwalk in the farthest aft and starboard corner of the ship.

It took just a minute to lower the box into the hole, and when the section of catwalk was lowered into place there was no way of telling except under a very close examination that anything could be beneath them except the stinking bilge.

"Now let's have some lunch and something to drink," Zimmer said, clapping his hands. "I think a celebration is in order before we have to hide the four of you."

"How soon can we set sail?" Speyer asked.

"We'll be gone by dinnertime."

"Good," Speyer said. "After lunch Ernst can return the car to Hertz and we can settle in. I for one am ready for a relaxing ocean cruise. A couple of uneventful weeks."

"And then what?" Lane asked.

"Then you'll be a rich man." Speyer grinned. "We'll all be very rich."

6

M/V *MARIA*

Their most pressing concern on the trip across the Atlantic was making mealtimes which, for Captain Zimmer, his officers, and guests, were served in the expansive, tastefully furnished officers' mess one deck below the bridge. The crew was international, but Zimmer insisted on German efficiency in everything. He had become somewhat nervous and not quite himself, however, as they approached their destination.

He came in a couple of minutes after noon and the stewards began serving the first soup course. "I thought you should all know that we'll be in Havana tomorrow about this time."

"Well, that's a bit of good news," Speyer said. "And nobody is breathing down our necks hunting for us."

"I wouldn't be so sure of that, Helmut."

Speyer smiled patiently. It had been a nearly constant theme of the captain's over the past few days, ever since they had passed south of Bermuda. "Unless you're carrying something you shouldn't be, which you assure me that you are not, there was no reason for the customs authorities in Hamburg to give your papers more than a casual once-over."

"It was too easy."

"If the BKA was on to us because of Neubrandenburg it would not make sense for them to let us simply sail away, would it?"

Zimmer spread his hands in frustration. "That might depend upon what you brought aboard in that precious metal box of yours."

"It's nothing that they would bother themselves with."

"They might be waiting to find out where you're taking it," Zimmer said. He was becoming agitated.

"They can't touch us once we reach Cuba. So what's your point?" Speyer turned to Lane. "What's he trying to tell me, John?"

Lane looked up from his excellent vichyssoise. He had an idea what Zimmer was getting at, but he feigned indifference. "The good captain might be worried that once someone notices that we're not heading for Miami as it states in our papers, but instead trying to make a run for Cuba, the U.S. Coast Guard might want to ask us a few questions."

"Something like that," Zimmer said.

"This is not a U.S.-registered ship, we're in international waters, and we're doing nothing illegal under U.S. law, so where's the problem?" Speyer asked.

"The problem is whatever's in that box."

Speyer put down his soup spoon. "We have come a long way together, Horst, as business associates and friends. Nothing is any different this time to change that. Believe me. There'll be other assignments for you. Lucrative assignments."

The captain poured some wine. "That's just it, Helmut. This trip *is* different."

"I fail to see how—"

"Having you aboard, for starts. You're a wanted man in Germany." Zimmer's gaze slid to Lane. "And this one. I don't know anything about him. I don't think you do either." He glanced at Gloria, who was seated between him and her husband, but he said nothing. For some reason she'd cleaned up her act on the voyage, cutting out almost all alcohol and cigarettes, eating tiny portions at meals, and spending almost all of her waking hours in the exercise spa that Captain Zimmer had set up across from the ship's chart room. The physical changes were dramatic, though she maintained a distant, disdainful attitude toward everyone, especially her husband.

She gave the captain a supremely indifferent glance, and held out her wine glass. "Since we're so close, why not celebrate a little?"

Zimmer poured her wine. He smiled at her, his intentions completely obvious.

"Do you know what I hate worst?" she asked.

"No, what?" Zimmer said. He was captivated by her performance.

"Cowards." She arched her left eyebrow. "Are you a coward after all, Captain Zimmer?"

Zimmer reared back as if he had been slapped. "Bitch."

"Yes, I am. But we were discussing your qualities just then, not mine." She tried her wine, but made a face, put it down and got to her feet. "Just get us to Havana and leave the thinking to my husband. You'll get your money and you can sail off to wherever it is people like you sail off to, until we need you again."

Zimmer started to rise, but the look on Speyer's face stopped him cold.

"It's good advice," Lane said. He wiped his lips and put his napkin down. "I'm getting paid off in Havana, and then getting out. I've had my fill of excitement for the time being. I suggest that you do the same."

"It's easy for you to say. Nothing's holding you back. But I have a ship to run."

"Change careers or get on with it," Lane advised. "But don't get greedy. You might lose everything."

"Don't threaten me on my own ship, you son of a bitch."

Lane shook his head. "You guys are all alike. Nothing ever changes." Gloria had already left. He looked at the others around the table, including the Greek first officer Spiro Metaxas, and shook his head again. "Do you see what you've done?" he asked. "You've ruined my appetite." He got up and left.

"Everything's going to be fine, Horst, I promise you," Speyer said. He got up, too, and followed Lane out.

Gloria had gone directly up to the exercise room. Lane went up after her and lounged against the door frame. She took off the light cotton print dress she'd worn at the lunch table. She was wearing spandex exercise shorts and a sports bra underneath. She sat down and exchanged her sandals for low white socks and jogging shoes then started on the exercise bike.

"You pushed the good captain pretty hard down there. Why?" Lane asked. In less than two weeks she'd gotten her muscle tone back, and she was looking very good.

"The man's a pig."

"He's a friend of your husband's."

She laughed as she looked at his reflection in the floor-length mirrors on the wall in front of her. "How very perceptive of you."

"He also has a crew of sixteen men and officers, but there's only four of us. Maybe you should think about cutting him a little slack. At least until we're ashore in Havana."

"He wouldn't dare try anything."

"Are you sure about that?"

"Very sure," she said, without breaking stride. "We

have a lot of friends in the most interesting places, and he knows it."

"There's no reason to provoke him," Lane cautioned. She had changed not only physically in the past ten days, but her entire spirit had changed as well. In the States and again in Germany she had been a lush, soft and unfocused around the edges. Now she was as hard as nails. It was almost as if she was playing a part, he caught himself thinking.

"John is right," Speyer said from the corridor. Lane moved aside for him. "There're less than twenty-four hours to go, why don't you leave the poor man alone."

"Because it amuses me thinking about what he would like to do."

"Maybe I'll let him do whatever he wants. Perhaps that will amuse me."

Gloria laughed again. "You may be capable of many things, Helmut, but that is not one of them." She glanced at Lane. "My husband is very protective of his possessions."

Lane took Speyer back out into the corridor. There were no crewmen up here at the moment. "Where's Ernst?"

"Downstairs finishing his lunch. What is it?"

"I think that until we reach Havana one of us should stick close to your wife at all times."

Speyer gave Gloria a glance. "Do you think he'll try something?"

"He's your friend. You tell me. But I wouldn't take odds on him keeping his hands off her. Or at least trying to make a move."

Speyer thought about it for a moment. "There's no use in asking for trouble this close."

"That's what I was thinking. But once we get to Havana, then what?"

"That's up to you. But you've been telling everybody that you want to get paid and then you're leaving."

"Yes, but that's going to take time. Selling the diamonds, I mean."

Speyer shook his head. "That part's already been arranged. We can pay your share into any bank account that you want, worldwide. Twenty-four hours tops."

"Won't you have to get the money from the German government first?"

"Like I said, all that's been taken care of. I hand over the diamonds to the Cubans and we get paid."

"Three hundred million?"

"At least," Speyer assured him, grinning. "You're going to be a rich man."

"How about you?" Lane asked. "Have you already got a place set up in Havana?"

"Outside the city, actually."

"What about your Montana operation?"

Speyer gave Lane a hard look, his eyes narrowed. "I don't care for these questions."

Lane shrugged. "Maybe I'll get bored and want another assignment. I'd have to know where to find you."

"You found me the first time. I don't doubt that you could find me again if you used your imagination," Speyer said. "But I don't think it'd be wise of you to return to Kalispell. Not unless you change your appearance."

"If you're not going to be there, why bother."

"Well, I'm not going to be there, but the people who will be wouldn't take kindly to someone like you barging in unannounced."

Lane looked in at Gloria, who was in her own world, a blank expression on her face in the mirror.

"She had trouble in Montana. I'd be surprised if she lasted a year in Havana."

"A lot of money can perform wonders."

Lane turned back to him. "I meant socially."

"So did I."

Baumann came around the corner. He looked surprised when he saw Speyer and Lane together.

"What'd the good captain say after we left?" Lane asked him.

Baumann exchanged a quick look with his boss, then shook his head. "Nothing much. He's pissed off, but he won't give us any trouble."

"John thinks that you're wrong," Speyer said. "He thinks that we should take turns keeping an eye on my wife."

Again they exchanged a look. "If you think that it's necessary, Herr *Kapitän*."

"It can't hurt. Maybe Horst has finally gone off the deep end."

Baumann laughed nervously. "I see what you mean," he said. "He would like to see you on the bridge sometime this afternoon."

"Did he say why?"

"Something about clearances to enter Cuban waters."

"I'll go talk to him now. In the meantime you can stay with my wife until Horst and I are finished discussing our business."

"If anyone cares I'm going back to my stateroom to pack," Lane told them. "Then maybe I'll go for a turn on the deck. I could use the fresh air. If you want some help baby-sitting just ask."

The screws holding the small ventilator grille were exactly as Lane had positioned them. No one had found his hiding spot. He reached inside and pulled down the compact Russian-made PSM semi-automatic pistol. It was only a 5.45mm, and he had no spare ammunition, but it was better than nothing. On the way out Speyer had made him turn over the Beretta, but he'd kept the PSM which he'd picked up as insurance on their last morning at the chalet. Now he was glad that he had, because something was rotten in Denmark, as his father used to say. Whatever deal Speyer had with the Cubans did not involve three hundred million dollars U.S. There wasn't that much hard currency available on the entire island. He stuffed the gun in his pocket, replaced the grille, then went out on the deck into the warm, sultry afternoon to wait.

Speyer left Gloria and Sergeant Baumann together in the spa and went directly to the bridge. The second officer and a helmsman were the only crew on duty. They ignored him. The afternoon was hazy, the horizon indistinct, and there were very little wind or waves, which was to his liking. It was ten minutes before Zimmer showed up, and he looked angry. "We have to talk."

"You're damned right we do," Speyer agreed. "Let's go to your cabin."

They went across to the captain's neat, very well furnished quarters, where Zimmer poured them each a schnapps. "Your boy is starting to get suspicious. Why the hell haven't you killed him? What are you waiting for?"

"In the first place, your crew would ask questions if something happened to him."

"You let me worry about my crew. I've got just as much at stake in this project as you do. In the meantime he could cause us no end of trouble."

"We have the only guns on the ship."

"That's right, so let's use them." Zimmer checked his watch. "In a little more than twelve hours this ship will be on the bottom in five hundred fathoms of water. There'll be no survivors. No mayday will be sent. No one will suspect a thing until we're reported overdue in Miami. By then we'll be long gone. I don't want anything screwing up my share of this operation."

"Mr. Browne is going down with the ship."

"I don't have any argument with that, Helmut."

"When the ship sinks he's going to be very much alive. Locked in his cabin. Knowing that there's not a thing he can do to prevent his own death, with plenty of time to think about how he got himself into such a deadly predicament."

Zimmer gave him an evil grin. "You're a sadistic bastard, I'll give you that much. What'd he do to you?"

"He interfered in places he should not have interfered."

"What the hell does that mean?"

"He went to bed with my wife."

Zimmer started to say something, but then thought better of it, and just shook his head.

"Are we on schedule for our rendezvous?"

"We'll be there at two this morning, which means we have our work cut out for us starting at one."

"We'll meet back here then," Speyer said. He tossed off his schnapps and left.

The first officer, Spiro Metaxas, listening on the ship's phone which Zimmer had left on, came in. He looked nervous. "Crossing that bastard is a risky business," he said. He was short, gnarled and misshapen like an olive tree, and just as dark and tough.

"You worry too much. That's my concern," Zimmer told him. "We're going to come out of this in good shape. Once we get the diamonds up to Washington and the organization pays us off we'll be on easy street."

Metaxas, who was a hard-headed Greek and had seen just about everything, wasn't convinced. "Killing the crew isn't going to be so simple either."

"One of the main charges will go off right below the crew's mess deck. All you have to do is get them there, just like we planned. Make some excuse to get the hell out, and . . . boom."

"Then what?" Metaxas asked sourly. "After Washington, I mean."

"Then I never want to see your ugly face again." Zimmer laughed. He poured a schnapps for his first mate and another for himself. "Relax, Spiro. When this is over you'll be a millionaire. You can go anywhere and do anything that you want. You'll be a free man. You can buy your Greek island and be king."

They had their dinner at 8:00 P.M., the tension in the dining room so thick that it could be cut with a knife. Afterward Lane went back out onto the quarterdeck to be alone and to smoke a cigarette. He was getting the feeling that they were never going to make it to Havana. It was the way Zimmer and Speyer kept exchanging glances, making offhand comments like schoolyard bullies trying to keep a secret about who they were going to pound next. Something was going to happen in the middle of the night, maybe a mutiny or something.

Once the ship had settled down for the evening, he was going up to the radio room to find a ship-to-shore phone. Florida was just over the horizon to the northwest, and sometime between now and the dawn he figured he was going to be needing help a lot more than he needed answers.

"What are your plans once you're no longer impecunious?" Gloria asked, coming up behind him.

She wore another sundress, her shoulders bare, the neckline very low. The lights from the ship's superstructure and from the stars were perfect for her. She looked fifteen years younger than she was.

"I thought that I would throw a big party. Copacabana, maybe."

"Sounds wonderful," she said, smiling wistfully. "I'm getting tired of Montana."

"You'll have Havana, if that's any consolation."

She pursed her lips seductively and inclined her head. "I lied to the captain when I told him that the thing I hated most was a coward. What really gets to me is boredom."

"Then change your life."

"I'm trying to, John, but it's never that easy."

"I'm sure that your husband's lifestyle provides plenty of excitement. Germany and now this, wherever it's leading you."

The captain came out on deck and didn't see them standing at the stern rail. He got what looked like a grappling hook and a coil of line from a locker, and when he straightened up he spotted them.

"Good evening," Lane said.

"Excuse me," Zimmer replied. He nodded and ducked back inside.

"Strange—" Gloria said.

"Gotta run," Lane told her. "Ta-ta." He followed the captain inside in time to see the hatch leading down to the catwalk between the double hull close.

Captain Zimmer stopped in the darkness to listen. He'd thought that he'd heard the hatch above closing and then footfalls on the stairs, but all was quiet now except for the ship's noises, and he wasn't sure what he'd heard. It was rotten luck that Browne had spotted him, but the bitch would keep him occupied. And none of them would matter when the rest of his plan was put in place.

He hurried the rest of the way down into the bowels of the ship, opened the bottom hatch, and ducked inside the passageway between the hulls. The stench was nearly overpowering; he kept reminding himself of the millions he was going to make.

He pulled up the grate at the turn of the hulls and then dropped the grappling hook into the stinking bilge, paying out the line with his fingertips.

He snagged one of the handles on the third try and, putting his back into it, pulled the box up out of the bilge. It was a damned heavy thing. He had to wrestle with it to get it up on the catwalk and remove the grappling hook.

He hunched down on his knee and rubbed some of the slime away from the lid. There was no lock or hinges. A bead of solder ran around the top edge, completely sealing whatever was inside from the air. Funny, he thought. Diamonds were supposed to be indestructible. But then the old Nazis had done some crazy shit, especially near the end of the war.

He dug in his pocket and pulled out a folding knife; he was about to start on the solder seal when he heard a movement behind him. He looked up, startled, as Browne came into view.

"What the hell," Zimmer cried out. He reached for his pistol, but Browne held a small pistol pointed right at the captain's head.

"You'll be dead before you get it out of your jacket," Browne warned, his voice perfectly calm, as if he were discussing the weather.

"Okay, you win, Mr. Smart Guy," Zimmer said, spreading his hands.

Browne motioned with the pistol. "Drop the knife into the bilge, like a good man."

Zimmer did as he was told. "Now what?"

"Now the gun. Take it out of your belt, very carefully, and slide it over to me."

"This isn't a very big ship and you're outnumbered. Sooner or later we'll get the drop on you. So maybe we can make a deal."

"The gun first," Browne said reasonably.

Zimmer considered his options, which for the moment amounted to zero. He did as he was told, easing the big Glock 17 out of his belt, laying it on the grating, and shoving it toward Browne. He watched as Browne scooped up the gun, checked the safety, and stuffed it in his belt. He was a careful man. "Same question as before. Now what?"

"Does Helmut know that you're down here?"

Zimmer shrugged. "I didn't stop to discuss it with him."

"Maybe you should have. According to him, opening the box will destroy a substantial portion of the value."

"What does it matter? The box is heavy, so there're a lot of diamonds inside. Even at a discount they have to be worth millions."

"Helmut promised me ten percent. What's your offer?"

"Exactly zero," someone said behind him. Lane recognized the first officer's voice by the rough accent.

"Shoot me and your captain dies," Lane warned.

"Maybe," Metaxas replied from the darkness. "But you'll die, too, with a bullet in the back of your head. Put the gun down."

Lane tried to judge the distance. Zimmer looked up at him with a big grin on his face. Lane finally nodded. "As you wish," he said. He bent over and placed the PSM on the floor grating.

"Hold up, Spiro, he has another gun in his belt," Zimmer cautioned.

"Look, I don't care who wins. I just want my money," Lane said.

"Yeah, right," Zimmer smirked. He stepped forward as Lane spread out his hands. "Don't try anything. Spiro is a very good shot."

Zimmer reached for the Glock, which was a mistake. Lane grabbed him and spun him around to act as a shield as he pulled out the big gun and thumbed off the safety.

Metaxas fired two shots, both of them wide for fear of hitting his captain. The bullets fragmented on the steel plates, the jagged pieces of shrapnel ricocheting down the passageway. He disappeared into the darkness.

Lane fired one shot, then held up and listened.

Zimmer shoved an elbow into Lane's ribs, and managed to break free at the same moment Metaxas fired two more shots, one of them buzzing past Lane's head, the other hitting Zimmer in the neck, knocking him backward in a spray of blood.

Lane grabbed a handle of the box, hefted it and stumbled as fast as he could into the darkness around the turn of the hull directly at the stern, firing three shots as fast as he could pull them off behind him.

Metaxas hunched in the semi-darkness at the foot of the stairs, holding his side. In the dim light from the open hatch above he could see that he was bleeding, but it wasn't too bad. He'd been hurt a lot worse in barroom brawls.

Captain Zimmer had gone down. He'd seen that much before Browne started shooting back. So now the *Maria*, the plan, and the diamonds were his.

"Listen up, Browne, can you hear me back there?" he shouted.

"I can hear you," Lane called back. "Your captain's dead."

"I know. So now I am the senior officer, and I'm willing to make a deal with you."

"Why the hell should I listen to you? As soon as you got the chance you'd kill me."

"No, I wouldn't, because I need your help now just as much as you need mine," Metaxas shouted. He moved along the passageway, his right hand trailing on the inner hull.

"What are you talking about?"

"I heard them talking up in the captain's cabin. That's why I followed him down here. I knew that he was coming for the diamonds. We're meeting up with a yacht tonight. They were going to kill the entire crew, me and you included, and then sink the ship."

"Then what was Zimmer doing down here by himself? And why was the box moved? This wasn't the same place we put it when we boarded in Hamburg."

"I only heard part of their conversation. I don't know the whole story. I swear it on my mother's grave, on the heart of Jesus." He edged farther along the passageway to where Zimmer's body lay in a heap next to the open grating. The box was gone. His stomach rebounded sourly and a black rage came over him for just a moment until he got hold of himself.

"If you want to make a deal, toss your gun down and come back here where I can see you," Lane instructed.

"How do I know you won't kill me and keep the diamonds for yourself?"

"Like you said, we need each other."

Something cold and hard touched Metaxas on the back of his neck and he stiffened. "Move and you're dead," Speyer warned softly.

"I'm waiting," Lane called.

"Just a minute, John, I'm getting the situation under control here," Speyer shouted. He relieved Metaxas of his gun.

"Did you hear his story, Helmut?" Lane asked.

"That's just what it was, a story. They'd hatched their own plan to kill us all and take the diamonds for themselves. Speaking of which, where are they?"

"I shoved them back into the bilge. I figured they'd be safer there. He moved them."

"I see that he did," Speyer said. "Okay, I have the bastard's gun. You can come out now."

"What if he was telling the truth?"

Speyer motioned for Baumann to go across to the stairway on the port side of the ship in case Browne should try to get out. Baumann immediately understood what was required and he hurried away noiselessly into the darkness.

"We've come this far together without mishap. Like you said, I'm not a man who throws away a valuable asset."

They heard a bump and then a splash as if a section of grating had been opened and something had been thrown into the bilge.

"Come on now, John, time is running out," Speyer called.

Lane sprinted back to the starboard stairs and took them two at a time to the main deck, taking care to make as little noise as possible. The thwartship corridor was empty when he peered out. He dashed across to the forward stairs and slipped inside, leaving the door behind him open a crack so that he could watch what happened.

Seconds later Baumann emerged from the port stairwell, a Glock 17 in his fist. He rushed down the corridor and cautiously opened the starboard stairwell hatch. He listened for a few seconds, then disappeared inside.

It would take them only a minute or so to discover that Lane had gotten past them and come looking. In the meantime he had to get a message off to the U.S. Coast Guard in Miami, and then warn the crew that they were all about to be killed. But he still had no idea what Speyer's real plan had been all along. He was sure that it had absolutely nothing to do with the Cuban government redeeming a bunch of Nazi diamonds. But he didn't know what else it was. It depended on what was really sealed inside the box.

He stuffed the Glock into his belt as he hurried upstairs. He didn't want to confront the crew until he'd sent off his radio message. If he ran into one of them while toting a pistol, questions would be asked that might slow him down. He was pretty sure that the crewmen were innocent, and he wanted to keep the casualties to a minimum.

He had to cross a thwartship corridor at each level, but he didn't see anyone. It was as if the *Maria* was a ghost ship.

When he reached the bridge deck he stopped for a few seconds to catch his breath. The bridge was forward, down a short corridor. To the starboard were the chart room, exercise room, and the radar power supplies and control units. To the port was the radio room. The cabins for the officers and guests were along the thwartship corridor here and one deck down, where the officers' mess and galley were located.

From his vantage point amidships he could see straight down the short corridor onto the bridge and, through the windows, the star-studded sky. But he couldn't see anyone.

Keeping an eye on the bridge, Lane went to the radio room door, listened for a moment, knocked once and let himself in. The room was in total darkness.

Finding the switch, Lane closed and locked the door and flipped on the lights. All of the radio equipment was dead. The switches were all in the ON position, but the dials and indicators were dark. The big circuit breaker panel on the rear bulkhead seemed to be intact, but there was no power to it either. The circuit had probably been cut below in the ship's electrical generating plant adjacent to the engines.

But they were still sailing, which meant there still had to be power to the bridge.

Speyer lowered his gun when it was finally clear that Browne had slipped past them. "It's up to you, Spiro. Either you're with us or you're not."

"It was that bastard Zimmer—"

"I don't care whose fault it was. What's it going to be? We still need your help."

Metaxas was a practical Greek. He glanced at Baumann, then back to Speyer. The wound in his side ached, but it had stopped bleeding. It was just a scratch. "What do you want me to do?"

"Good man," Speyer said, and he handed the first mate's gun back to him. "I'm going to retrieve the diamonds. You and Ernst are going to find Browne. I don't want him killed unless it's absolutely necessary." Speyer gave Baumann a hard look. "You understand, don't you, Ernst?"

Baumann nodded.

"He's probably on the bridge deck trying to radio for help."

"Power's been cut to the radio room, and all the antenna leads have been cut," Metaxas said.

"But the bridge still has power," Speyer said. "As soon as you've taken care of Browne we're going to blow the ship and take the captain's launch out to the rendezvous point. We'll sink it, too, so there won't be any evidence."

"Digging out Browne might not be so easy as all that," Baumann warned.

"There are two of you," Speyer shot back. "And as soon as I'm done down here I'll come up to help out if need be. Just watch yourself. We're almost home free."

The bridge was deserted, but there was power to all the controls and panels, and both radar sets were up and operating. They were just outside the Gulf Stream off the Florida Keys where shipping was fairly heavy. Although he couldn't spot any running lights out the windows, the were several targets on the radar screens.

Lane closed and dogged the hatch, then quickly studied the controls. The *Maria* was on autopilot, steering a course a little south of west, and making fifteen knots. The primary GPS showed the ship's latitude and longitude.

Lane cranked the autopilot to a new course well north of west, which headed them directly across the shipping lanes toward the coast of Florida fifty or sixty miles away. If Speyer cut the engines now, or sank the ship, the course wouldn't matter. But in the meantime they were headed in the right direction.

Power was still connected to the two VHF radios on the overhead. They were low wattage with a range of twenty-five miles or less, but there were ships that close.

Lane keyed one of the mikes. "Mayday, mayday, mayday, this is the motor vessel *Maria* calling the U.S. Coast Guard Station Miami or any ship within hailing distance, we are sinking. Our position is twenty-four degrees fifty minutes north, eighty-one degrees twenty minutes west, heading northwest across the Stream. We have been hijacked by an unknown number of heavily armed men. Mayday, mayday, this is the motor vessel *Maria*."

Baumann and Metaxas, their guns drawn, had positioned themselves on either side of the bridge door. They could make out Browne's voice, though not the words.

"He's calling for help," Metaxas whispered.

"I thought you said that the antenna leads were cut?"

"They are. Nobody's going to hear him. But he's changed course. Northwest, it feels like. Toward Miami. Puts us across the shipping lanes. Means it's not going to be such a good idea sinking this ship with witnesses."

Baumann thought it out. He didn't want to get caught and thrown in jail, not now that they were so close. He was too old to go to prison. "Is there another way out of there?"

"Captain Zimmer had me fix the port and starboard wing hatches so they couldn't be opened from the inside in case we had trouble up here with the crew. This is his only way out."

"Where the hell is the crew? I haven't seen anyone since dinner."

"Sealed in the crew's mess. Four steel doors, all welded shut."

"Jesus." Baumann had always thought that he was tough, but this was way over the top.

"Don't give me that look," Metaxas said defensively. "It was your captain and minc who cooked up that scheme, not me. Besides, they won't drown. When the plastic explosives go up they'll all be killed instantly." Metaxas grinned. "It's more humane that way."

"Captain Speyer is probably launching the gig. Get down there and tell him what's going on. I'll hold Browne here until you get back."

Speyer and his wife were on the port quarterdeck swinging the captain's gig over the side on her electric davits when Metaxas showed up. "Where's Ernst?"

"He's got Browne cornered on the bridge." Metaxas explained the situation. Gloria looked at him as if he were something she'd found under a rock. He wanted five minutes with her, just five, and her attitude would definitely change for the better.

"Get back up there with a welding torch and seal the door. As soon as you're done we'll blow the ship and then get the hell out."

"Don't be late," Gloria said, smiling. She was enjoying herself. "We wouldn't want to leave without you."

Metaxas shot her a dirty look, then hurried back up to the bridge deck. He pulled a small acetylene torch from the emergency stores locker and wheeled it back to where Baumann was stationed by the steel hatch to the bridge.

"He's still on the radio," Baumann said, eyeing the torch. "Hurry." This was a bad business. He had developed a lot of respect for the South African. But orders were orders.

Metaxas cracked the gas lines, held the torch away from his body, and lit it with a scratcher. When he had the mix right he pulled on a pair of dark goggles. Holding a welding rod at the seam just above the door lock, he drew a couple of quick beads to hold the door from being forced open. Then he started the full weld from the top.

Baumann called from the other side of the door when the welding was done. "Sorry about this, John."

"Yeah, I know. It's nothing personal, just orders, right?" Lane said. He had checked both wing doors. They were sealed, too.

"Something like that. You would be in the way. You couldn't be a part of our plans. Not this."

"What about the crew?" The only way out of here was through the windows. But they were probably polycarbonate plastic, almost impossible to break. They were designed to take waves breaking over the decks.

"They're going down with the ship, too," Baumann said. "But they'll be dead first."

"I'm sure that's a comfort for them," Lane said. When Baumann didn't reply, Lane went back to the door. "Wait a minute, Ernst," he shouted. "Did you find the diamonds? Can you tell me that much?"

"We found them. Helmut fished them out of the bilge."

"I've radioed for help," Lane called, but there was no answer. "Ernst!" He put his ear to the door but there were no sounds except for the distant vibration of the engines.

He wanted to believe that there was no reason for the bastards to kill the crew. But if he was a man in Speyer's position he knew that he would have to do the same thing.

Saving them was going to be impossible, but he would be damned if he was going down with the *Maria*. Speyer and company had not seen the last of him. Not yet.

Gloria was safely aboard the launch, Baumann at the wheel, when Metaxas emerged from the port quarter hatch, an evil grin on his face. "Three minutes," he said.

Speyer, waiting by the rail, raised his pistol and shot the first officer in the face, knocking him off his feet.

He cocked an ear to listen, but he couldn't hear a thing except for the ship's engines. He'd actually done it; against all odds, and despite Thomas Mann's warnings, he'd pulled it off.

Stuffing the pistol in his belt, Speyer dragged the first officer's body back inside the superstructure, then closed and dogged the hatch. It wouldn't do to have the odd body floating around out here. There would be debris, and an oil slick, of course. But by the time the authorities came out here to investigate, the Gulf Stream would have carried the evidence far to the north. Still, there was no need to take chances.

He hurried down the boarding ladder to the launch which was bobbing wildly on the waves streaming past the *Maria*'s hull and jumped aboard. He released the line and motioned for Baumann to head off.

"Where's the Greek?" Gloria asked her husband.

"Unfortunately he won't be joining us. He had a little accident." Speyer caressed her cheek. "You did a good job for us, sweetheart."

"Some of it wasn't acting, you know," she replied. He grinned and looked back toward the *Maria*, missing the angry expression on her face.

They were a long ways off when Speyer checked

his watch. He looked up as the dark outline of the ship seemed to shiver and a low-throated thump like very distant thunder came to them.

"Did something go wrong?" Gloria demanded.

"Look," Speyer said. Already the *Maria* was sharply down on her lines, down at the bow where some of the explosives had blown a huge hole just beneath the water line. The engines were still driving the ship forward, and they would help propel her underwater very quickly now.

Speyer clapped his hands in delight, missing another odd look from his wife and one from Baumann. But even if he had seen them he wouldn't have cared. He was going to be the king.

Lane had discharged the second fire extinguisher against the port wing window when the explosions seemed to lift the big ship five feet straight up into the air, knocking him sideways. He regained his balance, turned the fire extinguisher around, and slammed it against the window. A spiderweb of cracks appeared. The tough polycarbonate plastic had been weakened by the extreme cold of the carbon dioxide. He smashed the base of the fire extinguisher into the window again, completely shattering it like an automobile window in an accident.

The ship was already well down by the bow, water already up to the level of the first containers lashed on deck, when Lane grabbed the half-dozen life jackets he'd strung together and tossed them out the window.

There was no chance that the crew could be saved now. There'd been explosions all through the ship. No doubt they'd been herded somewhere central, maybe the crew's mess, where they'd been locked in. They were all dead, or soon would be, and there wasn't a thing that he could do about it. For that, if for nothing else, Lane swore that he would personally deal with Helmut Speyer and company at the first possible opportunity.

He stuffed the Very signal pistol into his belt and loaded a half-dozen of the big starburst shells into his pocket, then climbed out the window.

Water covered the entire deck forward of the superstructure and all but the top row of containers. There were no other ships in sight, nor could he see the captain's gig, which had to be out there somewhere. But they were probably running without lights, and despite the bright starlight the horizon was impossible to define; there was nothing but an indistinct blackness where it should be.

The stern of the ship had lifted about twenty degrees when there was a tremendous crash below. Some heavy machinery was breaking loose and the ship started listing to the left.

Lane snatched the bundle of life jackets, scrambled down the stairs to where the water had risen to within two levels of the bridge, kicked off his soft leather Gucci half-boots and jumped in.

The ocean was surprisingly warm, but he was swimming through a thick oil slick, the smell of diesel fuel so strong he could taste it and feel it in his mouth. It made him sick to his stomach, and burned his lungs.

By the time he got fifty yards out of the slick only the antennae and radar masts at the very top of the superstructure stuck up above the water. Seconds later they were gone.

Through the night Lane watched a steady stream of ships passing on the horizon to the west. Some of them headed north, while others were southbound, but all of them moved shockingly fast. Their lights came into sight in the very far distance and within minutes disappeared in the opposite direction.

He'd used five of the six starburst shells within the first couple of hours, then laid back to rest until morning. He would save his last shell until a ship came close enough that he could shoot the damned thing directly at the bridge.

Just before dawn a thick cloud raced toward him, blotting out the stars to the east and engulfing him in a downpour so heavy he had trouble breathing. It only lasted a couple of minutes. Afterwards he was struck first with severe leg cramps, and then chills that made him so weak he could do nothing to help himself.

For a time he thought about sharks—these waters were notorious for them—but then he concentrated on Tommy Hughes and Frannie back in Washington. When the *Maria* was reported overdue in Miami sometime today they would start the wheels in motion to find him.

With that comforting thought he laid his head back, his weight well supported by the half-dozen life jackets, and managed to nod off.

It was seven o'clock in the early evening after a very long, hot day, when the Coast Guard helicopter came out of the sun from the west. Lane heard the heavy drumbeats of the big rotors before he could pick out the machine, but by the time he could fumble the Very pistol out of his belt the chopper was directly overhead. The heavy downdraft flattened the seas in a big circle.

He looked up in time to see a Coast Guard crewman in a crash helmet and another man, bareheaded, looking down at him. He let the Very pistol slip out of his grasp and waved.

"You silly boy," Tommy Hughes's amplified voice boomed. "Don't you know that you shouldn't go for a swim without a proper bathing costume?"

PART TWO

Three Days Later

7

MONTANA

Konrad Aden parked his metallic green Mercedes 500SEL in a gravel lot above the Flathead River west of Hungry Horse and walked down to the water, where Kalispell Chief of Police Carl Mattoon was having a smoke. He was puzzled by the urgency of Mattoon's phone call last night, all the more so because of the confusing events of the past couple of weeks. Nothing added up, and Aden intensely hated disorder.

At forty-seven Aden was a highly respected attorney and real estate developer in Helena. His rugged good looks combined with his outdoorsman's physique and perfect English to make everyone believe that he was a native Montanan, a belief he never disputed. Actually he'd been born in Leipzig in what was then East Germany. He'd distinguished himself in Gymnasium there and then college in Berlin, getting his law degree when he was only twenty-three. He came to the attention of the Russians because his father had been chief of Leipzig Stasi operations, and because he was bright. They brought him to Moscow, where he studied international law and relations at Patrice Lamumba University. Upon graduation he spent one year at the KGB's School One outside of Moscow where he was taught tradecraft: everything from secret writing and codes to hand-to-hand combat and the skills with which to kill a man in several dozen different ways. Later he worked undercover out of the United Nations in New York and Geneva and finally as a special political officer for the Stasi in Berlin until the Wall came down and he was able to escape to the U.S.

He'd been one of the founding fathers of the Friends, and had stationed himself in Montana because no one else wanted the assignment, and because he wanted the uncomplicated wide-open spaces for a change of pace. His wife loved it here, as did their three children who'd all been born over in Billings.

Carl Mattoon was from Knoxville, Tennessee. He had come to Montana six years ago to escape a dead-end career with the Knoxville PD and two ex-wives, both of them cops. He'd been hired as a Yellowstone County deputy sheriff in Billings, which brought him to Aden's attention; Aden made it his business to know something about all the cops. Almost immediately Aden spotted the man's three major weaknesses: women, gambling, and money. From that point it took less than three months to buy the man, lock, stock, and barrel. Two years later Mattoon, under Aden's guidance, was assistant chief of police in Kalispell. A year and a half after that, he became chief when the old chief of police was killed in a tragic car accident on a mountain road.

Aden had gone through all this trouble because Helmut Speyer had taken up residence outside Kalispell, and Friends protected friends.

"Good morning, Carl. You called and here I am. I hope it's important enough to have dragged me all the way up here this morning."

Mattoon turned around, obviously troubled. "I think we got ourselves a problem, son," Mattoon said. "Fact of the matter is I don't know what the hell is goin' on."

"Is the FBI bothering you again?" Aden asked. "If

they are, just tell them what we agreed on."

"It's not them yet, but it's sure gonna be, because now I have to call them back up here. They know Helmut's real name and they want to talk to him about that cocked-up shooting."

"They have to find him first. But if they had any proof there'd be a federal warrant on him. And there's been no such thing."

"Like I said, I'm going to have to call that FBI bitch down in Helena because I think Helmut came back last night. A friend of my cousin's works in Flight Service at the airport. He called me and said that the Gulfstream landed out at the compound about one this morning."

"Okay, Carl, assuming they're back, just do your duty and call the Helena FBI office. Where's the problem?"

"That's the trouble. I'm supposed to be investigating the thing at the Grand Hotel. But wherever I turn I'm being squeezed from both ends. You want me to drag my heels and lose evidence so that nothing connects to Helmut. The Bureau wants to take the case away from me, and I can't give either of you an answer because there just plain aren't any."

"We're working on the Goldstein thing."

"There was a murder in that barroom, that's for sure. The forensics folks in Helena finally got back to me with the DNA results from the blood samples we picked up off the floor. It's human blood, all right. Type A negative. And according to Interpol it's a match with the live Goldstein in Vienna." Mattoon shook his head. "Now ain't that just a bitch. We got a murder without a body, and proof positive that the victim was never in that bar and is still very much alive. Now what the hell am I supposed to tell the FBI?"

"Exactly what you just told me," Aden said, his mood darkening. The incident in the barroom had been some sort of a set-up, a sting operation. But there was nothing in the FBI's or CIA's computers that his contacts had been able to find. If there was such an operation it would have shown up. Or at least there would have been hints of something in the wind.

"That's another thing. The Bureau is on my ass about Willy Hardt. Nobody's buying accidental death. Too many coincidences. How the hell Charlie Parker came up with that one goes way over the top."

Parker, the coroner, was one of Aden's people and so far he'd done exactly as he had been told to do. But even he didn't know anything about Goldstein, and the situation was starting to unravel.

"What's your point, Carl?"

"I don't know what the hell is going on with Helmut, and I don't think you do either. But the Bureau is interested because they've been asked by the German police to find him."

"Tell him that."

"His wife is back, but according to her Helmut's in Washington."

"For some reason you didn't believe her?"

"As a matter of fact I don't. So what am I supposed to do here? If I don't start doing my job, the FBI will have my ass. But if I do go out there and try to pick Helmut up for questioning he'll have me killed, or you will."

"I think that you have to decide who your friends are, who you can trust."

"Maybe I'll just go down to Helena and tell them everything. About Helmut, about you, about Willy."

Aden shook his head sadly. "I don't think that's such a good idea for the simple reason you don't know all the facts. Talk to them and you'll end up in a federal prison somewhere." Aden smiled. "Trust me, Carl, inside the penitentiary or out of it, you would most definitely end up dead."

Mattoon turned away in disgust. "Now ain't that just a plain load of horseshit."

"If it's any consolation I don't know what the hell is going on either," Aden admitted. "But I will find out and fix it."

"What about me?" Mattoon asked, turning back.

"Has the FBI given you proof that Helmut is who they say he is? I mean enough proof for you to arrest him?"

"That's what I'm supposed to come up with."

"Well then, your job is easy. Find the proof or try to. In the meantime cooperate with the Bureau. Tell them what you know, and what you don't know. They can't jail you for being confused, now can they?"

"No, but they can take a long, hard look at me."

"They won't find anything. And that you can take to the bank."

She had wanted to sleep late, but Gloria Speyer woke up with a start and looked at the bedside clock. It was a few minutes after ten in the morning. She lay back and closed her eyes. It was good to be on solid land again, even if it was Montana. But she was unsettled.

Coming back here was a part of the deal, and according to Helmut everything was going exactly as he had planned it. Germany had been dreadful, though. The weather had been horrible, the food fattening, and the tension so bad that she'd wanted to scream or slit her wrists; something, anything to make it better. But once they'd boarded the ship and headed across the open Atlantic she'd suddenly found her stride. She stopped drinking, she ate better, and she got back into the swing with her exercise program.

She felt good. And she knew that she looked good.

But the problem was what would come next. She knew none of the details of Helmut's plan except that it was very dangerous, it would end their lives here in the States at least for several years, but it would make them fabulously rich. Almost anyplace would be open to them, according to Helmut. She could imagine a lot of nice places and nice things. Clothes, cars, mansions. Maybe on the Côte d'Azur. Maybe the Costa del Sol, or the Caribbean or even Australia's Gold Coast.

The sun blasted through the open windows, the mid-morning mountain air fresh and sweet. She was alone in the big bed. Helmut had come to her a couple of hours after they'd gotten back, but she pretended to be asleep until he left. He was more disappointed than angry this time. She'd watched him leave through half-closed eyes and for just a moment she'd almost felt sorry for him. She was horny, no doubt about that, and Helmut was a reasonably capable lover, but she'd kept her silence.

She reached under the silk sheet and touched her breasts. The nipples were hard and extremely tender. She noticed Ernst and some of the other men around the compound giving her the look. But none of them were in the least bit interesting to her, not like Browne. She closed her eyes and she could see him naked in the shower.

Her vagina was wet. She spread her legs and began to masturbate as she imagined John coming through the door, yanking back the sheet and raping her, as her father had. She hadn't locked the bedroom door, in fact she'd left it slightly ajar so that anyone could look in on her. She'd had the same fantasy about other men including poor, hapless Willy the bartender for whom she'd felt some motherly affection. But never had her feelings for a man been so strong as they were for Browne.

Now he was dead, his body at the bottom of the Atlantic.

She squeezed her eyes shut, threw her head back and arched her body as she climaxed. When she was finished she was able to relax, but she was left with a terribly empty feeling, dissatisfied, an achy, hollow sensation in her belly. She needed a man inside of her. But not just any man. She opened her eyes.

Helmut stood at the open door looking at her, a dreamy expression on his face. "Are you finished?"

"Yes," she said coolly, which was an act. She was embarrassed. "I would like my privacy. Next time knock."

"Next time lock the door." He came in, shut the door, and went to the windows. It was a beautiful morning. "What did that idiot Mattoon want last night? You never did tell me the whole story."

"He wanted to talk to you, so I told him that you were still in Washington like you asked me to say."

"What were his exact words?" He was angry and he turned around stiffly. "Can you remember that much? You weren't drunk for a change."

"He said, 'Welcome back, Mrs. Sloan. Sorry to bother you at such a horrible hour, but is your husband handy? I'd surely like to have a chat with him.' Or something to that effect."

"And you told him?"

"Well, I'm sorry, Chief, but he's still in Washington. Business. Should be back in a couple of days, maybe sooner. Anything I can help you with?"

Speyer waited.

" 'Tell you what, why don't you ask him to give me a call when you hear from him. Sorry to bother you ma'am. You have a great day, hear?' "

"He didn't ask where we'd been?"

"No," Gloria replied. She was getting bored with his questions. She threw the sheet back and padded into the bathroom where she perched on the toilet without closing the door. "I'm hungry this morning. Tell cook I want a big breakfast. And mimosas, I think, or Bloody Marys. Afterward I'm going riding, and then into town to gawk at the natives." She laughed at her own joke.

"I want you to start packing your things," Speyer told her.

"We just got back."

"All your things. We're leaving here in a few days and we're not coming back for a long time, if ever."

Gloria was interested now. "Where are we going?"

"You'll see," Speyer said. He gave her a backward glance and left.

Maybe she wouldn't go into town today. Maybe she would just stay here and do as Helmut said, pack her things. Of course little she owned was worth the effort of taking, so the job wouldn't be taxing. The only problem was their ultimate destination. Beach wear, big city wear, she didn't know. But it would be interesting, she had to give him that much.

Aden walked back up to the parking area with Mattoon, but remained behind as the cop drove away. He made a call on his cell phone to a friend in Denver Air Traffic Control and gave him the Gulfstream's tail number. Two minutes later he got the answer he was looking for. The Gulfstream had flown direct from Miami International Airport last night. No stops.

He sat in silence for several minutes, looking out across the rocky slopes of a series of hills that rose to the snowcapped mountains in the distance. The view this morning didn't seem so nice as it usually did; in fact, the countryside looked ominous. How many secrets were buried in America's wild west mountains? How many should be?

He called Thomas Mann's encrypted number in Washington. "Good morning, General. I hope that I'm not interrupting anything important."

"On the contrary, Konrad, it's always good to hear your voice. Have you heard from Helmut?"

"That's why I'm calling, sir. I think that we might be facing something serious."

"Are you at a secure location?"

"Yes."

"Very well. Proceed."

"The FBI is apparently pressing its investigation into Helmut's connection with the shooting on the fourth," Aden said.

"Did you get that from your chief of police?" Mann asked.

"Yes. And frankly from some of what he told me this morning I think that he may develop into a separate problem as well. Possibly a serious threat, and certainly a delicate one to resolve."

"Is he beginning to fall apart?"

"He mentioned making a clean breast of it to the authorities," Aden confirmed.

There was a silence for a moment, until Mann was back. "I will leave the handling of that matter entirely to your discretion. After all, he is your creation." The message was clear. Mattoon was Aden's problem, and not the problem of the organization.

"I understand, Herr General."

"Now, tell me what the other problem is, and how I may be of assistance."

"There most definitely was a shooting at the Grand Hotel, but the body disappeared from the hospital's emergency room and no one knows how that could have happened. The blood at the scene has been positively identified as Meyer Goldstein's. But the old Jew is still very much alive in Vienna. In fact he never left there."

"It would seem that Mr. Browne is a confidence man."

"That's the conclusion I've come to. But I can't find so much as a hint about such an operation in the CIA's or FBI's files. Nor have our German contacts turned up anything. If Browne pulled off the stunt alone, he is a very adept independent operator. If he wasn't working alone I don't know who helped him."

"It's the last part that concerns you most."

"It's too coincidental. Just the right man for Helmut's German operation shows up at just the right time and supposedly kills an old Jew."

"Helmut was in Germany as of two and a half weeks ago, but he dropped out of sight," Mann said.

"He's back here. Or at least his wife is. She showed up last night aboard their Gulfstream which flew in from Miami. She told Mattoon that Helmut was in Washington, but their plane made no stops so I suspect he's out at the compound as well."

"At least that much bodes well," Mann said. "His operation in Germany apparently went without a hitch; otherwise I would have heard something."

"What exactly was his operation?"

"I don't know all the details except that Helmut stumbled across some Nazi documents that pinpointed a large cache of diamonds in a flooded bunker. Worth somewhere in the neighborhood of three hundred million dollars. Quite a considerable sum."

Aden was impressed. "Of which the Friends would get ten percent."

"When the time is correct."

"Someone must have known about the diamonds

and sent Browne and the Goldstein impostor out here to get inside Helmut's organization. The Russians?"

"It's a possibility that we must consider. I'll look into it from here. Lukashin is an open book. But that still doesn't address the larger problem."

"No. If Browne works for the FBI, Helmut won't be the only one with a problem. They could be working with the BKA and all of us could be in trouble."

"If Berlin had anything other than suspicions about who Helmut really is, they would have acted by now. I was thinking about the Israelis. The Mossad. We've seen this sort of thing happen before."

"Yes, we have," Aden said. In each case when the Bureau or the Israeli intelligence agency or some other law enforcement organization got too close, the Friends arranged a fatal accident for their own man rather than let him fall into the wrong hands. Everyone who signed on for protection understood the risks.

"I have a friend in the Bureau. I'll ask him to make some discreet inquiries. Perhaps we can get to the bottom of this mystery. For Helmut's sake. For all of ours."

KALISPELL

Back in his office Chief Mattoon took a couple of Tums, shut his door, and sat down to have a think. He was bright enough to know that he was in way over his head, but he didn't know where to turn.

So far as he could figure it he had several options; trouble was that none of them was foolproof. If he went to the FBI and told them everything they might offer him a plea bargain; maybe a couple of years at a federal country club somewhere. After all, he hadn't killed anyone, not even Dick White, his old boss. But Aden warned that inside prison or out, someone would get to him. Talk and he was a dead man. He had no illusions that the FBI could protect him forever.

If he stuck with Aden and did everything he could to protect Speyer, the FBI just might find out the entire story on their own. At the very least they would nail him with accessory to murder. Maybe even conspiring with a bunch of foreigners to commit treason. Hell, he might be a bad cop but he wasn't a traitor.

The third option would be to go through the motions of the investigation while *appearing* to cooperate with the FBI and with Aden. In the meantime he would cover his own ass.

He picked up his phone and called Special Agent Linda Boulton down in Helena. "Good morning. This is Carl Mattoon. I might have something for you."

"Good morning yourself, Chief," Special Agent Boulton said. "Have you made an arrest?"

"Nothing so exciting as all that. But it looks as if our own friend Herb Sloan and his wife are back in town."

"That's good news. Have you gone out to talk to him?"

"Not yet. They just flew in last night."

"From where?"

"That I don't rightly know yet. But I'm checking. But I was wondering if you wanted to come up here and sit in on the interview."

"Arrest him."

"You see that's just the point here, Special Agent. I can't go around arresting our prominent citizens without some kind of evidence. Might be I could bring him in for questioning, but that's all. I was hoping that you might be able to provide me with something I could charge him with. Something that'd stick. He's got a damned good lawyer down there in Helena."

"Who's that?"

"Konrad Aden."

"I know the name," Linda Boulton said. If she knew that Mattoon was playing games with her, she didn't let on. "Okay, I'll see what I can come up with. Meantime you sit tight up there. I don't want Sloan running off again."

"I surely hear you," Mattoon said. "I'll keep my eyes open."

HELENA

Linda Boulton hated men. They were all slime. As a woman she'd endured her share of shit at the FBI's school in Quantico, and even more shit, though of a subtler variety, during her nine years on the job. The fact that she'd made SAC of an office—even such a remote one as Helena, Montana—without sleeping with someone was an achievement in itself. One that she and her live-in lover were proud of.

That Mattoon was in league with Helmut Speyer and his mob up there in Kalispell was a foregone conclusion in her mind. She saw all the signs. The son of a bitch was protecting the Germans, probably for money. The chief had been spending more than he'd earned for about five years now. But even more interesting to her this morning was the addition of another name: another scumbag, this one a prominent attorney and businessman right here in her own backyard.

She telephoned Tom Fletcher in Washington. He was the deputy director in charge of the Bureau's Espionage and Counter-Intelligence Division, and one of the very few men who weren't out to screw the world. He was gay, which meant he was able to see what she thought of as the "big picture" when it came to relationships between people. His only fault was that he hadn't come out of the closet.

"How's it going," he said when Linda Boulton's call was transferred to his office.

"Good morning, Tom. Have you got a minute?"

"For you, kid, anything. What's up?"

"It's the Helmut Speyer investigation. I'm at a crossroads and I could use some help. Or at least some wise words."

"The Germans have backed down, if that means anything, so I don't know that we have an active investigation other than the Fourth of July shooting."

"I've put too much work into this, so I'll pretend I didn't hear that. Does the name Konrad Aden mean anything to you?"

"No. Should it?"

"I want to take a close look at him and I want your help."

KALISPELL

After lunch Helmut Speyer walked down to the firing range and confidence course where Sergeants Carl Heide and Hans Rudolph were running the men through the usual weekly small arms and hand-to-hand combat drills.

Besides Ernst and the air crew, there were thirteen members on his staff at the compound, led by his two top sergeants. All of them were members of the Friends, of course, and therefore perfectly trustworthy. Most of them had been here less than six months.

Speyer watched the automatic weapons rapid-fire practice for a couple of minutes then waved Heide down from the spotting tower.

"They're looking good, Sergeant." Speyer had to shout over the noise of the gunfire.

"Thank you, sir. They haven't lost their edge. Welcome back, Herr *Kapitän*. Your mission was a success?"

"It went without a hitch. But now we need to start on the second phase. Have Sergeant Rudolph take over here. I have another job for you."

"Yes, sir, just give me a moment. He's down on the wall. I'll call him on the field phone."

Speyer watched the men shooting. They were very good, their training superb, in fact. He would match them against the elite force of any country, including the U.S. Navy SEALS. But then German soldiers had always been the superior fighting machine when compared to any army on earth. Given the right leadership they were invincible.

Heide switched on the red flashing light down range and the five shooters stopped instantly. When they spotted Speyer they snapped to attention, their weapons at ready arms, and saluted. He came to attention and returned their salute. Really fine men, he told himself.

"Sergeant Rudolph is on his way."

"We'll go over to the hangar," Speyer said. "We have much to do and everything must go according to a very precise schedule."

"I understand, *Kapitän*." Heide was like Baumann. They were both cut of Prussian stock, and had they been born fifty years earlier they would have gone far in the Wehrmacht or even in the SS. Heide was tall, solidly built with a high forehead, blond hair, blue eyes, and a rugged, very capable demeanor. Set him to a task, any task, and you could consider the job as good as done. No delays, no excuses. All of the men here were like that, but Sergeant Heide was about the best behind Baumann.

They headed up the hill, out of the woods past the Bell Ranger parked on the helipad, toward the big hangar. The Gulfstream was still parked on the apron, the hangar doors closed. "Are you going to miss this operation up here?" Speyer asked.

"I won't miss it, and I don't think the men will either. But this place has been good for us. With no outside distractions there has been plenty of time for training."

"Now that phase is coming to an end."

"Yes, and naturally they're starting to wonder to what use they will be put." Heide gave Speyer a shrewd look. "When the weapon has been carved out of a block of steel, and loaded, it's of no use to anyone to leave it in storage."

"I couldn't agree more."

Sergeant Heide nodded in satisfaction. "From the nature of our training, I'll assume that this will develop as an urban operation."

"Most definitely urban, and against a numerically superior force. But you will have the element of surprise and vastly superior training on your side."

"And an escape route, *Kapitän*? A fall back?"

"Yes, to Eden."

Heide smiled. "That's a happy thought. R-and-R in a rear echelon paradise."

"It'll be better than you can possibly imagine, just what the name implies."

"Do we have a time line that I can share with the

men? They'll want to know when to start getting ready."

"Three to seven days, so I'm canceling all town leaves as of now. Will that be a problem?"

"None whatsoever, *Kapitän.* What about battle dress?"

"Civilian clothes under white coveralls. I'll issue breast pocket patches and back logos as they're required."

"Weapons?"

"One personal choice of handgun, but nothing less than nine millimeter, with fifty rounds and silencers. Knife or stiletto for those proficient. And for the main weapon, the nine millimeter suppressed version of the Steyr Aug Para submachine gun with the optical sights."

"If noise will be a problem we'll use subsonic ammunition," Heide suggested.

"Supply the men with both, as well as a four-man rifle grenade unit."

Again Heide nodded his satisfaction. "Night vision optics?"

"Of course. And body armor."

"Then we will present a formidable force."

"A force that I will do everything within my power to avoid using," Speyer said. They stopped. "I want you to be perfectly clear, so there will be no misunderstandings if it comes to a battle. Every single shot fired will take us one step *farther* from Eden."

"I understand."

"Even the threat of deadly force might interfere with our mission."

"But we will be there if you need us, Herr *Kapitän,*" Heide said. Like most good soldiers he abhorred violence, though he and the men he trained were masters at it.

* * *

When they reached the hangar, Speyer unlocked the service door and flipped on the strong overhead lights. The back of the hangar was partitioned off by tall accordion doors. Speyer opened these and they went inside. "This should be right up your alley. It's one of the reasons that I selected you."

An eighteen-wheel truck with the ADM AGRIBUSINESS logo was parked lengthwise across the back of the hangar, its rear doors opened and a ramp lowered. On the other side of the hangar an oddly shaped low-winged, two-seat small airplane with an angular canopy was parked diagonally to accommodate its stubby wingspan. A gleaming stainless steel three-blade prop was attached to a very large businesslike radial engine. This was obviously not a pleasure aircraft.

"*Gott in Himmel,*" Heide said. He looked at Speyer for approval, then walked over to the airplane and ran his hand tenderly along the leading edge of one of the propeller's blades. He went around the starboard wing, examining the control surfaces, then the landing gear and oversize tires. He checked the fuselage, which was a little more than thirty feet front to back, and studied the heavy-duty tail surfaces. The airplane was meant to maneuver in very tight places, pulling more Gs than an aerobatic craft.

"She's an Ayres Bull Thrush," Speyer said. "Built in Georgia. We got her fresh from the factory."

"Yes, sir, I know this airplane." Heide looked up sheepishly. "I meant I know of it. We never had such equipment as this."

One of Heide's jobs with Stasi in East Germany had been patrolling the borders with West Germany by air. He'd flown similar planes to this one that could not only stay aloft for a very long time because of their large fuel capacity, but could turn, climb, and dive in very sharp radii. Much of the border cut across hilly farmlands punctuated by stands of trees, small forests, and tiny towns with tall church spires that seemed sometimes to pop up out of nowhere. Most airplanes of this type were also equipped with armor plating on the bottom and a very effective crash cage of metal tubing surrounding the pilot, and in this model a passenger as well.

"Do you know this type of airplane well enough to do some work on it? It needs some modifications. Nothing too terribly difficult, I should think for a man of your abilities."

"I could try, Herr *Kapitän*," Heide said. "But I would have to know something about the mission."

They locked up the hangar and walked up to the house. Speyer got them each a beer before they went into his study. "I want the job done as soon as possible, even if it means working around the clock."

The airplane's blueprints were spread out on the desk. Heide studied them for a few minutes, shifting from one set of sheets to another. "What do you have in mind, sir?"

Speyer pulled out a second set of blueprints, these showing the airplane in its agricultural spraying version. "We need to add the fiberglass hopper, the stainless plumbing, pumps, fans, gates, and the spray-booms, plus the controls."

"That would have been easier done at the factory."

"The end use was none of their business. Can you do the work?"

"I don't foresee a problem."

"There'll be another modification, but not until later. This has to be done first. When can you start?"

"Are the equipment and tools here?"

"Yes, in the hangar."

Heide glanced at the blueprints again. "I'll need Hans to help me, but I think that we can finish by to-night, or first thing in the morning." He looked up. "Is this to be flown somewhere? Do you need a pilot?"

"Eventually. But when you're finished with that job, I want the airplane disassembled and packed into the truck."

A sudden understanding dawned in Sergeant Heide's eyes. "We'll have to remove the propeller, the wings, and the tail surfaces. I assume that the wiring harnesses have quick disconnects. The whole job of disassembly and packing shouldn't take more than a few hours. Put-ting it back together will take even less time because we'll know in advance how everything fits."

"I'll leave it to you, Sergeant. If there's anything you need, Ernst will arrange it." Speyer folded up the blue-prints, placed them in a large leather portfolio, and handed them to Heide. "I want you to start right now."

"Yes, sir. But I would like to ask a favor."

"What?"

"When the mission develops, I would like to be considered for the pilot's job. I know that airplane."

"I'll think about it."

Heide clicked his bootheels, saluted crisply and marched out.

WASHINGTON, D.C.

Thomas Mann's stomach was sour. Instead of lunch he went into his study and poured a Napoleon brandy in a Baccarat snifter and stared fondly at the Van Gogh that he'd practically stolen from Christie's in New York. Very slowly he calmed down, feeling an inner peace for the first time since Helmut started with his nonsense. Mann's father, a Prussian general from the old school, had cautioned that decisions made under uncontrolled stress were less than worthless, and in fact could be potentially deadly.

His father was killed on the Russian front in the winter of '42–'43, while his son was a Hitler Youth leader in Dresden. Difficult years, Mann remembered. Years that he would not care to repeat in prison somewhere.

He picked up the phone and called Speyer, who answered on the first ring, as if he had been expecting the call.

"Yes."

"Good afternoon, Helmut. Are congratulations in order?"

"Herr General, I was just about to call you. We got in late last night. But, yes, congratulations are most definitely in order. The mission to this point has been a clean sweep."

"I am happy to hear that. What about Mr. Browne? Konrad has expressed concerns that he could present a problem to us."

"That's been taken care of. He need not worry you any longer, nor should the Russians. Browne is dead and Lukashin has been well taken care of. He knows the consequences for him should he try anything. All the bases are covered."

"There is the business with the Fourth of July shooting. The FBI is very interested in you."

"That was all Browne's doing," Speyer said. "But it makes no difference. We're leaving here in a few days and we won't be coming back."

"Where are you going?"

"Eden."

On the surface that was good news to Mann. But there was more here than Speyer was telling him. "When will you be settled? I would like to visit."

"Give me a week, General. Perhaps a day or two longer, and we'll have a celebration dinner that you will never forget."

Mann telephoned his contact at the FBI. As with Speyer, it seemed as if he had been expecting the call.

"Do we have a problem on our hands in Montana?" Mann asked.

"I have an SAC out there who wants to beat the bushes. She called me this morning and asked for some help."

"What did you say to her?"

"That the German government has all but given up on the investigation. But somehow Konrad's name came up."

"You know where to lead her," Mann said. "Konrad is a good and loyal American."

"Of course he is," Tom Fletcher agreed. "As all of us are." He chuckled. "Don't worry, Herr General, Special Agent Boulton will cause us no trouble. But maybe you could convince Helmut to get the hell out of there for the time being."

"Consider it done."

"Then it's settled."

"One further matter. Have you come up with anything on the man I asked you about?"

"John Edward Browne. South African Intelligence, or at least he was until he got fired. Since then he's dropped out and no one's heard from him."

"He's legitimate?"

"So far as I can tell."

"Keep checking, please. He must have surfaced somewhere in the past few years. Men like that don't simply retire, they find new masters. I want to know who his are."

8

WASHINGTON, D.C.

After three days in the hospital, his wounds stitched up, inhalation therapy to soothe his lungs which were burned by the diesel oil fumes, Bill Lane was not only ready to break out, he insisted on it. He was still in pain, which he couldn't conceal as he pulled a Riscatto Portofino soft beige summer sweater over his head, but it was manageable.

"I think you're dotty checking out so soon," Tom Hughes told him disapprovingly. "Speyer's not that important."

"Yes, he is," Lane said, slipping into his hand-sewn Italian loafers. "He killed the innocent crew aboard the *Maria*, and you said yourself that he gunned down Otto Schaub at the chalet outside Neubrandenberg. They were friends."

"Yes, and he won't hesitate to kill you the moment that you pop into view, dear boy."

Lane grinned, pocketing his wallet, comb, handkerchief, and a few dollars, then putting on his Vacheron et Constantin watch. "That's the beauty of it, Tommy. They think that I went down with the ship. I'm dead."

"You survived the deep dive into the bunker, the ambush when you surfaced, the gun battle aboard the ship, the sinking, and then twenty-four hours floating about in shark-infested waters. Even your luck will run out at some point."

"Low blows, all of them, and from you of all people," Lane said. "I'm a master diver, a good shot, an escape artist, a strong swimmer, and you were waiting for me in Miami. What could possibly have gone wrong?"

"Plenty, unless you take off your clothes this instant and get back into bed," Frances said from the doorway.

She wore a muted yellow silk suit, no blouse, a subdued print Hermès scarf, and low-heeled sandals. The sight of her attractive, warm face and bright green eyes, flashing now with barely suppressed anger, never failed to please Lane, and he smiled.

"It's the woman's primitive side that I love most," he said to Hughes.

"I'm dead serious, William," she said sternly. She came in, gave him a kiss on the cheek, and then gave him a critical once-over. "And where'd you get those clothes?"

"One of our bright people, whose name shall forever remain a secret, broke into our house while you were out and got them for me." Lane took his 9mm Beretta from beneath his pillow, checked the action, and slipped it in the quick-draw holster beneath his sweater at the small of his back.

"Bloody hell."

"Not now, Frannie," Lane said seriously. "I'm a little sore and stiff, but we have work to do and I have a feeling that the clock is against us."

"I worry about you," Frances said, softening. She turned to Hughes. "He's a stubborn man."

"Indeed he is, which makes the two of you the perfect pair," Hughes told her.

They made it past the nurses' station and took the elevator down to the parking level. "Speyer and his wife and probably Ernst Baumann took the captain's gig before the ship went down. Have they been spotted in Havana?" Lane asked.

"They're back in Montana," Hughes said.

The news was unexpected. Lane's eyes narrowed. "Why didn't you tell me?"

"They didn't get there until late last night, William," Hughes said. "And I was about to tell you but you wouldn't listen.

"Did they fly in on the Gulfstream?"

"Direct from Miami."

Lane thought about that for a moment. "They've been out of sight for a full three days. It's a safe bet that they didn't take the captain's gig ashore anywhere in Florida; there's too much Coast Guard and DEA activity up and down the coast. They probably went to Cuba and flew from there to Mexico City and then into Miami."

"If recovering the diamonds from the bunker was the whole mission, they would have stayed in Cuba," Frances said. "Coming back to Montana means there's more."

"Bingo," Lane said, half to himself.

They got over to the office a few minutes before six. The unit's secretary, Agnes Warhurst, was the only one who hadn't already left for the weekend. She was a large woman in her mid-seventies who'd been the executive secretary to four FBI directors before her mandatory retirement. She knew just about everybody in the Washington area who was involved in law enforcement and intelligence. Her manner was gruff, but her heart was solid gold. Everyone on the staff loved her.

"What are you still doing here?" Lane demanded.

She gave him a critical look. "I knew they weren't going to keep you over there much longer." She handed him a dozen phone slips. "It looks as if someone is trying to stir the pot over in the Bureau and maybe at Justice. Do you know Tom Fletcher?"

"Espionage and Counter-Intelligence."

"He's a little shit, but he does a pretty good job, at least he has until now. All of a sudden he's put the brakes on the Kalispell investigation. I'd say someone got to him."

"Probably Thomas Mann," Lane said. The slips were phone messages from a dozen different sources that Agnes had approached around town. The Bureau had lost interest in the shooting. Their investigation was parallel to the Room's, and had been conducted along more conventional channels. But for them to have backed down meant somebody had gotten to somebody . . . as a personal favor.

"Mann is quite the bon vivant about town," Hughes said. "He knows a couple dozen senators and twice that many congressmen. Charities, boards of directors of a half-dozen major corporations, Kennedy Center advisory committee, some well-placed investments. And, interestingly enough, he makes and receives several encrypted telephone calls each day."

"Any luck breaking the program?"

"Not yet," Frances said. "It's a very good one. I asked Tony Bosons to lend a hand, but so far he's come up with nothing." Bosons was Britain's leading cryptographer.

"If and when he manages to break the program we might learn something from Mann's phone calls," Lane said. "In the meantime, have you come up with anything new on Reichsamt Seventeen?"

"Nothing," Hughes admitted. "But I'll tell you one thing, William, the Germans know what's down there. I'd bet the farm on it."

"Why aren't they talking? They want us to bust Speyer for them."

"I can't get a straight answer out of them. It seems as if there's a big mystery surrounding the place." Hughes shook his head. "One thing's for sure, diamonds were not used as a catalyst for anything they might have been doing down there. Whatever you brought up in that sealed box wasn't engagement rings."

"The *Deep Sound II* just happened to be in Sarasota," Frances said. "She should be about where you think the *Maria* went down by now. Thc ocean is terribly deep out there, perhaps five or six hundred fathoms, but if any ship is capable of finding the downed ship it'll be the *Deep Sound.*"

"The box should still be down there," Lane said. "I stashed it in a fire equipment locker. But at the end when I asked Baumann if they had found it, he said they'd fished it out of the bilge."

"It could be the reason Speyer returned to Kalispell," Frances suggested. "He failed and he came home to lick his wounds."

"In that case, I think that we should go out there and see for ourselves just what kind of a mood Herr Speyer is in," Lane said. "Bad, he's lost; good, he knows something."

"I can't believe what I'm hearing," Hughes protested. "The moment that you're spotted they'll kill you, no questions asked."

"That's why I'm taking Frannie with me. She'll provide the needed diversion," Lane said. "In the meantime, I want to have a word with the FBI agent in Helena."

Agnes had listened to everything. "That's plain crazy," she opined.

Hughes shook his head in defeat. "Welcome to the nut house, my dear."

ALEXANDRIA, VIRGINIA

Tommy's wife, Moira, and the girls were fixing a big welcome-home dinner for Lane, and since he wasn't flying to Montana until morning he couldn't refuse. He and Frances had just enough time to get home, change clothes and drive back.

"They're going to dote on you all night, and you're going to let them," Frances warned. "Knowing Tom he's probably told them everything so they'll have plenty to say. And you'll take it."

"Yes, dear," Lane said.

Frances started to laugh at his long face, but stopped herself. She became serious. "Speyer's a very bad man, isn't he."

"I don't know if that's the right word. Maybe indifferent."

"If he didn't hesitate to kill his friend in Germany, or the crew aboard the *Maria*, one wonders what's next on his agenda."

Lane gave his wife a sharp look. When they got married he knew that she would not give up her intelligence service career. She was a strong, bright, capable, independent woman. He knew that from the start. It was one of the many reasons he fell in love with her. And one of the first set of reasons that the President of the United States and the Prime Minister of Great Britain had agreed to include her in the creation of the special trouble-shooting unit called "The Room." That did not, however, stop him from worrying about her going into harm's way.

"A ha'penny, love," she said.

"Just what you wondered," he answered. "What's next on Speyer's agenda."

"Come on, there's more than that."

"No matter what happens, we have enough on Speyer and Baumann already to turn them over to the BKA, and be done with them."

"That wouldn't be very sporting, would it?"

"What do you mean?"

"We were asked to do a job. We're not finished yet. Arresting Speyer and deporting him is only half the business."

"It would take him out of circulation."

"That's all it would do, William. In the meantime we might never know what he was planning." She smiled her secret smile, which meant that she wasn't happy but she would bear up. "I'm to go out there and play goo-goo eyes with the monster, while all the while you want to put a bullet in his brain. That frightens me."

"Scares me silly, too," Lane admitted.

HELENA, MONTANA

Lane took a cab from the municipal airport to the federal building downtown. The late morning was bright, which was opposite his mood. Returning this close to Speyer's operation was like plunging headlong into a dark maelstrom. Frannie had been right last night. He did want to put a bullet in the bastard's brain and leave it at that. Very simple, very tidy, and very complete. But not very sporting.

His hanging bag was at the airport, but he had retrieved his gun from inside his laptop computer.

Linda Boulton was just coming out of the front door for an early lunch when Lane came up the long walk from the fountain. She looked just as angry as she did in her Bureau photograph.

"Special Agent Boulton?" he asked, coming up to her.

She stopped, her eyes narrowed in suspicion. "What can I do for you?"

"I know who shot Meyer Goldstein up in Kalispell on the Fourth. Interested?"

She nonchalantly unbuttoned her blue blazer. "I'd say that it was one of my priorities. May I have your name?"

"I'm Bill Lane and I work in Washington. Are you carrying a cell phone?"

"Let's see some identification."

"If you have a cell phone, I want you to call the White House switchboard, identify yourself, and ask to speak to twenty-seven blue ranger." He took out his wallet and handed it to her.

Keeping a careful eye on him, she checked his ID, then got out her cell phone and got the White House number from information. The call went through, she spoke the code, and he watched as her eyes widened.

"Yes, Mr. President, I recognize your voice. My name is Linda Boulton. I'm the special agent in charge of the FBI's Helena, Montana office." She gave Lane a sharp look, then nodded. "Yes, Mr. President, he says that his name is William Lane."

She was silent for several seconds. The president was telling her something. She nodded again. "Yes, Mr. President, I understand." She broke the connection, and hesitated for a few seconds, as if she was trying to come to a difficult decision. She seemed to be even more suspicious and angry than before the call. Something was eating at her, but she seemed to be resigned. "Okay, what the hell is this all about?"

"The name I used in Kalispell was John Clark. But believe me, no one was actually killed. In fact, the man posing as Goldstein is a friend of mine and is at this moment very much alive in Washington."

"That's just great," Special Agent Boulton said disgustedly. "Obviously I don't know what the hell I'm doing out here. Leastways that's the way I'm being treated."

"Take it easy. We're on the same side. It's Helmut Speyer who's the bad guy, and he's why I came out to talk to you." Lane took his wallet from her and they went over to the fountain, where they sat down. He offered her a cigarette, but she angrily declined.

"A simple email would have worked wonders," she said bitterly. "Somebody could have told me and I would have backed off."

"It's not that easy. Speyer has a lot of friends in Washington, and out here, I suspect."

"Yeah, Carl Mattoon, the chief of police up there. How'd you get this one by him?"

"No one expected a corpse to get up and walk out of the morgue," Lane said. "You sure about Mattoon's connection with Speyer?"

"Pretty sure. Along with an attorney right here in town. Konrad Aden."

"We'll check on him. In the meantime, you were asked to investigate Speyer as a routine request from the German Federal Police about three months ago, right?"

She nodded. "But we didn't find much, not until the shooting, and then what we did have started to make some kind of sense."

"That's why we engineered the operation, so that I could get close to him. We didn't think that you were going to get very far."

"And?"

"We're still in the middle of our investigation. Now Tom Fletcher has told you to back off."

"Is he one of yours?"

"No. But he could be working with Speyer, or with people who are protecting Speyer."

This last news seemed to deflate her. When she looked up her anger was all but gone. "I'm not even going to ask what agency you work for, because you probably wouldn't tell me. But what am I supposed to do?"

"Do you have enough evidence to prove the man is really Helmut Speyer? DNA, maybe?"

"We've been trying to get a hair sample or something, but without Mattoon's cooperation it's been impossible."

"Okay, keep trying. Just do your job."

"Do you want us to continue investigating Mattoon as well?" she asked.

"Wherever your police work takes you. But I don't want you to make any arrests just yet. Put some pressure on them, but that's all. In the meantime I'll be going through the back door."

"I hope you know what you're doing. If this guy is who I think he is, he's bad news. The Germans didn't have anything good to say about him."

Lane gave her a sympathetic look. She was caught between a rock and a hard place. Her boss wanted her to back off, and yet her boss might be one of the bad guys. "He's all of that and more," Lane said. "So watch your own back."

KALISPELL

Hughes arranged for Lane to pick up a Tradewinds luxury motor home in Helena complete with a dirt bike attached to the back. By the time he was checked out in the plush rig and had retrieved his bag from the airport, he didn't get out of town until late. It was around midnight when he reached an isolated spot to pull off outside Kalispell and get some sleep. Frannie drove up at 9:00 A.M. in a Nissan Pathfinder she'd picked up at the airport.

She came in and gave her husband a kiss. "How'd it go in Helena?"

"Special Agent Boulton is one troubled lady."

"Just lately you seem to be attracting your share of them, darling," she said. She took a look down the corridor to the palatial master bedroom. "How soon did Tommy say we had to return this?" she asked.

"Too soon," Lane said. "Have you had your breakfast?"

"On the plane. Don't remind me. It was horrible."

"You'd best start on the topographic maps, and I'll put on the tea."

"Sounds good," Frannie said. She went to the dining table where Lane had spread out the geodetic survey maps of Speyer's six-hundred-acre compound and the area around it. This operation had been laid on too fast for her to familiarize herself with the terrain. She got to it now in earnest. Her life depended on it.

Speyer's compound lay in the valley defined by the Middle Fork and the South Fork of the Flathead

River, between the towns of Columbia Falls and Hungry Horse. Dozens of mountain lakes fed the river from the north and east, just below the Continental Divide and Glacier National Park. Forests to the west and north led up into the Whitefish range and Big Mountain Ski & Summer Resort. A month from now the first snows would begin at the higher elevations, but for now skiing was out and mountain gliding was in.

"He must have had visitors before," Lane said.

"I would expect so, William," Frannie agreed, studying the map. "It's a little too far for the hang-gliding set, but at just about the right distance for the rigid-wing planes."

Lane pointed to the Big Mountain Resort. "Like the ones they rent up there. If you don't make the airport and the road looks dicey you'd naturally set down on Speyer's airstrip."

"But it's marked private in big red letters on the chart. I'm sure they warn everyone to steer clear."

"I'm sure that they do. A man is entitled to his privacy."

"No telling how he might react if someone were to simply drop out of the sky unannounced. Especially now."

Lane had thought about that serious problem, and he'd come up with the solution. "You'll radio a mayday, or better yet, a PAN, and tell the tower in Kalispell that you're running out of altitude, you've got a safe landing strip in sight and you're going down. It'll take them at least a half-hour to get someone from Big Mountain to come fetch you. In the meantime Speyer's people would have monitored your distress call."

"Maybe I'll convince Mr. Sloan to invite me to dinner, maybe even stay for the night," Frances teased. "I'd like to find out just how good a bridge player his wife is."

Lane got even more serious. "Don't fool around, Frannie. Just get in, find out what kind of a mood they're in, and get out."

"What about you?"

"I won't be very far away."

She gave him a worried look. "That's what I'm afraid of."

Lane locked up the motor home and took the dirt bike cross country a couple of hours before dusk. The bike was new and the muffler was very good; even so, it was shocking how loud the engine sounded in the deep woods. He was still tender from his injuries, but he put the pain out of his mind. It was easy to do when he thought about Otto Schaub in Germany. Speyer had gunned the man down, probably to make it look like Schaub and the Russian had had a shoot-out.

He was dressed in Navy SEAL camos he'd picked up before he left Washington. If the need arose, he could go to ground and a hundred searchers could all but step on him without seeing him. The only thing that he could not get past were motion detectors or infrared sensors. But he doubted that Speyer had gone to that much trouble to protect his privacy. The deer and the bear roaming around out here would be setting off the alarms constantly, driving his troops batty.

He crossed a small creek, then spit dirt as he climbed the steep hill on the other side. He had to work his way around a series of fallen logs until he came to the crest of a second, smaller hill where he pulled up short.

Directly below him, about six or seven hundred yards away, was the end of the paved runway. The

Gulfstream was parked in front of the hangar but there didn't seem to be any activity there or at the barracks beyond.

Lane shut off the bike, stashed it behind one of the logs, then, lying prone on the forest floor, studied the compound through binoculars. He spotted three men up by the house. One of them looked like Baumann. They seemed to be arguing about something, and when they broke off Baumann went inside and the other two headed down to the hangar.

He took out the handheld VHF and switched it to the Kalispell tower frequency, then settled down to wait.

The old, but still sleek and graceful German-built Sportavia one-seat glider was a delight to handle and for the moment at least Frances was having the time of her life. She had learned to fly when she was stationed in Australia with the RAF, and built up several hundred hours in the Midlands when she came back to England. But she'd never done any serious mountain flying where updrafts of more than one thousand feet per minute were common along ridge lines, and where the scenery was nothing short of fantastic as it was here.

She banked to the east, away from the sun, a large boulder in the middle of the Flathead River stationary just off the tip of her low wing as she made a slow, graceful clearing turn. Off in the distance, perhaps seven or eight miles, was Speyer's compound. She could make out some of the buildings, the bizjet parked in front of the hangar, and the long concrete runway. But she was too far out to see any activity, nor of course could she spot William, though she knew that he was down there in the woods somewhere.

She was a little over five thousand feet above the published altitude of Speyer's runway. Continuing her turn, she pulled the spoiler handle back two notches which reduced the lift of the long wings, and the glider began to sink.

A line of hills ran north and south. She headed toward them so that if anyone on the ground was watching they would see her trying to find lift, but not doing a very good job of it.

The altimeter continued to unwind slowly as she flew back and forth along the ridge line. She had to pull out more spoiler to decrease the wings' lift even farther at one point when she did find an updraft.

As she wheeled and soared above the tree line she kept looking off her left shoulder at the setting sun beyond the runway, then back to the unwinding altimeter, judging the distance and her altitude against precisely how much lift and therefore glide ratio she could coax from the airplane. The flight master up at the resort had been skeptical when she'd shown up and asked to rent the Sportavia, especially so late in the afternoon. But after they talked for a few minutes and she'd shown him her Australian, British, and American flying licenses, plus her log book, he was more than happy to accommodate her. She was an expert pilot on paper and in fact. The first time that she'd taken William up in England, she'd tried to make him sick by doing loops and aileron rolls. But instead he demanded that she teach him how to fly, and their love affair had begun in earnest.

She grinned, thinking about it now, as she radioed Kalispell airport.

"Kalispell tower, this is Sportavia Nancy-seven-seven-niner, declaring an emergency. Copy?"

"Nancy-seven-seven-niner, this is Kalispell tower. What's your problem?"

"I'm out of altitude. I'm up by Crazy Horse just west of the Flathead. I have a paved runway in sight, I'm going to have to put her down."

"Copy that. We'll inform Big Mountain Air Charters, and we'll try to contact the owner of the private strip. Give us a call when you're on the ground."

"Will do," Frances radioed. "Nancy-seven-seven-niner, out."

Frances eased back on the spoilers as she made a gentle banking turn toward the distant runway. Almost immediately the glider felt lighter in her hands. She glanced at the ridgeline in her rearview mirror. There was plenty of lift there; enough for her to make the Kalispell strip twice over. Her pride was a little wounded, and the resort's flight master would probably never trust a woman pilot again, but that was a small price to pay if she could get what she came for.

The sun was just dropping behind the mountains as she lined up with the end of the runway, and waggled her tail and wings to make sure that she was loose and that the aircraft's controls were in working order.

Two men in a jeep came down from the house and headed to the far end of the runway where the glider would end up. As she came over the threshold she glanced down at them. They were dressed in what looked like fatigues and carried a pair of rifles in a rack behind the seats.

She pulled the spoilers fully out as she came into the ground effect and the glider flared out and floated at a crabbed angle a few feet above the runway. Within five hundred feet the center wheel touched down and she began feathering the hand-brake, steering a straight line with the rudder pedals and keeping the wings level with the stick.

The two men got out of the jeep and came over as she slowed to a halt, but they didn't bring their rifles.

It was something, she thought, as she popped the catch, opened the clear Lexan hatch, looked up and smiled.

"Sorry to drop in like this, gentlemen, but I really didn't have a choice."

Lane watched Frannie climb out of the glider, her white silk Versace jumpsuit practically fluorescing in the deepening dusk. He could not hear what the two goons were saying to her, nor did he recognize either of them, but it was clear by their body language that they were not happy with her presence. It was also clear that they weren't going to do her any physical harm. Anybody who monitored her emergency call knew where she was. Speyer and his people knew this.

He checked his position on his tiny GPS navigator and entered it as a waypoint so that he would have no trouble finding his way back to the bike in the dark. Next he telephoned Tommy back in Washington.

"She's in."

"Has there been any trouble so far?"

"They're not happy, but she's okay for now." Lane looked again through the binoculars. Frannie was climbing into the jeep with the two men. She said something to one of them and he shook his head. They started away from the runway up to the house. "It looks like they're taking her to see Speyer."

"He's not going to be a happy camper. Especially if they were planning on making their move tonight."

"That's nothing compared to how he's going to feel when I get done with him."

"I looked into Konrad Aden's background," Tommy said. "He's squeaky clean. Practically an all-American boy scout."

"Yeah, the same as Thomas Mann. But they're both involved up to their eyeballs with Speyer, which means that their organization is tight. Could be the group that the Germans told us about. Thc Friends."

"They've apparently learned a thing or two about security from their predecessors, the Odessa. Wouldn't it be grand to not only take Speyer down, but to get the entire organization?"

"The same thought occurred to me. I can provide the eyewitness link between Speyer and Mann, and if Mattoon is working for them, he might be able to provide us with the link to Aden."

"I'll get on it," Hughes said. "From where you are, can you see any signs that they're getting ready to bug out?"

"If they are, they're being quiet about it. Nothing much is moving down there."

"Maybe they're staying after all."

There was still some daylight left in the hills, but the valley was dark, and lights were coming on up at the house. They had thought about equipping Frannie with a wire so that they could monitor her situation. But they'd decided that it was too risky. If Speyer's people detected it she would be in immediate trouble.

"I'm going to take a closer look," Lane said. "If Frannie does get into trouble, I want to be right there."

"Don't take any unnecessary chances, William. You already have a measure of the man. You know what he's capable of, what he's already done. If it comes to a showdown, shoot first and we'll put the pieces together later."

"Don't worry, Tommy, I won't be cutting him any slack real soon."

Lane checked the load in his Beretta, screwed a silencer on the end of the barrel, and blackened his face with camo grease. He took one last look at the way he had come in, memorizing the path, then turned and headed silently down into the valley.

The man they identified as Ernst Baumann met them at the door, an impatient, suspicious expression on his Teutonic features. He dismissed the two guards and escorted Frances into the soaring living room.

"You can wait here, Miss . . . ?"

"Frances Lane. Are you the owner?"

"No, that's Mr. Sloan," Baumann said. "We've notified the Kalispell tower that you landed safely and telephoned the Big Mountain Resort. They're sending someone for you and your aircraft."

"If we can leave it parked here for the night I can get a tow back into the air first thing in the morning. The thermals are really quite terrific just after dawn."

"Work lights are being set up now, and your glider will be disassembled by the time the truck arrives." Baumann gave her the faintest of smiles. "May I offer you a glass of wine?"

"Sure. In the meantime, is Mr. Sloan here tonight? I'd like to thank him in person."

"I'm sorry, but Mr. Sloan is—"

"Right here," Speyer said, coming into the living room. Like the others, Baumann was dressed in fatigues, but Speyer wore faded jeans, a UCLA sweatshirt, and moccasins. He looked preppy in the clothes, almost boyish, and, Frannie thought, almost handsome. He also was very happy, practically bubbling over with good cheer and enthusiasm.

"Mr. Sloan, I'd like to thank you, sir. You're a lifesaver. If there's anything I could do for you."

"Anything to help a pretty lady, which is reward enough of itself." Sloan kissed her hand and grinned as if he had said something super-charming. "Was it harrowing, your landing?"

"It certainly could have been dicey without your runway. Quite stupid of me, actually."

"Yes, it was," Gloria Speyer agreed as she came languidly down the stairs. She wore soft pink satin lounging pants, matching low-cut blouse, and high-heeled slippers. She looked ludicrous, and Frances stopped herself from laughing.

A look of irritation briefly crossed Speyer's face. "Darling, come say hello to our guest, Miss Frances Lane."

"I think that you've already said hello for both of us." Gloria gave Frannie a critical once-over as only one woman can give another. Frances, a half-smile on her lips, did the same.

"Good evening, Mrs. Sloan. A lovely outfit."

Gloria's lips tightened, but she nodded curtly. "Do all lady pilots dress like you?"

Frannie's jumpsuit was skin-tight and left very little to the imagination. It had had the effect she'd wanted on the two men at the airstrip, on Baumann and now on Speyer, who couldn't keep his eyes off her. Speyer's wife knew it.

"I fly a glider, Mrs. Sloan. Excess weight is very important." The comment was meant to be vicious considering the differences in their ages and physiques, but Frannie couldn't help herself.

Baumann had gone to fetch the wine. When he came back, Frannie gave him a sweet smile.

"I think it might be best if I pop back to the runway and help with my airplane," she said.

"That's a ducky idea," Gloria said, and a faint suggestion of recognition came into Speyer's eyes but then was gone.

"Thanks again for your hospitality, Mr. Sloan," Frannie said.

"My pleasure," Speyer mumbled, and Frannie left with Baumann. She half expected to be called back. It was her damned accent. It was possible that they'd heard her talking to the hotel clerk at the Grand just before the shooting. She'd seen the spark of recognition in Speyer's eyes. But he wasn't sure.

"Don't try to land here again, Miss Lane," Baumann warned her on the way down to the airstrip. "Your reception might not be as warm next time."

Lane dropped to the ground and froze as a half-dozen floodlights switched on at the end of the runway. He was in the scrub brush and rocks between the barracks and the house.

Two more men came out of the hangar and drove a golf cart to the glider, which was lit up as bright as day. A minute later Frances and Baumann pulled up in a jeep. It quickly became clear that neither Frannie nor the glider were staying the night, as the two men began removing the starboard wing. Someone from the resort was probably coming down with a truck to haul the glider away.

Making sure that no one else was coming down from the house, Lane eased farther back into the darkness, and then, keeping low, raced to the rear of the barracks. He peered in one of the windows. A dozen men, some of them in their skivvies, lounged around. Some of them watched television, one of then was shining his boots, and four were playing cards. It did not look as if they were planning on going anywhere soon.

He backed away from the window, and took a couple of minutes to make certain that there were no guards out and about. All the activity was taking place at the end of the runway, where both wings were already folded back. Frannie stood to one side watching.

He circled around behind the house, keeping well away from the spill of lights from the windows, and headed straight across to the hangar. The windows across the back of the big structure had all been painted over on the inside, and a rear service door was locked, so he made his way to the front.

The Gulfstream was parked on the apron between him and the men working on the glider, partially masking his movements. The main doors were partially open, but the inside of the hangar was in darkness. There was nothing inside except for what looked like a couple of big tool carts and a pickup truck.

He was about to slip inside to get a better look when he happened to glance over his shoulder in time to see one of Speyer's people heading up from the glider with the golf cart.

He ducked around the corner of the building and raced to the back, where he settled down to see what would happen next.

Speyer stood at his bedroom window drinking a dark beer and smoking a cigarette as he watched the activity at the runway. The truck from Big Mountain Resort had arrived and they were lifting the disassembled glider onto its flatbed.

The more he thought about it, the more he suspected that the woman's landing here as she had was not an emergency. It had been a contrived act. And her voice—he had heard it somewhere before, but for the life of him he could not remember where or when.

"You should have insisted that she stay the night," Gloria said from the door.

Speyer didn't bother turning around. He could see

her reflection in the dark window glass. She had brought a bottle of champagne and a glass up from the kitchen. It looked as if she was already well on her way to becoming drunk. "Perhaps I should have."

Gloria kicked off her slippers and padded across the room to the chaise longue where she flopped down. "Look at me when I'm talking to you," she demanded.

Speyer turned to her. Her eyes were starting to go fuzzy and her face was becoming slack. He hated her like this, and she knew it. "You're drunk."

She chuckled. "No, but I'm getting there." She focused on him. "Did you want to fuck her, Helmut? Peel that cutesy little jumpsuit off her hide. Have her whisper sweet nothings to you in that fake accent of hers?"

"The thought occurred to me." He looked out the window. A group of them were standing around the truck talking.

"I'll bet it did."

They were breaking off now, the truck driver and another man, plus the woman climbing up into the cab of the truck. "Go to bed, Gloria. We have a busy day ahead of us."

"She was at the hotel when John killed that old Jew."

The truck was heading out, and the others were heading back to work in the hangar. Ernst was on his way back to the house. What Gloria had just said suddenly penetrated, and he turned back. "How do you know that?"

"I recognized the voice. She called the clerk 'ducky.' "

Speyer remembered, too; a very cold knot formed in his stomach. He slammed his drink down and raced downstairs as Baumann came in.

"Call out the guard," he shouted.

Baumann stopped in his tracks, confused. "Sir?"

"The woman was a diversion. We've probably been breached."

Baumann went to the phone on the hall stand. "Should we stop the truck?"

"No. It'd cause too many complications. But I want every square centimeter of the compound searched. Now!"

Lane waited until the truck was gone before he retraced his path from the hangar, behind the house, past the barracks, and across the field that sloped down to the apple orchard. Lights suddenly came on all over the compound and men poured out of the barracks. They were fully dressed and even from where Lane crouched in the trees he could see that they were armed.

He speed-dialed Frances and she answered on the second ring.

"Hello."

"They're on the move. Are you at the highway yet?"

"Oh, hi, sweetheart," she said without missing a beat. "I'm just fine. Not even a scrape. As a matter of fact we're on the highway now. Should be back to the resort in a half hour or so. How about dinner?"

Lane grinned in the darkness. He was married to a remarkable woman. "Sounds good, love. But I have to run now. Ta-ta."

"Should I ask Tommy to join us?"

Speyer's troops were concentrating around the house and the hangar for the moment. "I don't think so. See you in an hour."

"Take care."

"You, too."

9

WASHINGTON, D.C.

The flight was long, and Frannie didn't seem to be herself. She was withdrawn and Lane couldn't get much out of her except that she was tired.

It was Saturday afternoon, the weather delightful and traffic light as they took a cab straight to the Naval Observatory where Tom Hughes was waiting for them.

"I'm glad that you're back in one piece. I was damned worried about both of you the entire time."

"There wasn't an exciting moment," Lane told him. "The only part that made me nervous was Frannie's landing right at dusk. She cut it a little close, and they sure as hell weren't going to turn on the runway lights for her."

"I had all the lift in the world," she said absently. "And I got to speak to Speyer just as we hoped I would."

"Are you going to keep me in suspense, my dear?" Hughes asked.

Frannie gave him a wistful look, then went into the back room where she got a paper cup of water and took a couple of aspirin. They were waiting patiently for her when she got back. "Headache," she explained.

"I shouldn't wonder, with all you've been through," Hughes said.

"Helmut Speyer is one jolly soul, though I wouldn't give you a farthing for his marriage." Frannie shook her head. "Whatever happened aboard that boat was not a disaster for the man. He got what he was after and he's on track. Either that or he's a very good actor."

Lane perched on the edge of Hughes's desk. "It didn't look like they were getting ready to bug out any time soon either. And that doesn't make any sense to me. If he got the diamonds to Cuba he would have stayed there. Unless he's up to something else."

"But you said you hid the box in a locker and Baumann knew nothing about it."

"He told me that they fished the box out of the bilge."

"Maybe they switched boxes," Hughes suggested.

"There was no reason for Speyer to do something like that. Not unless he was planning to kill Horst Zimmer and the crew from the start."

"That's a distinct possibility we should consider, William," Hughes replied earnestly. "Let's turn it over to the Germans right now. We've gone far enough."

"My pig-headed husband isn't about to do anything so sensible as all that," Frances said.

Lane was taken aback by the bitterness of her remark. "Are you okay, Frannie?"

"I'm just saying that Tommy is dead on. We're simply not equipped to fight an entire army."

"I'm not going to let it go after we've come this far. Even the Germans seem to want to sweep this under the rug. We can't get anything out of them about what really went on down there in that bunker."

"You're going to follow this wherever it leads?"

"That's what we're in business for."

"We're in business to serve Great Britain and the United States of America," Frances flared. She was on the verge of tears.

"Speyer is operating on U.S. soil. He had the bartender at the Grand murdered. And he's probably got the help of the Kalispell chief of police and maybe a high-ranking FBI officer. That makes it our business."

"Okay, kids, time for a truce," Hughes broke in. "The ink is barely dry on your marriage license and you're arguing like an old married couple."

"Sorry," Frances mumbled.

"Me, too," Lane said.

Hughes was troubled by the outburst. "What do you have in mind, William? What's our next step?"

"There are three possibilities. If Speyer switched the boxes as you suggested, he either took the diamonds to Cuba, or he brought them to Montana. Short of that they're still on the bottom of the Atlantic. That's going to be the easiest to check out. As soon as Tony locates her I'm going down in a submersible and take a look in that locker."

"There's a fourth possibility, William," Hughes suggested.

"What's that?"

"The one thing that we haven't thought of yet, because it hasn't occurred to us."

"We'll take them one at a time," Lane said. "In the meantime I'm going to take my grouchy wife home, feed her dinner and put her to bed."

Hughes clapped his hands in delight. "Good idea. I'll call you as soon as I hear something from the *Deep Sound*."

GEORGETOWN

They got their Range Rover from underground parking, and he drove Frannie back to their small, but very well furnished, three-story brownstone on Rock Court in Georgetown. All their calls were forwarded to The Room when they were gone, so there was nothing on the answering machine in the hall, and only a couple of bills and a few magazines including *Time, Scientific American*, and *Foreign Affairs* on the floor in the front vestibule.

"I'm going to draw a bath," Frances said, heading upstairs.

"Red or white?"

"White," she said.

Lane left their bags in the hall and made sure that the house had not been disturbed in their absence. He got a nice bottle of vintage pinot grigio from the wine locker, opened it, got a couple of glasses, and went upstairs.

Frances was in the bathroom, the door half-open. Lane could hear the water running as he poured a couple of glasses of wine, kicked off his shoes, and went in to her.

She was naked, standing in front of the full-length mirror looking at her body while tears streamed down her cheeks.

"My God, Frannie, what's wrong?" Lane demanded, setting the wineglasses aside and taking her into his arms.

"I'm ugly," she sobbed.

"Don't be ridiculous, you're beautiful."

"I'm fat."

"You're not."

She looked up into his face. "I'm preggers."

After their bath they made slow, gentle love on the big bed while Tchaikovsky's violin concerto played on the stereo. "We're getting a little long of tooth to be starting a family," she said, her head on his chest.

"Nonsense, I'm forty and you're barely thirty-six. I'd hardly call that doddering."

"You know what I mean. Having kids is for younger people in different sorts of occupations." She looked into his eyes for his reaction.

"Well, you're going to be out of the business, at least for the time being."

"Like hell I'll quit, you sexist pig."

"One word to Moira and your goose is cooked."

"She already knows," Frances said. "And she agrees with me that unless you and Tommy get all stupid on me, I'll do field work until my seventh month, and office work right up to term."

"And that's another thing, I want those nasty comments to stop, hormones or not."

She softened. "I am sorry, William."

"Pickles and ice cream?"

"Gads, no. But maybe a peanut butter sandwich . . . with anchovies."

He caressed her face. "I love you, Mrs. Lane."

She smiled. "And I love you, Mr. Lane. But at this moment I'm starved out of my mind."

They put on robes and went downstairs, where Frannie sipped her wine, the last, she promised, until after the baby was born, while she sat at the counter watching her husband fix them a light supper of toasted french bread, thinly sliced salmon with cream cheese, capers, onion slivers, and corchinons.

"What happens if the box is where you hid it, but when you bring it up it's empty?"

"Then we go to plan B, which is putting pressure on Speyer and his merry band to see what shakes out."

She shuddered. "I see why you think diving in a couple of thousand feet of water is the easier alternative. People could start getting killed."

"Which is why you're on the sidelines as of now."

She held her peace, watching him, but when the time came she would damned well make up her own mind.

VACA KEY

Lane hitched a ride to Key West aboard a Navy VIP Beechcraft bizjet, then rented a Chevy Caprice for the forty-five mile drive back up the Overseas Highway to Marathon. The Augusta-Bell Jet Ranger helicopter was sitting on the pad at the Vaca Key Oceanographic Institute when he got there just before noon. The day was brutally hot, no breeze, the ocean a hazy flat calm blue. The chopper's pilot, dressed in shorts, a T-shirt, and a baseball cap, was doing her walkaround. Lane watched her for a couple of minutes. She was young, very tall and thin with a runway model's figure, but she moved around the machine with an air of experience and confidence.

He got out of the car, the heat immediately plastering his Abercrombie and Fitch short-sleeved safari shirt to his back, and walked over to her. "Good morning. Are you my pilot?"

The woman glanced over her shoulder at him, and then went back to what she was doing, checking the fuel filters for water and other contaminants. "I am if your name is Bill Lane."

"In the flesh. And you're Ms. . . ?"

The woman buttoned up the access hatch and turned with a smile. "Actually it's *Doctor* Susan Hartley. I'm the chief scientist here."

"Open mouth, insert foot," Lane said with a grin.

"Sorry about that, but nobody told me." They shook hands.

"No problem, Bill. I'm not the usual pilot, but I was heading out to the *Deep Sound* anyway, so I decided to hang around until you showed up."

"This isn't a scientific mission, Doctor."

"It is now," she said. She glanced at the overnight bag he carried. "Is that all your gear?"

"I travel light," Lane said. "This could get a little dicey."

"That's what Tony told me. Maybe you can explain the deal to me on the way out."

OVER THE STRAITS OF FLORIDA

The haze began to clear ten miles off shore, and at three thousand feet there was some relief from the heat, though not much. Dr. Hartley was a relaxed, competent pilot. But Lane didn't want her on this mission.

"Are you going to tell me exactly who you are and what's going on?" she asked. They wore headsets so they didn't have to shout.

"We're going after a cargo ship that sunk last week in about six hundred fathoms. There's something aboard that I have to bring up."

"They found her yesterday." She gave Lane a pensive look. "Funny, there was nothing in the newspapers about it."

"It's going to stay that way. And once I get what I came for, the *Deep Sound* is getting the hell out of there before the Cuban navy comes sniffing around."

"Why don't you ask our Coast Guard for help? That would hold the Cubans at bay."

"We don't want to advertise what we're doing. The *Deep Sound* is a research vessel out there doing science and nothing more."

She nodded as if Lane had given her the answer she'd expected. "That's good, because I'll really be doing research. We're catching sharks for Mote Marine over in Sarasota." She looked at him again. "You work for the government. CIA?"

"Something like that," Lane said. "But I want you to drop me off and then get back to the institute. You can have your ship back tomorrow."

"Not a chance," she said easily.

"This isn't going to be fun and games. The captain and his entire crew went down with that ship. They were murdered. The people we're going up against aren't screwing around."

Dr. Hartley concentrated on her flying for a minute, obviously working out what she'd just been told. When she turned back to Lane she had a nervous but expectant look on her narrow but pleasant face. "Unless you mean to swim down to the wreck, you're going to need me," she said. "I'm the submersible driver."

DEEP SOUND II

A slight swell was running in the Gulf Stream, but the 230-foot research vessel held her position with bow and stern thrusters. The speed and direction of the ocean currents, the size and bearing of the waves, the speed and direction of the wind, and the picture from the sonar showing the exact location of the wreck were all fed into a computer which in turn controlled the thrusters.

Dr. Hartley planted the Bell Ranger's landing gear firmly on the rear deck helipad, and even before the rotors came to a complete halt a couple of crewmen were chocking the wheels and tying the chopper down.

"The captain's up in the center," one of the crewmen told them. Dr. Hartley led the way up to the research center on the bridge deck. Captain Tony Riggiro and another man were studying a large-scale chart. A half-dozen technicians and scientists were monitoring a lot of expensive-looking electronic equipment jammed into the big room.

Riggiro looked up with a big grin. "About time you finally got here." He and Lane, who towered a full head over him, gave each other a warm hug. "How's Frannie?"

"Fine. We missed you at the wedding."

Riggiro was sharp, and very good looking with his dark hair and dreamy Italian eyes. "I didn't want to give my girlfriends any ideas." He glanced over at Dr. Hartley. "Bill and I go a long way back. He saved my life."

"We saved each other's lives," Lane corrected.

"I'd like you to meet Gary Lenz, my first officer. He keeps me sober and honest."

Lenz looked like a football halfback, with a friendly smile. "Nice to meet you," he said, shaking hands. "But unless you've got jet lag or something, I think we should jump on this right now."

"We might have some company," Riggiro explained. "There's been a Cuban gunboat sniffing around just over the horizon since before dawn. We picked up her lights while it was still dark, and our radar detectors have been going crazy since then."

"I'll get *Sounder* ready to dive," Dr. Hartley said. "Is there any special equipment we'll need?"

"That depends on how the *Maria* is lying," Lane said.

Lenz pointed to a position on the chart. "She's in five hundred-eighty fathoms of water, listing about eighteen degrees on her starboard side." He handed Lane a couple of photographs taken yesterday afternoon from an unmanned submersible. "She looks to be pretty well intact. Whatever happened blew the bottom out of her about midships, and punched a smaller hole in her bow. The props were probably still turning as she started to go down which drove her bow first. But she somehow straightened out before she hit bottom and stayed more or less in one piece."

"We didn't see any bodies," Riggiro said. "What happened to the crew?"

"I'm not sure, but I think that they were sealed in the crews' mess, amidships, when the explosives went off."

Riggiro and his first officer exchanged a significant look. "Whoever pushed the button was a bad man."

"That's why I'm here, Tony." Lane showed one of the photographs to Dr. Hartley. "What I'm looking for is stashed in a fire equipment locker on the bilge deck just to the port of the center line aft."

"Maybe we can get to it down one of the passageways from the main deck. What is it?"

"A metal box, about two feet on each side. Weighs about a hundred pounds."

"Take a heli-arc torch and cut a hole in the hull," Riggiro said. "Bill can go in with the dizzy." The deep sea environmental suit, dizzy for short, was designed by NASA to take a man to depths of three thousand feet or more. It was constructed like a space suit, except that its rigid body was made of a superstrong and very light titanium alloy. The National Security Agency had asked for the suit to retrieve a spy satellite whose top-secret core had splashed more or less intact into the Indian Ocean.

"Have you ever used one before?" Dr. Hartley asked skeptically.

"Bill helped design it," Riggiro said.

Dr. Hartley grinned. "Open mouth, insert foot. I believe that's the proper phrase," she said. "I'll get *Sounder* ready."

The *Sounder* was an oddly shaped submersible designed for depths well in excess of ten thousand feet. It looked like an insect with two very thick bubble eyes made of a transparent metal alloy, a number of legs which were actually sensors and tools, a pair of skids to set down on the deck, and ten electrically driven ducted propellers for maneuvering. Divided into two sections, the upper two-thirds was for the pilot, crew, and passengers. The lower section, built like a diving bell, contained two diving suits along with some other diving and emergency equipment, and a large well that could be opened to the sea.

Lane climbed into the seat next to Dr. Hartley as the hatch above them was sealed and she put pressure in the craft. They donned headsets. "We're going to be at thirty-five hundred feet, so everything that you do has to be exactly correct. One mistake and you're dead. No second chances. Have you been there before?"

"Once or twice," Lane said.

"I want you to do everything exactly as I tell you. My life depends on your actions as well. Tony gives you high marks, but he'll be safely topside."

"I have a job to do down there, Doctor. I neither like it, nor am I looking forward to making the dive, but it has to be done. I'm not here to interfere with your science or to give you a hard time."

"Okay," Dr. Hartley said. "Anyway, the name is Susan."

"Fair enough."

Susan Hartley opened the channel that provided a comms link with the *Deep Sound II* via the tether. "*Deep Sound*, this is *Sounder*, how do you copy?"

"You sound good, Susie," Riggiro came back. "I'm showing a green board."

She scanned her instruments. "So am I. Let's go diving."

"Stand by."

A big deck crane lifted the *Sounder* off her cradle, moved her into position over the broad slot in the hull, and lowered her gently into the water. For the first thirty or forty feet there was plenty of light, but it began to grow dim out their windows below 150 feet, and by 500 feet it was hard to see much of anything. At 1,000 feet they were in an alien world of perpetual darkness.

"We'll be approaching the bottom in fifteen minutes," Susan Hartley said. "I'll wait until then to turn on the outside lights. We don't need them now."

"I'll go below and get suited up," Lane told her.

"Like I said, Bill, by the numbers. We're not here to take unnecessary risks."

Lane climbed down to the lower compartment, sealing the massive hatch above him. "I'm sealed," he said into his mike. "The pressure is coming up."

"I'm showing green," Susan Hartley came back.

Because of the light alloy it was made of, the dizzy weighed only one hundred pounds, but it was bulky and had to be put on one section at a time, starting with the torso shell. The chamber was warm because of the increasing pressure. Lane was sweating profusely by the time he had donned all but the helmet.

"How are you doing?" Susan Hartley asked.

"I'm suited up except for the helmet. But it's hot down here. I could use a cold beer."

"I'll buy you one when we get topside," she promised. "I have the ship on sonar now. I'll switch on the lights. You have a TV monitor in the overhead equipment bay."

"Got it."

"I'll pipe the picture down to you."

"We're going to have company real soon," Lenz said, looking up from the radar screen.

"The Cubans?" Riggiro asked.

"I think it's one of their foil boats. She's doing forty knots." Lenz studied the horizon to the south through binoculars. "There," he said after a couple of minutes.

Riggiro took the glasses and studied the oncoming ship. "Cuban navy all right," he said. "She's a Russian-made *Turya*-class hydrofoil cutter. Even if we wanted to, we couldn't outrun her."

"Guns?"

"A pair of twenty-fives forward, and a pair of fifty-seven millimeter cannons aft," Riggiro said, lowering the binoculars. "That's not counting four torpedo tubes and a crew of thirty."

"Do we call in the reinforcements?" Lenz asked. The other crew members and technicians shot them worried glances.

Riggiro shook his head. "We'll trust Bill on this one for the moment." He looked at the others. "We're a research vessel doing legitimate science in international waters. *Capisce?*"

They nodded.

"Make sure that we're ready to send out a distress signal the instant I give the word, though," Riggiro said as an aside to his first officer. He picked up the mike and called the *Sounder* as he watched the Cuban warship closing with them. "Susie, are you at the wreck yet?"

"Just got there."

"We have company."

"Who is it, Tony, the Cubans?" Lane's voice broke in.

"It's a Turya-class cutter coming in fast on our starboard bow."

"Have they tried to make contact by radio, or blinker lamp?"

"Not yet."

"Okay, you know the drill. No gunplay. We're scientists on a legitimate mission."

"Don't drag your feet, they might want us to get the hell out of here."

"I'm sure that's exactly what they're going to want," Lane said. "Stall them."

"I'll do my best."

The light from the industrial cutting torch, along with the massive amount of gas and debris it produced, was enough to completely blot out the image on Lane's monitor.

"The steel plate is very thick here," Susan Hartley said.

"Not as thick as it would be if it weren't a double hull. How much longer?"

"Five minutes, so you'd better get ready."

Lane donned the helmet, cocking it thirty degrees to the right until the collar threads were engaged, and then he twisted it left and engaged the locking slides. The suit automatically pressurized with the same oxy-helium mixture as the *Sounder* was on. It made their voices sound like Alvin and the Chipmunks.

Once he left the *Sounder* he would not be tethered.

He could still communicate with the submersible via aquaphone, but that would not work very well once he got inside the *Maria*'s hull. For all practical purposes he would be on his own.

The picture on the monitor cleared as the *Sounder* backed off, showing a man-size black hole that Susan Hartley had cut into the hull. Lane plugged in his temporary comms link.

"Good job," he said. "Have you ever thought about going into construction?"

"Only when a paper I submit to a research journal gets rejected for another rewrite."

"I'm told that doesn't happen much."

Susan Hartley laughed. "Our skids are about eight feet off the bottom, and it looks as if we got lucky—it's sand, not much silt."

"Don't leave without me," Lane said. He unplugged his comms link, grabbed the overhead hand rails, and stepped out into the well. When he was in position, he let go and sank slowly into the ink black water lit only by the powerful lights on *Sounder*'s bows.

His buoyancy was only slightly negative so his landing was easy, and he headed immediately for the stern of the *Maria*, less than thirty feet away.

When he was out from under the submersible, he looked back. Susan Hartley waved from the left bubble and he waved back.

"Copy?" he asked.

"You sound like you're underwater," she replied, her voice distorted but understandable.

"What was your first clue, Doc?" Lane laughed. He turned, made his way across to the ship and shone his lantern into the opening. An involuntary shiver ran up his spine. He was not particularly claustrophobic, but there were seventeen dead men entombed here. And he had come very close to being one of them. Now he was back.

The hull plate had fallen away from the ship, indicating there might have been an air bubble inside the hull, but Captain Zimmer's body, which was on the other side of the ship, had not been forced out.

Lane gingerly jumped up to the lip of the hole, steadied himself for a moment, then ducked inside. He was on the port side of the bilge deck at the stern, his back facing the bow. He took a few moments to orient himself; his underwater light penetrated only fifteen or twenty feet and the ship was lying partially on her side. But there didn't seem to be much damage back here, or at least none that he could see, and very little debris.

He turned to face the bow, when a hand reached out and touched his face plate. He scrambled back, his heart in his throat, and swung his flashlight in an effort to ward off the apparition floating in front of him.

It was Captain Zimmer, the back of his head partially blown away, his eyes open, his mouth gaping as if he were screaming in shock and horror.

Slowly Lane's heart slowed down. Bile was bitter in the back of his throat. This was Speyer's doing. The entire affair. There was no way he would let the bastard get away with it. No way in hell.

Lane eased the captain's body aside, and the beam of his flashlight fell on the fire equipment locker where he had stashed the box.

He half shuffled, half slid down the sloping walkway to it, released the catch and opened the hatch. The box was where he had placed it, wedged behind a large coil of fire hose.

Clipping the light on his right arm, it took him only a few moments to pull the box out of the closet, turn and struggle with it back to the strong lights at the opening in the hull. He let it fall outside to the ocean floor, then jumped out after it.

He gave Susan Hartley the thumbs-up sign. "Got it," he said.

Twenty minutes after they had first spotted her, the Cuban navy cutter with the number 193 painted on her bows was stopped one hundred feet off *Deep Sound*'s starboard side. Riggiro and Lenz studied her through binoculars. There were at least a dozen armed men on deck in addition to four or five they spotted on the bridge and bridge wings.

"Should we try to call them?" Lenz asked.

"Not yet. They're here and watching us. They can see the cable so they know that we have something down. And we're not trying to run. But we're in international waters so we have just as much right to be here as they do."

"Where I come from the guys with the guns usually have the most rights," Lenz said. He was an ex-Special Forces sergeant, and he'd been born and raised in the Bronx.

Riggiro called down to the *Sounder*. "Susie, is Bill back aboard yet?"

"He's under the skirt now. He's got the box."

"The Cuban navy is parked right next to us. We're going to start pulling you up as soon as Bill's aboard."

"Give us a couple of minutes."

"Will do," Riggiro said, and replaced the mike. He turned to Lenz to tell him to have the winch operator stand by, when the Cuban cutter hailed them by radio.

"*Deep Sound Two*, this is the Cuban patrol vessel off your starboard side. We are sending a boarding party across to check your documents. Lower your ladder."

"Negative, negative," Riggiro radioed. "We are a scientific vessel engaged in legal pursuits in international waters. Permission to board is denied."

"*Deep Sound Two*, we will fire on your vessel if you do not comply immediately. *Comprende?*"

"Oh, oh," Lenz said.

Two large rubber boats were launched over the side of the warship. They both started across. In one were a half-dozen armed men and two officers in white uniforms, sidearms strapped to their hips. In the other were a man at the outboard, and two men outfitted with diving gear.

"Okay, call the Key West Coast Guard," Riggiro told Lenz. He got on the ship's PA. "Scotty, we're going to have company. Lower the starboard ladder and then stand by the *Sounder*'s winch. We'll be bringing them up."

The others on the bridge and in the Research Center were looking at him.

"Nobody raises so much as a finger," Riggiro said. "If they ask a question, answer it, and then shut up."

They nodded.

He got on the comms link to the *Sounder*. "Is Bill aboard yet?"

"I'm here," Lane came back.

"They're sending over eight armed men to check our papers. But it looks like they mean to put a couple of divers into the water, too."

"Susan, are we secure to start back up, even with the lower hatch open?" Lane asked.

"My board is green," she said.

"Okay, we're bringing you up," Riggiro said. "And we're calling Coast Guard Key West."

"Good, the timing should be just about right," Lane

said. "Listen to me, Tony. Don't give those guys any trouble. Do exactly what they tell you to do."

"That's my plan."

"And no matter what happens, keep hauling in the tether."

"What are you talking about?"

"They want the box, but I'm not going to give it to them. Just keep hauling on the cable, no matter what."

Sounder started up almost immediately. Riggiro was wasting no time. Down here they were vulnerable, but as Lane hurriedly stripped the diving suit from his body he understood that the captain of the Cuban warship was covering all his bases by not only sending someone aboard the *Deep Sound* but by sending a couple of divers down to meet the submersible on the way up.

"Are you ready to depressurize and come up here?" Susan Hartley asked.

"No," Lane said. "Can they monitor our conversation topside?"

"Not now."

"Good, then this is exactly what we're going to do . . ."

As the Cuban boarding party came up the ladder, the two divers in the other inflatable entered the water and disappeared.

"Bill, the divers are in the water," Riggiro phoned the *Sounder*. But the circuit had been switched off.

"What the hell is he up to?" Lenz asked.

Riggiro shook his head. "I don't know, but whatever it is, it'll be good." He watched as the six Cuban navy ratings stayed on deck while the two officers made their way up. "Just make sure that Scotty keeps hauling on the cable." He looked at the others. "Keep your cool, folks. Our coast guard is on the way."

The two officers came through the door, looked with interest at the equipment and technicians in the research center, then came forward to the bridge. The taller one, lieutenant's bars on his shoulder boards and an insolent sneer on his narrow mouth, came first.

"Who is the captain of this vessel?" he demanded.

Riggiro looked the man up and down. "I am," he said at length. "And I will register a complaint with my government about this illegal boarding. We are a legitimate research vessel on a scientific mission."

The officer was unimpressed. "You are diving on a wreck that is the property of the Cuban government."

"Not in international waters."

"We'll see," the Cuban said disdainfully. "Come with me."

Lenz stepped forward, but Riggiro held him back. "Where are you taking me?"

"Down to the main deck to await the arrival of your submersible," the Cuban said. "Where else, *Capitán*?"

"We have notified our coast guard."

"We know that. But our business here will be finished before they arrive." The Cuban officer stepped aside. "After you, *Capitán*."

The depth gauge approached a hundred feet. Lane had donned scuba gear including mask and fins. The water in the open well at his feet was a bright swimming pool aqua. He checked to make sure that the large dive knife was free in its sheath on his chest.

"I see them," Susan called down. "They're just above us. Maybe thirty feet."

"Count to ten and then get out of here."

"I think you're crazy."

Lane chuckled. "Flattery will get you everywhere, Doctor," he said, and he stepped out into the well and started down.

Before he cleared the *Sounder*'s skids, he adjusted his buoyancy control vest so that he was slightly negative, then he curled up in a fetal position as if he'd been injured, or as if he was suffering from the bends. His right hand curled around the grip of the dive knife.

At the count of ten he heard the *Sounder*'s electric motors come to life, and felt the backwash from her propellers. He let his body go completely limp and he slowly tumbled in the turbulence.

The two Cuban divers were about twenty feet above him now and to the right. They watched as the untethered *Sounder* headed to the north, away from the *Deep Sound* and the Cuban warship whose hulls loomed directly overhead.

Lane continued to turn slowly end over end. The next time he was upright the divers were heading his way. They were about five feet apart, one of them a little above the other.

When he was facing downward he slipped the foot-long razor-sharp knife from its sheath, and tensed, ready to spring.

The first diver to reach him grabbed his vest and pulled him around. Moving deceptively slowly, Lane reached up and cut the diver's air hose. The man reared back, his eyes wide in panic, but Lane held him as a shield against the other diver who realized what was happening and was bringing his spear gun to bear.

He fired wildly, the spear embedding itself in his dead partner's thigh. Lane cut the man's weightbelt free and the body shot toward the surface.

The second diver frantically tried to reload his

speargun as Lane came at him. At the last moment he dropped the gun and reached for his knife, but it was too late. Lane batted the diver's hand away and cut his air hose.

The Cuban fought like a wild man, knowing that his only hope for survival was getting free and making it to the surface. But Lane spun him around and held him by the valve on his tank so that he couldn't pull himself free.

This was no innocent navy diver, Lane told himself. These bastards were working with Helmut Speyer. Thirty-five hundred feet below them seventeen men were locked forever in the wreck of the *Maria*. And these two had come down here to make sure that Lane and Susan did not survive.

After a minute the diver's struggles stopped. Lane cut the man's weightbelt and the body shot to the surface as the first one had.

One of the Cubans at the rail shouted something and pointed to large air bubbles coming to the surface.

The officer with Riggiro ran over to the rail as the first diver's body came to the surface facedown, arms and legs splayed out. He was obviously dead.

Something was going on that the officer could not understand. First the cable winching up the submersible had gone slack, and now this. An accident?

A second air bubble broke the surface and a minute later the body of the second diver appeared a few feet from the first. It wasn't an accident. It was a trap.

The officer spun around as he yanked out his pistol. "*Bastardo!*" He fired a shot that ricocheted off a bollard as Riggiro ducked behind the winch.

The other men took up defensive postures and held their weapons at the ready, but they didn't know what was going on, or who they were supposed to shoot.

The two divers were dead and one of their officers had apparently gone loco.

"Miguel," the second officer shouted as he raced down from the bridge. "We must go. Now!"

The cutter's whistle shrieked, the noise rattling the glass in the *Deep Sound*'s bridge windows, but before the officer on deck could react, a deeper, mind-numbing roar blotted out every other sound.

He looked up as a pair of F-14/D U.S. Coast Guard Tomcat fighters came thundering in very low from the north, Phoenix and Sidewinder missiles attached to their wing racks.

When the jets started their inbound turn two miles out, the Cuban warship's whistle sounded the recall again. All of the *Deep Sound*'s crew and scientists had ducked out of sight, and in the water the divers' bodies were being recovered.

"*Bastardos*," the officer muttered, holstering his pistol. He headed with his men for the boarding ladder.

When the Cuban warship left, Lane swam over to where the tether had been lowered into the water. Susan edged the *Sounder* slowly into position and he attached the big hook and comms cable. Moments later the submersible started up and he rode on top with it, acutely aware that he had killed two men and that it was another thing he would have to live with for the rest of his life.

The sun was setting and the *Deep Sound* was heading back to the institute on Vaca Key. The *Sounder* was attached to her cradle on deck and the helicopter was secured on the pad.

They were gathered around a big tank of fresh water on deck in which the metal box Lane had pulled from the wreck had been placed.

Susan Hartley kept glancing at Lane as one of the technicians used an underwater saw to cut the seal holding the lid. "I couldn't believe what I was seeing," she said.

"They would have killed both of us."

"How do you know?" she demanded, her voice low so that the others couldn't hear her over the noise of the saw.

"I just know," Lane said. "But I'm sorry that you had to see it. If this were a perfect world, things like that would never happen. But this is not a perfect world."

"No, it isn't," she said, looking away.

The technician set the saw down and carefully eased the box open with a small pry bar. One of the others took the lid from him and set it aside.

"Rocks," the tech said. He took one of them out of the box and pulled it out of the water for them to see. It was about the size of a grapefruit, but flattened, its edges smooth and rounded. "Granite, maybe. River rock, I'd guess, though I'm not a geologist." He shook his head. "One thing's for sure, Mr. Lane, these sure aren't diamonds." He looked back at the box. "And another thing I'd be willing to bet money on. This box is no more than a couple of years old. It sure as hell wasn't lying around underwater for very long."

"A decoy?" Riggiro asked.

"Looks like it," Lane said. "The problem is, what was the Cuban navy doing out here?"

"Legitimizing your search," Tom Hughes said on the phone ten minutes later.

"That's what Tony thinks, and I have to agree with both of you," Lane said. "Send somebody out to Kalispell to take a quick look at Speyer's ranch. If he's still there, watch him to see what he does."

"How about if he's already packed his bags and headed for the hills?"

"If there's nobody out there, it might be worth our while to take a quick look around. They might have left something behind. Check with Linda Boulton, the Bureau's SAC at Helena. She might be able to lend a hand."

"When are you coming home?"

"We should be back to the institute sometime in the morning."

"I'll send a jet to pick you up."

"Good. Now let me talk to Frannie."

"She and Moira are out shopping for baby clothes," Hughes said, obviously delighted. "Welcome to the club, papa."

10

KALISPELL

Helmut Speyer decided as he was placing the last of his confidential papers into his attaché case that he would miss the serenity of this place after all.

Gloria was already down at the airstrip aboard the Gulfstream ready to leave, and there was no one else left in the compound. He took a moment to step out of his study onto the second floor veranda and drink the last of his wine. The mountains were beautiful at this time of the afternoon.

He smiled. The operation was proceeding exactly according to his plans. The only glitch was the stupid research ship stumbling onto the *Maria*. His military contact in Havana had assured him that the scientists would never get near the wreck, but even that was of no real consequence, because there was nothing aboard, except for a few bodies. And there were no witnesses.

Baumann parked the jeep in the driveway, spotted Speyer on the balcony and came up. He'd left with the ADM truck earlier today.

"They got clear without notice?" Speyer asked, stepping back into his study.

"Yes, sir. I followed them all the way down to Interstate Ninety, and watched them head east. There was no trouble whatsoever."

Speyer closed and locked the sliding door, finished his wine, and set his glass on the side table. "Excellent, and is everyone else gone?"

"It's just us, Herr *Kapitän.*"

"A search has been made for anything that might . . . hinder our plans if found?"

Baumann nodded. "All that is left are legitimate business documents."

"What about the confidence course and firing range? Have they been cleaned up and converted?"

"Yes, sir. We have been fond of four-wheeling and of running dirt bikes."

"The barracks?"

"It takes a large staff to run a ranch this big."

Speyer locked his attaché case and got his jacket from the arm of the couch. "What about Browne's car?"

"The explosives and weapons have been disposed of, and we dug a trench with the backhoe and buried the entire vehicle to the west of the orchard. Someone might find it if they look hard enough. But it would take a lot of time."

Speyer looked around his study. "For all practical purposes by the time someone does come out here to snoop around, all they will find is what we want them to find. We're obviously away on vacation. But it'll be just as obvious that we intend to return."

"I hope they hold their breath waiting," Baumann made a little joke.

Speyer clapped him on the shoulder. "You have done well, Ernst. Military commanders from Sparta to Berlin understood that the men keeping their armies together were their sergeants. It is no different in my little army."

"Thank you, sir," Baumann said. "But there is the other problem we discussed."

"Konrad will clean up any lingering problems. That's what friends are for," Speyer made his own little joke.

"No, sir, I meant the woman. The glider pilot who landed here. We received a possible identification this morning. I didn't get a chance to tell you before I left with the truck."

Speyer looked at him with some interest. Although she'd probably been the woman in the lobby of the Grand Hotel on the morning of the shooting, they had found no evidence that their perimeter had been breached the afternoon of her landing. "Who is she?"

"Her name might be Frances Shipley. Our contact in the Bureau fingerprint section was a little vague because we managed to get only a partial print off the glider canopy while she was here at the house. But if he got that right, then she worked for British Intelligence until last year."

This news was totally unexpected and it took Speyer momentarily aback. "Whatever she came looking for, she couldn't have found it. She wasn't here long enough. Was there any connection between her and Browne?"

"None that we can come up with so far."

"She might have been working for the Germans," Speyer said. "No matter, though. In ten minutes we'll be gone from here forever. And by next week, perhaps sooner, we'll be completely out of their reach."

NEW YORK

It was 2:00 A.M. when the Gulfstream touched down at La Guardia Airport. They'd managed to get a few hours sleep on the flight, and even Gloria, who had stayed off the booze, managed to nod off. This would be the last flight in or out for the night.

"You know what to do for us in Washington,"

Speyer told his wife. "I'll join you and the others sometime tomorrow."

"Do you want me to send the plane back for you?" she asked. She was like an actress playing an earnest part in a bad movie.

"Send it to Miami. If anybody is looking for us, that'll throw them off in the wrong direction."

"What about the crew?"

"Ted knows what to do," Speyer said. "Don't worry about that part. Your job is to make sure that the safe house is ready for us."

She reached up and touched his lips with her fingertips. "We're almost finished with this, aren't we, darling?"

"Soon."

"All this running around and uncertainty is very hard on my nerves. I don't know how much longer I can stand it. We need a little fun in our lives again, like the old days in Hollywood."

Speyer smiled although he didn't mean it. He'd had just about enough of her to last a lifetime. "It's only a matter of a few days now, *Liebchen*, you'll see."

Baumann came to the door of the plane. "I have the car," he said.

"You shouldn't run into any trouble. Just stay put," Speyer told his wife.

"Anything could happen—"

"Do as I say."

The Japanese cargo vessel *Akai Maru* was tied up to the Brooklyn docks below Red Hook. Speyer and Baumann arrived in the rental Mercedes E320 a little before 3:00 A.M., the deadest hour for traffic in the entire five boroughs. They parked just outside the security gate. Speyer called the ship's captain, Shintaro Kato.

"You are on time, Mr. Speyer," the captain said. He'd been waiting for the call. "Do you have the remainder of the money?"

"Yes."

"Very well. In five minutes you may proceed through the gate onto the dock. My first officer and I will meet you in front of the warehouse directly across from my ship. It is thirty-seven B."

"What about customs?"

"The package has already been cleared. Be there in five minutes." The captain hung up.

"All he wants is his money and we'll get it," Speyer told Baumann.

"I don't trust the bastard."

Speyer chuckled. "You don't trust anybody. The good captain neither knows nor cares what's inside the box. He's just interested in getting paid."

Baumann started to object, but Speyer held him off.

"If Kato had wanted to double-cross us, he could have taken our money when he picked us up after the *Maria* went down, killed us and let our bodies go down with the captain's gig instead of taking us to Miami. The only reason he took a chance bringing the box here to New York and clearing it through customs was for the second half of his money. He's not going to do anything to jeopardize his position now."

Baumann held his silence. He was glum.

"The next twenty-four hours will be the most difficult. After that we'll really be on our way."

The security guard raised the barrier to let them through without asking to see their passes. Baumann drove down the lane between warehouses, across three sets of railroad tracks, beneath the legs of a gigantic crane, and onto the docks. There were a lot of lights and activity at a couple of ships farther up the quay, but here the night was quiet. The *Akai Maru* had already been unloaded, and was waiting for clearance before leaving.

The service doors to warehouse 37B were slightly ajar. Baumann parked the Mercedes in the deeper shadows on the south side of the big building and they went the rest of the way on foot.

"Did you bring a weapon?" Speyer asked.

"Naturally."

"Good. But don't even think about using it except as a last resort. All Kato wants is the money." Speyer raised the small leather bag he carried. It contained one hundred thousand dollars in one hundred dollar bills.

"If he sticks with the plan, he'll get no trouble," Baumann said menacingly. "If not, I'll kill him."

The captain and first mate were waiting for them in the darkness just inside the service doors. Kato was typical of many Japanese, short and slightly built. He wore wire-rimmed glasses and was dressed all in black. His mate was huge, built like a sumo wrestler, with a permanent scowl etched on his broad features. He, too, was dressed in black.

"Where is it?" Speyer demanded.

"Inside," Kato said. "Did you bring the money?"

Speyer held up the leather bag. Kato reached for it, but Speyer pulled it back. "Let me see the package first. An even trade."

The first officer, whose name they never learned, looked as if he was ready to tear them apart. Baumann was to the left of Speyer and half a step back. He would have only a moment to draw his gun and fire if the big Japanese started to make a move.

But Kato smiled. "Of course. It is business," he said. "Just this way, gentlemen."

They followed him and the mate into the dimly lit warehouse. Crates and pallets of boxes and what looked like machinery were stacked in long rows, sometimes all the way up to the rafters twenty-five feet overhead. One corner of the warehouse was screened off from the rest as a bonded holding area, secured by a heavy mesh door that was padlocked. Inside they could see crates and boxes marked with the brand names and logos of expensive products; Hermès, Cristal, Baccarat, Louis Vuitton.

Captain Kato unlocked the door and the mate stepped inside and brought out an olive drab duffel bag stamped U.S. ARMY. A customs clearance tag was attached to it. He set it on the floor, opened it and pulled the bag down around the metal box with the skull and crossbones and the single German word VORSICHT!

"This is what I believe you want returned to you," Captain Kato said.

"Yes, and this is yours," Speyer said, handing the leather bag to the captain.

The first mate stepped back so that Baumann could inspect the box, and then resecure the duffel bag as Kato opened the leather bag and checked the money.

"Everything is in order?" Speyer asked.

"Yes. And it would be to our mutual benefit if this transaction were never to be spoken of again."

Speyer nodded to Baumann, who hefted the duffle bag and slung it over his shoulder. It weighed one hundred pounds, but Baumann didn't let the effort show. The first mate had tossed the duffle bag around with one hand as if it were a loaf of bread.

"You cannot know how correct you are, Captain," Speyer said. "Give us a couple of minutes to get out of here. It wouldn't do for us to be seen together."

"As you wish."

MANHATTAN

Thirty minutes later they were across the Manhattan Bridge and had picked up East River Drive heading north. Almost all the traffic at this hour were trucks.

"Are we being followed?" Speyer asked.

Baumann, who was driving, had been checking the rearview mirror since they'd left the docks. He shook his head. "You were right about the money."

"Yes, I was, Ernst. But you were just as right to be cautious. It could have gone either way."

"They didn't tamper with the seal. I checked."

Speyer chuckled. "Kato wouldn't have answered his phone had they opened the box."

Baumann shot him a sharp look. "Do you know that for a fact, Herr *Kapitän*?" No one knew what the box actually contained except for Speyer, though Baumann had guessed some of it.

Speyer was too keyed up to let Baumann's tone of voice irritate him. "If you would like to check it out we can pull over and you can open the box. Only you'll be good enough to let me get upwind of you first. Three or four miles, perhaps."

"No thanks," Baumann said.

They took 79th Street west through Central Park, coming out by the American Museum of Natural History, and drove up to West 86th where they got lucky with a parking spot in front of a fashionable four-story brownstone a half block west of Columbus. The only thing moving was a garbage truck in the next block.

Baumann shut off the car and started to open the door.

"Wait," Speyer said.

They sat for a full five minutes. The garbage truck finally turned left a couple of blocks away. A cab cruised past, and the street was quiet.

"It would be good to have Browne with us now," Baumann said softly.

"He asked too many questions."

"He had a conscience."

"Yes, it was too bad," Speyer said, missing Baumann's meaning.

They locked up the car and went inside. Speyer dropped their overnight bags in the front stairhall, and went with Baumann, who carried the duffle bag down into the basement.

Speyer had arranged to buy this place and have it remodeled three years ago for this operation. He and Gloria had come out here a few times since then to shop and see some Broadway shows, so the neighbors were used to the place being empty most of the time.

He unlocked the steel door at the end of a short corridor, flipped on the lights, and stepped aside. Baumann brought in the duffle bag and set it on a bench in the middle of the small room, which was no more than twelve by twelve with a low ceiling. It was crammed with state of the art scientific equipment, including a powerful microscope connected to a computer via a CCD, or charge-coupled device, so that whatever was being studied could be manipulated on the computer monitor. There was a mass spectrometer, a powerful centrifuge, a cryogenic unit that used liquid nitrogen to quick-freeze and hold samples, and a very sophisticated laminar air flow glove box in which samples could be isolated from the outside air, and yet be safely manipulated by the operator.

All of it had been purchased at various times by dummy labs and research institutions and shipped here over the past eighteen months. No matter how thoroughly any one checked the records, none of this equipment could ever be traced here.

Knowing about the disassembled agplane heading east by truck, listening to Speyer's comments and now seeing this set-up, Baumann put it all together.

"This will be worth more than three hundred million dollars, if we can pull it off," he said, awed.

Speyer smiled with pleasure. "A whole lot more. But you haven't seen everything yet, because when you do you won't be asking *if* we can pull it off, but *when* we'll do it." He clapped Baumann on the shoulder. "Let's have something to eat, and then get a few hours sleep. The next twenty-four hours are going to be busy.

Speyer, dressed in a dark tweed sport coat, polo shirt, and tan slacks, headed on foot down Columbus behind the museum. It was four-thirty in the afternoon and he was well rested. Despite his tension he'd managed to sleep most of the day. Baumann stayed behind to keep watch. Everything was proceeding according to his plans.

There were a lot of shops on this street, restaurants, small specialty grocery stores, and a few bars, some with apartments above and others with private clubs in the basements, holdovers from the speakeasy days of the twenties and thirties. Below a shop selling German cookware and foodstuffs was the German-American club that the locals called the Bund. Speyer was well known here, stopping by whenever he was in New York. Six months ago he'd asked the manager, Rudi Steiner, to keep his eye open for a guy with the right background for a little job of work that would pay very well.

Three months ago Steiner had come up with a good

possibility and he'd begun working the mark. It was his call that had allowed Speyer to start on the final stages of his operation: finding a diver, setting up the German end of the mission including finding the ex-KGB officers, and finally arranging for the two ships to get him and the box back to the States.

The barroom was dark. Four men played cards at one of the tables. In back someone was playing *Füssball*; he could hear the click of the ball and the thumps as the paddle handles were slapped sharply. Four men were scattered at the bar, drinking beers while watching the German television program *Deutsche Welle*.

Rudi Steiner had worked undercover for the Stasi at the United Nations before the Wall came down. He looked like a character from a movie about the *Afrika Korps*, blond, blue-eyed, with craggy, weather-beaten good looks. "*Willkommen, Herr Kapitän*," he said as Speyer took a seat at the bar.

"Not too busy this afternoon."

"Sometimes it's for the best." Steiner nodded toward the end of the bar. "That's him at the end. Name's Bernhard Metzler. Associate professor of molecular biology at New York University."

Metzler was a stoop-shouldered man with long gray hair in a ponytail. He was hunched over his beer.

"What's his story?" Speyer asked.

"He should have made full professor five years ago, but he's been passed over every year." Steiner smiled. "He's a bitter man."

"What'd you tell him about me?"

"That you're a wealthy eccentric, and you need some work done by a competent man. He practically jumped over the bar trying to get me to give him your name and address."

"What's he drinking?"

"Weiss Bier."

"Send us down a couple." Speyer got up, walked down to the end of the bar and took a seat next to Metzler.

"What the fuck do you want?" Metzler demanded, looking up.

"The right man for a difficult assignment," Speyer said. Steiner came with their beers, and he gave Metzler a nod.

"There I go with my big mouth again," Metzler said, sheepishly. "Sorry about that."

"No problem. Rudi tells me that you're a molecular biologist and that you'd be willing to take on a little job for the right price."

Metzler eyed him speculatively. He was hungry. "How little a job, and how much money?"

"The work might take you a couple of hours, and I'd be willing to pay you fifty thousand dollars. For your discretion as well as your expertise."

Metzler practically fell off his stool. "Where and when?"

"About two blocks from here and right now if you're sober enough to do the work. It's delicate."

Metzler shoved the beers aside and held out his right hand. It was as steady as a rock, and Speyer nodded.

"Very well. We'll see if we can't get you home in time for dinner a richer man than you are right now."

Speyer had been gone less than a half hour when he returned to the brownstone with Metzler. Out of old habits he scanned the street for the out of place car or pedestrian, the rooftops for the glint of binocular lenses, and the windows of the houses for surveillance. He spotted Baumann at a second floor window. The curtains had been drawn aside, and when Baumann stepped back the curtains remained open. It was the signal that all was well.

He mounted the stairs, opened the door with his key, and showed Metzler inside. Baumann was just coming down.

"Ernst, this is Bernhard Metzler. He's come to do the work for us," Speyer said, locking up.

"Pleased to meet you," Baumann said, shaking hands with the biologist. "Rudi Steiner gave you high marks."

"He said you guys were okay, too." Metzler was looking around the stairhall. "I'm going to do the work here?"

"Yes. We have a small laboratory set up in the basement. I think that you'll find it's more than adequate."

"Well, if I'm going to get home by dinner like you promised, let's get started." A crafty look came into his eyes. "How about the money?"

Speyer opened a small leather bag on the hall table and showed Metzler the money. The man practically licked his lips.

"It's downstairs," Speyer said. "I'll show you what I want you to do for us."

Speyer and Baumann waited in the doorway while Metzler inspected the laboratory equipment. He was impressed by what he saw, but he kept glancing nervously at the metal box with the skull and crossbones and warning in German.

"This is first-class stuff. Looks like it's never been used."

"We tried to think of everything that you might need," Speyer said.

"So what's in the box? Obviously a biohazard of some sort, but what?"

"It's a virus. But I'm not really sure what kind, or even if it's deadly or not. But I don't want to take any chances."

"What form is it in? Gas, liquid, powder?"

"I don't know. That's one of the things I want you to find out."

"What else?"

"The money I'm paying you is just as much for your discretion as anything else," Speyer warned.

"Look, I don't give a shit if you dump the lot into the reservoir. Once I get paid you can color me gone, because I'm getting out of this shithole of a city before the sun comes up again."

"What about your wife? Your family?"

"I don't have any. I was a hatchling."

Speyer gave Baumann a look. Metzler's situation was better than he'd hoped it would be. No one would miss him.

"I need to know exactly what we're dealing with for starts. Then I want a sample prepared for shipment and the rest of the material placed into the two air tanks next to the cryogenic unit."

Metzler looked at them. "Nitrogen. It's inert so no matter what form the material is in the gas won't affect it, and yet when you want it released all you'll have to do is open the valves."

"That's the plan."

Metzler gave Speyer a hard look. "One hundred thousand dollars," he said. "For my discretion, because the work isn't going to be all that tough."

"Very well. Ernst will see to it when you're finished."

"Then it's settled," Metzler said, rubbing his hands. He took off his jacket and had Baumann help him place the metal box into the chamber of the glove box. He put the two nitrogen tanks inside along with a half-pint air bottle for the sample, a battery-driven cutting tool, a pry bar and some wrenches, as well as the CCD microscope.

As the unit pressurized, he switched on the computer that was connected to the microscope, then pulled on the crisp white biohazard suit with a small air bottle. He sat in front of the box and placed his hands in the gloves, the sleeves coming all the way up to his shoulders.

"Are you going to tell me where this came from?"

"No," Speyer said. "I believe that you already have enough information."

"Just curious," Metzler said. He had the seal cut and the cover removed in less than ten minutes. The box was divided into four sections, each containing what looked like a small air cylinder with a standard high pressure metric laboratory valve. Each section was filled with a clear liquid.

"Feels like oil or maybe glycerine," Metzler said, removing the bottles. He used a small wrench to crack the valve on one of the cylinders and held a glass slide in front of the nozzle opening for a second, before closing the valve again.

He mounted the slide on the microscope's stage, then as he adjusted the focus he looked over his shoulder at the computer. The screen was filled with thousands of hook-shaped stick figures. Even as they watched, the figures started to come to life, twitching and moving after lying dormant for nearly sixty years.

"Jesus Christ," Metzler said softly. He looked at the bottles in the glove box and then back at the computer screen.

"What is it?" Speyer asked.

"I don't know," Metzler said, shaking his head. "I mean I don't know the strain; you need to have an infectious disease expert look at this. But it's an arbovirus, you know. It's got RNA and it's usually transmitted by a bug; mosquitoes or ticks. And it's damned active."

"Deadly?"

"Give you hemorrhagic fever. All the capillaries in your body start blowing out and you bleed to death internally. Kidney failure. It's not pretty."

"Do you have to get bitten by a bug to get it?"

"No," Metzler said. "My guess is that this was engineered, like a vaccine. Infect a host, then reproduce the virus from their blood. In this form spraying it into the air would work." He gave Speyer another hard look. "This came from a military lab somewhere. It's a goddamn weapon."

"Do you have a problem with that?" Speyer asked.

Metzler shook his head. "No, but I think that two hundred fifty thou might be a little closer to the mark."

"I can give you one hundred fifty; that's all we have here. But you may have this equipment."

"Not a chance. I'll take the money and run, but I wouldn't touch this stuff with a ten foot pole."

"How do we proceed?"

"I'll need a meter or so of high pressure hose and the valve caps that match the nitrogen tanks, the virus bottles, and the sample bottle."

"I think we have everything that you'll need here."

"I'll empty one of the nitrogen bottles, transfer all the virus material into it, then mix the gas from the second nitrogen bottle. When we're done both bottles will be charged with the virus and enough nitrogen to release it. I'll transfer some of that mix into your sample bottle." He shook his head again and glanced at the computer screen. The virus was very active. "I hope that whoever you send that little bottle to knows what the hell they're doing. Because it'd probably be enough to wipe out a couple city blocks if it got loose and the wind was right."

"Won't the outside of the bottles be contaminated?" Speyer asked.

"We'll wash everything down first," Metzler said. "Don't worry, I know what I'm doing, and believe me, I *will* be careful."

It was after ten by the time Metzler finished the job and the inside of the glove box was washed clean with an extremely powerful virus-killing antiseptic. He removed his hands from the gloves, took off the biohazard suit, then sat back and lit a cigarette as Speyer came to the doorway.

"Are you finished?"

"Finally," Metzler said. "Two of the old valves were stuck and I nearly stripped them."

"Is it safe to handle the bottles now, without having to wear a suit?"

"Completely." Metzler stood up and got his jacket. "Now, if you don't mind, I'll take my money and I'll get out of your hair."

"I want you to open the glove box first."

Metzler chuckled. "I guess I can't blame you." He stuck the cigarette in the corner of his mouth, depressurized the cabinet, and opened the front cover. He took out the sample bottle, laid it on the table, and then took out the nitrogen bottles and set them on the floor. He dusted off his hands and held them out. "Germ free. But before you move this shit around I'd suggest you put some tape on the valves in case they get jostled."

"You've done good work here," Speyer said.

Metzler's eyes narrowed imperceptibly. "Aren't you going to give me the speech about forgetting that

I ever met you or you're going to send big Ernst to break my legs or something?"

"You're a bright man. I don't think a warning is necessary."

Baumann appeared in the corridor behind Speyer. He was not carrying the leather money bag.

Metzler casually picked up the sample bottle. "Like you say, I am a bright man. By the time old Ernst there pulled out his gun and shot me, I would have opened the valve and we'd all die."

Speyer gave him an appraising look. "I don't think so."

"Your choice, pal. But if I'm going to die anyway, I might as well take you nut cases with me."

Baumann stopped in his tracks, uncertain what to do.

"Tell you what," Metzler said. "We're all going upstairs where you're going to get my money. Then one of you is going to walk up to Columbus with me where I'll catch a cab. Once I'm inside the cab I'll exchange the sample bottle for the money. Everybody wins. And best of all I won't have any reason to open my mouth because if I do I'll lose the money. You get what you want and I'll get what I want."

Speyer was vexed but it was clear that he couldn't see a way out of the impasse. He nodded. "Very well. But I will give you a warning after all. We have many friends. Open your mouth and you're a dead man. Sooner or later someone will catch up with you."

"I get the message," Metzler said. "Now, if you don't mind, I want to get out of here. This place gives me the creeps."

Speyer got the leather money bag and walked up to Columbus Avenue with the biologist while Baumann wrapped the two cylinders in blankets and took them out to the trunk of the Mercedes.

Traffic was still fairly heavy, and it took only a couple of minutes for Metzler to hail a cab. When he got in, he exchanged the small cylinder for the money bag.

"Best you not forget what I told you," Speyer said.

"Believe me, I won't," Metzler said.

Speyer pocketed the cylinder, turned and walked back to 86th, and for the first time since he'd seen the images on the computer screen he sighed in relief.

It was eleven by the time they stopped in front of the Hayden Planetarium. Speyer dropped the package containing a letter and the sample cylinder into a Federal Express collection box. It was free of fingerprints, the FedEx account number was untraceable to him, and it was addressed simply to: The White House, 1600 Pennsylvania Avenue, Washington, D.C., 20502.

"Do you think they'll go for it?" Baumann asked.

"They'd be fools not to." Speyer stared out the window as they headed north on the Henry Hudson Parkway to the George Washington Bridge and I-95. "Seventy-two hours," he said. "If they don't pay us by then we'll spray one bottle over Washington and sell the other bottle to the highest bidder. And believe me, Ernst, there'll be plenty of bidders."

WASHINGTON, D.C.

The package, along with seventeen others, was delivered to the White House Mail Center in the Old Executive Office Building at one in the afternoon. Mary Wilcox, chief postal receptionist on duty, passed each package and letter through the Advanced Threat Evaluator, a complex piece of electronic hardware that checked for chemical, biological, or nuclear hazards.

The cylinder showed up on the X-ray and ultrasound scans, but the sensitive gamma ray and neutron detectors showed nothing. Nor did the chemical or biological sensors pick up a thing.

Nevertheless she stopped the conveyor and picked up the phone. "I might have something for you."

A minute later, Tom Walton, the chief Secret Service agent on duty, came across the hall from his office and studied the image on the screen for a minute. "I don't like the look of it," he said.

"What do you think it is?" Mary Wilcox asked. She was thinking bomb.

"I don't see any detonator circuits, but that might not mean a thing," Walton said. "Get your people out of here for a few minutes." He called his boss, Leonard Sills, who was chief of White House security, and then called the bomb squad from next door.

Both arrived at the same time, and Sills gave the okay to move the package and open it inside a blast box that was permanently set up in the hall. Everyone backed off to give the demolitions lead officer, dressed in a heavily padded and armored disposal suit, plenty of room to pick up the package carefully and walk with it out into the hall. When it was in the blast box they all breathed a sigh of relief.

Sills said something into his lapel mike, then nodded. "Give me five," he said. He looked over at Walton. "POTUS is enroute by chopper. I asked them to hold him for five minutes." POTUS was the Secret Service designator for the President Of The United States.

"Good idea."

"I have the package open," Martin LeRoche, the

demolitions officer, radioed. "No wires, no circuitry, no external power source."

"Any label on the bottle?" Walton asked.

"No, but there is a letter."

"Leave the bottle, bring the letter," Sills instructed. He took out a pair of surgical rubber gloves and put them on as LeRoche came back across the hall with the standard business-size envelope in his thickly gloved hand.

"It's addressed to the president," Sills said, carefully opening the envelope. It took him a minute to read the short note and for the words to register, but when he was finished his lips compressed and he looked up.

"What is it, Len?" Walton asked.

"Some nut case says he's sent the president a sample bottle of bugs. Call Bethesda and get the CDC's rapid response team over here on the double." He turned to LeRoche. "I want this wing evacuated and sealed right now." He got on his radio. "Thunder, this is Sills."

"Copy."

"We have a possible Mars One threat. Confidence is high. CDC is on its way."

"Copy that. We're diverting POTUS to the secondary."

"We should be clear within the hour. But this one came with a note."

"Fax it."

"Will do," Sills said, mindful of all the wheels that had been set into motion and hoping that this wasn't the big one.

DECATUR, GEORGIA

Dr. Theodore Osborne, director of the Centers for Disease Control laboratory division was about to sit down at the dinner table with his wife and teenage son when the phone call came for him. It was the lab where the cylinder had been brought.

"It's not good news, I'm afraid," Lieutenant Colonel Jan deHuis said. He was chief of the biological threat research section.

"Good God, don't tell me that it's legitimate?" Dr. Osborne said. He was a good Christian man who in his heart believed in the basic goodness of man.

"It's an arbovirus. Like ebola and some of the other African hemorraghic strains."

"Active?"

"Very," deHuis said. "But this one's in none of our databases. It's brand new."

"Did you find any biological tags?"

"None. But if I had to guess, I'd bet a year's pay that this was cooked up in a military laboratory somewhere. Maybe Iraq. But I just can't be sure. It's not very sophisticated but I expect that after we run our live tests we'll find that it's deadly."

"We'd better inform the president this evening," Dr. Osborne said.

"It's on your computer."

"I'll look it over and send it up. Thank you for the fast work, Jan."

WASHINGTON, D.C.

President Reasoner's National Security Council members got to their feet when he entered the situation room beneath the White House and took his seat at the center of the long table.

"I trust that everybody has read the letter that came with the cylinder, as well as the CDC's report."

"We have, Mr. President," his national security adviser, Leslie Newby said.

"Very well, what do we do about it?" The president glanced at the wall clock. It was 8:30 P.M. "We have a half hour before the son of a bitch calls us, and I'm going to have to make some tough decisions."

"We don't know who they are, what they want or how long they're going to give us," FBI Director Dale McKeever said. "None of that was mentioned in the letter. So our first job is to agree with everything they demand, but to stall for time."

"Does the Bureau have any leads?"

"There were no fingerprints on the letter or the cylinder. The paper was standard twenty-pound copy paper that you can buy from any office supply house. We'll have the brand later this evening, but I doubt that it'll help much. The printer was an older Hewlett Packard DeskJet that you'll find in about a quarter of all the households in this country. The cylinder is a laboratory item, manufactured two years ago by Western Laboratory Products in Waco, but distributed to nearly every lab supply company in the country. We're checking, but if the bottle was purchased through an intermediary or through a blind, it'll be a dead end." McKeever checked his notes.

"The package was picked up at a FedEx drop box outside the Hayden Planetarium in New York City, but we can't narrow the time it was placed in the box closer than six hours. We're canvassing the neighborhoods immediately around the box for witnesses." McKeever looked up. "There's more of the same, but the fact of the matter is that we need time."

The president turned to his CIA director, James Flynn. "Have your people turned up anything that might help?"

"If, as Dr. Osborne suggests, it's a military virus from an Iraqi lab, we're out of luck for the moment. Since the inspections were blocked again we've been unable to place an effective agent inside the country." He spread his hands. "Given the time we might be able to find out something."

President Reasoner's eyes were hard. "How much time?"

"Months, Mr. President, certainly not days or hours."

"They've covered their bases very well," the president said. He looked at the note that had been sent with the cylinder. It was short and to the point. The virus was deadly, the terrorists had much more of it, and they would release it in a major U.S. city unless one very simple demand was met. A call would be made to the White House situation room at precisely 2100 hours EDT.

The sweep second hand of the wall clock came up to 9:00 P.M. and one of the incoming lines lit up. The Marine technician let it ring twice then made the circuit. They heard the warbling tone of a computer and the call was switched to the laptops in front of everyone at the table.

"Good evening, Mr. President and members of

your security council." The words appeared on the LCD screens.

The president hesitated a moment, and then typed his reply. "You have our attention. What do you want?"

"No later than seventy-two hours from now, your government will deposit $10 billion in U.S. funds into the following seventy-three off-shore bank accounts."

A series of countries, banks, account numbers, and amounts, beginning with several deposits in the Grand Cayman islands totalling around $250 million, scrolled down the screen.

"Do we have a trace on him?" the president asked.

"No, sir," the Marine said. "The call is coming from an anonymous remailer in Switzerland."

"We can break that, but it'll take us several days, up to a week if the remailer is good," McKeever said.

"That means he could be anywhere?"

"Anywhere in the world."

The president turned back to the laptop. "Who are you?" he typed.

"That is of no consequence. You will be trying to find us, of course, mobilizing all of your military and law enforcement agencies. Under the circumstances I cannot wish you luck, but your chances are not very good. What you must not do is go public. Besides causing a panic in every major U.S. city, we would be forced to demonstrate our resolve."

"Son of a bitch, that's his weakness," McKeever said. He looked at the president. "Somebody knows these people. Neighbors, coworkers, somebody. That's why they don't want us to take our investigation to the public. He's afraid that someone will come forward and identify him."

"What do we do?" the president asked.

"Stall him."

"We need more time," the president typed. "One week."

"Seventy-two hours."

"Why are you doing this?" the president replied angrily.

"For the money, of course."

"If you go through with this, we will hunt you down."

"Surely you must have learned by now that any leader's power—even a great leader—is limited. We will be quite safe. Seventy-two hours."

"We will find you," the president typed.

"The connection has been terminated, Mr. President," the marine said.

11

WASHINGTON, D.C.

CDC Drs. Osborne and deHuis flew up to Washington to brief the president. They were seated across from him sipping coffee at 1:00 A.M.

"It's a manufactured virus, Mr. President, there's no doubt about it now," Osborne said. "It's equally obvious that it was designed to be a weapon, which in a perverse way works somewhat to our benefit. Once it hits the environment it has a life span of less than six hours. Quite ingenious, actually."

The president exchanged a glance with his national security adviser. So far the CDC had not been made aware of the terrorists' threat. "Would gas masks be effective? Or can the disease be spread by contact with other infected people?"

"The most effective way to deliver it would be by an airborne spray. Maybe out of an airplane. Or a canister with a timed release, say on top of the New York World Trade Center towers. Gas masks would not work."

"But it could also be spread through a building's or even a city's water supply," deHuis said. "In fact the virus might live a little longer in cold water than in the atmosphere."

"In that case we're only talking about a one-time limited effect, is that what you're saying?" Newby asked.

"Yes, sir. That's one of the reasons we believe the A virus was designed as a weapon. It could be used on a battlefield, but the soldiers could go in a few hours behind it to mop up the survivors."

"The A virus?" the president asked.

"A for antique," Osborne replied. "It's an old strain, one that we couldn't immediately find in our databases. It's manufactured, we knew that for sure almost immediately; there are certain aspects of its makeup that are giveaways. The thickness of the cell walls for one, and its reaction to some of our antiviral bullets. Modern-day viruses have learned not to react."

"I thought that this branch of biology was modern, since the seventies or eighties," Newby said.

"Actually virology got its name and its real start in the thirties in Germany," Dr. Osborne said.

It took a moment for what the doctor had said to sink in fully, and a look of surprise crossed the president's face. "The Nazis?"

"It's our best guess," deHuis said. "My grandparents and my father were taken from Amsterdam and placed in a concentration camp. My dad was the only survivor. When I was little I would sneak downstairs at night to listen to the stories he told my mother about medical experiments. He actually knew Mengele."

"I'm sorry . . ."

"I didn't mean to ask for sympathy, Mr. President. I grew up with the stories so when I went into medicine I specialized in biological killers, which led me to the CDC. I did a college paper on the virology research of the era, and this strain has all the earmarks of the weapons the Nazis were working on."

"How the hell did it get over here?" Newby asked, but the president cut him off.

"That'll come later. What I want to know is what

would happen if it were to be released, let's say from a skyscraper in New York, as you suggested."

"It would depend on which way the wind was blowing. But assuming the worst case scenario and the virus was blown across Manhattan, a lot of people would die. The virus sample sent to us could conceivably kill a couple of thousand people. Three or four pounds of the stuff could kill hundreds of thousands, maybe millions."

"Nor would their deaths be anything that you would want to witness," Dr. Osborne said. "I worked on a couple of outbreaks in Zaire and the Congo, and I saw firsthand what hemorraghic fever does to the human body." He averted his eyes. "Fever, sweating, palsy. Then nausea, weakness, diarrhea, vomiting. The patient bleeds internally. His organs, starting with the kidneys, fail. Excruciating pain. Bleeding inside the brain. Within twenty-four hours the patient is not only coughing up blood, he's sweating blood. It oozes out of his pores." Dr. Osborne looked up. "A half-million hemorraghic fever victims in Manhattan would be even worse than the Nazi death camps. It would be nothing less than a nightmare from hell."

"No preventive measures?" the president asked. "No antidotes?"

"No, sir."

The president nodded. "Thank you for the CDC's fast action. I have to order you not to tell anybody about this. That includes families."

"If there is an outbreak, we'll have to be notified."

"Of course."

"May I ask a question, Mr. President?" Osborne said.

"Yes."

"Is this an actual threat? Has someone threatened to release the virus in a big city?"

"I'm afraid so," the president said. "But we don't know which big city."

Dr. Osborne thought about it for a moment. "Well, sir, we have to stop them."

"We're working on it, Doctor."

Tom Hughes was awake when the call from the president came at 2:00 A.M. He'd not gotten much sleep since they'd lost track of Lane off the coast of Florida. Now that William was back safely from that operation and the one in Kalispell with Frances, he was still unable to get a full night's sleep. Something was about to happen. He just knew it.

For the past three days Moira and the girls had all but tiptoed around the house when he was at home. Something was bothering him and they gave him all the peace and quiet they could. What the president was telling him confirmed his worst fears.

"We not only know where the virus came from, Mr. President, we know who is planning to use it," Hughes said.

"How in God's name did you know, and why didn't you do something about it?" President Reasoner demanded angrily.

"We thought that it was something else. Diamonds. And we're still working on the project. It was something that the German Federal Police asked us to help with a few weeks ago."

"I want the three of you over here as soon as possible. We can exchange information," the president said. "We don't have much time."

Moira had turned on the light, got out of bed, and put on her robe. "Shall I make coffee, Thomas?"

Hughes looked at his wife and a wave of love came over him. He shook his head. "There's not enough time," he said. He'd never heard the president, any president, speak with so much fear in his voice. "I would like you to call William and Frances for me. Tell them that I'm on my way to fetch them. It has to do with Reichsamt Seventeen."

Lane was up and dressed in Armani slacks, a light handmade sweater he'd picked up in New Delhi a few years ago, and Bruno Magli loafers, when Hughes arrived at the house. Frannie, dressed in light silk slacks and a cream-colored blouse and flats, wasn't happy that Hughes was here. But Lane was ready to go. "What's this about Reichsamt Seventeen? Something new?"

"It's a deadly virus, not diamonds, and Speyer apparently means to use it. The president wants to see us immediately."

"No wonder the Germans wanted our help, and yet they didn't want to cooperate with us," Lane said. "They would have had to admit they were covering up their knowledge of what really was in the bunker. Did Speyer give a deadline?"

"The president didn't say," Hughes said. "But he sounded—"

"Frightened?" Frances asked.

Hughes nodded. "He did indeed sound frightened."

It was a few minutes after 3:00 A.M. when they were admitted through the west gate. They left their car under the portico and were immediately escorted to the Oval Office where the president and his national security adviser were in shirtsleeves, waiting. They looked as if they hadn't slept in days.

"Thank you for coming out at this hour and on such short notice," the president said tiredly. "Now maybe we can start to get somewhere. You say that you know about the virus and who has it?"

"A former Stasi captain by the name of Helmut Speyer," Hughes said. "But it was William who infiltrated his organization three and a half weeks ago."

The president turned to Lane. "Tell me."

Lane quickly told the president and his adviser everything, starting with the German federal police request to find Speyer and Baumann, all the way to his rescue in the Gulf Stream by the Coast Guard, and his and Frannie's entry to the Kalispell compound.

"That's quite a story," the president said, impressed. "But then I wouldn't have expected anything less from you. Where did he go with the captain's gig after the *Maria* was sunk?"

"It's a safe bet that he didn't take the gig to Miami. He would never have gotten the box through customs. He might have gone to Havana and from there to Mexico City. But he did show up in Miami three days later where he and his wife and the sergeant took the Gulfstream jet back to his ranch. How he got the box through customs is something we haven't figured out yet."

The president sat forward. "Good lord, is he still there?"

"No. He and all of his people left the day after William and I were there," Frances said. "The FBI office in Helena has been watching his operation, but Speyer somehow slipped through their fingers when they were looking the other way. The Gulfstream showed up at New York's LaGuardia forty-eight hours ago, dropped off two people, then flew down here to Dulles where a woman got off—presumably the man's wife—and then continued on to Miami where the crew disappeared."

"Was anything found aboard the airplane?" Newby asked.

"No, sir," Frances said. "Not even fingerprints. The entire aircraft was wiped clean."

"Nothing since then on Speyer?"

"We haven't come up with anything," Hughes said. "But under the light of present circumstances that is a task for the FBI. I'm sure that somebody has seen something."

The president handed Lane a file folder. "This is what we have so far. The note that came with the sample bottle, the CDC's findings, and a transcript of the computer conversation I had with him."

Lane quickly read through the material and handed it to Frannie and Hughes. "Well, his demands have certainly risen. When he was telling me that the box contained diamonds he was going to sell them back to the German government for three hundred million. Now he wants thirty times that much."

"The Bureau and the CIA are working on this, I would assume," Hughes said.

"Yes, but of necessity they're going about their jobs quietly. It's hampering their effectiveness, as is the deadline, but for the moment we have no other choice but to accept this madman at his word." The president glanced at his desk clock. "We have less than sixty-four hours, and we don't have an idea where to start."

"I'm sorry to disagree, Mr. President," Lane said. "But Speyer has inadvertently given us some very good clues. I'm guessing that he went to New York to pick up the virus where it came in on the ship that met him in the Gulf Stream. He's going to release the virus right here in Washington, and when he's done he's going to Cuba. Eden, he calls it."

"What if we don't pay him?" Newby asked.

"It doesn't matter to him," Lane said. "If we do pay him he'll give us the virus. I'm pretty sure of that much. But if we don't pay him, he'll release some of it in Washington. If it works, he'll take the rest of it to Cuba where he'll sell it to the highest bidder."

"Good Lord, the man is worse than crazy," the president said. "He's a sociopath."

"Much worse," Lane agreed. "But we'll find him. In the meantime don't tell the FBI or CIA that we're in the mix. It might leak and then the game would be up for us. At least for now."

"Very well," the president said. "Then there's nothing left but to put this in your hands." He smiled wryly. "But that's why I created The Room and hired you in the first place."

Back in their offices at the Naval Observatory Hughes telephoned BKA Chief Inspector Dieter Schey in Berlin. It was after 8:00 A.M. in Germany. He put the call on the speakerphone.

"We're running into a problem with Helmut Speyer and his people," Hughes said.

"What sort of problem, Herr Hughes?" Schey asked. They could hear he was under a strain.

"Well, as you know he made it back here to the States with whatever it was they brought up from Reichsamt Seventeen. We wanted to give him some room, you know, to see what he was up to. But he seems to have disappeared. With the box."

"*Gott in Himmel,*" Chief Inspecter Schey said softly. "Your man should know more about this than I do. He was there."

"He doesn't know," Hughes said. "Dieter, this is very important to us. To all of us. What was in the box they brought up from the bunker? What were the Nazis doing down there in the forties?"

"I will have to get back to you with that information."

"Quit stalling, we're under the gun here."

"I'm not stalling. It's that I do not know myself what went on in Reichsamt Seventeen, except that it was very secret. I will talk to my superiors. The decision will be theirs. You must understand this."

"Get back to me as soon as you can," Hughes said.

"I will."

Hughes broke the connection and looked at Lane. "They know about the virus."

"No doubt about it. And they're not going to help us."

"That's monstrous," Frances said.

"It's politics."

The regular staff wouldn't be in for a few hours yet, so Hughes and Frannie powered up two of the terminals. Lane looked over their shoulders.

"Where do we start?" Frannie asked.

"The box came to New York by ship. Let's start with that," Lane said. "After the *Maria* was scuttled Speyer made a rendezvous, transferred the box, and then either headed off to Cuba, or sunk the gig and came aboard with his wife and Baumann."

"He didn't go to New York with the ship," Frances said. "That doesn't make any sense. Why did he go all the way back to Miami just to fly to Kalispell, and then fly back to New York?"

"Maybe the ship that picked them up made a stop in Miami first," Lane suggested. "Maybe he and his wife and Baumann got off, but the box was sent on."

"There won't be many ships that fit that profile," Hughes said.

"If it was Gloria who got off here in Washington she might still be here getting ready for the attack," Frances put in.

"A gold star for the mom to be," Lane said.

"If you keep that up I'm just as likely to brain you as thank you."

"Ta-ta, kids," Hughes said. "Okay, what am I looking for exactly? If it's merely a safe house you're after, that could be anywhere within a fifty mile radius, and we would have to be very lucky indeed to stumble across it. Could be a rental under God only knows what name. Or, they could have purchased a house months ago, and under an assumed name."

"This will have to be a very special place," Lane said, pacing. "It's probably a rental unit, something that they picked up within the last six months. Speyer was starting to pinch pennies, so I don't think he would have spent the money to buy a house. It'll be off by itself to give them privacy. They don't want snoopy neighbors watching their comings and goings, especially not if they brought their storm troopers with them."

"We're looking for a place out in the country. Some woods, maybe. Near a highway, but not on it."

"That's right. And it'll have an airstrip on the property, or it'll be very near a small regional airport."

"You don't think this will be a static release, like off the Washington Monument?"

Lane shook his head. "Too many things could go wrong. Too many people, tourists as well as park rangers. And they would be at the mercy of the wind. Only the half of Washington downwind from the monument would be affected."

"There was no evidence that their Gulfstream jet had been fitted out to accept an external spray mechanism."

"See if there are any agricultural spraying companies in the area. Maybe he's talked to them about a job."

Frannie looked up from her computer. "It's too bad

we can't tap Thomas Mann's telephones. If the ever-alluring Mrs. Speyer is indeed here in town, she might telephone the dear old man."

"I don't want to get the Bureau here in Washington involved," Lane said. "It's too risky. If Speyer does have an informer inside the FBI the inquiries could get back to him. Besides, we haven't had much luck decrypting their telephone programs. Not without the CIA's computer system."

"So we do it the old-fashioned way," Hughes said. "I have a friend at the phone company who has done me a favor from time to time. Even if we cannot decrypt their conversations, maybe we can trace the calls."

"Clever man—" Lane said, when Frannie let out a little shout of joy. She was beaming.

"With child I may be, but dumb I'm not." She looked up. "Your ship is the *Akai Maru*, love, out of Nagasaki. Captain Shintaro Kato. At this moment she's at the Brooklyn docks, but she's scheduled to sail at noon."

"What do you have, Frannie?"

The figures were scrolling up the screen. "Nagasaki to the Panama Canal and from there through the Florida Straits to Miami where she dropped off six containers of Sony electronic equipment and Japanese furniture. The times match, and she was a couple hours behind her ETA."

"She's listed as a general carrier," Lane said. "And there's nothing about three passengers."

"Convenient," Frannie said. "Should I keep looking?"

"I don't think it's necessary," Lane said. "See if you can round me up some transportation to New York, and a car when I get there. Then you can help Tom."

"Why did I know that you were going to leave me home?"

"Don't fret, my dear girl, lunch is on me," Hughes said without missing a keystroke.

NEW YORK

At ten o'clock Lane showed his Immigration and Naturalization Service identification to the gate guard and was directed to the *Akai Maru*. The Brooklyn docks were alive with activity; trucks came and went from the warehouse in steady streams while front-end loaders darted about like angry wasps. Giant cranes unloaded some ships, while others lifted containers onto outbound vessels. Pallets of goods from around the world were piled everywhere in seemingly haphazard jumbles.

Lane parked his government Ford Taurus across from the Japanese ship and, attaché case in hand, went up the boarding stairs to the port quarterdeck. The ship was down on her lines, which meant that she was fully laden, her hatches dogged down and deck containers securely chained.

A Japanese man in spotlessly white coveralls came on deck from the superstructure. "No visitors are authorized," he said in reasonably clear English. "You must go."

Lane held out his INS identification. "I'm Agent Bob Salmon. I want to see the captain."

The crewman looked nervously from Lane to the picture on the ID and back. He took out a walkie-talkie and spoke rapid-fire Japanese to someone.

He got his reply in a moment, and motioned for Lane to show his INS identification again. He read the name and badge number back, and got another reply.

"Captain says there are no passengers on his ship. We get ready to sail now. You must go."

Lane suppressed a grin. He'd not said anything about checking for passengers. "Tell Captain Kato that if he does not wish to speak to me now, I will unfortunately impound this vessel and it may be days or weeks before the paperwork is completed." Lane didn't think that the crewman understood all of that, but he spoke at length into the walkie-talkie. He got his reply immediately.

He nodded. "The captain is coming down to see you." The crewman stepped aside, but kept a wary eye on Lane.

Captain Kato, a slightly built man wearing wire-rimmed glasses and dressed in khaki trousers and a yellow Izod polo shirt, came on deck. His mood was impossible to read from the bland expression on his round face.

Lane showed the captain his government identification. "You are carrying three passengers. I want to meet with them now and inspect their papers."

"There are no passengers aboard my ship."

Lane took photographs of Speyer, Gloria, and Baumann from his attaché case and handed them to the captain. "These three were reported to be aboard."

"By whom?"

"That information is confidential. Are these people aboard?"

"No."

Lane put the photographs back in his attaché case, smiled and glanced toward the bow of the ship, as if he were coming to a decision. When he turned back, the captain was watching him with interest.

"Look, captain, I know that keeping to sailing

schedules is very important. If need be I will impound this ship until it can be searched top to bottom. That might take days. But the fact of the matter is I don't care about your involvement with these people. I merely want to know if they are aboard at this moment. And if they're not, where did they get off? And where is the package that they brought with them? When I have that information you will be free to leave. You have my word on it. The INS does not care about your ship, we only care about these three illegals."

"They are not aboard."

Lane shrugged. "As you wish—"

"They got off the ship in Miami, seven days ago."

Lane gave him a hard stare. "Where did they board?"

"We picked them up in the ocean, in international waters between Florida and Cuba. Their small boat was sinking and we rescued them."

"Why didn't you inform the U.S. Coast Guard?"

"We were asked not to do so."

"What about the package?"

"They took it with them," Captain Kato said.

"Not in Miami, they didn't," Lane said. "Did they come here for it?"

The captain hesitated for only a second, but then he nodded.

"How was it passed through customs?"

"I don't know."

"When was this?"

"Two days ago," the captain said. "I have cooperated with you; now get off my ship, please. I have done nothing illegal."

"I sincerely hope that you have not lied to me, captain," Lane warned. "If I find out that you have lied, then the next time that you enter U.S. waters you and your crew will be subject to arrest, your vessel and cargo impounded."

The captain nodded gravely. "No lies."

Lane allowed a faint smile to curl his lip. "Except about the money." He turned and went down the boarding ladder.

WASHINGTON, D.C.

Hughes pushed away from the computer terminal and stretched his back. "Our jobs are certainly cut out for us."

Frances looked up from her terminal across the narrow hall. "Have you found something?"

"Enough to know that we might be looking for the proverbial needle in a haystack."

She got up from her desk and came over. "What is it?"

"In a fifty mile radius from downtown Washington there are no less than twenty-seven airports. That's not counting Dulles, Reagan, Baltimore, and the other big commercial airports, or the military bases or even the small private grass strips. I'm just adding up the regionals."

"What about crop dusting companies?"

"That reduces the number of airports to two, neither of which meets William's other conditions. Too big, too busy." Hughes shook his head. "If this was the Midwest where there was more farming it would be relatively easy to hire an ag pilot. But not here."

Frances looked out the window toward the vice president's residence. "Maybe he's not going to hire an airplane. Maybe he has his own."

"The Gulfstream is out, and the Bureau says that

his Bell Ranger is still tied down at his Kalispell ranch."

"I mean a crop duster."

"Somebody would have flown it out here," Hughes said, then he gave Frances a smile. "That's a new angle. I'll check to see if any new airplanes have arrived at any of those airports in the last few days. But you and William saw no sign of such an airplane out there, did you?"

"No. And airplanes are tough items to hide. But it's worth a try."

"That it is."

PHILADELPHIA

Bernhard Metzler had agonized about his decision on the train all the way from New York, and he was no closer to knowing what to do than he had been two days ago as he walked into the Federal Building on Seventh and Arch Streets a few minutes before eleven. But he was here, carried almost as if against his will, to do the right thing.

He took the elevator to the third floor, walked into the FBI office and stepped up to the receptionist, an older woman, who looked up.

"I want to report a terrorist attack that's probably going to happen in New York pretty soon," Metzler said. "A lot of people are going to get killed unless the Bureau does something damned quick."

The woman's eyes never left Metzler's as she snatched her phone and called Special Agent in Charge Michael Hood. The heads-up on the biological threat had been sent to every Bureau office in the world, and this was possibly the break they were hoping for. The lengthy confidential directive had forbidden any publicity whatsoever, which hamstrung their investigation. As the clock continued to count down, everyone was getting desperate.

Hood and two agents, their hands inside their jackets, came from the offices in back.

"What's your name, sir?" Hood demanded.

"Bernhard Metzler. I know something about the guys you're probably looking for. It's about a hemorraghic virus, right? And unless I miss my guess these nut cases have already threatened somebody with it. Am I right, or what?"

"How do you know about this?"

Metzler smirked sarcastically. "I'm the one who loaded it into the big air bottles, and pumped a little of the shit into a two-hundred-fifty-milliliter sample bottle." He shook his head. "Did I come to the wrong place, or do you guys want to talk to me? Maybe we can save a few lives here. I can be the hero for a change."

One of the agents came over. "Spread 'em," he said. He quickly frisked Metzler for a weapon. "He's clean."

"We certainly do want to talk to you, Mr. Metzler," Hood said.

"Dr. Metzler."

WASHINGTON, D.C.

At 11:45 A.M. the first flash traffic on Bernhard Metzler came into the FBI's Special Investigative Division, under the heading "Extremely Confidential."

At that same moment a computer in Tom Hughes's office warbled a warning tone. One of The Room's special intercept programs was getting the same message. The moment he realized what was happening, he picked up the phone and called Bill Lane.

NEW YORK

Lane was on the Brooklyn-Queens Expressway heading back to La Guardia when Hughes called him with the news about Metzler. "If Speyer has an informer inside the Bureau he knows about it now, and he'll have the man killed. Call the White House and have them order the Philly SAC to move Metzler to a safe house, right now."

"Are you going down there?" Hughes asked.

"I'm about fifteen minutes from the airport. As soon as you find out where they've taken him, let me know. And let the SAC know that I'm on my way."

"Did you get anything from the *Akai Maru*?"

"Speyer, Gloria and Baumann were aboard all right. They got off in Miami, and the package was taken up here, just like we figured," Lane said. "Any luck on the safehouse?"

"Nothing yet. And no mystery phone calls to Mann."

"Keep on it, Tommy."

12

PHILADELPHIA

Bill Lane was delayed a half-hour at LaGuardia so that by the time he touched down at Philadelphia's Northeast Airport and taxied to the government hangar, Frances was waiting for him with a car. He was vexed and he let it show.

"Don't pout, dear, you'll trip over your lower lip," she told him. "My jet has a fax machine and yours doesn't, so Tommy sent me what he's managed to dig up on our professor."

Frances had directions to the FBI safe house, so she rode shotgun while Lane drove the plain gray Ford van with government plates.

"Has Tommy come up with anything yet on where Speyer is hunkering down?"

"He's still working on it, but he's not going to make much progress unless we catch a break. Maybe Metzler is just the ticket."

"Don't count on it too heavily, Frannie. If Metzler knew anything that could interfere with Speyer's plans, they would have killed him."

"Maybe they tried and he got away. That's why he came to the FBI."

"That's possible. Maybe he *is* our only real lead."

They took U.S. 63 down to I-95 and headed south. The Bureau's safe house was actually in New Jersey, across the river from Philadelphia near Camden. Traffic was heavy but moved well.

"What'd we come up with on him?" Lane asked.

"He's apparently quite bright, but the lad is a chronic complainer," Frannie said. "He's been an associate professor of molecular biology at New York University for the past five years and that's as far as he's going to go because he doesn't know when to keep his mouth shut. He was born in 1970 in Milwaukee, second generation German with ties to the former East Germany. His parents used to send care packages to relatives behind the Wall. University of Wisconsin, then Heidelberg for his master's and back to Wisconsin for his Ph.D. He did one year of postdoc work at Columbia and then moved over to NYU. He's up for tenure but he probably won't get that either and he knows it."

"So he's a bitter man," Lane said.

"It would seem so."

"Money and revenge. Pretty powerful motivations. What else?"

"We don't know what he told the Bureau except that he's the one who loaded the virus into a pair of air bottles filled with nitrogen and the sample bottle which was sent to the White House. So we have no idea how Speyer found him, or what kind of a deal they struck."

"Evidently he thinks that Speyer is going to release the virus in New York City, which is why he got out."

"A little misdirection."

"Good move on Speyer's part," Lane said. "He would view it as insurance in case Metzler did exactly what he's done."

"Speyer may be a bastard, but nobody's accusing him of being stupid," Frances said. "So far he hasn't made many mistakes, and the clock is still running."

"It's compartmentalization. The old Russian cell system in which only one person knows the entire plan. Each cell knows one bit, but nothing more. Metzler is a one-man cell. He'll know something all right, but not the entire plan."

"Might be that he knows something, or saw something, or heard something that doesn't seem important to him, but that might help us."

Lane glanced at his wife, a glimmer of another idea coming to him from what she just said. Maybe there was someone else out there who could help them.

WEST FRIENDSHIP, MARYLAND

The country house was situated on the northeast corner of fifty acres of woods twenty miles west of Baltimore and thirty north of Washington. Speyer bought it three years ago about the same time he'd picked up the New York brownstone after he'd completed his operational planning. Like the Kalispell ranch, this place afforded him almost complete privacy for his men.

He was watching CNN for news about the virus threat when Baumann came in from making his rounds. It was 3:00 P.M. "Our perimeter is secure, and the landing area has been prepared."

"There's been nothing on the news, so they're taking us seriously after all." Speyer lowered the volume and went to the sideboard where he poured them each a cognac. "It won't be long now and we'll be home free. How many of the men will stay with us afterwards?"

The question caught Baumann momentarily off guard, but he recovered nicely. He'd been with Speyer for a long time. He knew when to tell the truth and when to lie. "Maybe half, if you really mean to retire to Cuba."

"That's about what I thought. What if I don't retire?"

"Maybe about the same number. Half of them want to finish this mission and get back to their families. The other half will want a new assignment."

"There's plenty to do."

"But not for us," Baumann said. "This is the big one. Your identity will come out eventually."

Speyer shrugged. "It wouldn't be difficult. A little plastic surgery, alter my fingerprints."

"DNA doesn't lie."

"That's true. But in order for them to match my DNA they would have to get a sample from me, which I would make very difficult for them."

Baumann thoughtfully sipped his cognac. "Are you thinking about another mission, Captain?"

"Nothing immediately."

"It would depend on what happens in the next forty-eight hours," Baumann suggested. "If the government pays us the ten billion, then we can pack up and leave as planned. But if they don't we'll have to go to stage red. If we're forced to go that far the situation will be much different. Money is one thing, but the murder of several hundred thousand civilians is something totally different."

"It would earn us respect, Ernst," Speyer said.

Baumann's eyes narrowed. "It would earn us more than that, Herr *Kapitän*. We would become the most hunted men on earth."

Speyer laughed and dismissed Baumann's objections with a wave. "The U.S. Navy went after Gaddafi and missed, and the entire U.S. military went after Saddam Hussein and missed again. I'm not overly concerned."

He offered another cognac but Baumann shook his head. He was clearly troubled.

"You think that I am wrong?"

Baumann put his glass down. "Permission to speak freely, sir?"

Speyer didn't want to be bothered with petty objections at this stage of the mission, but he nodded. Baumann was a good man, if a bit overcautious.

"State-sponsored acts of terrorism, or even wars are one thing, but killing American civilians in such large numbers on their home ground is something else."

"They haven't gotten bin Laden yet, and there's a five million dollar bounty on his head."

"He never killed tens of thousands—"

"That will be enough, Sergeant," Speyer said sharply. "I want the men assembled in the dining room in one hour." He looked at his watch. "At sixteen hundred."

It was clear that Baumann wanted to say something else, but he nodded curtly, and left.

Gloria hadn't bothered to unpack. They wouldn't be here for very long, and she was starting to get worried that Helmut was about to do something very stupid and dangerous. She watched from the front bedroom window as Baumann marched toward the horse arena across the paddock where the men were billeted. He looked resigned.

"I want you to make us dinner tonight," Speyer said from the doorway.

"Get your own goddamned dinner," she replied without turning away from the window.

Speyer came across the room, grabbed her arm just above the elbow, and yanked her nearly off her feet. "The truck will arrive in a couple of hours, and there'll be twelve hungry men plus Ernst and myself. We'll have potato dumplings, würst, lentil soup, spaetzle, and brown bread plus beer."

His tone of voice was calm, but there was something in his eyes that she hadn't seen before. Not anger, or even hate. Maybe indifference, and it frightened her all of a sudden. She nodded. "I'm sorry."

Speyer changed out of the slacks and shirt he was wearing into khaki trousers, a short-sleeved safari shirt, and boots. He always wore the quasi-military uniform when he wanted to emphasize the military command structure of his organization. Gloria had always thought he was being theatrical.

"How much longer are we going to be cooped up here, Helmut?" Gloria asked.

Speyer pulled on a shoulder holster and Glock 17. "Two days, and then you can go back to being a movie star." Something in the way he said it was hurtful, and she knew that he'd meant it that way.

The truck had not arrived yet, but it wouldn't be seriously overdue until midnight, so Speyer was not overly concerned yet. In fact, everything had gone according to the mission timetable so far.

Eight men plus Baumann assembled in the dining room got to their feet and snapped to attention when Speyer walked in. "As you were, gentlemen," he said. They sat down as he took his place at the head of the long table.

"Hoffmann and Schneider are on guard duty," Baumann reported.

"Very well. Has there been any interest from the neighbors, the townspeople, or the local authorities?"

"None."

"Let's keep it that way. You're all restricted to the compound for the mission duration which I estimate to be forty-eight hours, plus or minus four. Has transportation been converted and secured?"

"Yes, sir," Sergeant Fredrichs said. "The new registrations are valid, the tanks are full, and PM routines have been completed." They had two Toyota minivans and three SUVs, all purchased through legitimate sources. They'd been used to transport the men across country under one set of licenses which had now been changed. Once the ag plane took off, the men would head immediately to Baltimore where they were booked on commercial flights to Montreal, Mexico City, and Paris. Even before the first of the virus was released, if the mission developed to that point, they would be in the air and heading out of the country.

Until then, their primary function was guarding the compound and the airstrip and, when the ag plane arrived, defending it with their lives if need be until it was away.

"I want weapons and surveillance systems checks completed no later than twenty hundred hours, and that will include our perimeter point defense system."

"Yes, sir," Baumann replied.

"I want a final check on travel documents and identification papers by oh-eight hundred. Nobody is going to get arrested on the way out. You have all worked too hard to blow it at the end. Three days from now we'll be doing some serious R & R on a tropical beach."

The men around the table grinned. Most of their missions had been in East Germany, a long ways from any tropical beach. And they had spent the winter training at the Kalispell compound.

"What are the chances of an incursion by hostiles within the next forty-eight hours, Herr *Kapitän*?" one of the men asked.

"Very low, if we continue to maintain a low profile," Speyer said. "But not zero." He looked at each of them. "If it comes to that, you will be released from your duties once our mission strike aircraft is airborne. At that point you will be on your own until you reach one of the emergency rendezvous points. If you manage to get that far, you will be picked up by friendlies."

"Any further question?" Baumann asked. When no one responded, he dismissed them.

CAMDEN

The FBI's safe house was actually a room in a Motel 6 on I-676. The place was run-down, but under reconstruction, the smell of fresh paint and plaster dust thick in the air. There were a few semis parked in back, and by tonight the place would be filled with truckers. There was a Denny's next door, a 7-Eleven across the frontage road, a package liquor store nearby, and a large truck stop a quarter mile away. The interstate on/off ramps were under repairs, too, and along with the constant traffic the area was a confused, dusty mess. Anonymity in the midst of chaos.

Lane and Frannie were met on the second floor landing by two FBI special agents who checked their identification. They were expected.

The Philadelphia SAC Michael Hood was waiting in 207; Metzler was in 208. Hood did not look happy. He was mystified by what the White House chief of staff had told him.

"Now maybe we can get this mystery cleared up," Hood said once the introductions were made. He was a tall man, with a solid football player's build, and a wide, pleasant face.

He reminded Frannie of a Labrador retriever: honest and friendly.

"There's no time for the long version, so I'll give it to you straight out," Lane said. "You know, of course, the threat we're facing. To complicate matters, we believe that there's a mole in the FBI. Someone highly placed who may be feeding this terrorist information."

"We'll skip over the part about my skepticism. If you're right, it means someone may be on the way here to silence our informant."

"That's why you were asked to move him," Lane said.

"How much time do we have, can you tell me that much?"

"Fifty hours."

"Then we'd better get to it," Hood said. He had Metzler brought over. The molecular biologist gave Frances an interested once-over, and then smirked at Lane.

"Who the hell are you, then, another government man here to waste time?" He was frightened and indignant because of it.

"We're the ones who're going to save your life for cooperating with us," Lane said pleasantly. "You were moved to this shithole because the people who hired you are not happy. They've sent someone to kill you."

Metzler glanced nervously at Hood and the other two special agents. "I turned myself in because the crazy bastards already tried to kill me once. And the shit they've got could kill hundreds of thousands, probably millions of people."

"We'll help you, but you'll have to help us, too," Frances said. "We want to know everything that happened."

"I've already told them—"

"I meant *everything*, Dr. Metzler, no matter how seemingly insignificant it might seem to you." She gave him a warm smile.

His lips compressed, and then he nodded his head. He looked as if he hadn't slept in a week; his eyes were red and his hands shook as he lit a cigarette. "It started about three months ago with Rudi Steiner, who owns a place on the upper west side called the Bund."

They were recording Metzler's story but one of the special agents was also taking notes. For the most part they let him tell his story, but a couple of times Lane interrupted him to clear up a point.

"Why did you come to the FBI?" Lane asked when he was finished.

"I wanted to get out of New York as soon as possible, before they did their thing."

"Yeah, but why did you blow the whistle?"

He glanced at Frances, and then shook his head. "I can be an asshole sometimes, I know it. But I'm no Tim McVeigh."

Frances smiled. "Just maybe you have saved the lives of a great many people, Dr. Metzler. I'd say that makes you one of the good guys."

They got a street map of midtown Manhattan north, and Metzler pinpointed the locations of the brownstone where the lab was set up in the basement, and the German-American club on Columbus. When he was done they took him back to his room.

"It would be a lot easier if we could use Washington on this," Hood said. "But if you're right, and there is an informant inside the Bureau, we'd be wasting our time. Which we might be doing in any event, because there's probably nothing left at the brownstone and this Rudi Steiner is probably long gone by now."

"We don't have any other choice," Lane said. "Who do you know in New York who's not busy right now, and who'll keep their mouths shut?"

"That depends on what you want to do. If we go in there guns blazing, there's no telling what we might run into. Booby traps, maybe. And considering the stuff Metzler says he loaded into those tanks, I for one wouldn't want to be anywhere near when they went off. Hell, maybe they're leaking."

"The lab will be our first stop," Lane said. "I'll have a CDC team meet us, but in the meantime we have to stake out both places. Very quietly. If the media gets wind that something's up, it might end up on television, and it's a safe bet that Speyer is watching."

"Do you think that he'd actually pull the plug?" Hood asked.

Lane nodded. "Yes, I do. And completely without remorse."

"I'm coming with you."

NEW YORK

Speyer's brownstone on West 86th looked empty, and no one answered the door when Lane walked up and rang the bell. Hood and the two New York FBI agents stood to one side with Frances, while the pair from the CDC waited in a van across the street. Columbus was busy, but only the occasional pedestrian or cab went by here. It was 7:00 P.M., only forty-eight hours to go.

"No one's home," Lane told the others. He took

out a lock pick and had the door cracked in under forty-five seconds.

"Easy, William," Frances cautioned.

He extended an eighteen-inch pointer and ran it slowly around the edge of the slightly ajar door feeling for trip wires, switches, or fail-safes. So far as he could determine, the doorway was clear.

"So far, so good," he said. "Stand by." He eased the door the rest of the way open, stepped inside the stairhall, and cocked an ear to listen. The house was quiet. There was a musty smell in the air, as if no one had lived here for a long time.

He took out his pistol, went to the end of the short corridor, eased open the basement door, and turned on the lights. "Anyone home?"

There was no noise. Not even the sounds of the air conditioner, or a clock chiming; the house was dead.

Frannie and the others came to the front door. "William?" she called.

"Check upstairs and in back," Lane ordered. "But it looks as if they're gone."

"Watch yourself," Hood cautioned.

At the bottom of the stairs, Lane flipped on the corridor light. A steel door at the end of the corridor was open, and he approached it cautiously. The layout was exactly as Metzler had described it. He found the lab's light switch and flipped it on. His eyes were immediately drawn to the glove box and the open steel container inside with the skull and crossbones symbol and the single word: *VORSICHT!*

CDC field agents David Holt and Deena Goldman wore biohazard suits and every move they made was methodical and very careful. One slip-up could mean death. Metzler told them that he'd washed everything down, but they were not going to bet their lives that he hadn't made a mistake.

Hood and the others were upstairs, leaving Lane and Frances alone for a couple of minutes in the corridor outside the lab.

"Is that the box you brought up from the bunker?" she asked.

"One and the same," Lane said. "It's a good thing that I didn't do what I wanted to do."

"What's that?"

"Open it to see what was inside."

Frances shivered. "It's good for you that I taught you how to listen to your instincts, love."

Lane had to laugh despite himself, and despite the gravity of the situation. Frannie was dead serious. Like every woman Lane had ever known, she felt that it was her God-given duty to change the man in her life. And she had, of course, but he wasn't about to give in so easily just yet.

"What's so funny?"

"Later," he said.

Holt took several samples inside the glove box and mounted them on the microscope's stage while Deena Goldman powered up the computer. The images that appeared were all hook-shaped stick figures. None of them were moving.

"This is the same as the sample," Holt confirmed.

"Are they dead?" Lane asked.

"Yeah. The inside of the box is loaded with disinfectant. Nothing could possibly live in there."

"Is there any way of telling how much of the virus there was?"

"Not really. It depends on the concentration inside the four bottles. But even at low pressures there could be a lot of it. Plenty to wipe out a good-size city." Holt looked over at Lane and Frannie. "That's just a wild-ass guess, but I think that if I'm mistaken it's on the low side."

Hood came to the head of the stairs. "It's all clear up here," he informed them. "Anything down there?"

"Nothing we can use," Lane said. "We'll be right up." He turned to the CDC agents. "Take whatever you need and then get out of here."

"We'll be here another twenty hours at least," Holt said. "We need to call for a backup—"

"We're walking away from this house in the next ten minutes. That's how long you have," Lane said. "If the news that we've been here leaks, the game is up."

Holt wanted to argue, but he looked around the lab and nodded. "I understand." He said. "We'll be out of here in ten."

The German-American club was obviously closed. A metal accordion gate was drawn across the door, and a couple of old men stood out front talking, while another rattled the lock. Lane, Frannie, and Michael Hood were in the back of the plain gray New York FBI van parked across the street. Special Agents John Tremain and Floyd Rudy had come down at Hood's request to help out. It was about the way Lane figured it would be. But he wanted to see for himself.

"There's probably a back way, if you want to get in there," Tremain suggested.

New York was a dead end after all. "There'll be nothing inside that'll help out," Lane said.

"We can keep someone here around the clock."

"Don't bother. I don't think anybody's coming back here. Ever."

The two New York FBI agents exchanged a look. "Can you tell us what we've been doing here tonight, with the CDC and all?"

"We were following up a lead we had in Philly," Hood said. "But it looks like we're too late. If you can run us back out to LaGuardia we'll get out of your hair."

"How do we log this, Mike?" Tremain asked.

"You don't."

WEST FRIENDSHIP, MARYLAND

The ADM Agribusiness truck finally arrived a few minutes after ten. The pilot Sergeant Heide was driving, and Sergeant Rudolph rode shotgun. They had taken their time coming east, avoiding most of the state truck weigh stations, and sticking strictly to the speed limits, despite that they had been stopped three times for log book checks.

The guards on the long driveway radioed to the house, and Speyer and Baumann drove down to meet the truck at the big barn. "Gentlemen, it's good to see you," Speyer told them. "Did you have any trouble?"

"Nothing more than we expected," Sergeant Heide said.

The barn doors were opened and Heide backed the truck inside almost all the way to the rear. He shut off the engine and he and Rudolph climbed down from the cab and stretched.

"It's good to finally be here," Heide said. The center of the barn was set up as a workshop with all the tools and equipment needed to put the agplane back together and to carry out the final modification.

"There's dinner waiting for you up at the house," Speyer said.

Heide eyed the long bench and the toolboxes. "Thank you, sir, but we had dinner on the road and

I'd like to get the aircraft put back together first."

"There'll be a modification, as I told you in Montana, but it shouldn't be terribly difficult."

"That won't be a problem, Herr *Kapitän*. How about the men?"

"They're ready, Carl," Baumann assured him. "We did a weapons check at twenty hundred hours, and they'll have their travel documents in order no later than oh eight hundred."

"There was no news on any of the radio stations we picked up on the way east. Are we on schedule, sir?"

Speyer gave him a vicious smile. "Forty-five hours and counting." Sergeant Heide was the only one who knew the whole story now other than Baumann.

"The aircraft will be ready to roll before dawn," Heide promised. "Are the plans and the parts for the modification here as well?"

"Yes, but there is one problem that must be rectified."

"What is it, sir?"

"I need a pilot."

A grin spread across Heide's face. He looked like a kid on Christmas morning. "I think that we can take care of that small problem, Herr *Kapitän*."

"Good man," Speyer said, clapping Heide on the arm. "I'll have Mrs. Speyer bring down your dinners."

Heide's smile died. "That won't be necessary, sir," he said carefully. "As I said, we had our dinner on the road just a couple of hours ago."

Speyer suppressed a momentary flash of anger, then nodded. "Very well. If you need anything, Sergeant Baumann will be at your disposal." He turned and walked off.

* * *

Baumann helped open the truck's door and lower the big steel ramp. "If I were you I'd watch myself when he talks about his wife."

Heide and Rudolph looked at him. "Are they having it out again?" Rudolph asked.

"Worse than ever." Baumann looked over his shoulder to make sure that Speyer hadn't returned. "I wouldn't be surprised if he kills her before this mission is completed."

Heide laughed. "It might be for the best all around, if you know what I mean."

The three of them removed the tie-downs holding the airplane in position. On the count of three they lifted the tail. The Bull Thrush was not a small aircraft. Even without its propeller, wings, and tail feathers, and empty of fuel, oil, and payload, it weighed nearly four thousand pounds. But it was well balanced on the main landing gear, and came out of the truck and down the ramp without too much effort.

When they got the plane to the middle of the barn, Heide chocked the wheels and got out the tools he would need. Baumann and Rudolph brought out the rudder and vertical stabilizer, and the elevators and horizontal stabilizer. They brought out the two wings with great care not to cause any damage and laid them out on either side of the fuselage. Last, they muscled the heavy three-bladed stainless steel prop out. They slid it onto the hub once Heide packed it with grease and placed the splice keys in their slots.

"This is a beautiful machine," Heide said earnestly as he worked.

"It's ugly, it looks like a big bug." Baumann laughed. "Now the Gulfstream, that is a pretty machine."

"It's a matter of function, Ernst. The Gulfstream

could not carry out the mission this one is designed for."

Baumann stopped what he was doing and stared at the back of Heide's head. He wondered if Carl truly understood what he had just said. If the White House decided not to pay the ransom, then this machine that Heide thought was so beautiful would be used to kill a great many people.

Heide turned and caught Baumann's expression. "What is it, Ernst?"

"You understand the full consequences if the mission develops?"

Heide shrugged. "I don't worry about things like that. I have a job to do and orders to follow. That's enough for me." He chuckled. "The rest of it gives me a headache."

Rudolph was checking one of the landing gear struts. He looked up. "You should take the advice, Ernst, and stop worrying like an old woman. The captain has not let us down yet. In a couple of days we'll be out of here and safe."

"And warm," Heide said. He made the shape of a woman's curves with his hands. "Very warm."

Speyer came down to the barn with the Mercedes. The agplane's tailfeathers were on, and Heide, Rudolph, and Baumann were working on the starboard wing, getting ready to lift it into place. "How much longer?"

"A couple of hours, Herr *Kapitän*," Heide said, wiping off a wrench. He was in his element.

"Have you started the modification yet?"

"It's almost finished. The plumbing's already installed along with the controls inside the cockpit. I mounted the delivery lever on the opposite side from the throttle so there can be no error. Once the wings are in place and secured, the wiring harnesses connected and the rest of the plumbing led out, we'll install the wing rack to hold the bottle, the control servo to open the valve and the spray nozzles. When I'm finished here, I'll start a weather track. This operation won't maximize if the winds aloft are wrong."

"The weather is supposed to hold for the next forty-eight to seventy-two hours."

"Good. Then all that's left to do is set the mission parameters. I'll need a flight path and alternatives, along with two landing zones."

"We'll work that out tomorrow after you've finished here and gotten some sleep," Speyer said.

"What about the weapon? When will I be allowed to inspect it?"

"Right now," Speyer said. He motioned to Baumann, who popped the Mercedes' trunk, brought out one of the bundles, and laid it on the workbench.

Rudolph stepped back a pace, but Heide gingerly approached the table, and carefully unwrapped the bundle. He had a great deal of respect for what he was handling; they all did. The cylinder's valve was sealed with duct tape, but that precaution was not very reassuring.

"It's okay to handle this without special protective equipment?" Heide asked.

"Yes. But be careful of the valve," Speyer warned. "It's very deadly stuff."

"I will be careful, Herr *Kapitän*, believe me." He shook his head. "To think that they developed this sixty years ago. If it had gone operational we might have won the war."

"Well, we're going to win a war of a different kind this time."

Heide grinned. "Yes, sir. We will even the score. Just a little."

WASHINGTON, D.C.

A few minutes after midnight Tom Hughes walked across the hall into the operations center where Lane and Frannie were poring over satellite images of the greater Washington-Baltimore area. They were looking for private grass strips that would not show up on any FAA list of small airports.

"Any luck?" he asked.

They looked up. Frannie's hair was a little disheveled, but Lane still looked matty in his light madras sweater and hand-tailored natural linen trousers. "Nothing yet, how about you, Tommy?" he asked.

"We might have caught our first break. Frank Lee finally got back to me. Thomas Mann has three phone lines and a pair of cell phone accounts. All of them are encrypted, but we have taps on them now. When someone calls we might not know what they're saying to each other, but we'll be able to tell where they're calling from."

Lane sat back and stretched his back, the only sign that he was as tired as the rest of them. "If I were Speyer I wouldn't allow any outside calls. It would be too dangerous." He frowned, and then a sudden grin spread across his face. "I just had another thought. You'd have to think that Mann knows where Speyer is holed up. They're pals, after all. We just have to force him into making a call."

"He'd have to know that making that call would be risky," Frannie pointed out.

"That's right, but there are risks, and then there are calculated risks. And he believes that his phone lines are secure."

"Well, arresting him and questioning him wouldn't do any good," Hughes said. "As soon as Speyer found out he would pull the pin. It would take something important to happen to force Mann to call."

"Give the man a cigar," Lane said. He snatched the phone and dialed the home number of the FBI's Helena SAC Linda Boulton. He held his hand over the mouthpiece. "If Chief Mattoon was arrested by the FBI tonight and held incommunicado, the word would get back to Washington. If there is an informer inside the Bureau, he would call Mann."

"That might work, William," Hughes agreed. "They might see Mattoon as a weak link. That's information Speyer would have to have. But it could cause him to make his strike early—that is, assuming the president decides not to pay the ransom."

"We all know the answer to that one, even if the president and his cabinet don't yet," Lane said. "But if this works, we'd be killing two birds with one stone; finding the informer and Speyer's location."

WEST FRIENDSHIP, MARYLAND

Gloria feigned sleep when her husband finally came to bed around three in the morning. She'd gotten a couple of hours sleep earlier in the evening, but impressions and worries and thoughts and fears were popping off in her brain like flashbulbs at the premiere of a major motion picture, and she was wide awake.

She got out of bed, put on her robe, and quietly left the bedroom without waking Helmut. Downstairs in the kitchen she opened a bottle of Dom Perignon and sat down at the counter to consider her situation.

Helmut was on the verge of doing something really stupid. She was convinced of it. Killing the men in Germany and even killing the crew aboard the ship were only a prelude to something much bigger. She was off balance and truly frightened for the first time in her life. If men wanted to kill each other, that was okay with her. She really didn't care. But now she was beginning to believe that her own comfort and maybe even her own life were in danger. That, on the other hand, was completely unacceptable.

When she'd left Hollywood she had burned a lot of bridges; told a lot of important people what they could do to themselves in very clear anatomical language. Her brothers and parents thought that she lived on another planet. And there was no one else. No close friends, no former lovers or ex-husbands whom she could count on for help.

If she tried to run now she knew that she wouldn't get very far. This place, like the Kalispell compound, was guarded by Helmut's toy soldiers. Thugs, actually. Although they might not hurt her, she had little doubt what Helmut would do when they brought her back. She shuddered. There was a sadistic edge to her husband.

There was only one person she knew who had any influence on her husband, and who would listen to her. And calling him would not be seen as an act of betrayal because he was a friend and a mentor to Helmut.

She dialed Thomas Mann's number by heart and it was finally answered after four rings.

"Yes?"

"Hello, Thomas, this is Gloria. I'm really sorry to call you so late like this, but I'm frightened and I just have to talk to someone."

"You should not have called here, *Liebchen*,"

Mann told her sternly. "But since you have, tell me your problem. Has something gone wrong with Helmut's mission?"

WASHINGTON, D.C.

The computer running the search engine on Mann's phones warbled. Hughes scooted over to the monitor that had picked up the incoming call, identified the number and was searching for the location. "We have a hit already, children," he called out.

Lane and Frannie came across the corridor on the run. "They couldn't have picked up Mattoon yet," Lane said.

"It's an incoming call," Hughes pointed out. The computer was chewing on a location. Hughes hit a few keys and a map of the countryside along the Interstate 70 corridor west of Baltimore popped up.

"There's lots of small grass strips up there. Might be what we're looking for," Lane said.

"It's coming," Hughes said. An irregular area about five miles wide and fifteen miles long was highlighted on the screen. As the computer continued its search that area got smaller and smaller, until a pair of addresses showed up. One of them was for a post office box in the small town of West Friendship, which was the billing location, and the other was for a rural delivery route on county road 144.

"Bull's-eye," Hughes said.

They went back to the maps in the operations center, where they found the address just west of the small town. There was no indication of an airstrip on the satellite images, but there were two wide open fields that would easily accommodate a small plane.

"So what do we do now, William?" Frances asked. "If we call in the troops, Speyer is just crazy enough to release the virus, according to what you've told us about him."

Lane glanced at the clock. It was 3:30 A.M. "We have a little more than thirty-nine hours, which gives us some leeway if we don't press him." He looked at his wife and friend and an instant message passed between them. They didn't have to ask what the next step would be. They knew it.

Speyer had to be stopped. And it was up to them to stop him.

13

THE WHITE HOUSE

Lane did not trust anybody's telephones now. If there was an informer inside the FBI, there could be another inside the White House. He showed up at the west gate a couple of minutes before four, and it took the Secret Service fifteen minutes to verify who he was, wake the president, and escort him inside.

When Lane was shown into the Oval Office a White House steward was pouring coffee for President Reasoner, who looked tired, but fit and alert. His anger had been replaced with determination. The bastards might be pounding at the gates, but the fort would hold if the president had anything to do with it.

"Good morning, Mr. President."

"Good morning, Bill," the president said. The steward left. "You wouldn't be here at this hour unless you had some news, and you weren't willing to trust anyone to give it to me."

"Yes, sir. We think that we know where Helmut Speyer is located. It's a farmhouse about twenty miles west of Baltimore."

"Thank God," the president said. "Now we're finally getting somewhere." He reached for the phone.

"If we send the police or the military up there Speyer will react by releasing the virus," Lane said.

The president hesitated. "If he finds out what's happening in time. We have some pretty good people."

"He'll have security measures all over the place.

It'd be very tough to take him by surprise."

"Very well. How do you suggest that we proceed?"

"First of all, we need some accurate intelligence. How many people he has with him. Where the two tanks are physically located, and how tight the guard is. Maybe they're booby-trapped. We just don't know."

"Go on," the president said. He wasn't happy.

"Speyer knows that we're looking for him; he'd be a fool to think otherwise. But to this point he doesn't know how close we are. I want to go up there and make a quick pass. Depending on what I find out we'll decide if we send the troops in, or if I go back and make a surgical hit."

President Reasoner looked down for a long moment, organizing his thoughts. When he looked up, he seemed even more resolved than he had a moment earlier. "If you fail or if you're delayed for some reason, we'll have no other choice but to make a strike. A very strong strike."

"I understand, sir. But the advantage is on our side this time. Speyer doesn't know that we're coming, and we have a day and a half."

"Then I won't keep you," the president said. "God speed."

"Thank you, sir," Lane said. At the door he hesitated and turned back. "Are you planning on paying the ransom if this doesn't work?"

The president shook his head, a hard look in his eyes. "Not a chance in hell."

WEST FRIENDSHIP, MARYLAND

Gloria was still sitting at the kitchen table when Speyer came down around 6:00 A.M. just before dawn. They sky to the east was becoming pale, and in the dim light she looked sickly. She'd been drinking but she wasn't drunk. Speyer gave her a disgusted look then went and put on the coffee.

"How long have you been down here?"

"I don't know, a few hours," she said. "What are you doing up so early?"

He took down two cups and got out the cream and sweetener. Now that they were this close he was tense and mellow at the same time. His nerves were jumping all over the place, which made it impossible to sit still, let alone sleep. Yet he was at peace, like General Rommel before a desert battle, sure of his coming victory. "There'll be plenty of time to sleep later. Right now I have too much on my mind."

"I'm frightened."

He chuckled. "Of what? If anything goes bad you'll be in the clear. You're just an innocent victim."

"I'm frightened of you."

"That's an acceptable fear," he said indifferently. "Live with it."

"Thomas agrees with me," she blurted.

Speyer gave her a hard look, then glanced at the telephone. "Is that what you did down here by yourself in the middle of the night? Get drunk and then make telephone calls? Disturb our friends when they were sleeping?"

"Just Thomas. He's not the enemy."

"Are you the enemy, Gloria?" he asked, his tone deceptively mild.

She shook her head, then flinched as he came to her. "I don't know what's going to happen."

"We're going to become very rich, my dear. Rich beyond even your wildest dreams." He took her by the shoulders and began to squeeze very hard. "What did you and the general chat about?"

She tried to squirm out of his grip, but he was far too strong for her. "You're hurting me, Helmut."

"Yes, I am. What did you tell him?"

"That you were about to do something crazy. Get us all arrested or killed."

"What else?" Speyer kept up the pressure, and he could see the pain and fear in his wife's eyes. It excited him.

"Nothing."

Speyer squeezed harder. If need be, he decided, he would break both her collarbones. That pain would be a reminder to her for a long time of exactly who was in charge. She whimpered. "I told him about Germany, and then about the sinking of the ship."

"What did he say?"

"Please—"

"What did the general tell you?"

"That I wasn't to worry. He has faith in you and I should, too."

Speyer smiled, released his iron-hard grip on her shoulders, then reached down and kissed her on the cheek. "Good advice, sweetheart."

She pushed him away, then rubbed her shoulders. There would be bruises by this afternoon. She hated that almost worse than the pain. "You're a bastard," she said.

"Yes, I am. But I'm the bastard who's in charge. Never forget it."

The sun was up by the time they passed through the tiny town of West Friendship and took the country road to the west. The morning was quiet, only the occasional tractor or farm truck on the road. Lane drovc thc Land Rover, Frannie rode shotgun, and Hughes sat in back with his wireless laptop. They came to the anonymous-looking driveway with the fire number 46-144 that had shown up after the phone intercept, and Lane pulled over to the side of the road a half mile beyond it.

"Not exactly a hotbed of activity this morning," Hughes said. He was connected with the main computer back at The Room. No further phone calls had been made since they left Washington.

Lane looked at the driveway reflected in the rear-view mirror for a long time. In passing he'd not spotted any of Speyer's guards, but that didn't bother him. Driving up to the Kalispell compound he'd not spotted any of the lookouts either. They were professional, and had been well hidden. He expected nothing less of them here.

What was bothersome, however, was the driveway itself. No one had come that way for a long time. The gravel was overgrown with grass. Undisturbed grass. Not flattened by the passage of a single vehicle anytime recently.

"What is it?" Frances asked.

"We may be on a wild goose chase," Lane said. "Are we sure that this is the right location?"

Hughes brought it up on his computer. "Forty-six, one forty-four. Unless someone switched signs, this is the place."

Frances suddenly realized what her husband was getting at. She turned and looked back down the road. "The driveway hasn't been used lately. Maybe there's another way in."

"Not according to the map," Hughes said. "And we didn't see anything on the satellite shots." He held the laptop up so that they could see the image on the screen. It was a topographic map of the immediate area west of the town and south of the Interstate. There was no other way into that piece of property.

"Write a message for the president," Lane said to

Hughes. "He knows that we're out here this morning. Tell him that we're in trouble and we need help right now." He put the Land Rover in gear, made a U-turn on the narrow road and headed back to the driveway. "But don't send it until it's necessary."

"Already on it," Hughes said.

Lane and Frances exchanged a glance. She took out her pistol, checked the load, and set her purse aside. She grinned. "You sure know how to show a girl a good time."

Lane laid his own gun on the seat beside his leg as he slowed down and turned onto the driveway. In the time since they stopped and turned around, no other traffic had come by. The morning continued to be lovely; a warm, gentle breeze came from the south, carrying the noise of insects and birds and maybe the very distant noise of a farm tractor. The countryside was rolling hills and patches of dense woods punctuated by the occasional farm field under cultivation, or fields left for grass.

"All set to send," Hughes said. "Are you sure that barging in like this is such a good idea?"

"We're a couple of investors being shown a piece of property by a friendly real estate saleswoman," Lane said. "What could be more natural?"

"Unless Herr Speyer and his merry band happen to be in residence," Frances pointed out. "They would certainly be surprised to see me again. But that's nothing compared to how they would react seeing you back from the dead."

"In that case, Tommy sends the SOS while I turn around and you start shooting at the bad guys."

Frannie's window was open. She checked the safety catch on her pistol and gave her husband a wicked grin. "Peachy," she said. "Maybe the inestimable Gloria Speyer will also be there. Bridge indeed."

The unused driveway cut through the woods for a few hundred yards where it followed the bottom of a low hill before coming out over the top. The two grass fields nestled between the hills were just as they had seen them in the satellite photographs. But the satellite shots had been taken at high angles and hadn't given a very clear indication of the elevations. Seeing them now in person Lane could see that, because of the sharp slope of both fields, it would take a hell of a pilot to land or take off from there.

There was a house, however, and a large barn plus some other outbuildings, the set-up nearly perfect for what Speyer was trying to pull off. But there was no sign of his troops or that this place was occupied.

Lane stopped at the crest of the hill, still within the dense woods. "Let's take a look before we drive down there," he said. He got out of the car and Hughes handed him a pair of powerful Steiner military spec binoculars.

The house stood out in sharp detail in the glasses. Some of the upstairs windows were broken out, and he spotted dozens of bullet holes in the wood beams of the front porch. Hunters, probably, with nothing better to do than shoot up posts. A NO TRESPASSING sign on the front door was half shot away, too. The barn and other buildings were in the same condition, or maybe even a little worse.

"Nobody home," Lane said.

"What do you want to do?" Frances asked.

"We've come this far, we have to check it out."

"With care, William," Hughes warned. "This could be a blind. And there is a lot at stake."

* * *

Sergeant Erwin Meitner was on west perimeter duty when he spotted sunlight glinting off something metal in the woods above the house across the creek. He turned his head toward his lapel mike. "Base, three, I have a possible contact west of my sector. Six hundred meters."

"What do you have?" Sergeant Baumann came back.

"Something on the driveway in the woods above the Hansen house," Meitner radioed. "Stand by." He raised his binoculars in time to see a Range Rover emerge from the woods and start down the driveway to the abandoned farmhouse. A RE/MAX REALTY sign was on the passenger door. "It's an SUV, real estate agent. Two people. A man driving, a woman in the passenger seat. Maybe a third person in the back."

"Are there any other vehicles?"

"No."

"Keep an eye on them. I'm on my way down."

Lane pulled up in front of the farmhouse. It looked in even worse shape close up than it did in the binoculars. A section of the roof had collapsed, and the entire building looked as if it was about to collapse in on itself.

The nearby barn was a wreck, too, as were the other buildings. It had probably been thirty or forty years since anybody had lived here.

"Not exactly a retirement palace," Frances said.

"Speyer may be desperate, but not this desperate," Lane told them. "He and his people aren't here." Lane sat back in his seat and stared at the house. They were missing something. Speyer might be a megalomaniac, but he wasn't stupid. He'd been well trained by his Russian masters, and had the Soviet Union not fallen apart, and the Berlin Wall not come down, Speyer would have risen very high in the Stasi. The place was significant.

Hughes was doing something on his laptop. He grunted in satisfaction. "Okay, this is the right location," he said. "Nobody has tampered with the signs and this is definitely where the telephone call originated."

"Could it have been a cell phone?"

"Land line," Hughes said.

"There are no phone lines coming to the house. They would have led along the driveway."

"Maybe they're buried underground," Frances suggested.

"Not out here, and not thirty or forty years ago."

"This is the right spot, William," Hughes said. "The phone call this morning originated from right here."

"Then we'd better take a closer look—" Lane said, when Hughes's computer chirped.

"Hold on," Hughes said. His fingers raced over the keyboard. "It's an incoming call from Thomas Mann. Encrypted."

"Incoming here?"

Hughes looked up and nodded. "Right here, William. Thomas Mann is having a conversation with someone in this house at this moment."

"Stay here. If there's any trouble beep the horn." He and Frances got out and, guns in hand, went into the house, holding up in the entry hall.

Stairs were to the left, living room to the right, dining room and kitchen farther back. The place was deserted, there was no doubt of it, yet the computer was telling them that Thomas Mann was talking to someone here and now.

Lane motioned for Frannie to cover him as he went back and eased open the door to the cellar. Light came from two broken-out windows. The stairs were gone, and the basement floor was under at least a half-foot of water.

They quickly checked the rest of the ground floor, leapfrogging from room to room; first Lane in the lead and then Frances.

Finding nothing, they took the stairs to the second floor as quickly and as quietly as possible. In a back bedroom Lane pulled up short. An electronic unit, about half the size of a VCR, was wired to a six-inch dish pointed out a broken window. Several green lights flickered on the front panel.

"Damn," Lane said, pushing Frances back out into the corridor and out of any sight line through the window.

"What is it?" she demanded.

"They're across the creek. Tommy was right, this place is being used as a blind." He holstered his gun at the small of his back and hustled her back downstairs. "That was a microwave relay for telephone calls."

"They know we're here."

"Unless they stationed someone on this side of the house they wouldn't have gotten a clear look at our faces. They might think that we're doing nothing but looking at a piece of property for sale."

"That explains why the driveway hasn't been used recently. They came over here on foot to set up the equipment. What do you want to do?"

"We're here to look at property. So that's what we're going to do. When we're done, we'll drive off and come back tonight."

"Let's not make them nervous," Frances said.

"Anything but," Lane agreed.

* * *

It seemed like a waterfall was roaring inside of Speyer's head. It was hard to think, to keep on track. What Thomas Mann was telling him seemed to be nothing short of impossible. "There's been no mistake, Herr General, you're certain of it?"

"I don't have all the details because Konrad is on the run now, and he won't surface until he's sure that he's in the clear," Mann said. "But that fool cop of his in Kalispell was shot dead this morning by the FBI."

"But why? What happened?" Speyer felt the pressure increasing inside of his head.

"I don't know, Helmut. My contact inside of the Bureau is just as much in the dark as we are. But the FBI was investigating him because of the shooting of that Jew in the Grand Hotel. For whatever reason, Mattoon decided to shoot it out."

"Then there's no problem, Herr General. Mattoon was a loose cannon. Now that he's dead he can't do us any harm."

"You're wrong," Mann roared. "Mattoon's death is a problem. Not only your problem, but mine as well. When the connection between him and Aden is made, it will undoubtedly lead back to me. Which is why I am going to ground myself."

"But there's no direct connection to my operation. At least nothing that would lead the authorities out here."

"You're wrong again," Mann said. "It's the old Jew. The shooting was faked by your Mr. Browne."

"Browne is dead. I saw him go down with the ship with my own two eyes."

"It's likely that Browne was an impostor. He either worked for the American government or for the Germans. Either way he wasn't working alone, which means that your name is known and almost certainly known in connection with your little project."

"Shit. Shit," Speyer said. He wanted to lash out, hit something, destroy somebody, anybody.

"Take my advice, Helmut, and get out of there while you can. Forget the project, just run."

"I can't—" Speyer said, but he was talking to a dead line. Mann had hung up.

Because of the angles Baumann could only see the back half of the Rover that was parked in front of the Hansen house. The man in the rear seat was large, but that's all Baumann could tell from this distance and because of the way the sun reflected off the windows.

"How long has it been parked there?" he demanded.

"Just a couple of minutes," Sergeant Meitner replied.

Baumann swung his glasses to the open bedroom window again. He'd thought he'd seen a movement, but it had been just a fleeting glimpse and now he wasn't sure if he'd seen anything. He could see that the microwave dish had apparently not been disturbed, however.

If they were in fact real estate agents and had spotted the equipment, they wouldn't know what to make of it. Maybe a college experiment. Something to do with a physics class, perhaps, though it didn't matter. This mission would be fully developed by tomorrow evening, and if the authorities showed up the entire operation could be moved out with just a few minutes' notice. Any cops unlucky enough to cross the creek would run into a maelstrom.

Baumann turned back to the Rover in time to see it back up and head left. He caught a quick glimpse of the front passenger, but he was unable to tell anything except that the passenger was female, or at least a person of very slight build.

"See, sir, they're from a real estate company," Meitner said.

Baumann could read the RE/MAX sign on the Rover's passenger door, but that meant nothing. What were they doing out here at this moment? Why not next week? Why today? He did not trust coincidences.

"Does anyone else have a twitchy feeling between their shoulder blades?" Hughes asked as they drove over to the barn.

"They know that we're here, all right," Lane said. "The question is what are they going to do about it?"

"I'd rather not remain long enough to find out," Frances put in.

Lane drove around to the front of the barn, putting it between them and the hill across the creek where the microwave dish was pointed. He pulled up and stopped.

"If the fiction is holding, we have a couple of minutes while they think that we're checking the barn," he said. "We know where they're holed up now, but we still don't know the layout up there."

"If the Marines come barging in, he's just likely to release the virus, isn't he," Frances said.

"In a perverse way that might be the least horrible thing he could do," Hughes told them. "If he gets it to Washington, tens of thousand of people, maybe more, are going to die. But if he releases it here, depending on which way the wind is blowing, maybe only a few hundred or a thousand will be infected. One wonders if the president will take that as an acceptable trade-off."

"He's not going to pay the ransom, so it might be his only real option," Lane said.

"Does he actually think that he can get away with this?" Frances asked.

"I think so."

"If he does plan on releasing the virus over Washington tomorrow night as he says he will, then he's facing another problem," Hughes said. "Mainly how to make his escape. He must have a plan."

"His Gulfstream is being watched; he'll have to accept at least that much," Lane said. "So unless he has another plane stashed somewhere he'll have to go commercial at some point. Baltimore would be the first guess, about the same time the gas is being released and everyone's attention is focused on getting survivors out of there."

"If he is as devious and heartless as you say he is, there is another option open to him," Hughes suggested. "He might send his men in one direction while he gets out in another."

"Sacrifice them?"

"It would be tidy for him."

"We'll have to find that out as well," Lane said. "Tonight."

Baumann watched them through the binoculars as the Range Rover emerged from behind the barn and headed up the driveway. When the car made the turn toward the hill there was a moment or two when he got a good look at the driver and passenger. He thought that he was hallucinating, that the strain of these past few months on the project had finally gotten to him. The business aboard the ship had been a nightmare, but it was nothing compared to what the captain was planning for the people of Washington.

His knuckles turned white and his hands shook so that he had to lower the glasses.

"What's wrong, Sergeant?" Meitner asked, concerned.

Baumann took a moment to frame his answer. "Nothing. *Alles ist in Ordnung.* Do you understand?"

Meitner nodded uncertainly. Did Baumann mean the language or the situation?

"If they come back, or if anyone else shows up, radio me immediately."

"Yes, sir. Of course."

The highway followed the valleys through the hills for another mile before it crossed over the creek and took a jog to the north. They came to a gravel driveway leading into the woods. This one was well traveled.

"That's it," Lane said, as they passed without slowing.

"I didn't see anything down there," Frances said.

"You wouldn't have. But they saw us."

Three-quarters of a mile farther, Lane pulled off to the side of the road. Hughes was working at his laptop, his fingers flying over the keyboard.

"Here it is," he said. "Purchased three years ago by Donald Smith, Redman, Arizona. Damn. My mistake, William, I should have caught it earlier. The brownstone in New York was purchased about the same time by a Robert Smith, Redman, Arizona."

Lane used his cell phone to speed-dial a special White House number. "Don't beat yourself up, Tommy. There had to have been tens of thousands of real estate transactions around the country in that month, or any other month for that matter. And don't forget, it was I who told you to look for a rental."

The president himself answered. "Ycs."

"Mr. President, Bill Lane. We've found them. I'm in my car on Maryland Highway 144 a few miles west of West Friendship. The farmstead we thought they were using turned out to be a blind alley. But we know where they are now. I'm going to send you an email with a map showing their exact location."

"Good work, Bill. What do you want us to do?"

"We still don't know their set-up. But we still have a little time. I'm going in after dark to see what I can find out. In the meantime, have the place put under surveillance. But they're going to have to stay out of sight, because if Speyer's people spot me they might shoot it out. But if they spot the Marines I think they'll release the virus."

"It's going to be the same deal as before, Bill. I want to know the exact moment you go in, and if you're not back at a specific time I'm sending in the Special Forces."

"Yes, sir. Has Speyer tried to make contact again?"

"No. Just the once."

"If he does, please let me know," Lane said. "I think that we were probably spotted up here. But if we're lucky they think we're real estate people looking at property."

"You know what's at stake," the president said. "Godspeed."

"Yes, sir. Thank you."

Baumann came up to the farmhouse from the western perimeter on the run. Speyer was hunched over maps spread out on the dining room table and Gloria was in the kitchen. Everyone else was either on guard duty or down at the barn.

"We must leave now, Herr *Kapitän*."

Speyer looked up, his complexion pale, an ugly expression in his eyes. He had already received some bad news. "What is it?" he demanded, his voice hard.

"Someone showed up at the Hansen farm, masquerading as real estate agents. They went into the house and the barn and then drove off. I think that it is a very good possibility that they saw the telephone relay equipment in the upstairs bedroom."

Speyer considered it for a few moments, then started to shake his head. But something in Baumann's expression stopped him cold. "What else, Ernst?"

"There were three of them. A man in the backseat, and a man and a woman in the front. The woman was the same one in the glider, the one who is probably a British intelligence agent, Frances Shipley."

Speyer put down the map. "Her being here now is no coincidence. Who was the man with her?"

"John Browne."

The news physically staggered Speyer. For a second it seemed as if his legs were going to buckle beneath him. "I'm not going to ask if you are certain—"

"It's either Browne or his twin," Baumann said. "We have no choice now, Captain. We must leave this place immediately."

"I don't understand how they could have found us."

"That doesn't matter. We have to abandon the mission and leave for Havana before we're trapped here."

Speyer's brain was going at light speed. His old look of cunning came back. "You're right, of course, Ernst. We're moving out immediately. But not to Cuba, not quite yet."

"Captain—"

Speyer turned back to the maps on the table and began feverishly rummaging through them. "Have Sergeants Heide and Rudolph report to me on the double, and then get the men packed up and ready to move out."

"To where?" Baumann demanded.

"I'll tell you that in thirty minutes."

Gloria came to the door five minutes later. She had a glass of champagne in her hand and she was already half drunk. Her lips curled into a sly smile.

"Did my ears deceive me, or did I hear Ernst say that John had come back from the dead?" she said.

Speyer had the solution, he was once again on track, in charge. He could see how the entire operation was going to work, no matter what anyone tried to do to them. He looked up from the maps. "Either that or someone who looked something like him. It doesn't really matter."

"No?" Gloria asked. She laughed. "He got your precious diamonds, or whatever they are, for you in the first place. And now he's come to get them back. And do you know what, Helmut?"

Speyer smiled at her. His decision was made about everything, and it gave him a great deal of satisfaction. "No, Gloria, what?"

"I don't think that there's a thing you can do about it now. I think that you're scared silly."

Speyer went to her and took her arm before she could back away. "Let's go upstairs," he said gently. "There's something I have to tell you, and then we're going to pack. We're leaving within the hour."

"Where are we going?"

Speyer led her to the stairs and they went up to the master bedroom. He took the champagne glass from her and set it aside. Gloria had an uncertain look on her face. She had been playing a dangerous game over the past couple of years, goading her husband, but she couldn't help herself.

"I asked you a question, Helmut—" she said, when he punched her in the face with his fist, breaking her nose and jaw, and knocking her to the floor. There was no pain, just a flat, very dull feeling in her face and neck, and a sick feeling in the pit of her stomach.

Without a word, or change of expression, he kicked her in the side just below her left armpit, next to her breast. This time the pain was immediate and immense, causing her to cry out with a muffled gasp.

He kicked her again, this time in her kidney. It felt as if her spine had been ripped out of her body. He stomped on her pelvis, she could feel the bones breaking, and on her stomach and chest, the pain mercifully fuzzing out with each blow.

She looked up at him, all of her hate and sarcasm gone. She felt a sense of wonder at how one human being could do something like this to another human being.

She saw the blunt toe of his boot coming toward the side of her head, but she couldn't do a thing to defend herself, and then the lights went out.

14

WASHINGTON, D.C.

President Reasoner and his hastily assembled National Security Council were seated at the long table in the White House situation room. It had taken less than a half hour since the phone call from Lane to get them here and up to speed with the latest development.

"We know where they are, but the problem still exists: How do we handle it?" the president said.

"With all due respect to Mr. Lane, he's acted like a maverick through all of this," National Security Agency Director Air Force Major General Thomas Roswell said. "He's ignored a lot of resources."

"I agree with you, he's all but thumbed his nose at us. But he's the only one who's gotten any results. And he's *my* maverick. If he tells us to move with care because this madman may release the virus at the slightest hint that we're getting close, then that's exactly what we'll do."

The president looked around the table. No one challenged him.

"How do we proceed?" he asked.

"Unfortunately we don't have a satellite in position, but we're going to have to throw a cordon around the farm and put a surveillance platform up," Roswell said. "I would suggest an *Aurora* out of Kelley in Texas. We can have it up here in ninety minutes which includes prep and actual flying time."

"Will Speyer's people be able to detect it?" the president asked.

"No, sir. It'll orbit the area at about one hundred fifty thousand feet. Even our Washington defense radars won't detect it. We'll get real-time images downlinked, which should help level the playing field somewhat."

"What about on the ground?"

FBI Director Dale McKeever spoke up first. "I think that whatever happens we have to make sure that they stay put up there. Worst comes to worst and Speyer actually releases some of the virus, it would hurt us a lot less in the relatively unpopulated Maryland countryside than here in the middle of Washington."

It was the same thought everyone had had the moment they'd learned Speyer's location, but McKeever was the first to say it out loud.

The president looked around the table for a consensus. When he had it, he nodded. "Agreed. I'll order the Andrews ASSAF unit to move out immediately. We should have the area secured by the time the spy plane gets up here." ASSAF was the All Services Special Armed Forces unit that had been created to combat the threat of terrorist acts on U.S. soil. Consisting of the crème de la crème of the special forces from each of the armed services branches, the unit was exquisitely trained, well equipped, and highly motivated.

"We have more than twenty-four hours," the president's national security adviser Leslie Newby said, glancing at the clock. "Maybe Lane will find something tonight when he goes in."

"Let's hope so," the president said. "Without him a lot of people could lose their lives."

WEST FRIENDSHIP, MARYLAND

"There has been a change in the mission plans," Speyer told Sergeants Heide and Rudolph. They had come up to the farmhouse on his orders. Baumann was assembling the others outside and getting ready to pull out.

"Is there a problem, Herr *Kapitän*?" Heide asked. Of all the men here, he was the most anxious for the operation to come off.

"Yes, there is. Which is why I'm pushing the mission clock up. Is the aircraft ready, the spray tank loaded on the wing, and the release mechanism operational?"

"Yes, sir."

"Very well. You and Sergeant Rudolph will remain here with the airplane until you receive radio orders from me, and only me. The rest of us will be moving out within the hour."

"We will be undefended here, sir, except for the two of us," Rudolph said.

"I understand that, but you won't be here for long," Speyer told him. They went to the maps on the dining room table. "I will send either code blue or code red," he said. He pointed to a small airport at Owings Mills just north of Baltimore. "If it's code blue, you will fly to Owings Mills where you will leave the aircraft. You can rent a car or arrange a ride to the Baltimore Airport where you will evacuate the area as planned." He looked up. "If it's a code blue it means that you will *not* release the virus. Are you clear on this?"

Both sergeants nodded. "What if we get the code red?" Heide asked.

"The winds are expected to remain out of the southeast for the rest of today," Speyer told them. He flipped to a large-scale map, this one showing only Washington and the area immediately around it as far out as the Beltway that completely circled the capital. "If it's red, you'll fly directly down to Falls Church and make your first pass over the city well north of the White House. You'll make your turn up here around Bladensburg, head south and start your last leg over the city so that you'll cross the river below the airport."

Heide took his time studying the map, memorizing the landmarks. Any mistake could be fatal.

"The effects of the virus won't be immediate so you'll have plenty of time to complete the mission, fly back across the river ten miles south of Andrews Air Force Base, and then head north again." Speyer pointed out the small town of Seabrook a few miles east of the interstate highway. "There's a grass strip you can use here. Someone will be waiting to pick you up and take you to Baltimore. By the time the first aches and pains and sniffles start in Washington, we'll be long gone."

Both sergeants looked up. "What are the chances that this will develop into a code red?" Rudolph asked.

Speyer considered the question for a moment. "Good," he said. "Very good."

Lane, Frannie, and Hughes stopped at a coffee shop in West Friendship. If Speyer's people left the farm, they would probably come this way because it was closer to the interstate highway. Before they went in, Lane called the president.

"A special forces unit from Andrews will be in place within ninety minutes, about the same time that an Aurora from Texas will arrive," the president said. "Has there been any movement out there?"

"Nothing yet, sir," Lane said. "Just make sure that the field commander keeps his people out of sight."

"The ball is in your court for now, Bill. But unless you come up with something tonight, I'm ordering the ASSAF unit to take Speyer's people by force."

"I understand, Mr. President. We'll do our best."

ANDREWS AIR FORCE BASE

Marine Major Jim Heinzman sat in the operations room watching the president finish his briefing on the closed circuit encrypted television link with the White House situation room. The Air Defense Command's 7777 Support Squadron, the "Lucky Sevens," had been given the heads-up on the developing situation twenty-four hours ago, so the president's message was not unexpected. What was coming as a nasty surprise, however, was the order that effectively tied their hands.

"Your people have to be put into place around the farm without disturbing so much as a mosquito," the president said. "If you are discovered, it's likely that Speyer will pull the plug. If that happens there will be casualties. Do you understand, Major?"

"Yes, Mr. President," Heinzman replied. He glanced at the others around the table, all of them his superior officers. They weren't going to like what he was about to say, but it was his life, and the lives of his men, at risk. "You're telling me, sir, that if we're ordered to go in and take the farm by force, that whatever else you have in place will have failed and we'll be doing our jobs not to eliminate casualties, but to minimize them. We will be expendable."

The president smile wryly. The circuit was two-way so he caught the angry reactions of the officers around the table. He held up his hand. "We can hardly fault an officer for telling the truth," he said. "The briefing book will be in your hands within ten minutes, Major. I want you up there in place by nine-thirty; that gives you about ninety minutes. Can you make it that soon considering your . . . restrictions?"

"Yes, sir. How soon can we expect the downlink from the Aurora? It would be a big help to have those pictures before we get close."

The president said something to someone off screen. "The Aurora will be airborne in just a few minutes. It should be over the farm in less than an hour."

"Very well, sir. We're on it."

"Good luck, Major."

"Thank you, Mr. President. In this situation I think we'll need it."

WEST FRIENDSHIP, MARYLAND

Baumann had finished briefing the men and checking out their civilian papers and travel documents in the great room at the back of the house when Speyer came in.

"Are we ready to leave? Papers in order, everyone clear on his orders and rendezvous point?"

"Yes, sir," Baumann said. Some of the men seemed disappointed.

"This element of the mission has been pushed forward not because of any mistakes that you have made," Speyer told them. "On the contrary, it is because of your training and skills that we're getting out of here early and without firing a single shot."

The younger men grinned, but a couple of the older ones looked skeptical.

"Your job now is simply to get out of here without being caught. The rest of the mission will go according to schedule, of course."

"What about when we get to Havana, Herr *Kapitän*?" one of the men asked.

"You will be met at José Marti Airport with sealed orders. They will speak for themselves." Once he was set up down there, he would need these men and eventually others as bodyguards. Cuba, despite Castro's propaganda to the contrary, was a dangerous place.

"Are you coming with us, sir?" another man asked.

"We'll be right behind you," Speyer assured him. He went to each man, clicked his heels at attention, saluted and then shook hands.

Speyer had left Heide and Rudolph to study the Washington map back in the dining room. They looked up when he came in.

"Are you ready?" he asked.

"Yes, sir," Heide said. "What about Washington's air defenses?"

"You'll be in a light plane, flying VFR at one thousand feet above the city, all legal and normal. They aren't expecting the attack until tomorrow night at the earliest. If it's a code red, we'll take them completely by surprise this morning."

Rudolph started to say something, but then he hesitated.

"What is it, Sergeant?" Speyer asked.

"If it's to be code red, Herr *Kapitän*, a great many people will die."

"That's correct," Speyer said, his irritation rising. "What is your point?"

"Why, sir?"

"Because the American government would have disregarded my instructions."

"No, sir, I mean why was the attack planned in the first place? The United States isn't our enemy."

Speyer nodded his understanding, keeping his anger in check. "They have been our enemy for sixty years," he said. "It's something that you should not forget." He gave Rudolph a hard look. "As for the attack, you may think of it as a demonstration. At the end of the war, Harry Truman had a choice to make with the atomic bomb. He could demonstrate it on an uninhabited island somewhere, or he could demonstrate it over a couple of Japanese cities. He chose the latter, and because of that choice no one on earth has ever doubted the reality or the power of nuclear weapons. We may do the same with our weapon."

"All we have to do is obey orders," Heide said. "Nothing could be easier."

Rudolph gave Heide an uneasy glance, but then he nodded. "We will follow our orders, Herr *Kapitän*."

"Good," Speyer said. "Change into civilian clothes now, and meet me in the barn in five minutes."

"Yes, sir," they said.

Baumann was supervising the men's departure when Speyer came out of the house. They were taking both minivans and two of the three SUVs. The third was parked in back of the house.

Baumann broke off and came over. "They're ready."

"Have all the airline reservations been changed without problems?" Speyer asked.

"No problems whatever."

"Send them off, then. I'll be finished in about ten minutes and we can get out of here." Speyer glanced back at the house. "Have you taken care of the extra tank?"

"It's going with our scuba equipment."

Speyer grinned and clapped him on the shoulder. "We're almost home free, Ernst. Just a little longer now." He turned and headed down to the barn.

The convoy was starting up when he entered the barn. He went immediately to a secret hiding place in a far, dark corner, and pulled out a bundle about the size of a carton of cigarettes from beneath a pile of debris. He went back to the agplane, where he stuffed the package completely out of sight behind the backseat. In order for somebody to find it, they would have to reach back and deliberately search for it. Short of that, they would have to unbolt the seat from the floor and remove it from the airplane.

He climbed out of the airplane and as he stepped back he reached inside a pocket, his fingers brushing the remote control detonator unit. When he pushed the button, the brick of Semtex plastic explosive he'd placed behind the rear seat would explode in thirty minutes. He would push the button the moment the agplane appeared above the treetops on its way down to Washington. Thirty minutes was plenty of time to complete the mission. Then, somewhere southeast of Washington, probably somewhere near Andrews Air Force Base, the plane would suffer a tragic malfunction and explode in mid air.

"*Alles ist in ordnung*," Speyer said to himself.

ANDREWS AIR FORCE BASE

Major Heinzman had thirty men under his command including the two chopper pilots. He had just finished his briefing in the Lucky Sevens' ready hangar, the pair of Bell UH-1 E/N Iroquois assault helicopters behind them ready to fly, when their two supply sergeants came in with their biohazard suits.

"We're going in with full gear, and it'll stay that way until the cylinder is secured," Heinzman said.

"What are the chances that the bad guys will give it up once they realize what they're facing, sir?" one of the men asked.

"Slim," Heinzman said. "Do not underestimate these men, people. They got their training from the KGB's old School One, and then from the Stasi's program. They are probably well-armed, and most definitely well-motivated. If you make a mistake they *will* capitalize on it."

The major never exaggerated. If he said they were facing a tough opponent, that's exactly what they could expect.

He glanced at his watch. "We should be getting real-time pictures of the farm in the next thirty minutes." He turned to the large-scale map on the briefing board. "Until we get those pictures we're not approaching any closer than five klicks." He pointed to an area well south of the interstate. "There's some public land down here consisting of a gravel pit and several open fields. We'll use it as our primary staging zone. The CDC is sending up a recovery unit that will meet us there. But nobody moves closer until we get the pictures."

"What about this civilian who's supposed to be going in for a look?" one of the men asked.

"Apparently he's not going in until after dark," Heinzman said. It was clear from the tone of his voice what he thought of civilians meddling in military operations. "It's my intention to make his incursion unnecessary. Do I make myself clear?"

"Yes, sir," the men shouted. They were pumped.

WEST FRIENDSHIP, MARYLAND

Lane, Frances, and Hughes sat in the coffee shop watching what little traffic there was pass by. The few regulars having their morning coffee paid them little or no attention. Lane was obviously brooding about something.

"What's the matter, William?" Frances asked.

"We can't wait here like this all day," he said. "They could just as easily go the other way and we'd miss them."

"Do you think they're starting to get nervous because they saw us out at the farm?" Hughes asked.

That's exactly what Lane had been thinking about. "It's a possibility," he said. He put down some money for the bill. "I'd rather wait out there where we can keep an eye on the driveway."

"I think you're right," Hughes said.

Sergeants Heide and Rudolph were holding up the convoy, talking to the men, when Speyer emerged from the barn.

"Why are they still here?" he shouted to Baumann. His nerves were jumping all over the place.

"They were just wishing us good luck, Herr *Kap-*

itän—" Rudolph said. Speyer cut him off.

"Get them out of here, Ernst." He turned to Heide and Rudolph. "Do you have your papers and travel documents?"

"Yes, sir."

The rest of the men had mounted up. They pulled away and headed up the driveway toward the highway. They would be at the Baltimore Airport within the hour.

"You're clear on your orders?" Speyer asked. "No questions? You know exactly what is expected?"

"Of course, sir—"

"I want you in the barn with the airplane ready to fly the mission the instant you receive my radio message. Is that also clear?"

Heide and Rudolph stiffened to attention. "*Jawohl, Herr Kapitän,*" they said.

"*Güt,*" Speyer snapped. "*Denn, gehen Sie. Jetzt!*"

Both men saluted, turned on their heels, and hurried down to the barn as the last of the convoy disappeared up the hill into the woods.

"They haven't thought it out," Baumann said. "The plane will be contaminated with virus. No one will be able to approach it."

"There must be sacrifices in war. Every soldier understands that fundamental fact." Speyer smiled sadly. "We will make a toast to them in Havana."

"Only two casualties is an acceptable price to pay."

"Only two, Ernst," Speyer said. They started to the back of the house where the SUV with their things was parked.

"What about Mrs. Speyer?" Baumann asked. "Is she ready to leave?"

"She won't be coming with us."

Baumann gave Speyer a worried look. "If she remains here won't she present a danger? If she is arrested she can be made to talk. It will come out where we've gone."

"Not to worry, my friend, I have taken care of it," Speyer said. "She won't talk. Not to anyone, ever again."

Baumann was struck more by Speyer's matter of fact tone of voice than what he said. "Yes, sir," he said softly.

They stopped to remove the RE/MAX signs from the passenger and driver's doors. Without them the Rover would be slightly less obvious to anyone who'd seen it earlier. Lane drove fast, worried that he was going to be late. He was probably wrong about them moving out so soon just because they'd seen someone at the next door farm. But warning signals were jangling all along his nerves, and he had learned to trust his instincts; they were right more often than not.

"I'm in the ASSAF squadron's database," Hughes said from the backseat, his computer up and linked to the mainframe at The Room. "They're mounting up now. Pair of Iroquois assault helicopters."

"Noisy beasts," Frances said. "If they get close the game will be up."

"Do they have a landing zone?" Lane asked.

"About three miles from the farm. They'll be well out of sight until they're needed—"

They came around a curve as two minivans and a pair of Toyota SUVs came from the opposite direction. There was nothing Lane could do except keep driving and keep his eyes straight ahead on the road. But it was obvious from the glimpses he caught that these were Speyer's men. They had the look. He thought that he might even have recognized a couple of them from the Kalispell ranch.

"Speyer and Baumann are not with them," Hughes said.

"Neither is Speyer's wife," Frances said.

Lane sped up around the curve. "Did they pay any special attention to us?"

"They didn't seem to be," Hughes said. "Should I give ASSAF the heads-up?"

"Not yet. I want you to follow them. My guess is that they're going to the Baltimore Airport to get out of the country. Which means that this is going down today, not tomorrow night."

"Why?" Frances demanded.

"I don't know. Maybe he thinks we won't pay him." Lane made a U-turn about fifty yards from the driveway to Speyer's farm. "It leaves the airplane," he told them, pulling over to the side of the road. "It's either still here with Speyer and Baumann, or his troops are heading to wherever it's hidden."

He got out of the Rover and Frances slid over to the driver's side. "Be careful, William."

"You, too," Lane said. "As soon as you find out where they're headed call in the Special Forces. But Speyer's people mustn't be allowed to reach the plane, if that's where they're going. And it'd be better if we could avoid a firefight in or around the Baltimore Airport if that's where they're headed. A lot of innocent people could get hurt."

"There's a lot of that going around these days," Frances said.

Lane slammed the door, stepped back, and waved them off. As Frances headed away he crossed the road and entered the woods, drawing his pistol as he went.

Baumann drove along an old horse path at the base of the hill behind the house that led down to the shallow creek and up the other side to the Hansen farmstead. The summer morning was delightful; warm, bright, only a few puffy white clouds in the sky, a gentle breeze and the smells of the country in the air. He decided that he could have been happy here. Far happier than in Montana or even in Germany. This was good land. He could have been a farmer.

He glanced over at Speyer. Staying here was not possible, of course, no matter how right the area felt.

"We've been through a lot together, old friend," Speyer said, completely misinterpreting Baumann's expression. "Now we've just about made it to the payoff."

Baumann nodded. "No more casualties then."

Speyer's expression darkened. "Don't be tedious, we've already covered that."

"No, sir. I mean Carl and Hans."

"They're dead men—"

"Only if you send them the code red and they release the virus. We don't have to do this. Send the code blue and we can all walk away from this with clear consciences."

Speyer laughed. "Only a fool has a conscience, Ernst." He shook his head. "You know the consequences in the German army for not following orders."

Baumann looked away. "Yes, sir," he said. He automatically scanned the treeline above the farmstead for any sign that Browne had come back and was up there watching them. In a way he wished that it were so, and that this insanity would end.

"You worry too much," Speyer said. "Leave that part to me."

"Yes, sir," Baumann replied. He drove up from behind thc ramshackle old house and parked in front, out of sight from the creek. They would wait here until the agplane appeared above the trees on its way to Washington. Speyer would push the button and they would drive immediately to the airport at Frederick, about twenty-five miles west, where a charter bizjet and pilot were waiting for them.

Nothing could be simpler, Baumann thought, than to follow orders. Except he couldn't shake the vision of tens of thousands of people filling the hospital emergency wards, too weak even to stand, dying horrible, painful, bloody deaths.

Speyer set up his laptop computer on the SUV's open rear hatch. He made the telephone link through the equipment in the upstairs bedroom and was connected with the first of his off-shore banks in less than three minutes. A minute later, after entering the proper identification code, he came up with his account, which showed no new transactions.

His lips compressed. He looked up at Baumann watching him.

"Nothing yet, Herr *Kapitän*?"

Speyer shook his head and brought up the next account. There had been no deposits to it in seventeen months. He tried a third and a fourth account with the same results.

"They have more than twenty-four hours to act," Baumann said.

"They're not interested in dealing with me, Ernst," Speyer said. He backed out of his account search, and brought up the White House number. "Sending Browne and that woman here after me proves that much, so before we give the code red we'll supply them with a little misdirection."

From where Lane crouched just within the woods he had a good view of the farmhouse, barn, and outbuildings. Nothing moved, which didn't mean a thing. At the very least Speyer and Baumann were down there and could be waiting out of sight. The airplane, if it was here, could be locked away in the barn. And there could be one or more of Speyer's men left behind to watch over it.

He was to the east of the driveway, the house one hundred yards directly below him, and the barn and other buildings on the other side. Keeping low, he emerged from the woods on the run, zigzagging left and right in an irregular pattern in case a marksman was trying to take a bead on him. He had run out of time for not taking chances. If they saw only one man coming they might not release the virus just yet, thinking instead that they could take care of him.

He reached the back corner of the house without shots being fired, however, and he stopped to catch his breath. The morning was very quiet. Only a few birds were singing, and if he held his breath and listened hard enough he thought that he could hear the gurgling of the small creek.

His eyes fell on a rutted track through the grass that led down the hill away from the house. The grass had been flattened very recently. As he watched, some of the taller blades started to spring back. Someone had gone that way just minutes ago. Speyer and Baumann, to the next door farmstead where the telephone equipment was set up.

Whatever they had planned was starting now. But he had to make sure that no one had been left behind. He didn't want to take a bullet in the back.

Around front he mounted the porch and tried the door. It was unlocked. He opened it, held up for a moment to see if he was going to draw any fire, then slipped inside, sweeping his pistol left to right.

Everyone was gone. The house was deathly still, though he could still smell the lingering odors of breakfast. If anyone was left at this farm they would probably be in the barn. He turned and started for the door when he heard a noise from somewhere upstairs. He spun around, his pistol at the ready, all of his senses alert. He held his breath.

It sounded like a kitten mewing, perhaps a small animal crying weakly. Whatever was making the noise, he decided, was in pain. As he started up the stairs he had a sick feeling in the pit of his stomach that he might know what it was.

Gloria, the side of her head beaten to a bloody pulp, a big pool of blood on the floor between her legs and smeared back across the floor to the middle of the bedroom, lay curled in a fetal position halfway out into the hall. Somehow she had managed to get the door open and crawl this far. Now she could only lie there and cry.

Lane holstered his pistol and dropped down beside her. Her eyes were open and when she saw who it was, she reached out for his arm.

"Who did this to you?" Lane asked, keeping his voice soft. A very hard knot had formed in his stomach. "Was it your husband?"

She blinked her eyes and managed to give a very slight nod. Her grip tightened on Lane's arm. "Is he gone?" she whispered.

"I think he went next-door with Ernst. Where is the airplane? Do you know?"

She blinked furiously as a spasm of pain hit her, and she coughed up a big glob of blood and mucus.

"I don't know how soon I can get you help, Gloria," he told her. "I think that they're going to use the virus soon, maybe even this morning. You'll have to hold on."

"Here—" she whispered.

He leaned closer to her. "I'll try to do what I can for you, but we have to stop them."

"Here," she whispered again. "The airplane is here."

"Where?"

"In the barn. Heide and Rudolph are with it." She panted, trying to catch her breath, but even more blood welled from her nose and mouth, and the pool of blood on the floor beneath her was growing.

Lane wiped her mouth with his handkerchief and gently stroked her face. He took his time with her, although he wanted to race down to the barn. She was only one woman dying here. There were tens of thousands of potential victims in Washington.

"He's crazy," Gloria said. She closed her eyes for a moment, then opened them again. "But I loved him—" Her eyes went unfocused, came back and then went blank, her body sagging loosely in death.

Lane sat back on his haunches, and studied her face. She had been a woman who had made bad choices all of her life. But they had been mostly innocent decisions, until she met Speyer.

He removed her hand from his arm and got to his feet. He took one last look at her, then pulled out his pistol and headed downstairs, his heart harder than it had ever been in his life.

WASHINGTON, D.C.

The Oval Office was filled with the president's advisers and most of his National Security Council, everyone talking at once when Leslie Newby's voice rose over the others.

"Mr. President, it's him on the computer."

The president's advisers had been arguing all

morning to no avail for the president to leave Washington. The room abruptly fell silent.

The president went to the computer on the coffee table in front of Newby and sat down at it. The message on the screen was simple and to the point.

"There are less than 34 hours remaining. Why have no deposits been made as instructed?"

A good deal of discussion amongst the president's advisers had been about the issue they were facing right now. Tell the bastard that he would never get any money from the U.S. government and that he would be hunted down like a rabid animal, or try to stall him by promising him whatever he wanted in order to give Lane and the ASSAF time to do their jobs?

The president typed his reply. "Why are you doing this? You know that you will get caught."

"That is my concern. Yours is the safety of the people who voted you into office. Where is my money?"

"We need more time."

"You have already wasted more than half of the generous amount of time that I allowed you, without so much as a token payment. WHERE IS MY MONEY?????"

The president glanced up at the expectant faces all watching him. He typed: "You will have your money before the end of your deadline. I hope you rot in hell."

This time the president broke the connection as everyone started to talk at once.

WEST FRIENDSHIP, MARYLAND

Lane approached the barn from the back where he could look through the cracks between the uneven boards. Speyer had beaten his wife to death with the heel and toe of his boots, by the look of the marks on her head and on her clothing. The woman had been a twit and a lush but nobody deserved a death like that, especially not at the hands of someone she loved. "You'll be dealing with me before this is over, pal," he said softly.

The agplane was parked in the middle of the barn, its nose pointed toward the big double doors, its canopy open. A pair of compact Steyr AUG 9mm Para submachine guns were propped against a tool case a few feet away. A cylinder about the size of a scuba tank was connected under the wing on the left side, and even in the imperfect light Lane spotted the plumbing connections attaching it to a bell-shaped set of three spray nozzles.

At first it appeared that the barn had been deserted, but then two men came into view from the front of the plane. He recognized both of them from the Kalispell ranch. This time they were dressed in civilian clothes, and they both looked angry, as if they had been arguing.

They spoke in German, most of which Lane could pick up.

"We can turn our backs on this, Carl, and you know it," Rudolph said.

"We would be on the run for the rest of our lives."

"Better than dead."

"You heard the *Kapitän*. We'll be long gone before

the effects are felt in Washington. By the time they know what hit them we will be in Havana."

"You dumb bastard, look at the nozzles," Rudolph shouted. "The entire side of the airplane will be contaminated. No one will be coming for us. We're dead men."

Heide studied the spraying arrangement under the wing, and after a few moments he nodded. "You could be right, unless the *Kapitän* has brought a neutralizing agent. Something to clear the way for us."

Rudolph turned away in disgust, his eyes falling on the crack in the boards where Lane was watching. He hesitated for just an instant before he turned away nonchalantly. Too nonchalantly. "Maybe you're right after all," he said, moving toward the weapons.

Lane sprinted to the front of the barn, flicking the Beretta's safety catch to the off position. He looked cautiously through a crack in the main doors. Heide and Rudolph, both armed now with the assault rifles, stood covering the rear wall.

Lane eased one of the doors open just wide enough for him to slip inside. He reached the side of the airplane before they heard anything, and Rudolph turned around.

"Nobody needs to get hurt here," Lane said.

Heide turned around, too, his eyes narrowed, obviously calculating the odds. There were two of them, trained soldiers armed with submachine guns, up against only one civilian armed with nothing more than a pistol.

"A prison cell is preferable to a slab in the morgue," Lane said.

Rudolph glanced at Heide. "Let's give it up, Carl—"

Heide started to bring his rifle up and Lane shot

him in the chest just below his breast bone, driving him backward off his feet.

Committed now against his will, Rudolph was bringing the submachine gun to bear when Lane switched aim and fired two shots, one catching him in the groin and the second in the chest in almost exactly the same spot Heide had been hit. He went down on one knee, an almost apologetic look on his face, and then toppled over.

Lane quickly checked to make sure that both men were dead, then checked the front to make sure that Speyer and Baumann across the creek hadn't heard the shots and were on the way to investigate. For the moment no one was coming.

Holstering his pistol, he went back to the airplane and inspected the plumbing and control connections to the tank. It was possible that by trying to disconnect it from the wing he might inadvertently allow some of the virus to escape. The CDC antiterrorist team would be better equipped and qualified for the job. In the meantime, he would make sure that the plane would not be flying any time soon.

He found a Zeuss fastener tool and quickly undid the twelve fasteners holding a section of the engine cowling in place. When he had it off, he found a pair of wire cutters and began cutting ignition wires and fuel lines and electronic wiring bundles. The job took less than five minutes, but it would take hours, perhaps days, to put the airplane back into flying condition.

When he was finished, he took one of the submachine guns, slipped out of the barn, and headed to the rear of the house and the path that led across the creek.

* * *

"The president said that we would get paid," Baumann tried to argue.

"He was lying," Speyer said. "Put yourself in their shoes. What would you recommend to the president? That he tell us to go to hell?" Speyer shook his head. "If they were going to pay us anything, they would have started the transfers by now. They're stalling for time."

"Then let's drive back to the farm, pick up Hans and Carl and leave. We can take both cylinders."

"You still don't understand, do you, Ernst," Speyer said tightly. It was almost impossible to keep on track, to keep from exploding with rage. How easy it would be to pull out his gun and put a couple of rounds into Sergeant Baumann's complaining face.

"You want to demonstrate the weapon, yes, I know this, Herr *Kapitän.* But those are innocent people in Washington. Women and children. And the sample we sent to the White House has been analyzed by now. They know what we have. No need for us to take any more risks."

"There will be no further risks to us," Speyer replied. "The weapon will be delivered, Carl and Hans will die, and we will be long gone before anyone is the wiser. Then, in a few months, we will open the bidding on our weapon from a position of safety."

"You're forgetting Browne—"

"If it was actually him, something I'm starting to find hard to believe, why hasn't he returned with the authorities?"

Baumann had no immediate answer.

Speyer keyed the walkie-talkie. "Unit one, code red. I repeat the message. Unit one, code red, code red."

Baumann shuddered, but then the moment passed and he looked down toward the line of woods where they would be seeing the airplane take off in a few minutes. "*Jetzt, er ist fertig*," he mumbled. Now it is finished.

Speyer was suddenly in good spirits. He packed up his laptop and put it and the walkie-talkie in the back of the SUV along with their luggage and scuba equipment. A little diving vacation. It was just what the doctor ordered, they would tell anyone who asked.

Baumann went into the house to get the telephone equipment while Speyer got out a pair of binoculars and scanned the tree line across the creek. He took out the detonator control and laid it on the open tailgate, and then checked the tree line again.

Patience was not one of his virtues. He had fought the problem all of his life. Most of the time he had been surrounded with stupid, dull people who were always a couple of steps behind him. He had learned to control himself, to slow down, to let them catch up. But it wasn't easy.

By now he was certain that he should be hearing the agplane's big radial engine. But the morning was quiet. Too quiet.

Baumann came out of the house with the telephone relay and small dish antenna. He, too, realized that something was wrong. He stopped and cocked an ear. "Maybe they are having trouble with the engine."

Speyer grabbed the walkie-talkie out of the back. "Hans, this is unit one, come back."

There was no answer.

"Hans or Carl, this is unit one, come back."

Still there was no reply.

Speyer tossed the walkie-talkie in the SUV, pocketed the detonator unit, and shut the tailgate. "We have to get down there. Something has gone wrong."

15

I-70 WEST OF BALTIMORE

Frances eased the Rover into the right lane a quarter mile back from the convoy. Traffic was moderate at this time of the morning so it was easy to keep up with Speyer's people. They passed a sign that said BALTIMORE-WASHINGTON INTERNATIONAL AIRPORT, 27 MILES VIA I-695. There was little doubt in her mind now that she knew what was going on. Speyer's people were simply making their escape. William, on the other hand, was in the middle of it back at the farm.

Tom Hughes was on the computer. He looked up as they passed the road sign. "It's the airport then."

"Are you still in the strike force database?"

"Yes, but they took off about twenty minutes ago."

Frances glanced over at him. "Have they reached the farm?"

Hughes brought up the Lucky Sevens' encrypted mission operation program overlaid on a grid reference map of the West Friendship area. "They're about three miles out from their staging zone."

"How long would it take them to get up here?"

"Not very long once I convince them it's what they should do."

"Get started, love." It was hard for her to keep her head focused on the task at hand, thinking about William up against Speyer and Baumann. She wanted to be with him more than anything she'd ever wanted in her life. Pregnancy does that to a girl, she thought wryly. And that was something that neither of them had planned.

Hughes's fingers flew over the keyboard, and after a minute he was into the squadron's voice circuits. "Good morning, I would like to speak with your commanding officer, Major Heinzman, please."

The face of a very startled gunnery sergeant came up on the screen. "Who the hell is this? You're on a U.S. military tactical circuit. Get off now!"

"Gunny, I don't have the time to have the nice chat that I know you and I could have, so I'm going to show you something," Hughes said pleasantly. He hit a key and the strike squadron's entire operations program was shut down, replaced by a rapid-fire profile of Speyer's entire operation and the role that Lane had in busting it up.

The data transfer took less than ninety seconds, and when the screen cleared again Major Heinzman, in battle fatigues, was there.

"Okay, Mr. Hughes, you have our attention, what can we do for you?"

"Are you in sight of the farm?" Hughes asked.

"No, but we're coming in on our staging area."

"I need you to divert your troops to my position so that we can avoid a bloodbath." Hughes quickly explained the situation to the Lucky Sevens commander. When he was finished he pulled up the mission map, expanded it, and pinpointed the convoy's location.

Major Heinzman was vexed. "You're going to have to show my people how you do that to our computers."

"Agreed," Hughes said. "How soon can you get here?"

"What about the farm?"

"Bill Lane will take care of that for the moment. We have to deal with this problem first."

Heinzman consulted with someone off screen and

when he came back the mission map insert at the bottom right of Hughes's screen showed that the helicopters were already turning to the east. "Our ETA is four minutes," he said. "Those are Captain Speyer's men, so I'm assuming that they are heavily armed."

"That's a good assumption."

"Okay, we'll make one pass from the rear and I want you to try to stop traffic if you can."

"We'll do our best. Good luck, Major."

"They're not getting to the airport, I can guarantee it, sir."

WEST FRIENDSHIP, MARYLAND

Lane had just crossed the creek and started up the path on the other side when he heard the SUV coming his way. He scrambled off the path and ducked into some brush and high grass, the Austrian-made submachine gun in hand.

The heavy sport utility vehicle was moving fast, and as it flashed past Lane, bumped across the creek and disappeared up toward the house, he caught a brief glimpse of Baumann at the wheel with Speyer riding shotgun. Neither of them looked particularly happy. Lane's guess was that they tried to make contact with the two men in the barn and were coming back to investigate what the trouble was. It probably meant that Speyer had given the order for the operation to begin. It was a chilling thought. But Lane didn't understand why Speyer and Baumann hadn't left with the others. Why had they stuck around at the next-door farm?

Lane got up and started after them. One tank of the virus was still strapped to the airplane, while the other was probably in the SUV. Talk about trotting down into hell, he thought. He was practically slavering to get there.

Baumann pulled up alongside the barn and parked twenty feet from the front. Speyer pulled out a Glock 17 and jumped out of the SUV. Baumann took out his own gun and joined him.

"They should have had the engine started by now," Speyer said.

They ran to the front of the barn, Baumann scanning the tree line up toward the highway for any sign of movement. He had a feeling in the pit of his stomach that Browne had come back, and that they were all in for it.

Speyer peered around the corner, then went to the big doors and looked through a crack. "*Verdammt*," he said. He yanked open the barn door and disappeared inside.

Baumann made a second quick sweep of the open fields around the farm, then followed Speyer inside. Part of the airplane's engine cowling had been removed and he could see that someone had made a mess of the wires. Heide and Rudolph lay in pools of their own blood.

Speyer went from the airplane to the two downed men, feeling for a pulse. He was beside himself with rage. When he looked up his face was that of an insane man's. "They'll pay," he said through clenched teeth.

"We can worry about revenge later, Herr *Kapitän*. We must leave now while we still can. We can drive to Frederick as we planned. We can be in Havana with the men by this afternoon."

"We're going to stay here and fix the airplane," Speyer said, getting up. "Thc mission is still a go. Especially now."

"Who is going to fly it? Carl is dead."

"You'll fly the airplane, Ernst."

"I'm not a pilot."

Speyer laughed. "Anybody can turn an ignition switch, taxi down a runway and take off. That's the easy part."

"I won't do this," Baumann said. Before Speyer could react, Baumann slipped outside and headed back to the SUV.

"Go, you bastard!" Speyer shouted. "Run! Coward!"

Speyer had gone completely mad. There was no reasoning with him now. The only hope was getting out of the country as rapidly as possible.

Lane came up behind the barn from the creek in time to hear the argument. He hurried around to the SUV, checked to make sure that the second tank was in the back, then took the car keys out of the ignition and ducked down out of sight as Baumann came charging around from the front.

When he was sure that Speyer wasn't coming immediately, he stood up and stepped around the back of the SUV, the submachine gun in the crook of his arm. "Good morning, Ernst."

Baumann stopped short, his left hand outstretched, and the pistol in his right pointing down toward the ground. "*Gott in Himmel,*" he said softly. "I knew it was you."

"He's gone completely around the bend, hasn't he?"

"Yes, yes. He meant to release the virus over Washington whether we got paid or not."

"Why didn't you stop him?"

Baumann shook his head as if the question was incomprehensible. "We were following our orders. It was very simple."

"All those people in Washington would have died."

"It's not my responsibility. I was following—"

"Yeah, I know, pal, you were just following your orders," Lane said harshly.

Baumann saw something in Lane's eyes and realizing all of a sudden that he was in trouble, started to raise his pistol. Lane pulled off two rapid shots both hitting the German in the heart, killing him instantly.

It was John Browne. Speyer recognized the voice. He stepped back from the barn door, the Glock 17 in his hand, his heart in his throat. He'd seen the bastard in action. They all had in Kalispell and in Germany and again at sea. He was a demon. He had shot Ernst to death, and now he was coming in here to finish the job.

Such a long time since Berlin. They had come a long way out of the ashes; too far for it to end here when they were on the verge of such a fabulous victory. This was the operation that would get the world's attention.

He glanced at the ruined airplane engine. That was too bad, but the two tanks of virus were still intact. Still just as deadly.

All that stood between him and success now was the one man. Only one.

Speyer turned and hurried back to the ladder up to the hayloft. He looked over his shoulder to make sure that Browne wasn't right behind him and then scrambled up as quickly and as silently as he could.

Lane came to the partially open door in time to see Speyer disappear up into the dark hayloft. There was still the tank hanging off the airplane wing. If Speyer was nuts enough he might just try to shoot at it. If it exploded there would be enough casualties several miles downwind to fill every funeral home and morgue from here to Baltimore.

He hurried around to the opposite side of the barn.

There were four windows along its length, along with a feed chute for loading hay aboard a truck or trailer. Laying the submachine gun aside, he climbed up on the chute and managed to crawl the ten feet or so to the swinging door. Lane eased it open and crawled inside. He was directly beneath the hayloft. The airplane was parked off to his left, and the ladder Speyer had used was to the right.

Speyer would be watching the airplane and the front door.

Lane took out his pistol, went quietly to the ladder, and climbed up to the loft. He hesitated just below the top, easing just high enough to see what was there. It took a few moments for his eyes to adjust to the darkness, but then he made out a form crouched behind a pile of hay bales ten feet away.

Legally the correct thing for him to do would be to give Speyer a fair warning: Give up, lay your weapon down, raise your hands over your head or I'll shoot you.

But then again Speyer was obviously completely insane, and there was no telling what a crazy man might be capable of doing. He ordered the deaths of all the crewmen aboard the *Maria*, and he certainly didn't give them any warning. Nor was it likely that he had warned Gloria to behave or he was going to cave in her skull with the heel of his boot. He'd even killed his old friend in the chalet back in Germany.

Give him a fair warning first? Give him a chance?

Lane smiled. "I don't think so," he said to himself. He rose up and fired three shots as fast as he could pull the Beretta's trigger.

Speyer rolled off to the side of the hay bales with a cry of pain.

Lane fired two more shots then scrambled up over the top, rolling left as he brought up his pistol.

Speyer, blood stains spreading on his right thigh

and high on his right shoulder, was whimpering as he desperately searched for his gun. He'd dropped it and couldn't find it in the hay.

Lane got up and went over to him.

Speyer looked up, his eyes wide and he started to cry and squeal like a pig being led to slaughter. "There's money for you. Millions, my God, I swear to Christ, you'll be a rich—"

"Right," Lane said. He raised his pistol and fired one shot, hitting Speyer in the forehead between his eyes, at the same time Speyer raised his left hand in supplication.

The morning was suddenly intensely quiet. Lane couldn't even hear the birds singing. He holstered his pistol and went to Speyer's body. The German had something clutched in his left hand. Lane pried open Speyer's fingers and took the small electronic unit out of his hand. It was about the size of a pack of cigarettes with a small antenna, and one caged button. The safety was up. Speyer had pushed the button.

Lane straightened up and looked down at the ag-plane, his blood running cold. The son of a bitch had sabotaged the plane to blow so that there would be no evidence, no survivors.

He had no idea how long the delayed fuse might be. The choice was searching for and disconnecting the explosive device in time, or risk releasing the virus by trying to disconnect the tank. He had to choose one or the other right now.

I-70 WEST OF BALTIMORE

Traffic on the interstate several miles west of the I-695 interchange had already started to back up when the pair of Iroquois assault helicopters passed behind the convoy of two minivans and two dark gray SUVs.

Speyer's troops, realizing that something was going on behind them, had sped up when the helicopters flashed across the highway about fifty feet off the deck.

"Break break, command one. Looks like they spotted us," the pilot of chopper two radioed Major Heinzman. "I have a clear shot."

"Stand by," Heinzman said. He directed his pilot to take them ahead of the convoy and threaten the lead car nose to nose.

"Okay, heads up back there," Heinzman called to the two door gunners. "If they so much as twitch you are authorized to fire."

"Roger that, sir," they said. They cycled the bolts on their 7.62mm machineguns.

"Unit two, command one. You are cleared for weapons hot."

"Aye, weapons hot," the copilot of chopper two replied. Heinzman's copilot gave him a questioning look. He nodded and the officer gave him the thumbs-up.

Each helicopter carried six Hellfire AGM-114A air-to-surface missiles, each capable of taking out a ceramic-armored tank. Laser guided, they could not miss. All six on each chopper were armed and pointed at the four vehicles below.

The lead chopper swooped low over the convoy and dropped down to ten feet above the surface of the highway about twenty yards ahead of the SUV. The pilot flew sideways, pacing the convoy, which had slowed way down.

Heinzman was looking directly into the eyes of the driver and passenger. He raised his right hand and motioned for them to slow down and stop.

He could see the indecision on their faces, which finally turned to resignation. They were professional soldiers and they understood that they were outmaneuvered, outgunned and outclassed.

The driver raised his hand in salute and slowed down. Within fifty yards the convoy had come to a complete halt.

The lead chopper turned to face the lead vehicle, its Hellfire missiles locked onto their targets. Chopper two took up position just behind and to the right of the last minivan in the convoy, at an altitude of no more than twenty feet.

Heinzman got on the loud hailer. "Dismount from your vehicles now, with your hands in the air. Leave all your weapons behind, and then get on the pavement facedown."

Slowly the ten men got out of the vehicles, their hands in plain sight, and lay facedown on the highway. In the distance from the east and west dozens of police vehicles, their lights flashing, were converging on the scene.

One of the door gunners, not realizing his mike was hot, safetied his weapon noisily. "Ah, shit, they gave up too fast," he said. "That's no fun."

WEST FRIENDSHIP, MARYLAND

Lane crouched under the agplane's wing, hurriedly tracing the plumbing and control lines that led to the tank. So far as he could tell, the tank's valve was in the open position. It meant that the spraying system was charged with virus-nitrogen mix. No matter if he closed the valve now; if he tried to disconnect the tank, whatever virus was already in the system would be released.

He stood up and looked at the plane. There were any number of ways to bring it out of the sky, but the simplest to control with a remote detonator would be an explosive device. Possibly Semtex. Easy to use and very powerful.

They were going to overfly Washington, spraying the deadly virus on the city, and then Speyer was going to kill them.

He started at the nose of the airplane, running his hands over and into every nook and cranny. A half-pound of Semtex would be more than enough to take off the prop, or blow the entire engine out of the plane.

He checked under the landing gear, and then back to the wing roots and tail surfaces, conscious that the plane could blow at any moment. But he couldn't simply turn his back and walk away. A lot of people would die if the virus were to be released, even out here in the country.

Lane climbed onto the left wing and started searching the cabin, reaching under the control panel, and under the seats. Ten minutes after he had come down from the loft his fingers brushed across the brick of Semtex under the backseat.

He gingerly eased it out and, holding it carefully in both hands, stepped back down off the wing and turned away from the airplane. There was an electronic fuse stuck into the plastic, but there was no way of telling if it was active, or if by trying to remove or disconnect it the thing would explode.

He nudged the barn door open with a hip, and then hurried around to the back, and down the path to the creek. He laid the bundle on the ground, backed off a couple of feet and then turned and walked off.

Sooner or later it would blow. But back here it would do no harm.

He shook his head. It was time for a vacation, he thought. A very long vacation.

The Semtex exploded with a flat bang thirty minutes after Speyer had pushed the button, but Lane didn't bother leaving his seat on the front porch. In the distance to the east he'd spotted the pair of Iroquois helicopters coming in just above tree level. Their part of the mission had to have been a success, too; otherwise they wouldn't be coming here now.

He'd gone back upstairs to have a last look at Gloria, to convince himself that she was really dead, and then had found a bottle of Dom Perignon in the kitchen. In a blue funk, he took the bottle and a couple of glasses out to the front porch to wait. Because of the baby, Frannie wouldn't have any wine, but Tommy would probably share a glass or two.

It was pleasant out here, he thought. Maybe something like this would be a relief from the grind of the city. At least for a while, until he got bored again.

The helicopters landed in the field across the driveway. Frannie jumped out of the lead one and headed up to the porch in her long-legged easy run, and Lane's heart swelled. He didn't think he could ever be bored so long as he had moments like this, with her coming across a field toward him.